THE FIRST AMERICANS
WHO BOLDLY CAME TO THE

FORBIDDEN LAND

TORKA—Skillful hunter, noble leader. Having defied the will of the tribe, he must face the cunning of his enemies. Refusing to sacrifice his children or compromise his beliefs, Torka boldly leads his family to a land where none before had dared tread . . . in the hope of claiming a new future.

KARANA—Torka's adopted son, revered as a man of magic. In the new land, Karana struggles to keep two secrets from his father: that his magic powers have dwindled . . . and that he knows the terrifying truth of his heritage.

LONIT—The graceful woman with the antelope eyes is Torka's wife. Brave and loyal, she has vowed to stand by her brave husband now and forever. But no matter how far they wander, she cannot forget the infant son she was forced to give up . . . and in her dreams she believes he still lives.

CHEANAH—Last surviving son of a woman whose family had always ruled the tribe, he was pushed by a scheming mother into driving Torka out. His wrath will follow them even into the Forbidden Land.

MAHNIE—Young, gentle, and pretty, she was Karana's woman—but the passion she felt for him was unrequited. In a new land, can the strength of her love sustain the man whose power will shape their destinies?

THE
FIRST
AMERICANS

FORBIDDEN
LAND

WILLIAM
SARABANDE

™

Created by the producers of
**Wagons West, Stagecoach,
White Indian,** and **The Badge.**

Book Creations Inc., Canaan, NY · Lyle Kenyon Engel, Founder

BANTAM BOOKS
NEW YORK · TORONTO · LONDON · SYDNEY · AUCKLAND

FORBIDDEN LAND

*A Bantam Book / published by arrangement with
Book Creations, Inc.*

*Produced by Book Creations, Inc.
Lyle Kenyon Engel, Founder
Bantam edition / September 1989*

ISBN 0-553-28206-9

Published simultaneously in the United States and Canada

Bantam Books are published by Bantam Books, a division of Bantam Doubleday
Dell Publishing Group, Inc. Its trademark, consisting of the words ''Bantam
Books'' and the portrayal of a rooster, is Registered in U.S. Patent and
Trademark Office and in other countries. Marca Registrada. Bantam Books,
666 Fifth Avenue, New York, New York 10103.

PRINTED IN THE UNITED STATES OF AMERICA

O   0 9 8 7 6 5 4 3 2 1

DEDICATION

To Carla . . . with memories of Hubert Howe Bancroft and all of the good books read and shared!

And in loving memory of my great-great-grandfather Brigadier General Wladimir Bonaventura Krzyzanowski—an immigrant to the New World whose travels and daring exploits of 1872–1874 first inspired this author's fascination with the history of the Far North.

"Everything was foreign to me," he wrote. "There was no hand to shield me from distress, there was no heartbeat of brothers or sisters which would have echoed mine. . . . I suffered through my distress with the hope that something better would grow, and I watered it with my tears."

A special agent of the United States Treasury, he was sometimes called the First Governor of Alaska, because he was often the only American governing official of rank within the territory. He rode the high seas and trails, from the customhouse of Sitka, to the upper reaches of the Stikine River and Fort Wrangell, to the goldfields of the Klondike. On behalf of his adopted country and its native Americans—whose rights and land he sought to protect against the smugglers, rumrunners, corrupt politicians, and gold-crazed prospectors—he fought the good fight as valiantly as he fought at Gettysburg, Bull Run, Chancellorsville, and the Battle of Cross Keys as commander of the Second Brigade, Third Division, XX Corps of the Army of the Potomac.

This book, *Forbidden Land*, is for you, Kriz, and for all of those "first" Americans who knew a wondrous land when they saw it, who had the courage to stay and water it with their tears and to protect it with their love and lives.

FIRE CIRCLES

Torka
Lonit, Iana, Summer Moon,
Demmi, Umak, Manaravak,
Swan, Stillborn Son

Grek
Wallah
Iana

Simu
Eneela, Dak, Larani, Nantu

Karana
Mahnie, Naya

Cheanah
Zhoonali, Xhan, Kimm, Mano, Yanevha,
Ank, Shar, Klu, Honee, twin sons, taken

Ekoh
Bili, Seteena, Klee

Teean
Frahn

GRAY-HAIRS
Zhoonali, Teean, Grek, Wallah

MIDDLE-AGED
Torka, Iana, Cheanah, Xhan

ADULTS IN PRIME
Lonit, Ekoh, Bili, Kimm

YOUNGER ADULTS
Simu, Eneela

ADOLESCENTS
Karana, Mano, Yanevha,
Mahnie, Ank

CHILDREN
Summer Moon, Honee, Demmi, Dak,
Umak, Manaravak, Nantu, Larani,
Seteena, Naya, Swan, Shar, Klee, Klu

R. TOELKE '89

PART I

UNDER THE SHADOW
OF THE BLACK MOON

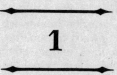

1

"Now!" The old woman's voice was as sharp as the ancient, taloned hands that pressed hard against the young woman's belly. "Bear down! *Now!*"

In the shadowed darkness of the hut of blood, Lonit obeyed. The child was coming, coming on a tide of blood and pain. She would not be here to greet it. She was too tired. Even though the midwives were holding her upright, she felt herself slipping away, drifting into delirium.

The two women who held her by her upper arms shook her. Jarred her. She was annoyed with them. The pain was passing. The tide of blood had brought no child after all. Why did they not allow her to lie down? Her blood ran down her legs and was seeping into the thick layer of grasses and lichens covering the floor. How she hated the sweet smell of blood and the rank, moldering scent of winter dark that filled the little hut. Just thinking of them sickened her, and she wished that the midwives would clear the soiled floor covering away and bring in fresh, which, unstained, would smell of the summer sun. Summer! How she longed for summer!

The gray lichens and golden grasses pricked the soles of her feet. She was too weak to stand, but perhaps it would not be so good to lie down. The floor covering had been spread to absorb blood and birth debris, not to provide comfort. That would come later, after the child was born. If it was *ever* born!

"Woman of the West, bear down, I say!"

Who spoke? Old, talon-fingered Zhoonali? Wallah? Iana?

Kimm or Xhan? Lonit could not tell. Around her, the overcrowded confines of the circular hut were a blur of sweating, watching women, as naked and painted with ash and rancid oil as she.

Above her, the interior framework of mammoth and camel ribs arched upward toward the hide-covered vault of the unvented roof. A jumble of thong-joined caribou antlers supported the ceiling. How she wished that one of the midwives would fold back a portion of the hides, allowing the smoke to vent and fresh, cold air to enter. It was so close, so dark—and so smoky that she could barely breathe.

Her eyes rolled back in her head. The ceiling appeared to float, high . . . so high. The racks of antlers seemed to move through mist, as though the spirits of the caribou were taking them up again and forming an invisible migration into the night. Lonit wondered if her spirit would follow. It would not be such a bad thing to die . . . to join her ancestors . . . to be away from pain, away from the probing eyes and hands of the midwives. She would follow the spirit caribou herds as her people had done since time beyond beginning—only this time she would go alone and not come back.

"No!"

Her own shout of defiance startled her. The ghost caribou fled into the night, and the antlered ceiling hung steady and unmoving. She was suddenly aware of the rich, acrid stink of burning bison tallow and knew that the moss wicks in the stone lamps were guttering—again.

How many times had they been replaced since she had been proudly escorted to the hut of blood by her man? How long had it been since she had entered the hut, stripped off her specially made waiting garments, and ceremonially fed them to the fire of new life coming?

The embers of that fire were cold now, as were the ashes that had been drawn from the smoldering fire pit to paint her body and the bodies of the midwives with symbols that honored the life-giving powers of Father Above and Mother Below.

Her mouth was dry. Someone gave her water from a bladder skin.

"Just enough to moisten the throat. There. No more."
Wallah smiled, but there were only sadness and empathy
in the wide, loving eyes of the aging matron.

Lonit was so exhausted she could barely swallow. She
closed her eyes. Since her labor had begun, the sun had
twice risen and fallen over the edge of the world. Now it
was night again—a long, cold Arctic night filled with the
sound of the wind and the slow, atonal chanting of her
people. She listened to them. It must be very late, for
only a few sang, and no children. Only the old ones. And
the wolves.

Wolves! She opened her eyes. She could hear them
clearly, close to her band's winter encampment. They
were hunting in packs now, running across the winter
tundra beneath the starving moon, seeking to take the
blood and flesh of their prey into themselves, even as she
fought to expel life from her body—without losing her
own life in the fray.

But she *was* losing. Two days and two nights were much
too long to be at the birthing of a child. Her pains had
begun close together, no more than the breadth of time
between heartbeats, it seemed. Right from the start, they
were savage pains, the sort that wore a woman down if
allowed to continue.

There was worry in the midwives' eyes, but Lonit was
too exhausted to worry with them and too weak to wonder
if they would consider the howling of wolves to be a good
omen or bad. She did not care; no omen could be worse
than the pain that was rising in her again. She drew in a
breath and held it, gritting her teeth and closing her eyes.

She tried to think of wolves, of *being* a wolf—not a
naked woman trapped within a fouled hut but a wild
thing, running free beneath the blue light of the starving
moon . . . running lean with the cold, clean breath of the
wind at her back . . . running hungry for life across the
wild, savage miles of the open tundra, in the shadows of
great, tumbled ranges and the glacial massifs of the Mountains That Walk.

"Bear down, Woman of the West!" Zhoonali commanded.
"You are first woman of our headman, but like the rest of

us you are only a woman. Cry out if you must, but bear down! *Now!*"

Lonit was young and strong, and it was not within her nature to cry. She willed herself to run with wolves across the open miles of her imagination. Her blood surged, and her heart pounded fast and hard. She was no longer a woman. She *was* a wolf! She was a strong and sleek wild animal, just like the wolf that had once leaped upon her and nearly claimed her life. Her arm bore the white lightning mark of a jagged scar inflicted by the tearing fangs of that wolf. Her man wore the skin of the beast, and its paws and fangs were around his neck. But now, as she ran, she was pursued by a terrifying white lion with a great black mane, a lion that roared within her.

"Torka!" From out of her very soul, Lonit howled his name in unspeakable anguish as another contraction transformed the supple muscles of her abdomen into a single oiled, ash-blackened strap that tightened, boring in and down upon her unborn child, crushing it—no!—forcing it from her body at last!

The baby was coming! She could feel the head burrowing deep, ripping her tender flesh, tearing her apart like a wolf trying to free itself of a trap—and failing. Never had she suffered such agony. Not at the birth of her firstborn child, Summer Moon, nor at the birth of her second daughter, Demmi.

Her eyes widened with terror. *Little ones! Will this woman ever look upon you and hold you close again?*

Beyond the winter hunting camp of her band, the wolves broke and scattered, disappearing into the far hills and the farthest reaches of her fevered mind. Her little girls ran with them, and her man followed. Only the pain remained. She tried to call out after the ones she loved—the wild wolves, her children, her man. But even as she attempted to form their names, light exploded within the little hut. Briefly she thought of the sun. She wondered if the intensified pain were its child; for with pain, always there was light, bright . . . glaring . . . blinding.

"Lonit! Come back to us!"

She did not want to come back, but Xhan and Kimm,

the two midwives who supported her weight, shook her again, hard.

"The child comes!" Xhan was shouting. "You must kneel again now. You must try harder!"

Lonit was beyond trying. She was not even a woman anymore. She was a spirit, running away into the face of the rising sun with the ghosts of the caribou. Why did the women not leave her alone? The child would come or not come. Her body would allow it life or not; either way, she had no control. None.

The fingers of Xhan and Kimm curled into Lonit's armpits. That caused a little pain, though of no importance. The contraction was building in waves as the midwives forced her to crouch and spread her knees wide.

"Push!" demanded Kimm.

Slumped in Kimm's arms, Lonit could not even try. The ebbing pain would come again. The next time, she knew it would kill her, and she would be glad.

Wallah knelt before her, shook her head, fixed Lonit with frightened eyes, and, with a sigh of regret, slapped her once, twice, and then again.

"You will *not* give up now, Lonit! The life you carry is the first to come forth in this new land. It will be a bad thing if it dies, and a worse thing if it takes you with it! Look at me, Woman of the West! You have never been lazy before! You must work *harder*!"

In a stupor of pain and exhaustion, her entire body was trembling as she crumpled forward, bent double against the agony of yet another contraction. Blood and fluid gushed again from her body, and still the child would not be born.

"Stand back and away!" Zhoonali's command was for Wallah as the old woman took the matron's place and reached out with taloned hands to part the curtain of black hair that had fallen before Lonit's face.

"This goes on too long. A woman can only take so much. You are young and strong. You have given life before, and if the forces of Creation allow it, you will give life again. But now the spirits have spoken with the voices of wolves—a very bad omen. The life in your belly must be taken now, before it *is* life."

Lonit blinked. The contraction was easing a little, just enough to give her time to focus her thoughts. The old woman's words had been spoken so softly, but with threat. She began to understand that Zhoonali was speaking of killing her unborn child.

Lonit stared at the old woman. She could see the pores in the creases at the sides of her wide, flat nose, and the painted patterns around her smoke-reddened, rheumy eyes had smudged and run together. But somewhere in that haggard, time-scarred face, the ghost of long-lost beauty lingered, and Lonit was not surprised to see genuine and deeply felt pity in the dirty, desiccated features. Zhoonali had borne many children, but only one had survived to offer comfort to her in her old age. The old woman was no stranger to pain or to death.

"No . . ." She sighed the word, moving back from the old woman and wrapping her long, slender arms protectively about the great, swollen mound of her belly. This was *her* baby! When her pains had first begun, a new star had shown itself above the western horizon. *A new star!* A tiny, glimmering, golden eye with a bright whisk of a coltish tail! It was the best of omens! The magic man, Karana, had said so.

Karana. Where was Karana? He should be here now, outside the hut of blood, making magic smokes, dancing magic dances, chanting magic chants for one who was as a sister to him. Had he left the encampment again, to seek the counsel of mammoths? Were Zhoonali and those loyal to her right about him? Was he too young and unreliable for the responsibilities of his position?

Lonit moaned. Within her belly, the baby moved. With or without omens or the presence of the magic man, her child lived, and Zhoonali had no right to speak of ending its life. The child would live or die according to the will of the forces of Creation. Apart from this, only its father and the magic man had the right to deny it a place within the band. This baby was Torka's child—perhaps Torka's *son!* And what man with only daughters at his fire circle would deny life to a son!

Pain was rising in her again, cresting, then crashing as Lonit felt her back and hips rent apart. It was excruciating, but she had no wish to evade it. This time when she gritted her teeth and closed her eyes, she did not think of wolves or spirits. She thought of her man. She thought of his child. *Their* child. And with a fully human cry, she bore down on the pain, pushing so hard that the world seemed to crack open all around her. She screamed until it seemed that her pain screamed back at her as she fell gratefully into darkness, into a thick, all-encompassing black lake of oblivion in which she would have drowned . . . but for the cry of a child. Her child!

"A male child!" The voice of Wallah was as full of pride as though she announced the birth of one of her own.

Relieved, Lonit managed a brief moaning tremor of a laugh. At last. She would look upon her infant and hold it to her breast! She had given birth to a son! Karana was right; the new star *had* been a good omen! Torka would be so proud!

She tried to open her eyes but failed; her lids were too heavy. It did not matter. The long ordeal of childbirth was over. The pain was over. The midwives were cleansing her, stroking her back. Old Zhoonali was gently kneading her belly, seeking to purge it of the afterbirth.

Strange: Her abdomen still felt swollen, and she could have sworn that the baby still moved and kicked within her.

But the black lake of oblivion was closing over her again. It was warm. It was deep. It was welcoming. It was good to drift in it, listening in supreme contentment as the midwives fussed around her.

Then she heard Zhoonali sadly say, "The infant son of Torka is strong and sound. The first infant born in this new and forbidden land is more beautiful than any boy this woman has ever seen. It is a pity that this child must die."

"*Why?*"

Torka's question rang through the encampment like the sound of a spearhead shattering against stone. Beneath the savage, black span of a moonlit, star-strewn sky, he faced Zhoonali. The wind was cold. His heart was colder. He felt the eyes of his people watching him in the winter dark, peering from their own huts.

Men, women, children, all had heard Lonit's terrible, anguished scream of life coming forth, followed almost immediately by the cry of a newborn child. After days and nights of waiting, the birth was finally accomplished.

But had it been a *good* birth? Had Lonit survived? In an agony of dread and anticipation, Torka had stumbled from his hut, with Summer Moon and Demmi, two tiny fur-clad shadows, close behind him.

"Is the new life here *now*, Father?" Five-year-old Summer Moon was petite, and as soft and pretty as her younger sister's buckskin dolls.

"Will Mother stop hurting now, Father?" Demmi was a bright girl for three, and as caring and full of love as her namesake, Torka's own mother, had been.

Torka had not replied. The answers had not yet been his to give.

He stood tall before the hut of blood while his people emerged from their shelters, drawn by curiosity into the cold, windy night. They stared at him as his daughters clutched the shell-beaded fringes of his wolfskin leggings. He locked his limbs lest the children feel his trembling and know he was afraid.

Zhoonali had already come out of the hut of blood with the infant. The overpowering moonlight flooded the world, defining every form, intensifying every shadow. Torka saw that the head midwife was naked and glistening within the folds of her time-yellowed, wear-worn bearskin robe. The ruffed hood of the robe had blown back, leaving her gray head bare and vulnerable to the winter wind. Nevertheless, she possessed an imposing aura of absolute authority. When she stood before him with the infant held outward in her hands and covered by a smooth, white skin of winter-killed caribou, he lost his breath to relief, anticipation, and dread. The caribou skin told him that his child lived; had it been stillborn, the hairs would have been facing downward. But was the child sound? And had its mother survived its birth? He stared down at Zhoonali, seeking answers in her eyes.

"The mother lives, but Torka must turn his back on the child," intoned the woman.

The words nearly struck him down. First with joy. *Lonit lived!* Then with grief. *The child must die.*

"Why?" he cried, and his people gasped at his audacity. No one ever yelled at Zhoonali. She was the daughter, granddaughter, and widow of headmen of legendary status, and she was so old that many believed that she possessed magic powers.

Her sunken, tired eyes were black pools that coldly reflected the stars and the nearly full face of the moon. Her head went high, and her chin jabbed the night defensively, rebuking Torka and reminding him that she was Zhoonali and would not be challenged.

But he was a man to whom challenge had become not only a way of life but the only way to survive. And he was not in a mood to be rebuked.

"By what right do you tell me to turn my back upon the life of my child? I am headman of this band, and only the magic man may so order me!"

Startled, she took a moment to regain her composure, then spoke slowly, with great emphasis. "I am Zhoonali. No one in this camp has seen as many moons as I, or birthed as many infants. Zhoonali is head midwife and needs no magic man to tell her that the forces of Creation will not allow this baby to live among the people."

Torka had learned early that when the lives of others depended upon his actions, he must master his impatient, restless, questing nature. It was not always an easy mastery, for he was the son of Manaravak and the grandson of Umak. The blood of many generations of headmen and spirit masters flowed within his veins. His life had been warmed by the midnight sun of twenty-seven summers and chilled by the endless dark of as many winters. His body carried scars inflicted by the fangs and claws of wolves and bears and lions, the tusks of mammoths, and the spears and daggers of men.

He was headman of this band; but these people were *not* his people—not in the way that generations of common lineage made a people one. They were survivors of four distinct bands; violent circumstances and natural catastrophes had forced them into a single hunting community. Internecine struggles that had begun long before he had known of the existence of any other band but his own had thrown them together. He had not coerced the other hunters into naming him headman over all. Grek, Ekoh, and Cheanah had each stepped aside and urged him to lead their three bands as one. He had been honored and flattered at the time; but he should have known long before now that cultural differences would prevent them from ever becoming one people. And not since leading them ahead of their enemies to safety here, in the Forbidden Land, had he felt as painfully aware of their many variances.

Within Zhoonali's hands, the white caribou skin moved. The baby moved. *His* baby moved. *His* baby!

"Torka would see his child."

Zhoonali took two steps back and glared at him. "Torka must not look at its face!" She was emphatic, and her face was set.

He knew that she was waiting for him to turn away and deny life to his newborn child. The realization repelled him. *If I must deny life to this infant, I must know why. I must see why or forevermore be haunted by the spirit of this life*.

He extended his hands to Zhoonali and made a considerable effort to gentle his tone. "Once more, Zhoonali, Torka asks to look upon his child."

Her head went higher, and she took another step back.

Suddenly he was filled with anger. Before she spoke or stepped out of his reach, he pulled the covering off his child and took the infant forcefully. Zhoonali screamed as though he had struck her, and a gasp of incredulity went up from all who watched.

From the night shadows that laked before one of the larger pit huts, Cheanah, Zhoonali's only surviving son, rose to stand belligerently in the moonlight. His broad features had the look of a riled, albeit cautious, bear. His three wolf-eyed sons came from the hut to stand beside him.

Torka paid them no heed. He held his child, braced to see the malformed and monstrous thing. Instead he stared at the bloodied, absolute perfection of his son.

The wind touched the flesh of the infant. The tender, unwashed skin prickled, and the little legs kicked. Arms shook as tiny fists clenched, and an equally tiny penis shriveled and turned blue. The fat little face contorted as, from healthy lungs, a ferocious squall of protest against the cold issued forth. Torka rejoiced in the warmth and voracity of the tiny life.

"It is not fit to live!" cried Zhoonali.

"It?" His anger toward Zhoonali was without bounds. She was reaching for the child. "You do not understand!"

Backhanding her away, Torka silenced her with a dismissal that allowed no argument. The wind took the unlaced edges of her robe and blew them fully back and off, revealing her scrawny shoulders and sagging, greasy, ash-painted breasts and belly. She cowered. She was so old. So tragically old. And so frail.

Torka felt sudden pity for her. He had no wish to strip her of her pride. Time allowed little enough dignity to those who managed to survive into old age. "This band has seen enough of death! Are you not weary of it, Zhoonali? This child that you have brought out to me, it is sound and male and has not taken the life of its mother. Look to the west, to the good omen of the new star, and welcome a new hunter into this band. Welcome the first child born in this new land!"

He held his newborn son high. His wide, strong, ungloved hunter's hands cupped protectively around its buttocks and the back of its head. The old ones said that cold put the first strong breath of life into little ones; it made them gasp and kick and cry for warmth. Torka drew the infant close. He breathed the warm breath of his life into its nostrils. He cradled it against his upper chest, enfolding it in his arms and the soft, golden warmth of his long-sleeved tunic of lion skins as he threw back his head and shouted with pride to the moon and the great black expanse of the star-strewn night. "Umak! Father of my father, hear me! May your life spirit flow now into the body of this child, to live once again in the flesh of one who will carry your name with pride. Umak, Spirit Master, is now Umak, son of Torka! Torka accepts this life! Umak, may the—"

"Torka! No!"

Zhoonali's shriek was enough to unnerve anyone in the camp. But the scream that followed it set terror and confusion loose within Torka's gut: It was the howling scream of the wanawut—the voice of a wind spirit, a monstrous, predatory animal that, legend claimed, was part flesh, part spirit, bear, and man. The beast had been born at the beginning of the world to give meaning to the word *fear*.

No more than a moment passed, yet it seemed forever. No omen could be worse than the howling cry of the wanawut. It was a beast that walked with death. The wanawut did not scream again, but from across the encampment, within the hut of blood, Lonit's cry of infinite pain rent the night.

Everyone gasped and ran to the clearing before that hut, where they stood looking at the hide door flap. Zhoonali, facing them, drew her robe back around her body and muttered that no child born to the screaming accompaniment of the wanawut could be accepted into the band, for it would guarantee death for them all. Nevertheless, it had been accepted. The child *was* a child now: It had a name, it had a life; it could no longer be taken from the encampment to become meat for beasts. Zhoonali looked up at the sky as a red, flowing aurora flamed across the night. The frozen skin of the tundra twitched and shivered with a minor earthquake.

The midwives came rushing outside, Xhan and Kimm wailing in fright. Only Wallah seemed contained. She looked up, shook her head, and gestured to Zhoonali. "Come. It begins again," she announced and, with a sigh, returned to the hut.

"Again?" Torka was confused. He felt the arms of his little girls tighten around his legs. They were so young, so small; yet they could sense the tension and the danger around them, not only in the burning sky, the trembling earth, and the cry of the wanawut, but in the eyes of the people.

"Why does Mother still cry?" Summer Moon whimpered.

"Perhaps she cries in fear of the shivering earth, my

little one." Torka touched the top of her head with his free
hand to calm her and wished that he felt as certain as he
sounded.

The wind was rising. The earth was still, but the thunder of panicked herd animals sounded across the tundra.
Dire wolves howled again in the surrounding hills, and
somewhere, far away within mile-high glacial mountains
that nearly encircled the tundral valley, an unearthly,
half-human scream rent the night.

Karana was out there somewhere, unarmed. Torka hoped
that the magic man was safe. He wished that Karana were
here beside him, affirming the right of his child to a place
within the band. He stared westward, looking for the new
star, but it was late, nearly dawn, and the star had slipped
over the edge of the world.

Torka held tiny Umak close. The single good omen that
had preceded the infant's birth had vanished, and in its
place were roaring beasts, an unstable earth, a burning
sky, and a screaming woman.

Zhoonali's face twisted, but into malevolence or pity, he
could not tell. "Your woman cries out because there is
another! Yes! A twin! Two lives coming forth from the
belly of one! It is *forbidden*! It is unnatural. It is what this
woman was trying to tell you!"

*Another child? Perhaps another son! Why should this
be forbidden?* Torka did not understand. "Twins are rare,
Zhoonali, but not unnatural or forbidden among my people. Does not the great bear birth twins, and the wolf
and—"

"Your people?" The stern voice of Cheanah was heavy
with threat, like storm clouds roiling and bumping and
growling with thunder. "We are your people now. Among
the bands of Cheanah, of Grek, and of Ekoh, no omen—
not even the rising of a new star—could justify the lives of
twins! Look to the sky! Father Above is angry. Feel the
movement of the earth! Mother Below is offended. The
wanawut howls in the distant hills, and as always, Lonit,
your favorite woman, takes too much upon herself! A
woman is *not* a bear! A woman is *not* a wolf! In starving
times, a woman with two sucklings grows weak. In the
time of the long dark, a woman with two babies in her

pack frame cannot carry her full share of the load when the band moves to new hunting grounds!"

His words were echoed by many mouths.

Zhoonali, head held high, nodded; her bearskin robe took on the color of watered blood beneath the red aurora borealis. She ventured close to Torka and allowed herself the privilege of touching him—the most tender and motherly of pats upon his forearm, as though he were the son of her own body. "Since time beyond beginning, this has been the way of the people, Torka! You are a man of the far west, and perhaps among those of your own band, it was different. But of Torka's band, only Lonit and Torka have survived. Perhaps because the spirits were angry with Torka's people for allowing the lives of twins—"

"My band perished when a rogue mammoth rampaged through the winter camp, not because our women were allowed to give suck to twins. We have all felt the earth shake before, and we have all seen the sky burn with red rivers of light. These are not starving times. This band grows fat in a camp full of meat. The time of the long dark is ending. We have no need to move to new hunting grounds." Torka turned to face the gathering. "It was said by Umak, grandfather of Torka, that in a new land, men must learn new ways! We are in a new land. We are one people now. We have survived the great falling and coming together of the Mountains That Walk. The way back into the land of our ancestors is closed to us—perhaps forever. In the meantime, I am headman, and while Torka is headman, the lives of infants are not thrown away. And only a magic man may interpret the omens."

Cheanah sneered. "How convenient for you that the magic man is never in this camp when he is needed."

"And if you wait on his word, your woman will surely die," Zhoonali warned.

If there was magic in the Forbidden Land, Karana, the magic man, could not find it.

For two brief, pale, sun-hungry winter days, he searched. For two long, black, star-filled nights, he hunted. And for all of that time, an inner and unwelcome voice bit at his throat and whispered in the winds of his mind: *You run*

*from your people when they need you, Magic Man. You
hide from your own inadequacy. Anyone could look at a
new star and say that it is a good omen. But can you be
certain? No! You are certain of nothing these days. You
will never find the magic. Never!*

The voice made him feel old and impotent. But he was
young, lean, and as powerfully made as a stallion—and
according to his woman, as restless and intractable. Across
the long miles, he thought of his sweet, young, patient
Mahnie, daughter of Grek and Wallah.

She had begged him not to go, warning him that there
would be trouble if he left. Too often was he away from his
people when they needed him, and too often was he away
from Mahnie herself.

He knew the truth when he heard it, but it chafed his
conscience far too much to admit that she was right. He
lengthened his stride into a lope and refused to think of
Mahnie. He named the unwelcome inner voice Liar until
it spoke no more. It was not the voice he sought, and so
he would not listen.

He carried no spear, no dagger, no snare nets for the
taking of food, and nothing to aid him in the making of
fire. He was alone with the great wolflike dog, Aar, and,
he hoped, courage and wisdom. With such companions,
he had no need of weapons. And the magic spirits with
whom he sought communion would not speak to a man
through a full belly or out of a warm and sated mind.

If he wanted to find magic, he must be an empty vessel,
open to the spirit wind that would come only when he had
put himself beyond the limits of flesh and blood and bone.
He traveled as the wind travels—neither eating nor sleeping nor choosing his course, but allowing his steps to be
directed by the unseen forces of the savage Ice Age earth
and sky.

Now and again, the dog looked up at him with questions
in its blue and watchful eyes. *Why do you run? What do
you seek? How much farther before you allow a friend to
rest and eat?*

"You may hunt and rest and feed as you will, Brother
Dog, but I will not rest until I find the magic. For *her*."

He passed Arctic lions, dire wolves, and a great short-

faced bear hungry after months of living off its own fat.
The predators watched but did no more, for the magic
man climbed into broad, spruce-fragrant hills of mammoth
country with a stride that had neither hesitancy nor ac-
knowledgment of danger in it. Like the wind, he bore no
scent of vulnerability. Like the wind, he was unafraid—
until now.

"Lonit!" He spoke her name aloud, and the unwelcomed
inner voice returned to stab him deeply.

Awash in the shimmering, blood-red glow of the northern lights, the wind blew his hood back from his face.
With his unbound black hair whipping in the rising wind
and his body encased in multilayered garments cut from
the skins of every animal that was food for his people, he
heard the distant scream of a woman and stopped dead in
his tracks as the earth quivered beneath his booted feet.

*You were wrong about the star, Magic Man! It was a
bad omen. You knew that all along but had not the courage to stay and speak the truth. You should not be here.
You should be with Lonit, who has been as both sister and
mother to you. You should be with Torka, who has named
you Son although you are not of his flesh. You should be
with your band, making spirit smokes and dancing ritual
dances, so the forces of Creation will be merciful to Lonit—
for you alone knew that two hearts beat within her belly.
It is because of you that the earth has shaken and the sky
has caught fire!*

He felt sick with guilt and shame. His need for self-
justification was so strong, he spoke aloud to the inner
voice.

"Had I stayed within the camp, my people would have
seen that I have no powers! I do not know how to make
true spirit smokes, dance true ritual dances, or chant true,
time-honored chants to ease the delivery of Lonit's babies!
I could have bluffed and blustered, and the people would
have been impressed, but the spirits and I would know
the truth of such trickery! I fear to act lest the forces of
Creation turn against those I love. I know that among my
people, tradition demands that all twins must die! But I
could not speak words that would deny the lives of Torka
and Lonit's newborn children! I could *not*! And so I look

for *good* omens instead of bad! Even if I do not find them, the midwives will tend to Lonit's needs, and the longer I stay away, the more likely the people will forget the tradition, or perhaps Torka will persuade the band to overlook it."

And if they do not? the inner voice asked. *When the worst has happened, Karana will be to blame.*

Even the dog cocked its black-masked, grizzled head and seemed to frown at him.

Karana seethed with frustration. As a boy, he had been able to summon the rain and call the lightning from the sky. Since his earliest childhood, he had been able to look into the eyes of men and beasts and know what was in their hearts. He could set his spirit free to roam across the world, to scout the land, to find the herds of caribou and bison and elk and entice them to the hunting grounds of his people.

He had been born to be a magic man! And, indeed, he was—until entering the Forbidden Land. Now the power of Seeing was gone, the gift of Summoning denied, and not one of his kind was alive to teach him how to renew his strengths or explain to him why he had lost them.

Beside him, the dog's ears went back, and a low growl formed deep within its broad, powerfully muscled chest. Karana, lost in thought, noticed no change in the animal. He was facing westward, staring back across the way he had come, waiting for Lonit to scream again. She did not. Had the birth been accomplished? There was a time not so long ago when he would have known.

He raised his head and like an animal sniffed the wind. It carried no scent of celebratory fires, smoke, roasted meat, or the habitation of men. He was far—too far—from the winter camp of his people. He closed his eyes and willed his spirit to fly across the tundra, to seek out the camp of his people, to discover if Lonit's delivery had gone well or awry. But his spirit remained locked within the shell of his body, and he had not the power to free it.

There is no magic in this land, he thought. *At least not for me.*

Why had he lost his powers? Old Umak and Sondahr would have known. But both were murdered by enemies before either could teach him all he needed to know. Umak, grandfather of Torka, was sage, teacher, and spirit master. Sondahr, wise woman, was seeress of the bands that convened at the Great Gathering. The pain of their loss was great in him.

"Umak! Sondahr!" he wept. "Speak to me from the spirit world. Help me! Put omens in my path that will tell me what to do. Return to me the gifts of Seeing and of Summoning so I may help Torka and my people! Help me to learn the proper way to chant so that Lonit and her babies will be strong through me. But by all the powers of the forces of Creation, do not ask me to be ultimately responsible for sentencing those babies to be abandoned as food for beasts!"

His sobs were so fierce with pain and need that the dog winced and backed away from him.

Ghosts whispered on the wind and taunted the magic man. *But that is the condition of your power. You are too weak to work the will of the forces of Creation upon a pair of spiritless sucklings. And so your powers are no more. We will not listen to your pleas. Lonit's twins will be denied life within the band. And you are not fit to keep the gifts of Seeing and Summoning. You will never find the magic you have lost because we, the ancients, have taken it away from one who is unworthy to possess it.*

Truth struck him hard, but anger struck him harder. The voices had not offered what he wished to hear, nor were they the gentle, guiding counsel of Umak and Sondahr. These were the ghostly voices of malevolent strangers. Was Navahk, his true father, with them? Navahk, the deceiver, slayer of women and children, murderer and manipulator of men—Navahk the beautiful, the treacherous, the fearless, who had dared to slay a wanawut and dance in its skin.

Yes! Even in death Navahk haunted his son and tried to deny him the shamanistic powers with which he had been born.

The dog was growling. Again the magic man failed to notice. The ghost wind was whirling away to the east, into that far portion of the world where the sun would soon rise over high, massively glaciated mountains. Under sim-

ilar ranges far to the west, Navahk lay buried under the
rubble of a collapsed mountain range of ice. Karana was
glad his father was dead.

He glared across the distances. The moon was setting,
soon to follow the new star over the western horizon. The
nearly full, pockmarked face of Father Above stared back
at Karana dispassionately, without interest, as Father Above
always did out of the black lake of the night. Only tonight
his face was red and bloated in the light of aurora.

"I have not asked to be a magic man!" Karana shouted.
"It is you, Father Above and all the powers of Creation,
that have made me what I am! I have not asked for these
heavy responsibilities. Give me signs so I may *help* my
people—not condemn their children to death, as I was
once condemned by Navahk, my own father!"

It was in this moment that somewhere in the snow-
misted highlands that lay directly ahead the scream of an
animal was followed by the screech of another.

Karana wheeled, his hunter's mind instantly categoriz-
ing the two distinct animal sounds: wanawut; leaping cat.

The first was close. The second was much too close and
moving fast. Beside him, Aar's tail tucked up between his
hindquarters, his head went down, and the hair along his
back stood on end.

Every nerve ending in the magic man's body cried
Danger! But it was too late. The dog was springing to the
attack, and Karana was knocked on his back, with the
great, fang-toothed leaping cat already on top of him.

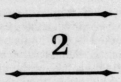

2

The light of the sun was barely visible at the edge of the world as Zhoonali reentered the hut of blood.

"Where is my baby?" demanded Lonit.

"It lives." The head midwife's tired voice was as cold and devoid of emotion as snowfall on a windless day. "Your man stands birth vigil in the light of the rising sun, but his fast is useless. Torka has broken with the ways of our ancestors. Against the will of the band and without counsel of the magic man, he has named your firstborn son Umak. He has put it to suck at the breasts of Eneela without the consent of Simu, her man. Now the wanawut howls with wolves and leaping cats in the distant hills. The sky is angry, and the earth trembles. Umak will live . . . but by the powers of the forces of Creation, this one that is not yet born will not!"

Frightened and confused, Lonit looked at the midwives. Zhoonali, her discolored bearskin robe cast aside, moved toward her. Wallah's mouth was set into a line of grim regret. Iana's sad eyes were filled with indecision. Xhan and Kimm edged forward with pinched faces, their fingers curled around thong nooses.

"Stay away from me," she snarled.

They ignored her, surrounding the clean, freshly laid mattress of grasses and lichens.

Lonit sat up, but the effort cost her. She was still exhausted from her previous labor, and now the pains were beginning again. She would bring forth a second child in as many days. It seemed impossible after the exhausting, excruciatingly painful birth of her firstborn son. Perhaps she carried a second son! The thought of having two sons filled her with pride. The corners of her mouth moved upward into a quivering smile of triumph. But what had Torka's acceptance of Umak cost him? The leadership of the band? She did not care—not now.

Her pain was growing, expanding. How she longed for Torka! How she yearned to rejoice with him, to be held in his strong arms as she put their newborn son to her breast! But no man could enter the hut of blood lest he contaminate his masculine spirit, and she could not suckle their firstborn until after the birth of its sibling.

The midwives were watching her closely. Tears welled in Iana's eyes. Wallah was shaking her head pityingly. Xhan and Kimm looked dangerous. Lonit bit her lower lip and paced her breathing. Fear for the life of her child inspired a granite-hard strength of will that allowed her to override her agony and focus her thoughts.

"Why?" she implored.

Old Zhoonali replied in a voice that held no inflection. Lonit listened but heard only in snatches. She was so tired . . . *too* tired. Zhoonali's words had something to do with twins, bad luck, and omens. With bright stars, red skies, a trembling earth, and howling beasts. But they did not matter, for Lonit knew only that her twins were not being born in starving times. In such times as these, when the encampment was full of meat, twins should be considered good luck, especially if one or both proved to be male.

Her pain was gone. She relaxed a little. Where was Karana? His soft voice and gentle hands could ease her pain. Her head swam, and the tips of her fingers felt numb. She looked up at the women through her long, uncombed hair. "Go. You give me no room to breathe."

Zhoonali did not move. She held the claw of taking. The long, bloodstained, use-worn claw of a giant sloth lay balanced across her palms. "We will not leave you. Before you die of this, we must end it. It must be done now."

Lonit's eyes widened. Zhoonali would use the claw of taking to pierce the child and then would wield it, in combination with the thongs, to draw the mutilated infant

from her womb. Few women survived the ordeal. Most
slowly died of fever afterward, screaming while their bellies bloated and their lips dried and their eyes bulged as
though they would pop from their sockets.

"Stay away," she warned Zhoonali.

"I cannot," the old woman replied with great empathy
and concern. "This birth goes on too long. It will kill you,
Lonit."

"This woman will take her chances. This woman will not
allow you to kill her baby."

"And this woman cannot allow such a risk to the headman's woman. Torka will be angry with Zhoonali if his
favorite woman dies. And for what? A spiritless suckling
that will not be allowed to live? No. An infant that takes
the life of its mother will bring bad luck to its people
forevermore. Everyone knows that! And even if Lonit
does not die, a second twin is a forbidden thing! Either
way, tradition commands that it must die. Torka has already offended the spirits by accepting the firstborn twin.
He will never be allowed to accept the second. *Never*. So
why should you die with it?"

"It?" Lonit's right hand rested protectively across the
taut span of her abdomen. In accordance with the traditions of her people, life came to a child along with its
name; before naming, it was nothing more than a piece of
meat that might be abandoned or, in starving times, fed to
the band.

Lonit frowned. Was it not already alive? The question
troubled her. She had nurtured four babies within her
belly, and each had seemed alive to her long before its
birth—except this last. The second twin must have lain
curled beneath the other all these many moons. It must
be very small. She had mistaken its heartbeat as merely an
echo of the firstborn's. The pains that announced its coming were few and far between, as though her body were
not certain the time was right for the birth. She was
grateful for that. It allowed her to rest. To think of life . . .
of death.

Beneath her hand, the baby moved. Lonit's heartbeat
quickened. It *lived!* It *was* a baby! Not an "it," not a
"thing," not a spiritless suckling, but a living child. It did

not heave and flail as its twin had done, nor did it stress and strain against her skin as though trying to explode through it. Its movements were gentle, sleepy ripplings that made her feel as though tiny fish were schooling within her.

Now, as she held Zhoonali's gaze, she felt an overwhelming protectiveness for the tender little life. "This child is mine," she proclaimed without flinching. "The customs of Zhoonali's people are good, as are the customs of Wallah's and Iana's. But they are not the same as those customs that bind Lonit. Without consent of the magic man or the headman, Zhoonali will not touch this baby or me!"

Zhoonali's head went high. "We will see." She nodded a signal to the others to close their circle.

Lonit felt like a cornered wolf. She showed her strong, white, even teeth. "Stay away," she warned still again, thinking that when they came close, she would spring at them. She would claw and gouge and bite to drive them off.

But her exhausted body was unable to resist. The women—all but Iana—closed their circle. Where was Iana? She was Torka's second woman and like a sister to Lonit, but she was not of their original band. Perhaps she believed that what Zhoonali was doing was right but could not bear to be a part of it. What matter? The others were holding her now, forcing her to lie back. Xhan and Kimm gripped her ankles and forced her limbs wide.

"Do not fight us, Lonit," implored Wallah, soothing her brow with gentle, loving hands. "This woman weeps for what must happen. But Zhoonali is right. You will die if this baby is not taken from you. And twins *are* forbidden. From time beyond beginning, among *all* people, it has been so!"

"Why?" shrieked Lonit, fighting, twisting to be free of their grip. "You cannot be sure that what you are doing is right—not without a magic man to tell you so!"

Xhan made no attempt to conceal her impatience. "The magic man is gone from this camp! As he is usually gone when anyone has need of him! Always you make trouble for us, Woman of the West. You talk too often with the tongue of a man, as if you had the right to speak and question and form opinions! Your skill with a bola shames your band sisters before their men! And when you think that no one is looking, you dare to touch the spears of Torka and hunt as a man beside him! All this is bad enough! But you cannot have two babies at one birth!"

"It is forbidden to your people, not mine!"

"We are *one* people now," reminded Zhoonali.

"And if you continue to fight us, Woman of the West, the claw of taking may seek too deeply and take your life along with the spiritless suckling's." Kimm's threat was unmistakable.

Lonit was light-headed, but she could sense Kimm's obvious pleasure. Lonit twisted violently, freed her ankle from Kimm's hurtful grasp, and kicked out, landing a solid blow to Kimm's jaw that sent the woman sprawling, spitting blood and teeth.

"I *can* bear this child! I *will* bear this child! And I will fight you to the death if you try to stop me!" Lonit cried, trying to kick free of Xhan's hold.

Zhoonali commanded Kimm to rise. The younger woman did so slowly, resentfully, glaring hatefully out of sharp little eyes beneath a narrow, furrowed brow. Her fat fingers explored her bleeding gums. "You will pay for this."

Xhan intervened. Of Cheanah's two women, she was the elder. As the mother of his three sons, hers would have been the higher status even if she had not been his first woman. When she told Kimm to shut her mouth lest the rest of her teeth fall out, Kimm glowered but did not argue. Xhan turned to Lonit and spoke persuasively. "Before Cheanah chose to walk with Torka as his headman—in the year of much hunger when the caribou did not return along familiar routes out of the face of the rising sun— Kimm opened herself to the claw of taking and sacrificed the life spirits of twin sons for the good of all. Her *only* sons!"

Lonit felt sick with fear for her child and for herself and with pity for Cheanah's second woman. So Kimm was one of those who had survived the claw of taking. Lonit was not surprised. It was no secret that the woman was barren. Only one child named her Mother: a fat little girl,

Honee, who had obviously been born before her mother had been unfortunate enough to bring twins to term under a starving moon. Remorseful, Lonit looked at Kimm now. The woman's face was swelling. Soon it would be difficult to open her mouth, but now Kimm had little trouble spewing her jealous anger.

"Why should Lonit be allowed to keep even one of her twins when Kimm could not? Both should die, as the twins of Cheanah died, for the good of the band!"

Lonit's sympathy toward Kimm was short-lived. "These are not starving times! How will the death of one or both of Torka's twins be for the good of this band?"

Zhoonali replied smoothly. "When the life of the second is no more, perhaps the fire in the sky will cool, the skin of the earth will cease trembling, and the wolves and the wanawut will disappear into the mists. But for now, that which cannot be born must die before it kills its mother and brings disaster to us all. Where is Iana? No matter. Hold her fast, and it will be done!"

Lonit screamed, but the women paid her no heed. Even motherly, loving Wallah gripped her shoulders hard as Xhan and Kimm pulled her limbs wide and sat upon her feet while Zhoonali crawled close. Her breath was warm between Lonit's thighs as she stretched forward and began to probe with the oiled tip of the blood-darkened claw. It entered and trespassed deeply as Lonit screamed and screamed until suddenly a male voice commanded: "Stop!"

The midwives turned and gasped. With the door skin held back and the red light of dawn glowing behind him, Torka wantonly broke every male-female taboo of his people. With Iana following, he came boldly into the hut of blood, pulled a protesting Zhoonali aside by her hair, and took Lonit in his arms.

"What happens here?"

Zhoonali sat in shock, her skinny, vein-scarred old legs splayed before her. "We do what must be done. Look at your woman. The spiritless life within her belly must be taken before it kills her."

Lonit burrowed her head into his chest. He should not be here! He was risking the wrath of the spirits by daring to enter. But she was so glad to see him, so grateful for the strength of his arms, that she could not speak to send him away. Tears were burning beneath her lids. She would not let Zhoonali or him see her cry.

"I will bear this child," she told him adamantly, "if they will only let it come from me as it will. . . ."

"They will kill her and the child if they use the claw of taking!" said Iana as she eyed the other women and knew that she had made enemies of all but Wallah, who seemed relieved.

Torka's stern gaze settled on the claw. "This is not the way of my people," he said coldly.

"It is the *only* way. Zhoonali speaks for the spirits and for the forces of Creation! You profane them all by your presence here! Disaster will befall us all because of your arrogance!"

Torka closed his eyes and, holding his woman in his arms, spoke softly in her ear. "Beyond the hut, the sun is rising. The fires in the night sky are cooling, the earth has ceased its trembling, and the wind-spirit wanawut has grown silent. Soon Karana will return with the magic he seeks—for you, for our children. He will tell them all that the spirits smile upon our children. Until then, rest easy, woman of my heart, for I will stay at your side until the baby is born."

"This baby will be the death of us all!" declared Zhoonali in the tone of one who has seen the future and knows what it will bring.

Lonit felt Torka's muscles bunch with anger. "Or of you alone if you come at my woman and attempt to kill this child again!"

The midwives gasped. Never had they heard Zhoonali spoken to in such a way. They stared, waiting for her to hurl invective at the headman. Instead, she stood calmly, regally, pondering the moment. The man was tired and irritable. And dangerous after a two-day fast. This was no time to challenge him. She bowed her head with utmost deference. "So be it, then. This is the will of Torka. The mother will live or not live; the child will be born or not born by the will of the forces of Creation and not through any interference on the part of this woman. Now before the wrath of the spirits falls upon us all, go out from among us, Headman, and know that Zhoonali has never broken her word. Whatever choices must be made concerning the life or death of this child will be made later by the magic man. *If* he is a magic man. And if he ever returns to his people."

"He will return," said Torka.

"We will see," replied Zhoonali. "We will see."

The great, lion-sized animal had come at the magic man at a dead run. Karana had gone down hard, and now the cat was on him, panting and snarling. He knew that he would surely have been dead had it not been for the thick layering of his clothes and for the valiant defense of the dog. It was Aar's leap that had alerted him to danger and given him a moment's warning—time enough to anticipate nearly three hundred pounds of animal slamming into him, time enough to turn and brace against his fall so that when the beast took him down, he was curled into a fetal tuck, protected against the penetration of tooth or claw that would leave him paralyzed and totally defenseless against the beast's mauling until the last agonizing moments of his death.

Death. The word echoed in the magic man's head. He was pinned down by a leaping cat, and any moment pain would flare and death would come. He would never again see his sweet, adorable Mahnie. He would never find the magic or the omens that he sought. He would never dance the dances or chant the chants that would help his beloved Lonit through the terrible ordeal of childbirth. Her fate and the fate of her doomed twin children would lie with the forces of Creation. He would not be able to change their destinies, but then perhaps he had known that all along.

The weight of the great cat was suffocating him. Its deep snarling seemed less sound than sensation as the beast pressed in on him. He felt the vibrations of its growls and thick, choked hackings emanating through its massive chest into his own skin. Without a spear or dagger, Karana knew that he had no chance against such an adversary. It would have been best if he had had no warning, if he had simply been pierced through the heart by the stabbing fangs of the beast, ripped apart, and consumed before he had a chance to visualize the sort of death that was to be his.

The magic man heard the barks and growls of Brother Dog. He sensed the dog's presence atop the cat, harassing the beast, biting and tearing savagely at its neck.

Aar, my old friend, run fast and far. You are no match for that which is killing me!

The dog did not run. Karana knew that it would not. Aar never ran from danger. In the past the dog had stood with him—as well as with old Umak, Torka, and its "man pack"—against wolves and bears, charging mammoths and woolly rhinos, lions and leaping cats. But always the man pack had been armed, so Aar, as a part of a team, had come away virtually unscathed. Now the dog was alone, and it was only a matter of time before the great cat arched its back and with one swipe of its paw sent the dog flying, yipping and bloodied, to its death.

Shame and frustration rose within Karana. It was *his* fault that the dog would die! What sort of arrogant fool would walk alone and unarmed from an encampment? What sort of idiot would wander the world with no thought of predators? What sort of a man would put his brother dog at risk?

A magic man? No man at all! No brother at all! No magic man at all! No wonder the spirits mocked and denied him. He deserved to die.

But deserving and desiring were two different things. Karana was young. He had no wish to die and could find no justness in the fact that the dog was going to die with him. The spirits were not being fair to him. They had invaded his life, walked in his dreams, and come to him in the guise of eagles and clouds and ragged bolts of lightning, to foretell the future through his mouth and to save his life a thousand times. Now, when he most needed them, they ignored him.

His anger, resentment, and despair stirred and congealed into the foul brew of rage. In rage there was strength, a bitter heating of the blood, a mixing of adrenaline with righteous indignation. He *had* possessed the powerful gifts of Seeing and Calling. True, he had hurled his spear at Navahk, his own father, but this act had been provoked, and in the days that had followed, the spirits had made him a magic man whose powers had stunned not only his people but himself.

Then he had entered the Forbidden Land, and his powers had dwindled into mere shadows. Now that he refused to stand before his people and command the death of Torka's twins, the spirits had abandoned him entirely. How could he condemn the babies of those whom he loved most in all the world? He could not! He *would* not! And if the spirits could not understand his reasoning, then he would die, cursing them all to the end.

Levering against the frozen earth, Karana pushed up with all his strength against the weight of the great cat and gained just enough space for his lungs and throat to form a shout.

"Father Above! Mother Below! Spirits of this world and the world beyond this world, if you are ever going to help this magic man, now is the time. I swear by the blood of my life, if I die now, I will come after you in your spirit worlds and make you pay!"

Suddenly the leaping cat drove him flat to the frozen ground—not with paw or claw or fang but with the abrupt collapse of its own weight. Air exploded from Karana's lungs. He waited for what he knew must follow: The cat would get at his belly and throat, rip through his garments, and feed on him. And he would lie opened and gutted like an antelope, twitching and staring and making garbled sounds until the end.

But the cat merely lay on him, breathing hard. Its stench was overwhelmingly foul. The stench of blood—his own blood, he assumed—was overridden by the stench of musty, old fur and sore-blistered skin, of thick mucus, infected gums, and of time-worn teeth thick with plaque.

Old! The cat was old! It must be so! Otherwise the curving, serrated fangs of the animal would surely have pierced clear through him by now. Hope flared within Karana. The spirits had listened! They had been impressed by his curse! If there had been enough breath left in him, he would have shouted with joy and gratitude. The cat was not killing him; *he* was killing the cat, not through any physical action but with the pure, driving thrust of his will. He could feel the life of the animal flow out of its body. He *was* a magic man, and his powers had saved him and Brother Dog from certain death! He had at last found the magic that he sought! And what an extraordinary magic it was!

With all the strength heightened by his rising sense of euphoria, Karana forced the cat's corpse to roll off him. After a two-day fast, the effort left him breathless and dizzy. He remained hunched on the ground, gasping and checking himself for injuries. He was infinitely relieved to find only a ripped surplice.

The dog was running in excited circles, then ventured to take brazen nips at the motionless cat. Karana saw blood on Aar's muzzle and shoulders—the cat's blood, for other than this well-spattered stain, the dog's coat was unmarred.

Brother Dog is lucky, running with a magic man whose powers are so great.

Karana felt smug. It was an emotion he always found repugnant in others; but with the cat dead at his side, he found the feeling sweet indeed. Instead of threats, he offered thanksgiving to the spirits; they, not he, had killed the cat. But they had done so at his command! The realization intoxicated him with pride and renewed purpose.

He rose shakily and stood leaning slightly forward, hands resting just above his knees, drawing in the welcome, pungent scent of the surrounding hills. The wind was pouring down from the heights. Cold, bitter, and thick with mist, it blew away the cat's stench and replaced it with the odors of ice and snow, rotting stone, lichens and mosses, spruce trees and the spoor of mammoths, and . . . something else that quickened the beat of his heart even though he could not identify it.

It was familiar and oddly soothing, yet threatening at the same time. It made him think of the smell of crushed tussock grass, a long-lost nephrite dagger, and silver eyes filled with reflected starlight. But whose eyes? He could not remember. His reaction made no sense to him. He told himself that he was not thinking clearly.

He shook his head and willed the beat of his heart to slow. It obeyed. He smiled. The spirits *were* with him. Calm satisfaction flooded him as he looked at the body of the cat.

It was larger than average and lay on its side. The last vestiges of life were still visible in its glazing yellow eyes and the twitching of its massive paws and short, lynxlike tail. Along its back were wounds inflicted by Aar's tearing teeth. But along its side were massive lacerations that gaped wide, allowing the guts of the animal to extrude in shining, bubbling, bloodied coils. No dog could have inflicted such injuries; it was as though the cat had been disemboweled by an animal of at least its own size or power.

Spirit power. The power of the forces of Creation. Yes! They had killed the cat, and they had done a good job of it! Karana had come too close to death not to be amazed and grateful to be alive. If he had survived the attack and willed the beast to drop dead, perhaps he could help Lonit, after all. Even without a complete knowledge of ritual, with the forces of Creation on his side, there was nothing he could not accomplish! Not even Navahk, his hated father and legendary magic man, had ever demonstrated such power! Men would sing songs of Karana's magic for generations to come!

He would skin this old, dead cat, using one of its own fangs as a tool, then hurry back to camp, resplendent in its skin and his renewed sense of worth! Men had called him Lion Killer once, and they would do so again! Let old Zhoonali and Cheanah and the other hunters doubt his powers now! A lone hunter, unarmed, and weakened by days of fasting, was no match for a leaping cat unless he *was* a magic man . . . a shaman . . . one who found favor with the spirits and could bend the will of the forces of Creation to suit his own desires! Lonit and Torka's twins would live! By the powers of this world and the next, he would see to it.

In that moment, the dog stopped circling and began to back up. Its lips pulled back to show its fangs as a dreadful growl of fear and terror reverberated within its throat.

"Aar?" Karana frowned and turned. Suddenly he was a boy again, speechless with horror.

The wanawut was moving toward him quickly, walking upright with an oddly rolling gait. In the wind-torn mists of morning its body seemed to be clothed, for it was thickly maned across its shoulders and along its spine, and its entire body was furred, with long, shaggy guard hairs that disguised the form of its enormous torso and made the entire beast appear frosted. Its massive neck sloped into equally massive shoulders from which long, powerful, shaggy arms swung and sliced through the air. Its hairy, blood-matted hands—not the hands of a beast but of a man, only three times the size, and clawed—were curled into fists.

Aar charged the creature. Karana watched in disbelief as, for one moment, Brother Dog was a snarling blur of fur leaping upward toward the wanawut; then Aar was flying through the air, turning head over tail and yipping.

The wanawut kept on coming, closing on the magic man without a break in stride. Karana stared, immobilized by terror. The features of the thing were clear now: a flattened, sloping cranium; mist-gray eyes set deeply beneath a projecting brow; pointed, grotesquely human ears, a bare, bloodied, cylindrical muzzle; and a broad-lipped mouth pulled back to reveal glistening canines that were nearly as massive as the stabbing teeth of the great leaping cat.

With a sick, sinking feeling that would easily become a faint if he allowed it, Karana knew that neither his threats nor his pleas had anything to do with the death of the leaping cat. This—the wanawut—was the spirit that had gutted the cat and sent it running in its last moments of life in blind panic . . . into the path of a foolish youth who had dared to imagine that the forces of Creation would care whether he lived or died.

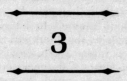

3

Beyond the shadowed confines of Torka's pit hut, the red aurora of the previous night had faded into the ripening morning—a benign gold-and-pink morning misted with low clouds of blowing ground fog . . . a morning devoid of omens . . . a morning that allowed the headman to retreat into his shelter in the hope of gaining a few hours of much-needed sleep until Lonit's labor began again. As the unsecured hide door snapped in the rising wind, light trespassed into the interior. It backlit Iana's long, loosely plaited hair and shimmered in the well-matched silvery lynx skins that formed her dress. She knelt before him, offering skewered wedges of roasted fat on a platter fashioned from a bison's pelvic bone.

Her voice was as soft and full of worry as her dark, perpetually sad eyes. "Lonit's pains did not begin again. Wallah gave her a horn of crushed green willow bark, blueberry root, and marrow broth, so she sleeps now. Xhan and Kimm have gone to tend to Cheanah and their children. Unless the magic man returns to make the baby-come-forth magic, Zhoonali says that it may be long before the second child is born. The second baby has yet to move into the upside-down, quick-to-come-out position. Now Torka must eat. It has been too long since he has gone without food and sleep."

In the rear of the hut, he sat cross-legged on his un-made bed of thickly piled caribou furs. His undertunic of bison calf skin, cured and chewed by his women to the softest consistency, kept him warm. In spite of his physical comfort, he had been too concerned about Lonit and Karana to sleep. He had been able to soothe his frightened little girls with wonderful stories of the beginning of the world, of First Man and First Woman, of adventure and magic, which distracted them from their mother's plight. Now, sprawled over his thighs and nestled in the hollow of his lap, Summer Moon and Demmi slept, curled like a pair of furless little cubs. Hungry and irritable from worry and lack of food and sleep, he waved away the woman's offering and made a conscious effort to distract himself from the rich smell of the heated fat. It was not easy.

The sounds and scents of a slowly stirring encampment were evident above the low but constant whine of the wind. With the rising of the sun and the cooling of the fires in the sky, the people of the encampment had sought sleep; because of painfully short days at this time of the year, however, the women were already awake, making their fires, cooking their meals, and tending their children and the needs of their men.

Iana had been at her cooking for some time now, and Torka had been disturbed by the sound of her preparations as she arranged her fire stones and the kindling of dung, dried tundral sods, and bones, and then hacked slabs of frozen fat into cubes with her broad-bladed stone knife. The whirring of her bow drill had been followed by the low cracklings of fire. When he smelled the oily, richly rancid fat, he had salivated, imagining the little cubes swelling, softening, dripping into the flames. He had envied the meal that his children and second woman would soon consume, never expecting that Iana would offer any food to him.

"Torka *must* eat," Iana said again. "Torka *must* have strength in the day to come."

"I cannot!" He was visibly annoyed. The fat smelled wonderful; his stomach growled. He absently stroked his girls' hair as he scowled at Iana. "*You* may eat! The *children* may eat. But Torka cannot! Iana must be very tired indeed to have tempted her man with food that is forbidden to him as long as his woman is in labor!"

His rebuke was sharp. She was cut by it even though it

had been spoken in little more than a whisper lest it rouse the children. She hung her head. He saw the weariness in her, the repentance, and something else—fear, intense fear. It paled her features and tightened the corners of her lips. He knew that she shared his worry over Lonit. He was sorry for having spoken so impatiently and was prompted to speak from his heart to his second woman. "We are both tired and filled with worry. Tell me, Iana, among your own people, have you ever heard of a birth taking so long?"

She shook her head, looked up briefly, and then hung her head again. "This woman cannot say. It is not one birth, Torka. It is *two*. Never was this allowed among the people of the band into which Iana was born or among any of the bands that Iana has ever known. As Zhoonali has said, such a birth was always ended before it was allowed to begin."

It was not the answer that he wanted to hear. He glared at her. "Then why did you practically drag me into the hut of blood to put a stop to such an ending? The claw of taking was unknown to the band into which I was born, so I had no idea that the old woman would try to take the life of the child. Had you not come, the second twin would be dead by now. Zhoonali would be happy. Everyone would be happy. Except Lonit and me."

She thought a moment. "Iana could not stand by and watch Lonit die. Torka now has one son. The fate of the second twin can be decided later by the magic man."

"Karana would not speak against the life of my child."

"He may have to. And it is not a child until it has a name." She paused, silenced by the sudden anger in his eyes. And he looked so painfully tired. Balancing the bone platter across her folded thighs, she went on, knowing that she must risk his anger: "This woman has not forgotten the ways of the people, Torka. But she wonders if perhaps the forces of Creation would not mind if Torka broke his fast just a little, between the coming of the babies. Today of all days the headman must have his strength and wits."

"When the second child is born this man will eat. Not before."

She drew in a ragged breath of frustration. "Zhoonali's

is not an unkind heart, Torka. She is a wise old woman who has come to know that traditions, no matter how painful, must be obeyed for the good of the band."

"I will not abandon my newborn children simply because the traditions of other people demand it. I am headman of this band. I care not for Zhoonali's understanding. I care only that she does as she is told."

"Zhoonali would never disobey the command of a headman—not when so many of her ancestors, brothers, husbands, and sons have been headmen themselves."

"She has made that clear enough, often enough," he grumbled. "As has Cheanah, the only son she has left. It must be a bad thing to live as long as Zhoonali, to see so many of her loved ones die and yet herself living on and on."

"Torka, you *must* listen. Iana has brought more than food to Torka. She has a warning."

"Of what?"

She swallowed, then spoke quickly. "In a camp without a magic man to confirm the rightness of the headman's decisions, Zhoonali's words are powerful in ways that frighten the people. Eneela trembles with dread as she suckles Torka's son against her will, and Simu, her man, turns his back upon her in anger."

"His anger will fade soon enough. When the second twin is born and Lonit has rested, she will suckle her own infants. Torka grows weary of your words, Iana. Eat. Rest. Renew your strength. Lonit will soon have need of you again."

"It is Torka who must eat! It is Torka who must renew his strength! And do not interrupt this woman again before she can speak her warning!"

Amazed by her uncharacteristic outspokenness, he stared wide-eyed at his usually subservient woman.

"While Torka rests within the darkness of his hut, Cheanah stands tall and bold beneath the light of day! While Torka fasts, Cheanah eats raw meat and draws his sons to him. The other hunters of the band circle close and listen to his words."

Torka's brow arched. "This birth vigil is mine to keep,

not theirs. They prepare to hunt before the dark comes down again. Before a hunt, men must eat."

"But what do they hunt, Torka? They sharpen no spearheads. They make no songs to the spirits of the game. They gather before the hut of Cheanah and talk low, like women gossiping over a flayed skin—Torka's skin! It is no secret in this camp that Zhoonali constantly prods Cheanah to think fondly of the days when he was a headman. Perhaps now that Torka has dared to challenge the forces of Creation, Cheanah thinks that soon he will be headman again. And if this happens, Torka will have no say in the fate of his children or of his women."

He stopped her with a scowl and a wave of his hand. Now he understood the fear in her eyes. His scowl eased as he looked at her with love—not the love of a man for his woman, for that love was for Lonit alone, but of a brother for a sister. In the years since Iana had come to share his fire, she had never been more than that to him. He doubted if she would ever be more to any man as long as she was allowed a choice, for men had used her cruelly in the past. At Torka's fire circle, the choice would always be hers; he had sworn it long ago, and she had wept in gratitude.

He gazed into her sad eyes, remembering that she had suffered more than most. In a world where starvation, marauding beasts, and natural disasters compassionlessly snuffed out the lives of boys and girls, men and women, most became inured to suffering. Others, like Iana, did not. Her wounds were concealed by her lovely, superficially imperturbable appearance, but Torka knew better. Nightmares frequently woke her in the early hours and caused her to stare wide-eyed in terror, panting like a panicked doe pursued by men who would tear her to pieces. She had lost to violence all her children and Manaak, the man who had sired them.

Torka saw the terror in her eyes. He reached to wipe it away with a tender touch. "Iana, you are Torka's woman. Whatever Cheanah may think, you are Torka's woman, not his."

"But he has looked at me. And if he and the others stand against you, with Karana gone from the camp—"

"Cheanah has an appetite for women. If you were meat, he would eat you all. But Iana will be Torka's woman until she willingly chooses another man."

The corners of her mouth quivered, but with relief or tension, Torka could not tell. "If Torka stays too long within this hut and grows weak from fasting, that choice may not be mine or his to make." Steadying the platter of fat with one hand, she reached with the other to trace the forms of the sleeping children. Her eyes caressed them with love, then moved to beseech Torka. "And so this woman says that although it is against tradition, Torka *must* eat, must put upon his body the paint and raiment of his rank. In the skins of lions, with the teeth and claws of wolves about his neck, Torka must go out to his people and show them his strength before it is too late for us all."

The cave was dark and rank with the stench of feces and urine, spoiled meat and moldering bones and grass, and something big and alive lurking close in the shadows.

Karana awoke with a start, sat up, banged his head, and fell back as consciousness spun away into dreams of a mewling beast leaning over him . . . breathing on him . . . lifting him with monstrous, gray-furred arms . . . drawing him close . . . and rocking him as a mother would rock an injured child.

Somewhere in the dream, a dog was growling, while the beast made low grunting sounds of deep distress as it exhaled meat-eater's breath across Karana's face.

"Wah na wah . . . wah nah wut . . ." the monster purred as it caressed his face with a bloodstained claw.

Karana lay still, willing the dream away, but it deepened, intensified, and the pain in his head grew worse. He continued to lie still, so still that it was an effort to do so. His muscles began to twitch, yet he forced them to remain motionless, somehow knowing that to do otherwise would bring about his death. His head hurt, and he could feel blood, warm and wet, seeping from the top of his scalp. He wondered if it was real or a part of the dream.

The monster continued to purr and stroke him, gently probing the gash in his scalp.

Suddenly Karana knew that he was *not* dreaming. He

cried out, and the beast, startled, winced and uttered high little hoots. It tightened its grip and rocked him faster.

Karana's eyes opened. The morning light outlined the beast's monstrous, powerfully muscled form in a silvery nimbus. The magic man needed no gift of Seeing to tell him that he was in a cave—the den of the wind-spirit wanawut.

Panic filled him. He could just make out the face of the wanawut. Its eyes stared down at him as if it were wondering if it had seen him before. Its long, bearlike muzzle worked as it drew in his scent. The long, wet glint of its teeth shone dully in the dark.

The size and closeness of those teeth set the panic loose within Karana. "Torka!" he screamed, and even as the scream left his lips, he knew that his adopted father could not hear him, let alone help him.

Karana tried to tear himself free from the grip of the beast, but it was no use; the monster held him fast in the curl of one arm, hooted, and grunted, then knuckled him hard in the belly with its other hand as if to say: *Lie still, puny one!*

It was all Karana could do to keep from screaming again as the beast began its strokings once more and continued to mew at him. It was better to be stroked than torn to pieces. But perhaps the creature was contemplating that. It may have fed on the dead leaping cat, then, as an afterthought, it had brought him here to be cached for future feedings. The magic man's heart lurched at the thought.

The wanawut showed its teeth. Was it smiling or grimacing? Karana could not tell. He felt sick. He wondered if the beast would be upset if he vomited; if he did, might it let him go in disgust? No. That was too much to hope for. This wanawut dwelled within a cave so foul, vomit would probably pass unnoticed.

Karana swallowed hard, resolving not to be sick, not to do anything that might anger the beast, for despite the strength of its hold on him, its mood was surprisingly passive. It was crooning in low, guttural sounds as it fingered him in the way a girl-child played with a favorite doll . . . lovingly.

Karana's heart pounded. *Lovingly?* He nearly gagged on the supposition. It was impossible! The beast was playing with him, as he had seen many a carnivore toy with its prey before settling in to its meal.

Yes, he was a magic man who would soon be meat. There was nothing he could do to save himself. Terror numbed him. He did not even know how he had come to be here. He could only remember the wanawut backhanding the dog, then pounding toward him with its great arms raised and its canines showing.

He knew now that he must have fainted. Being attacked by two man-eaters in one day had proved too much for him. So much for the powers of the magic man! So much for dressing himself in the skin of the leaping cat and swaggering into the encampment of his people! So much for helping Lonit! For all his bluster and bragging, he could not even help himself.

Somewhere beyond the thick, stinking blackness of the cave, the spirits of both worlds must be laughing—and Navahk the Spirit Killer, who had slain a wanawut and danced in its skin, must be laughing with them.

A thought more terrible than death struck him. Had Navahk sent the beast to slay him? No! Karana would not believe it! Not even Navahk could come back from the dead to work such a deed upon the living.

The wanawut, with no instigation from the ghost of Navahk, had followed the wounded leaping cat to make a meal of it and had found a man, had brought him up out of the hills and into a cave high within the clouded crags that its kind was known to inhabit.

Karana closed his eyes. How far was he from the encampment of his people . . . from Torka and Lonit and his beloved Mahnie? He could hear her voice: "Do not go! There will be trouble if you do."

Trouble! If only she knew the trouble he was in!

"Too often are you away from your people when they have need of you, Karana," she had said. "Too often are you away from me."

I will never see you again, my Mahnie. We will never make a child together. I will not hunt with Aar at Torka's side, hear the laughter of Lonit and sweet Demmi, or look

*upon the dimpled face of solemn little Summer Moon.
Zhoonali will see to it that the twins die. Torka and Lonit
will curse my name for not having tried to save them. I
will die in this stinking cave. The wanawut will eat my
bones, and no one will ever know what has befallen me.
And when my spirit walks the wind, Navahk will greet me,
laughing; because in the end, the son whose magic he
feared above all else will be dead!*

The beast's fingers were tracing his lids. There were
tears in his eyes. In terror he squinted hard, visualizing
his eye sockets pierced and his eyes ruined at the whim of
a creature that could use its claws to flick out his eyeballs.
More times than he could remember he had used his own
thumbs to gouge the eyeballs of animals he had killed.
Eyes were the best part of a kill. But he was not dead yet!
And he would not lie here waiting to be mauled and
eaten. Beyond the cave, there was light and clean, cold
air, and the sound of wind and the low, constant growling
of a dog.

Aar! Was Brother Dog alive? And was that a baby that
he heard crying somewhere in—or beyond—the darkness
of the cave? Perhaps he was not as far from the encampment as he had thought!

There was only one way to find out—only one way to
return to the world of the living—and that was to take the
risks of the living. Mahnie was waiting for him. Lonit
needed him. Her twins needed him. He had come out
across the land in search of magic and omens that would
allow him to stand against tradition without provoking the
wrath of the spirits. Had he succeeded and had not realized it until this moment?

Yes!

The magic and the omens that he sought were not in
the land or the sky but within him—within his love for
those he had left behind. What did it matter if he did not
know the proper rituals? He was a shaman, and he had
been trained by the best—by old Umak and the lovely and
wise Sondahr and, yes, in his way, by Navahk, too. If all
his instincts cried out that it was wrong to refuse life to
children simply because they were twins, then it must be
so! He had only to make up the words, conjure the omens,

dance, chant, and make the magic smokes in whatever way he chose. The people would believe him. He would *make* them believe him. The twins would live!

With a shout of defiance, he wrenched his body hard to the right. His movement was so quick and so violent that the startled wanawut loosed its hold with a frightened shriek as he went rolling into the darkness over jagged fragments of broken bones, grabbed at what had to be the femur of a large grazing animal, and sprang to his feet, holding the long, saliva-slick bone as a stave, ready to fight for his life.

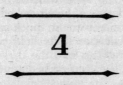

4

The baby came forth quietly, in a rush of blood and fluid, without any pain at all to its mother. Lonit awoke, aware that something had changed, and was amazed to see Zhoonali was kneeling before her, holding a newborn infant that was still red and glistening. Her child! Her *tiny* child!

Was she dreaming? No, she knew that she was not. Her heartbeat quickened with excitement as she raised herself onto her elbows. Suddenly dizzy, she fell back onto the bed of grasses. Her eyes strayed around the hut. It did not seem that much time had passed since she had fallen asleep. Xhan and Kimm had not yet returned. Nor had Iana. She knew that Karana had not come back to the encampment: Were he here, she would hear his magic chants on her behalf. Everything seemed the same, except that someone, most likely Zhoonali, had been burning dried sprigs of spruce and artemisias in the tallow lamp. Lonit's nostrils tightened against the sharply medicinal scent. In the hut's shadows, Wallah still snored. Lonit smiled tenderly as she closed her eyes and focused her thoughts upon the older woman.

"Another son," informed Zhoonali.

Lonit opened her eyes. All thoughts of the midwives vanished. She forced herself onto her elbows again, nearly swooning with weakness until pride and delight in the sight of the little one brought her strength back. What a tiny, skinny thing he was—yet perfect in all his parts and squirming like a cold little fish in Zhoonali's palms. Soon he would be warm. She would hold him close, and he would draw the warmth of life from her breasts. She exhaled a little sob of delight. There was no fear in her heart for this child—not since Torka had made it clear to Zhoonali that with or without the consent of the magic man, it was her obligation as head midwife to deliver the baby and not her right to kill it.

The old woman held the child up and glared at it with hard, critical eyes. "It is so small. Half the size of the other . . . almost as though it had not had the same father as the other, but a sire of smaller stature."

Lonit stared as something ominous stirred deep within her heart. Her breath caught in her throat. In the misted recesses of her still groggy mind, memories that she had not allowed to surface for many moons threatened her: memories of rape. Of mauling at the hands of a man dressed all in the white belly skins of winter-killed caribou. Of a man as strong and beautiful as a lion. And as deadly. *Navahk.*

Her eyes widened and fixed upon the infant. *Navahk is dead! And even if he were not, I could bear nothing with him! My body bled between the time of his rape and my reunion with Torka. Not much, but surely enough. I could not have carried his child!*

But even as she thought these thoughts, the memories mocked her. Her heart began to beat again, hard and sure, the blood to pound in her veins. She snarled at Zhoonali, "This woman would look upon her child!"

Zhoonali frowned, sensing the change in her, and displayed the infant before its mother.

Relief surged through Lonit. The little one had her eyes—unusually round and deeply lidded—but the baby had Torka's face! His mouth . . . his nostrils . . . the high, wide span of his brow . . . even his finely shaped, tight-to-the-skull ears. The resemblance was unmistakable. No one would ever question the paternity of this little one! *No one*—especially his mother.

She laughed aloud and reached out to hold her son. "Please put him into my arms. I would hold him."

Zhoonali shook her head. "Not until the father accepts it."

Lonit lowered her head and threatened: "Do not call my child 'it,' Zhoonali. He lives! Soon he will have a name! He is a member of this band!"

The old woman's face was devoid of expression. "You must rest now, Woman of the West. When the infant is accepted by the headman, then that to which you have given birth will be put to your breast."

Lonit lay back, exhausted but contented. Even though Karana had not yet returned to the encampment to override the cruel customs of the others, Torka would accept his son as he had accepted his twin. "With his brother," she said.

The old woman's face remained impassive, but the expression in her eyes became dark and sad. "Rest," she repeated, and rose. Holding the infant in the bend of her left arm, she took up her cloak, swung it on, and reached for the caribou skin that would be placed over the infant as it was carried out to its father.

Lonit sighed. In the shadows, Wallah was stirring, perplexed by the sight of the baby.

"What . . . how? . . ." she sputtered, backhanding sleep from her eyes.

Lonit beckoned her friend to come to sit beside her. "This one was born as easily as the dawn. Do not be angry that no one chose to wake you. This child was born without even waking *me*! The spirits smile upon him and show this woman that they are no longer displeased with Torka and Lonit for wanting to keep their twins."

Wallah frowned. "It is not good for a mere woman to say what pleases or displeases the spirits," she whispered.

Zhoonali's chin went high. She began to respond, then paused, changing her mind. When she did speak, her words were monotonal but oddly tense. "Stay with Woman of the West. Tend to her needs. She has suffered long, has lost much blood, and is very weak. She must drink from the healing horn and sleep for at least another day and night. Now Zhoonali will go out to offer that which Lonit has born to its father. If he accepts its life—"

"Torka *will* accept his *son*!" Lonit said hotly. She would have rebuked Zhoonali further had she not been so infinitely exhausted. Zhoonali was right; she did need to

sleep. She was actually grateful when the old woman
nodded her head in deference to the sharp reprimand and
continued calmly: "Zhoonali will do what must be done.
Stay here, Wallah, woman of Grek, and see to it that
Woman of the West is not disturbed."

She paused for a moment, her old eyes squinting in the
pale, tenuous light of the morning. Her small body was
wrapped in her great white bearskin cloak, and the infant
was held firmly hidden beneath it in the fold of her arm,
close against her side. Morning was all that there would
be of day. There would be no noon, no afternoon, no
dusk. Soon the sun would set without ever having fully
risen. The long dark would come down again, and it would
be night. By then she would be alone and far away.

Zhoonali's chin came up. Her fear and indecision were
buried deep; no one would have guessed that she was
capable of either. Anyone looking at her would have seen
her resolve. But no one saw her as she closed the door
skin and stood immobile against the shaggy, conical hide
walls of the hut of blood.

The encampment was full of life and wind-combed smoke.
Torka had the band's attention, and hers. He had taken up
the stance of birth vigil again. She felt her body respond
to the sight of him, for although she was old, she was still
a woman, and the sight of Torka in the full regalia of his
rank aroused a sexual awareness that would have stunned
and most likely appalled him had he known of it.

He was magnificent, this Torka, this Man of the West
whose totem was Life Giver—the great mammoth that her
people knew as Thunder Speaker—this Torka who was
called Man Who Walks With Dogs because of the magic
powers that allowed him and the members of his family to
command the spirits of the wild dogs of the tundra. He
was a tall man. Winter-lean and storm-strong, he stood
outside his pit hut, facing the rising sun, with his head
back, arms lifted, and limbs splayed wide. His hands were
curled tightly around the bone haft of his stone-headed
spear. Around his head was a circlet of feathers plucked
from the wings of eagles, hawks, and the great black-and-
white flight feathers of a condorlike teratorn. Around his

neck was a massive collar of intricately woven sinew strands adorned with stone beads and tiny fossilized shells. From this hung ornamental loops of braided musk-ox hair, which held the paws and fangs of wolves, as well as the claws and stabbing teeth of the great short-faced bear he had killed long ago in face-to-face combat.

Awash in the cool, lustrous opalescence of the morning, in his exquisitely sewn garments cut from the skins of dire wolves, caribou, and Arctic lions, with his thick, unplaited black hair loose and blowing in the wind, his was a posture of defiance, not of supplication.

Zhoonali's eyes widened. Was it any wonder that the hunters and the women and children of this camp observed him with awe and trepidation? What a man he was, standing against them all! Standing against the very forces of Creation for this woman! For his newborn son! And in hope of the life of this spiritless suckling, which, unknown to him, she held captive within the warm, sheltering fall of her cloak.

You cannot have them both! Her inner turmoil was great, the unspoken words fire in her throat. Her eyelids half closed, sharpening her focus as she scanned the band's people. Her eyes were barely visible between the thin, white screening of her lashes. *Is there not one man here bold enough to confront him? Is there not one man who will stand up to him, as this old woman tried to do, and tell him to his face that this birth vigil violates tradition? Twins are an affront to the forces of Creation! The acceptance of one might be tolerated, but the effrontery of Torka to ask for the lives of both is too much! Someone must tell him!*

They were all such strong, sinewy men. All of them, including the boys and old Grek and ancient, crooked-nosed Teean, were bold when hunting prey. But Torka was not prey; he was their headman—a man who had led them safely away from their enemies, around mountains that rained fire, through canyons of falling ice, into a new but traditionally forbidden land, which had proved a better hunting ground than any they had ever known before. And in this new land, Torka had hunted beside them and taught them the mystical power that lay in the use of spear hurlers. He had followed his totem, Life Giver, to this camp full of meat, where those who had so willingly walked with him now sat in their prime winter furs, with their bellies full, and their lips greased with fat, and their dark eyes fearful as they observed him from the semicircle that they had made around Cheanah's fire.

Zhoonali's mouth pressed back against her time-worn teeth. How small they seemed to her now as they hunkered close to the lee of Cheanah's large pit hut. Of dark, shaggy bison hides that were lashed tightly across a framework of mastodon bones, camel ribs, and caribou antlers, it suited the big man who had naturally commanded the loyalty of his fellow hunters . . . before Torka had overshadowed him.

Cheanah was talking with the hunters in low, insistent tones. Zhoonali saw the worry on their faces. Cheanah's alone seemed impassive, but she knew that her son was on edge. His mother had been challenged, her ways repudiated before the entire band. And no doubt Kimm had been whining about her bruised face, wheedling and reminding him of the twin sons that he had forced her to sacrifice for the good of all.

A man did not sacrifice sons easily—bravely, but never easily. Torka's adamant refusal to do the same was an affront to Cheanah, Kimm, their sacrificed twins, and the customs and taboos of their ancestors. It was no wonder that in the continued absence of the magic man, he had called the others together for man talk. Soon he would confront Torka with their concerns.

But Zhoonali had lived long enough to know the hearts of men. The magic man was but a youth, and Torka's adopted son. His heart was soft with affection for Lonit. If this power of Seeing had allowed him to know that two tiny hearts beat within Lonit, Zhoonali doubted that he would return until the fate of the twins was decided, lest he have to condemn them himself. It would take more than talk to force Torka to abandon his insistence upon keeping his twins alive—but she was not convinced that Cheanah was willing to do more th. that.

Shame was bitter in her mouth. It was an emotion that had been alien to her until Cheanah—with no advice or consent from her—had passively acquiesced to Torka's leadership. Never before had Zhoonali lived within a band over which one of her men—first grandfather, then father, husband, and sons—had not been headman. She thought it a pity that of all of her sons, Cheanah was the only one who had survived.

True, he had always been the most solicitous. She knew that his love for her was deeper than that of most sons for their mothers. Nevertheless, for all of his bearlike physical attributes and skill as a hunter, there was little aggressiveness in the man. Handsome he was, and more powerful than most, but like a bull musk-ox, his mind was a small, muscle-bound, herd-animal sort. Flexibility and abstract thought were beyond its capacity. It took extensive prodding to rouse anger in Cheanah, and then he became like a riled, rage-maddened bear; only when the herd—his sons, his fat little girl, or his women—were placed in imminent danger of a direct attack could he be provoked into action. He must be provoked now.

Shame became regret as she felt the small life within the crook of her arm flex with a yawn.

For the good of the band and for the sake of my son and my grandsons, this one suckling must not have life lest the forces of Creation bring death to us all as punishment for the arrogance of its parents!

She had promised Torka that she would not interfere with its birth. She had promised that the fate of this child would be determined by the magic man. But for the good of her son, Cheanah, her grandsons, Mano, Yanehva, and Ank, her granddaughter, Honee, and for all of the sons and daughters of the band, this she could not do!

She drew in a deep breath, seeking courage from it, turned on her booted heels, and hurried, unseen, from the encampment.

Come, spiritless suckling. This woman must take you far from this camp, to expose your flesh in a place where no man or woman will ever find your bones . . . or mine! For when my spirit walks the wind because of a child that should never have been born, my son Cheanah will remember that he is a man who was a headman to his people . . . a man whose anger will make him headman again.

Not even Torka will be able to stand against Cheanah when at last the bear within his grief-stricken spirit is riled.

The wanawut crouched in the shadows. The light from the fissure was still behind it.

The magic man's escape from the cave must be through the fissure, into the light. How was he to get around the beast without losing his life or being dismembered by a single swipe from the wanawut's great clawed arms? He swallowed, his heart seeming to lodge in his throat. He had heard it said that the spirit of a mutilated body was doomed to haunt the world of men forever, as it searched for its lost parts.

Karana felt light-headed. His choices were clear enough: stay and be consumed, or run for freedom and be killed, horribly injured, or escape through the fissure unscathed. He must focus all his thoughts and energy on getting himself out of this black, foul-smelling cave! He must face the beast wanawut and overcome it, with only a long bone to serve as a weapon.

He tightened his grasp on the bone. Its lightness told him that it had not come from a recent kill. It carried no scent of blood or tissue. The marrow had been sucked from its ends. From its length he judged it to be a leg bone of a camel, bison, horse, or . . . of a man? No. That could not be. As far as he knew, with the exception of his own band, there were no people in the Forbidden Land.

He swallowed. The hunters were far away, safe within the winter encampment. He willed his mind to focus on the threat at hand.

Karana, son of Navahk, your people call you Magic Man. If they are right . . . if there is any power in you at all, you had best summon it up now!

The beast was circling, making low, quick exhalations that betrayed its nervousness. Was the thing afraid of him? It growled but was not coming any closer. Had it been a man instead of a beast, Karana would have assumed that it was begging for conciliation, for its hideous brow was furrowed as though with concern, and its great arms were gesturing wide, almost in the manner of an old friend beckoning to another who has too long been an enemy.

The magic man found these thoughts preposterous. The beast in the shadows was big and powerful and dangerous, but it lacked one crucial weapon, which made it vulnerable to a man—the ability to reason.

Karana, hunching low, circled opposite the wanawut, warning it away with the long bone, jabbing at it with the end from which the ball joint had been chewed to dagger sharpness. The creature stayed back but continued to circle. It stared at the gnawed end of the bone as if it understood the threat.

The magic man smiled with relief. The thing could have had him by now, but for reasons that eluded him, it evidently feared him as much as he feared it. If the wanawut kept on circling, the fissure would momentarily be at Karana's back, and freedom would lie just beyond—if he could get through the opening before the beast made a grab for him.

The moment came. With the long bone in one hand, Karana reached back frantically to loosen stones from where the creature had wedged them into the fissure, to wall up the entrance to its cave. Only a few were small enough to move easily. His fingertips bled as they worked to move the large, cold, rough stones.

The beast was coming at him, its eyes wide with anger.

Karana screamed in desperation as he swung the long bone at the wanawut. The bone sang as it cut the air and cracked in half against the creature's forearm.

Startled, the wanawut screeched in pain, leaped straight up, and instead of falling upon Karana to make an easy end of his life, cowered back . . . back . . . into the thinning shadows.

The magic man stood in shock. Beyond the cave, the wind blew ice clouds away from the sun, allowing the full light of day to blossom across the world and stream into the den. Karana could see the wanawut clearly now, and he gasped in horror. The creature was female—hideously, grotesquely female—with long, swollen, milk-encrusted, hairless breasts protruding from her furred chest. She beat

her monstrous fists upon her thighs as she made high
grunting noises at him.

Behind her, he could see the back of the cave. It was
wet, slimed with multicolored algae and moss. Where the
ceiling met the bone-and-refuse-littered floor, he could
see a nest of spruce boughs and lichens, and in the nest, a
cub was stirring, wailing its protest at having been awakened from sleep—a little cub that was not a cub at all but,
impossibly, in all ways except for the gray fur that covered
it from head to toe, a female human child.

The beast saw his reaction and, sensing danger to her
offspring, ran to her nest, swept the cub into her massive,
hairy arms, and cradled it against her breasts as she sat
cross-legged in her nest. The thing took suck. Karana
could not tear his eyes from it. The wanawut was hooting
at him as she rocked and rocked, like a demented woman
begging for pity. He made himself look away.

And then he saw it: Spread out on a rack of its own
bones, a skin was positioned to keep the ceiling moisture
from dripping into the nest of the beast—the skin of a
man, boned and gutted, arms flung wide, head still attached, one eye open and staring hollowly . . . at his son.

Navahk's eye. Navahk's skin. The skin of Karana's father, whose body did not lie buried beneath the collapsed
ice walls of the far mountains, after all, but had been
brought here to this cave, to be preserved by the wanawut,
the beast that Navahk had seduced into following him
across the world like the hideous shadow of his own twisted,
malevolent soul. The beast that had borne him a child. A
cub. An animal that was Karana's half sister.

Revulsion and horror were so great in the magic man
that he acted without thinking. With a howling shriek of
rage, he charged the beast, flailing the broken end of his
father's leg bone. He would kill the cub with it. And in
the killing, the wanawut would end his life and his shame.

But the animal rose to deflect his blow and, instead of
attacking him, knocked him away gently. He fell. The
beast stood over him, mewing softly and touching him
with a tenderly reproving hand, as if he were not a man
and predator who would kill her and her cub if he could
but a long-lost mate.

Suddenly Karana was sick, violently and uncontrollably sick. Men had always said that he looked like his father—like Navahk, the deceiver, the treacherous, slayer of men and raper of women—who had, sometime before the end of his life, mated his power to that of the wanawut to produce an heir that was truly worthy of him. An animal.

The little thing was staring down at him now as its mother held it to her breast. The half-human beast was an affront to the very forces of life, and Karana hurled himself upward at the thing, intending to snap its neck. But the wanawut struck him again, hard this time. He crashed down and slammed the back of his head against a stone and knew no more.

Karana awoke in darkness. The sun was down. The cave was cold. The fissure had been closed by stones. The beast had gone out, taking her child with her.

Slowly, with grim purpose, sensing the hollow eye of his father staring down at him from its lifeless skull, he worked to remove the stones that blocked the den's entrance. It did not take him long to clear it, and although his fingers were bleeding and sore when he was done, the anguish within his mind was so much greater, he felt no physical discomfort.

Beyond the cave, the new star shone in the night sky, its tail upturned like that of a young colt frolicking across the summer tundra. Karana looked at it somberly. Was it a good omen or bad? He did not know. He did not care. His shame was so great that he did not care whether he lived or died.

Dog sign was everywhere. So Brother Dog *had* followed him! The ground outside the lair told him that Aar had been at the beast. There was blood on the mountain.

Karana tasted it. It was not Aar's blood; it was the blood of the beast. He closed his eyes and tried to use his powers to learn whether the creature was alive or dead, but nothing came to him except the small, hairy vision of the cub. He hoped it was dead, along with the monster that suckled it.

It did not take him long to gather up enough dry scrub

growth to fire the cave. His fingers were growing stiff, so it was no easy thing to start the fire. He stood and watched the flames draw life from the refuse that littered the floor. The flames threw red and yellow light, the color of the sun. Karana looked through the blaze at what remained of Navahk.

As the flames consumed the skin and skull of his father, he turned away and knew for a certainty that he would never find the magic; it was not meant for the sons of men who coupled with beasts.

In abject misery, he went down from the heights and strode across the hills. He did not know when Brother Dog joined him. They moved across the land together, loping aimlessly beneath the stars while a red aurora slowly washed the night in great, looping rivers that were the color of blood. Karana paid no heed to them. Somewhere along the way the dog cut across his path, forcing him to pause, warning him of dangerous terrain.

To calm the dog he changed his course until, at last, breathless and exhausted, he stopped. Something was coming. He knew it. He felt it. Minutes passed. The earth quivered ever so slightly beneath his feet. He could not have said when the mammoth appeared. Perhaps it had been with him all along, that great, towering mammoth that was Torka's and his totem. Life Giver . . . Thunder Speaker . . . the great one who had led them from their enemies to safety within the Forbidden Land stood before him, a living mountain, blocking his way.

The dog whined softly. The mammoth was so close that its breath was one with the wind, which stirred the ruined garments of the magic man. Tears rolled down his cheeks.

"I am not worthy of you, Life Giver. Go."

The mammoth did not go. Instead, it touched the sobbing young man, nudged him with its trunk, urging him on, westward, homeward, as, for the first time since entering the Forbidden Land, the spirit wind—that strange inner turbulence that always preceded Seeing—rose within Karana and made him know that he *was* a magic man. For the sake of those whom he loved, he knew he must hurry.

The great mammoth was leading, and he would follow, as he had always followed, for in the shadow of his totem, with the Seeing wind rising within his soul, Karana knew that his mystical power was restored.

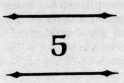

5

The first woman of Cheanah stood at the entrance to the hut of blood, holding the door skin back. The sky was afire behind her. "Where is Zhoonali?"

Wallah blinked, taken aback by Xhan's question. "Gone. A long time gone. To bring the child to its father."

"*Child?*"

"Of course! Why do you stare at me like that, Xhan?"

"The burning sky . . . the trembling earth . . ."

Wallah nodded. Fear was growing in her, also. The bad omens had returned, but the head midwife had not. In celebration of the birth of Torka's second son, the camp should be filled with the sounds of story chanting and revelry. Instead, an unnatural silence filtered through the doorway. Wallah's mouth puckered over her teeth. "How long must we wait in the hut of blood for Zhoonali to bring us word of the child's acceptance by its father?"

Xhan frowned. "It has been done. You know that."

Wallah felt irritable. Something was wrong here. But what?

On her bed of clean furs, which overlay a mattress of freshly laid grasses and lichens, Lonit backhanded sleep from her eyes, sorry that she had drunk so deeply from Wallah's healing horn; she had slept the entire brief day away without knowing the joy of holding her sons to her breasts. Now it was dark again, and again the sky had caught fire and the earth had trembled. In the eyes of the people of this band, this would bode ill, but Lonit knew

58

that Torka would allow no harm to come to his newborn sons. He had experienced and survived much worse and had come to believe that such phenomena were beyond the influence of men. The lives of men and women mattered little to such great powers as Father Above and Mother Below. Torka was strong in his opinion that signs read from the movement of the earth and sky should be interpreted, acted upon, not propitiated or sacrificed to. Karana, however, disputed this; Lonit was not sure of it; and every band that Torka had ever walked with had condemned him for his arrogance. Now, thinking of her man, she asked to hold her sons and was puzzled when Xhan scowled at her.

"*Sons?* What are you saying, Woman of the West? The one boy child that Torka unwisely accepted sleeps in the arms of Eneela. Your man continues to stand birth vigil for the second."

"But the second child was born in the light of yesterday's dawn," Lonit said, perplexed. She drew back the furs that covered her. "Look at me, Xhan. I lie on a clean bed. Wallah has taken away the fouled birth grasses and has washed my body. Look. My belly is flat, but my breasts are full and aching to give the milk of life to my sons!"

Wallah, frowning, looked at Xhan. It was quite clear from the expression of Cheanah's first woman that she had no idea that the second baby had been born. Rising groggily to her feet—Wallah had also drunk deeply of the healing horn and, after days of caring for Lonit, had slept long and deeply—she grunted. Her excess weight, from the prolonged good life in this camp to which Torka had led them, made upward mobility difficult.

Xhan's eyebrows joined across her narrow, almost bridgeless nose. "Zhoonali has not come out from the hut of blood with any second child."

"But she did!" insisted Wallah. "She *did*! And told me to wait with Lonit until—" The matron paused for a moment, gathering her thoughts and not liking them at all. "She told me to wait here . . . until she had done . . . what she *must* do. . . ."

And suddenly, as one, they understood what had happened: The old woman had despaired of the omens. She had taken it upon herself to expose the infant for the good of her people.

Xhan sucked in her breath, and Wallah looked thunderstruck.

Lonit stared at them both, and with her hand across her abdomen, she thought of that so very small little life. A single sob of longing escaped her.

"You have a son, Lonit. Be content with that," consoled Wallah, sweeping across the hut to squat beside the younger woman and take her hand. Her soft eyes brimmed with pity.

Xhan's mouth turned down, and although her eyes were hard, the words that followed were harder. "The old woman has risked her life because Torka and his first woman insisted on granting life to that which should never have been born. Cheanah will be very angry when he learns of this. The band will be angry. I think soon you will have *no* sons, Woman of the West, for Torka has proved himself unfit to lead. The forces of Creation, with their burning sky and trembling earth, have chosen Cheanah to be headman of this band!"

At Cheanah's urging, the men of the band followed the trail of the old woman. Although she had done her best to conceal her tracks, she was a female and had not the skills of a hunter.

"Zhoonali has gone far for one of her years," said Grek, impressed by the physical prowess of the old woman whose walk was leading them eastward into distant hills and difficult terrain.

"Why did she not simply take the thing from camp, pack its mouth and nostrils with moss, and leave it to suffocate while she returned safely to her people?" grumbled old Teean.

"She wanted to be certain that we would not find it." Simu's voice was firm and strong with youth, and with resentment as he glanced at Torka. "For the good of the band she wanted to be sure that under no circumstances would it be given life like the other . . . against the wishes of the people."

Torka did not flinch against the obvious rebuke. He looked at the young hunter evenly. "That decision, Simu, was not hers to make."

"You forced her to make it!" snapped Cheanah. He walked beside Torka, his face congested with rage. "If she has been hurt in any way, know now that I will have your life for hers."

Torka eyed him impassively. He felt no animosity toward Cheanah; they hunted well together and had shared many a kill, many a meal, and many a good night's talk while stalking the great herds far from the fires of their women. He understood Cheanah's mood. Torka had always found it admirable when a man cherished the woman who had given life to him. Many did not.

"If my infant is alive when we find it, I will overlook your words," he said.

"If your infant lives, I will kill it with my own hands!" Cheanah replied. "The sky burns! The earth shakes! The wanawut howls! And now an old woman risks her life with the hope that the forces of Creation will not destroy her people because Torka's arrogance will not allow him to admit that his twins are forbidden things, fit for nothing more than to be meat for wolves and dogs and the carrion eaters of the night!"

Torka stopped. No man could ignore such a threat, and no friend would make it. "The child that this man has put to suckle at Eneela's breast and the infant that Zhoonali has taken from Torka's encampment are my *sons*. And I warn you now, Cheanah, that I will make meat out of any man who tries to harm either of them."

Zhoonali was exhausted. She could not go another step. She put the hide-wrapped infant on the frozen ground at her feet and seated herself on an outcropping of rough, lichen-clad boulders.

The wind was rising out of the west—a cold wind with the bitter taste of distant smoke and snow in it. She drew her bearskin robe close about her scrawny, bone-weary frame and looked up at the high, thin ribbons of cloud lacing the sky. The aurora turned them red. Stars shone through, glinting dully like the mist-veiled eyes of the very old. She wondered if her own eyes looked like that. *No.* Her eyes were clear. She saw things sharply, as well as she had when she was a girl.

She sighed. Youth did not seem so long ago. She remembered it all. She could focus back through time to see her parents, to feel the strong, loving embrace of her first man, to hear the laughter of her long-dead children and grandchildren. Remorse struck her so deeply and suddenly that she gasped. So many children gone! So many good men lost to this world!

Zhoonali felt the spirits of the dead watching her, whispering in the late-winter dark—sons, daughters, lovers—calling her name on the vast, invisible tides of time.

Zhoonali!

Mother!

Beloved Woman!

Come! Join us! It is time!

She listened, but try as she might, although her sole purpose in walking so far from the encampment was to encounter death—it was the only thing that would motivate Cheanah into taking action against Torka on behalf of his people—she could not bring herself to yield passively to the spirit voices.

Die she would, and soon. She was old and tired, but she was still Zhoonali, and passivity was against her nature. She sat resolute on the boulder, glumly feeling tiredness ebb, wishing that it would not. Fatigue would help her to accomplish her purpose. But how did one die? She had seen the life spirits of ancient ones sometimes simply slip away. But how? Exactly *where* did they go?

She looked up, squinting, and tried to see the wind and the spirits of the dead and the invisible world they inhabited, but it was no good. The wind stung her eyes with cold and grit, reminding her that she had witnessed enough deaths to realize that the world beyond this one was an unknown thing over which the living had no control. Did the dead fare any better? Were they given choices in the spirit world? She did not know, and her lack of knowledge was more troubling to her than the actual premise of death.

Again she sighed. She had always avoided situations

that she did not understand. She had learned early in life that only through understanding could control be attained, and Zhoonali liked to control—people, situations, her own life, and the lives of those around her. Perhaps that was why she had lived so long. Perhaps that was why she had failed to control Torka—she had never been able to understand that man. But she did understand Cheanah, and so she knew that she had done the right thing.

"Soon he will come," she told the spirits of the wind. "But he will not find me. And in his anger, he will become the man that he was born to be—headman of his band."

The wind grew colder. She wondered how the smoke from the encampment could have come so far and still remain so sharp. The smoke had the smell of burned meat and the stink of feces to it. Somewhere close, a wolf lifted its voice, and far away, miles down on the rolling tundral steppe that she had left behind, another wolf answered, and then another.

Zhoonali listened. As she sat alone in unfamiliar country, the wolf song sounded hostile, threatening.

She looked down. At her feet, the infant kicked and fussed within its wrapping of caribou skin. It was such a little baby. And such a *good* baby! Not once had it cried. It had lain content in the fold of her arm all these many hours, making smacking sounds as it tried in vain to draw life from its own tiny fingers. Zhoonali sighed yet again. The baby would cry when the wolves came. She wondered if she would do the same.

The thought was intolerable. She snapped to her feet. No! She would not have such a death! Die she would, and what happened to her spirit after that, she could not say or hope to control. But she was still Zhoonali, daughter and granddaughter of headmen, woman of headmen, mother of headmen, and as long as there was breath in her body, she would order her life as she had always ordered the lives of those around her!

She bent and took the wrapping of caribou hide from the infant. The eyes of the newborn were still closed, but she could feel other eyes watching her—wolf eyes, spirit eyes. Hackles rose on her back and neck and along her arms as she placed the tiny form upon the frozen tundra

and rose, tossing aside the caribou skin. She had broken
her promise to Torka that she would not be responsible for
the life or death of this little one. Nevertheless, she would
not allow herself to participate actively in its death. She
would not break its neck or pack its mouth, nostrils, and
body cavities with mosses and lichens in order to suffocate
it, and also prevent its life spirit from escaping its corpse
as a crooked spirit, which might haunt those who had
denied it a place within the world of the living. At least a
portion of her promise would be kept; the forces of Creation would take the spirit of the little one.

She still sensed eyes on her as she quickly hurried
away. Soon the wolf would have the little one. She would
hide within one of the high mountain caves that she had
seen not far to the east. She would take refuge and die
there, her body safe from carnivores, herself in control to
the very end. She lengthened her stride, wanting to be far
from the spiritless suckling when the wolf came to feed
upon it. She did not want to hear its cries.

Instead she heard her own. Although she had not gone
far, she had come face to face with Death.

It loomed bigger than a man before her. But it was not a
man. Nor was it a spirit. It was huge and gray and female,
and the massive bulk of its hairy body smelled like the
combined refuse pits of every camp that she had ever
lived in. In abject terror, she fled, arms up, screaming its
name again and again until she collapsed in a heap and
could run no more.

She was still muttering its name when Torka, Cheanah,
and the other hunters found her: "Wanawut . . ."

The hunters listened as Zhoonali spoke the wind spirit's
name. Their hands curled tightly around their spears, and
their eyes shifted nervously in all directions.

Only Cheanah appeared unafraid, his concern focused
totally upon the object of his search. He found no cause to
conceal either his relief or joy as he knelt, scooped his
mother into his arms, and held her as though he would
never let her go.

Torka stood staring down at her. "Where is my son?"

She looked up at him, then away, burying her head in the wind-ruffled fur of Cheanah's surplice.

"Where is my son!" Torka demanded.

Zhoonali peered up at him, her eyes wide, the pupils dilated with terror. "Wanawut . . ." she whispered, and gestured toward the high, stony hills from which she had come.

Torka followed her gesture with his gaze. The expression of anguish on his face was such that Simu, standing behind Cheanah and directly across from the headman, found himself regretting his earlier hostility; he was deeply touched by the visible depth of the headman's pain. He could not help thinking of Dak, his own yearling boy. He pictured his fat, glossy-cheeked son snuggling close to Eneela's bosom. What if the consensus of the band had decreed that little Dak be taken from his woman's arms without either his knowledge or permission? What if it had been *his* son who had been taken across the wild hills, stripped of its swaddling, and abandoned upon the cold, compassionless earth to become meat for beasts and for . . . the wanawut? Would his face not look like Torka's—pinched and twisted with grief and frustration?

"Come, Mother. We will go back to the encampment now." Cheanah was helping Zhoonali to her feet.

She had caught her breath and recaptured her dignity. She stood erect in the shadow of her bear of a son, her head high, her eyes steady and cool as she looked from one hunter to another until, finally, her eyes rested upon Torka. "The forces of Creation have held against you, Man of the West. That which was born out of the belly of your woman has been put out from among the band, but still the sky burns and the wanawut walks the land."

The headman stood unmoving. His head was held as high as the old woman's, and his eyes were as steady—but they burned. "It was not for you to take the life of my child, old woman."

"It was *not* a child! It had no name, no life! And this old woman gave; she did not take. The spiritless suckling still moved and breathed when she left it, but the—"

"My child was *alive*? You left him alive, to be torn to pieces by predators?"

"It was born to be meat. What else should she have done with it?"

The coldness of Cheanah's query struck Torka with the force of a northern gale. Had the man been closer, Torka would have dropped him where he stood. As it was, he hefted his spear and threatened with it, his lips pulled back into a snarl of warning as Cheanah's sons formed a defensive circle around their father and old Teean reached out to grip Torka's throwing arm.

"Hold, Torka! Would you kill a brother over this?" asked the old man.

Torka trembled with rage. His eyes never left Cheanah's face as he said, "No brother of mine would speak as Cheanah speaks. And no child of mine is meat to be fed alive to animals."

"It is dead by now," assured Zhoonali, pity in her eyes.

Torka glared at her. "You cannot know that."

She shook her head. "What this woman knows or does not know is of no importance. What matters is that for the good of her people, Zhoonali has done what her headman and magic man would not do!"

"It is for this man to accept or deny life to his child!" Torka was emphatic. "And no child of mine or of my people, in starving times or in times of plenty, be the child perfect in all of its parts or blemished, will ever be abandoned alive to be food for beasts!"

"It is dead by now." Mano, Cheanah's eldest boy, echoed his grandmother, boldly answering Torka as he looked to his father for approval. Cheanah had no chance to give or deny it.

Torka's reply came quick and sharp. "Until I see the bones of my son, until I place his body to look upon the sky forever with my own hands, I will not accept the death of one whose name has already been chosen and whose spirit lives within my heart."

The hunters murmured restlessly in the rising wind. They looked up at the red sky, then at their headman. Then they looked at Cheanah as if they were not certain who should speak for them.

Zhoonali's breath caught in her throat as she waited for her son to draw himself up and speak as a headman once again. But the moment passed, and he stood silent. She looked ready to scream at him as he stood scowling above her.

It was old Teean who broke the silence. "If Torka goes into the country of the wanawut to seek that which should never have been born, he goes without this man."

His statement inspired others to voice their agreement. Torka eyed them all darkly. "Then I will go alone."

"No!" It was Grek who spoke. As bearlike as Cheanah but twice the age, he stood forth boldly in the meticulously pieced garments that Wallah, his woman, had made for him. "Torka is this man's headman. This man has chosen to walk with Torka across the long miles and has learned that Torka's ways are good ways. If Torka would seek the body of his son, Grek would walk at his side. Grek is not afraid!"

The others muttered in resentment of the obvious insult, and Zhoonali exhaled a low hiss, like a riled old gander, when Cheanah made no reply.

"So be it, then," said Torka, and, with Grek at his side, he turned and strode away.

At last the baby cried, against the cold, killing touch of the wind.

Crouching over the remains of the dead leaping cat, the wanawut stopped feeding. At her breast, her cub dozed contentedly, but there was no contentment in the cub cries that wailed upon the wind.

The wanawut, unmoving, was disturbed by what she heard. The distressed cries were much like those of her own cub. She hooted softly in confusion. How could this be? She had seen the last of her own kind slaughtered by the flying sticks of the dreaded beasts that walked upright in the skins of animals—beasts such as the one she had left within her cave, the one that had come back to life even though its skin shielded her nest inside the mountain cave.

A tattoo of excitement beat within her massive breast. When she had eaten, she would bring food back to the beast. When it had fed, the wildness would go from its eyes, and it would love her again, stroke her again. Then she would not be alone in the gray world, with only the cub to make the soft, golden breeze of happiness rise within her spirit.

Again the baby cried. A high, screeching spate of angry wails.

The wanawut stood, twitching against the pain that rose from a dog-inflicted bite high on her thickly maned shoulder, and listened intently to the cries of the baby. She sniffed the night and drew in the scent of the dark, the cold, the distant smoke, and the cub.

Whose cub? Hope filled her. Were there others of her kind left alive, after all? Others to hunt with, to den with? Had her mother returned from the dead to care for her, to share her joy and ongoing puzzlement in the strange, furry little life that had poured so unexpectedly from her body one day on the tide of a great, gushing cramp? *Mother!*

Ambling forward, her cub protected in the curl of her arm, she moved across the high, cold hills, scenting the crier, listening for its whereabouts. She stopped at last, cocking her head and making low grunts of puzzlement when she saw it. What was it?

It lay on its back. Its legs were bent upward and pulled over its belly. It was no longer crying. Its face was contorted. It was still, so very still. She was certain that the breath of life had left it.

Curious, she ventured closer and stood scowling over it. It was shaped like her own little one, but it had no fur except for a thick, black tufting like new grass on its head. And it was so *puny*!

She bent forward and sniffed, then drew back in revulsion, knowing from its bland stink that it was a beast cub, abandoned as the beast cubs were often abandoned.

It might make a meal, but she was not hungry and the meat of their cubs was soft and tasteless, as were their bones. Her brow worked. Beasts were cruel and uncaring of their own. Mother had taught her that. Her muzzle worked with disappointment. It was not one of her own kind, and it was not even worth eating.

She would have turned away and left the thing where it lay, but it moved suddenly and stiffly. Its tiny, clawless fingers flexed. A pathetic sheeplike bleat came from its blue little mouth. There *was* life in the thing. She could smell its warmth but little else in the bitter chill of the wind. She bent again, sniffed again. She poked curiously with the tip of her finger at the thing, toying with it, amused by its frailty until, to her amazement, the tiny hands grasped her finger and drew it forward into a fiercely sucking mouth. Amazed, she allowed the thing to have its way.

As it sucked, it did more than grip and draw upon her finger. It gripped and drew upon her maternal instinct, so that abruptly she squatted where she was, took up the little hairless sack of bones, and drew it close, warming it with her breath. And with a sigh of amazement and delight, she felt it latch hard and imperatively to her nipple . . . and to her heart.

Karana watched it happen. He froze where he was. The wind was in his favor, so the beast caught no scent of him. Torka's baby? It could be no other. So the birth had taken place.

Vision was swept to him on the Seeing wind: The firstborn was alive! A boy, as was the other twin a boy! He could see the firstborn now, sucking dreamily at Lonit's breast. And he could see Lonit's face—so sad, so infinitely sad. So they had allowed her one twin but had condemned the other.

Remorse swept through Karana. He should have been there; perhaps he could have saved them both.

Beside him, the dog growled as it caught the stench of the wanawut. It hunkered low and would have leaped to the chase had the magic man not stopped it with a single command.

Far below, Karana could see a group of hunters moving due west slowly and surely. He frowned. Zhoonali walked with them. He recognized her cloak. What was she doing so far from the encampment? Meanwhile, ascending into the high hills, Torka and Grek were coming toward him.

He frowned, knowing that there must have been dissension in the camp over the birth of the twins. Had Torka stood against the decision to abandon the second child?

Had he defied them? Yes, Karana knew that he had. Torka could not have done anything else.

Love and admiration for his adopted father filled him. He almost cried out: "Hurry! The baby still lives! The mammoth has called me home to help you! The forces of Creation have decided in favor of Torka's sons!"

He could have charged down from the high, misty neck of the pass in which he stood and scrambled madly across the gray, stony scree directly at the beast. He could have screamed and waved his arms, diverting the wanawut, frightening the creature off, and driving it into Torka's path, where the unerring spears of the headman and Grek would surely kill it.

But he did not move because he realized that after Torka and Grek killed the beast, they would discover the *thing* . . . and looking upon it, they would know that it was Navahk's child . . . Karana's half sister . . . an affront to life.

And when Torka saw it, their relationship would forever be different. When Torka looked at Karana, he would always see the *thing* in him and know that Karana was not his son but the son of Navahk, a man who coupled with beasts and had raped Lonit.

Shivering against shame and revulsion, Karana did not move. Torka and Grek had seen him. As his hand held the dog steady, he stole a glance at the wanawut. She was rising, ambling away across the slope, and the infant remained clutched in her arms, along with her own cub, as she disappeared into a deep, cloud-shrouded defile.

Aar trembled, bristling against the desire to pursue the beast.

"Let her go," whispered Karana. "Her and the monster she suckles. The baby she carries was doomed anyway, even before it was born."

Even as he spoke, he felt the Seeing wind ebb away within him as, on the misty spine of the ridge directly ahead and to his right, the mammoth Life Giver paused, looked at him, and turned away.

The magic man was sitting cross-legged in the mists when Torka and Grek finally reached him. His face was ashen, his eyes looked old, and in his lap was the bloodied caribou skin in which Zhoonali had carried the baby from the camp. The blood was Karana's, not the child's, but Torka never asked the question, and so the magic man kept the self-inflicted wound on his inner arm concealed and was not forced to speak a lie.

They stayed awhile on that high, cold hill while Torka mourned and brooded. The little one had died cruelly, and now, without a name, the child would never again be born into the world of men.

Torka listened to the wind and felt the weight of the gathering storm mists. From the very moment that he had known of the second child's existence he had known that it would be a son, and he had joyously, secretly named it for his long-dead father, Manaravak, a brave hunter killed by a great white bear so long ago!

Torka's heart went cold.

"Manaravak! Your spirit will live again in the spirit of one who has come after you! Manaravak! Father! Although his tender flesh and tiny bones lie in the black belly of the wanawut, the son whose life Torka could not save is named for you. Together may you walk the spirit world of mists and endless wind until, beneath a sky that shows favor to the People, Lonit may give life to you once again!"

In the silence the three men began the long walk back to the encampment. The storm was on them now, shrieking and wailing and driving hard, stinging pellets of snow before it. Only once did Karana look back. The heights were shrouded, but he saw what he did not want to see . . . yet would always see . . . a haunting that was not a haunting, a gray-furred beast veiled in the swirling clouds, the wanawut, holding his half sister in one arm and Torka's son in the other.

PART II

LIFE GIVER

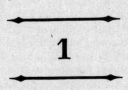

1

The wanawut watched the beasts disappear into the lowering mists. Seen from the heights, they appeared so small that she could make out no individual characteristics; they seemed no larger than the black, featureless shapes of birds winging by the bright yellow hole in the sky. She had been able to make out their throwing sticks. Her heavy, sloping brow furrowed. The beasts were dangerous. They were always hungry. Always hunting. Always ready to kill.

The sky was darkening. The underbelly of the clouds had a thick, milky, pinkish glow. The wind continued to rise, and the snowfall was intensifying. The wanawut longed for the shelter of her cave.

With a haunch ripped from the dead leaping cat held in the bend of one elbow, she walked easily through the storm. She was a creature born to the heights and their mists and the rough, cold scree slopes and mountain glaciers. Storms were more commonplace here than good weather.

Within the hairy protection of her arms, the two cubs suckled contentedly. She looked at them now and again as she walked, comparing the puny, hairless little suckling to her own large, sleekly furred cub. She saw similarities and noted differences—not only in the construction of their bodies but in their size, bone structure, and alignment of muscles and features. Indeed, on close observation, they seemed more like one another than like her. She grunted, not understanding.

Lengthening her stride, she remembered the beast that she had walled into her shelter. She did not know what to make of him. Was he the same beast that had killed her mother and danced in her mother's skin? Was he the same beast that had brought food to her when she was a cub, spoken to her in the odd voice of a beast, and stroked her and joined his body to hers? When he lay dying, she had inadvertently hastened his demise, then skinned him and brought him back to her cave in the hope that life would return to him so that she would not be alone. How could he hang over her nest while living in the skin of another? Or perhaps he was another? Perhaps he was Star Eyes, a beast that she remembered from the far land beyond the white mountains . . . a beast that looked like Mother Killer but was younger . . . a gentle beast in whose eyes the night swam with all of its stars . . . a beast who had looked directly into her eyes. Why, then, had he attacked her with the bone, stabbing and slashing and hurting her?

Because he *was* a beast. Beasts were killers. She would have to let him go or eat him before he turned on her and her cubs.

The thought of them was comforting. For the first time since the death of her mother, she did not feel alone. She was Mother now, and from the instant that the little hairless one had taken suck upon her breast, she had ceased to think of it as a beast. It was a cub, only a cub, and it was her cub now.

She turned her full attention to the icy path that she must follow to the cave. Her broad, well-arched, thickly callused feet did not lead her astray. Her acute sense of smell alerted her to danger. Burned grass. Burned bones. Burned refuse. Burned skin. She stopped, the odor offending her nostrils.

The cave! Fire had come to the cave! Fire terrified her. She had seen what it could do to the summer grasses of the tundra when it was given power from the crackling white fingers of heat that struck from the sky. Memories made her cry out as she hurried on, imagining flames and the captive beast blackened and smoldering.

Her breath was rasping in her throat and both cubs were crying when at last she reached her burned-out den.

She stood in the wind and snow, noting that the stones she had used to wall up the entrance had been moved.

She sniffed the rank air. The stench of the beast's fear was strong on the stones and on the ground all around the entrance to the cave. She bent to smell it. It was red with his terror, with his hatred of her, and with his intent to escape.

The wind was bitterly cold as it combed through her fur, parting the long, silvery, thickly shafted guard hairs and driving straight through her downy undercoat to her skin. She shivered, cooed softly to calm the bawling cubs, and went inside.

Now her mouth curled back in anger, for the beast's scent told her that he had set fire to her lair. She inhaled deeply through wide, splayed nostrils, and in the essence of his scent she could re-create it all: the thoroughness with which he had gathered dried scrub from outside, the way he had carried it in and viciously piled it all around her nest below the skin of Mother Killer, the way he had worked a stick around and around between his palms, faster and faster until they bled, the way the fire had taken life and scourged the cave and all that was in it.

Everything was black and fouled with the cold, acrid stench of smoke. The skin of Mother Killer was now a heap of ashes with a jawless, blackened skull gaping in the middle of it. Her caches of food—voles mostly, a few hares, a half-eaten, well-aged marmot, and a pile of dried berries, tubers, and well-aged animal droppings—had been reduced to a smear of greasy black powder, speckled with tiny traces of burned bones and teeth. She fingered it and growled. Beneath the ashes lay her man-stone dagger, the one that she had taken long ago from the ground near where she had discovered the wounded Star Eyes, beaten and left for dead by his own kind.

Suddenly tired and hungry, she put down the haunch of the leaping cat and sat at the back of the cave, rocking the cubs, urging them to suck while she used the man stone to cut away a slab of wind-dried, frozen cat meat.

She ate as the cubs slept in the warmth of her thick gray fur. Leaning back against the charred stone wall, she listened to the wind and gazed into the darkness. Her breath formed a mist before her face. She listened for the familiar drip-drip of moisture oozing through the ceiling, but it was so cold that the water had frozen. She dozed for a little while. The yapping of wild dogs somewhere far below the mountain awoke her. She thought of the wild dog that walked with Star Eyes. Would the dog and the beast come back, now that they knew where she took shelter? Would they come with flying sticks and man stones and other beasts to kill her and her cubs? She looked down with remorse at her sleeping cub and the beastling. The force of life was strong in this puny, ugly little thing.

Had the beasts she had seen on the lower slopes of the mountain been seeking it? Were they making certain that it was dead? Were they going to eat its tiny body? There had been such an urgency to their steps and a ferocity to the shriek of the one who had called out. She remembered the cry. *Man-ara-vak*. She imitated it. "Mah . . . nah . . . rah . . . vahk . . . mah . . . nah . . ."

She stopped. She feared this Man-ara-vak sound, because she instinctively understood that it had been a shriek of pain, a demand that the cub be returned to its pack—as if she would do that! They had abandoned it. She had found it. From the moment that it had eagerly sought the milk of life from her, she had known that it would be a part of her "pack."

And now as she drifted into sleep, cuddling her cubs close, she knew that this was the last storm she would endure within her cave. When the wind and the weather allowed, she would go from this man-infested land and would teach her cubs to live, to hunt, and to endure in the way of the wanawut.

The storm raged for a day and a night and well into the dull, bone-cracking cold of a sunless dawn. Within the hut of Cheanah, his three sons by Xhan played a sullen game of bone toss on their shared pile of sleeping furs as Honee, his daughter by Kimm, offered a compress of fat-impregnated willow leaves to her mother.

Cheanah lounged in the shadows on his own pile of furs, watching glumly as Kimm, by the light of Zhoonali's tallow lamp, accepted the poultice with no word of appreciation. With her short, plump fingers, she placed it into her mouth and bit down carefully, still managing to complain, through the mouthful, to her man.

"Look at me. My jaw remains swollen, and my gums still bleed where the woman Lonit kicked me. Two teeth are gone forever—two! Everything is bad—my pain, this storm; they will never stop because of her! Because of him! And here you—"

Cheanah's frown silenced her. His mood was as bleak and as chilling as the weather. Yet, although she wisely held her tongue, her unspoken accusation hung in the air for all to hear: And here you sit, you who were once headman, doing nothing!

Had she been sitting closer to him, Cheanah might have caused her to lose another tooth. He had never hit a woman before, but his hand twitched with the desire to do so now. What did she expect him to do? What could he do?

Torka, Grek, and the magic man had returned at the height of the storm with the wild dog but without the second twin or a word to anyone. They had gone to their own pit huts to sit out the blizzard, and the threats between Torka and Cheanah remained unsettled while the wind rose and howled.

Zhoonali's old eyes drew his gaze, which clearly indicated that his patience with his woman was wearing thin. She turned to look purposefully at Kimm. "A woman who loses a tooth is a woman who loses a year of her life. You can thank Woman of the West for that. You are right: It is bad. *Very* bad."

"She should be punished. If Cheanah were headman, he would make certain that it was done!" said Kimm petulantly, pressing her swollen jaw. She moaned and looked expectantly at Cheanah.

He glowered at her, thinking of striking the woman bare-handed across the face. She had been nagging him far too long.

Yanehva, Cheanah's middle and most thoughtful son, looked up from his game and took measure of his father's mood. He was a gaunt, stringy boy despite the fatness of this camp and the endless meals served by the women of his father's fire. "Woman of the West has been punished. She has suffered the death of a son."

Cheanah nodded, approving and agreeing. At eleven years, Yanehva was showing signs of maturity. His even-tempered, reticent nature pleased his father as much as it annoyed his mother, troubled Zhoonali, and irritated Kimm.

"What does a mere boy know of such things?" she snapped, glaring at the youth.

"It is said that when Karana was my age, he could call the rain and summon the game to die upon the spears of men, cause the—"

"*Karana!*" Kimm spat the name back at him. "That magic man speaks only for the good of Torka and Lonit—not for us! Woman of the West may have lost one twin to the wanawut, but where is the other twin? Kimm will tell you where it is—at Lonit's breast! Both twins should be dead, as my twin sons are dead."

Five-year-old Honee, as fat as her half brother Yanehva was thin, appraised her mother with infinite sadness. "I would be a son for you, Mother," she whispered. "Once, this girl asked Magic Man to make it so, but Karana said that my father would not have named my spirit unless he wanted me to live among his people. And so, because of this, Magic Man would not change me."

"Could not!" Xhan corrected the child disdainfully.

If Kimm was touched by the confession of her only child, she did not show it. She continued to hold her jaw and to moan, as though she had not heard the girl at all.

Mano pointed at his half sister. "Honee loves Karana! Ha! Some magic man he is! He disappears when he is needed! And now he hides inside his pit hut and will not speak, not even to stop the storm—"

"He could if he wanted to!" the little girl interrupted hotly.

"Ha!" goaded Mano. "Our father has wondered if Karana's powers are as juiceless as his manhood. What kind of magic man cannot even put a baby in the belly of his woman?"

Honee's backward-sloping chin trembled. "He could if he wanted to!"

Cheanah's features expanded with surprise at Mano's recollection of his words; he did not recall being in the presence of his sons when he had spoken them. He would have to watch what he said. Mano could just as easily have repeated his entire statement—including a strong willingness to take young Mahnie in trade for either of his women or simply to take her, with or without the consent of the magic man. He would accomplish with her what the magic man had failed to do.

"Karana can do anything! Anything!" There was unmistakable defensiveness as well as adoration in his little girl's quavering voice.

"Could he give you a chin and smaller ears?" taunted Mano cruelly, rolling away with giggling, six-year-old Ank on top of him while Yanehva struck out in annoyance at them both.

Honee wilted.

Cheanah saw her sideward glance at him. No doubt she was wishing that, just once, he would come to her defense against the endless teasing of her brothers. He did not. She was no longer the pretty baby who had proved an amusing variation in a family filled with the constant brawling and competition of Xhan's sons. Honee was no longer pretty at all. The realization disturbed Cheanah. He had come to care deeply for her, even though he had initially accepted her only with the thought that as his two women grew older, they would need assistance with their woman's work.

Kimm would just as soon have exposed her firstborn rather than waste precious boy-bearing time nursing a girl. Indeed, Kimm often displayed unveiled antagonism toward the child, as though it were somehow Honee's fault that she had not been born male.

Cheanah felt a growing hostility toward his second woman. She had grown too plump with the years, and too demanding. And while poor little Honee had taken on her tendency toward fat, she had inherited none of Kimm's one-time good looks. Nevertheless, Cheanah could see himself in Honee's wide features, and like his sons, she was a brave, strong little thing. He found it a pity that she was not a boy. But thanks to her brothers, she was fleet-footed, fearless in a fight, and as nasty as a badger when riled. She would have made a hunter with skills to envy. Unfortunately, despite her faith in the magic man, some things simply could not be changed. Honee would never be able to win a man with her appearance or personality; she would have to do it on strength alone, and so Cheanah made no attempt to interfere with her brothers' teasing. Their taunting would make her stronger than she already was, and Zhoonali could soothe the child later, as she always did.

Now Cheanah felt pride for the little girl as she glared defensively at Mano and informed him boldly: "This girl does not care what you say! Karana has said that the daughter of Cheanah is pretty! As pretty as Summer Moon! As pretty as—"

"And so she is, and so she is," interrupted Zhoonali with all the fervent love and blind-eyed assurance of a grandmother. "All of Zhoonali's children are beautiful! Since time beyond beginning always the people of Zhoonali have been beautiful people! Zhoonali herself, her daughters, her sons, her granddaughter . . . her grandsons . . . especially the twin sons whose lives Kimm so bravely sacrificed for the good of Zhoonali's band when Cheanah was headman. It is so! The twins were the most beautiful sons of all."

Xhan and her boys glowered.

Feeling the drag of the old woman's well-baited hook, Cheanah gritted his teeth, refusing to rise to it or be taken in by it.

Kimm wailed. "My babies! My sons! How can Cheanah rest when even one of Torka's twins draws the milk of life from his cursed, man-willed woman?"

Cheanah's brow came down. Could Kimm not see that her emotions were being led by Zhoonali? Of course she could. She was simply choosing to follow. He knew that Kimm was jealous of Lonit; she was jealous of every female who had ever caught his eye—and that had been quite a number over the years. He shared her resentment over Torka's insistence that Lonit be allowed to keep her twins. That demand had upset the entire band and nearly cost his beloved mother her life. But thanks to Zhoonali's brave unselfishness, one of those twins was dead. Nothing could be done about the other twin. It was a child with a name and a life now that it had been officially accepted by its father.

He said as much, and beyond the pit hut, the wail of the wind rose as Zhoonali shook her head. In the dull, oily, yellow light, her face was as worn and rutted as an outwash plain, but her eyes were sharp as they fixed him—penetrating, deeply contemplative, and demanding eyes that put an edge to his already well-honed irritability. "Think, Cheanah, think! The firstborn twin has been accepted by its father but not by the band. Kimm is right. The newborn must not be allowed to take its life among this people, or soon there will be no people."

Outside, the blizzard was still howling. Cheanah could not remember a worse storm or a more vicious wind. It was as though the forces of Creation were running mad across the world, trying to rip the pit huts from their stakes and blow them and the people away into the bitter dawn and off the edge of the world. Perhaps before the storm was over, the forces of Creation would have their way? If they did, Zhoonali would be proved right. But by then what would it matter? Because of Torka's stubbornness, for the sake of an arrogant woman and a child that should never have been born, they would all be dead.

"It is strange," said Zhoonali, narrowing her eyes at him meditatively. "You look like my son."

Cheanah felt the critical gazes of his boys upon him. He sat up very straight, threw out his chest, and squinted back at his mother, frowning in the way of a son who fears that a beloved parent is succumbing to the infirmities of her years. "Of course I look like your son! I am your son! The only one you have left!"

The old woman nodded and smiled with obvious relief. "Your response is what I had hoped for. You, Cheanah, were born to be headman of your people. You should never have chosen to follow Torka or allow yourself to be overshadowed by him. He is not of our people. He is an outsider. He is not my son!"

"Mother, I am your son, and you need fear nothing in all this world as long as you have Cheanah to protect you."

"But for how long shall I have you? For how long shall I have any of you? My *beautiful* children. My *beloved* children! Torka and his woman have defied tradition! If you are Cheanah . . . if you are my son, then you must challenge Torka! You must demand that he put aside both his twins! You have sacrificed your sons for the good of your people. So must Torka be willing to do the same. Now, before it is too late for us all!"

"No."

Torka's word was clearly and calmly spoken, yet it broke upon the assembled members of the band with more fury than the weakening storm.

In their heavy winter furs, with their hoods raised and their ruffs pulled forward against the wind while their children held fast to the fringes of their leggings, there was not a man or woman among the gathering who had truly expected him to say anything else.

"This will be settled now," said Cheanah.

Torka eyed the sky. "For a day and a night has this storm raged. Now it is dawn, the weather is clearing—all the more reason for Torka to stand firm. My child lives. The people live. The storm has not blown us away!"

Resolute in her bearskin, Zhoonali stood beside Cheanah. When he hesitated, she did not. "Do not mock the powers of Father Above and Mother Below, Torka. When you named your firstborn son, all bore witness to the burning sky and the trembling earth. For a day and a night this old woman has lain awake listening to the spirit voices of her ancestors. It was they who returned Zhoonali from the spirit world. It was they who put the wanawut in my path. It was they who brought Cheanah into the far hills to find me so that I might stand before you now. The storm is ending because of this old woman. The forces of Creation have sent the wanawut to feed upon the life spirit of your second son. Now the wanawut waits, hungering. Not until it has fed upon the flesh of Torka's other twin will it turn away, and if it does not feed, then the trembling earth will open to swallow the people, and the burning sky will fall upon us to bury our bones!"

Standing apart from the others, the magic man stiffened. The old woman was in good form, with her fiery-eyed, finger-pointing boldness. He could see Lonit peering wanly from the hut of blood, with Wallah at her side. Bundled in her bed furs, she caught her breath and hugged tiny Umak closer. Karana knew that she was not afraid for herself but for her child. Zhoonali's threat could not have been more strongly stated, and there was not a man, woman, or child who heard it who was not visibly impressed.

Except Torka. "Then the wanawut has spoken to you, Zhoonali? And Father Above and Mother Below, they have told you this?"

Now it was Zhoonali who hesitated—but only for a moment. "It has spoken. They have told me."

She is afraid, thought Karana, *but what does she fear? The beast? The forces of Creation?* He was not certain. He knew only that she was afraid. They were all afraid. Only Torka seemed untouched by the woman's words, while the tremulous whispers of the weak-kneed people ran in the wind like small, seed-eating animals scurrying through autumn grass ahead of a fire. The magic man recognized them for the potentially deadly things they could become if they joined forces against Torka. His stubbornness was feeding the flames of his people's terror. As Karana looked at their faces, he knew that if Torka could not ease their fears, they could destroy him and anyone who chose to stand at his side.

The magic man shifted his weight and folded his arms across his chest. All eyes were on him now. They waited for their magic man to speak.

But there was no magic in him. No power. No Seeing. He wanted to speak, but what could he say? How could he prove to them that the old woman was lying? For all he knew, she was speaking the truth. And so he said nothing —as he had said nothing, not even to Mahnie, since returning to the encampment.

When she had lain beside him in their pit hut, stroking him as she whispered words of love and gladness at his return, he had turned his back, because he knew that he was not worthy of her love and was sorry that he had returned. He had wished he were dead. He was Karana.

Son of Navahk. Brother of beasts. Killer of infants. Betrayer of friends.

And now, beneath the wind-tattered, rapidly clearing sky, he could see his precious Mahnie standing with the other women, staring at him as they all stared at him, waiting for him to speak, wanting him to speak, hoping for his confirmation of Zhoonali's condemnation of Torka's child or for his refutation of it. There was no way for any of them to know that he had already condemned one twin. Now they were demanding that he condemn the other or stand with Torka against Zhoonali and all the forces of Creation.

Deep within the magic man's gut, revulsion, shame, and guilt squirmed until together they bit deeply, hurting him with the knowledge that Torka's infant might still be alive had it not been for his own deception. Might be. He would never know. He only knew that his sister lived, drawing life from the milk made of the bones and flesh of Torka's son.

Karana felt sick. He also was Torka's son—in name only, but a son nonetheless. And as a son, he would not betray his father twice! But neither could he make a decision that might result in the destruction of the band that trusted him. He would prefer to walk off alone into the storm-whitened hills and feed his own life to the forces of Creation.

But no such sacrifice was required of him. The headman silenced them all with a wave of his arm.

"The storm is over," Torka declared. "Zhoonali is a fearful old woman plagued by bad dreams in the night. Go back to your hut, mother of Cheanah. Relax. Sleep. And as for the rest of you, what has been done has been done. Think no more of this."

In the growing light of day Zhoonali stared unflinchingly. She drew herself up lest her dignity wilt like a tender-leafed plant before the killing frost of Torka's dismissal. "To think no more of this is to die of this!" she shouted at him.

The people gasped in amazement. Females did not argue with males—at least not before witnesses. Only Zhoonali, the bravest and most reckless of women, would dare to believe that her years and impressive lineage would grant her the authority to shout at her headman before the entire band.

Torka leveled a measuring gaze at her. Between the rising of this dawn and the last, Zhoonali had dared a great deal with him. Because of Zhoonali, one of his sons was dead, his other son's life was threatened, and his control of the band was in jeopardy. Any other headman would have struck her down. Any other headman would have ignored the hulking, glowering presence of her son and proclaimed that given her age, gender, and behavior, she had forfeited her place within the band.

But Torka was not any other man. He saw Zhoonali as an old, inflexible woman so steeped in tradition that she was blind to the wisdom of other people. What she said and did was not motivated by avarice or cruelty but by her sincere belief that she was acting for the good of all. With these thoughts gentling what easily could have been hatred for her, Torka failed to recognize the one facet of Zhoonali's nature that was the most dangerous and selfish of all—her ambition for her son.

And so he spoke no harsh words of rebuke. To honor her with a response would be to acknowledge the status that she had conferred upon herself. Instead he looked at Cheanah and directed the reply to him.

"Zhoonali is an old woman whose years have allowed her to forget her place. You have called this gathering for her sake. Now, for her sake, call it off, and in the light of the newly risen sun, let us forget that hostile words have been spoken between us."

He reached back, drew up the black-maned hood of his lion-skin parka, and would have turned away, but Cheanah's strong hand stayed him. In that moment, whatever Cheanah might have said in the way of conciliation or further argument was lost as wolves began to howl in the distant hills, and from somewhere in the misted highlands, the voice of the wanawut was heard in the land.

Zhoonali tensed. Vindicated, she turned around and around, gesturing broadly to the people. "Listen! The wanawut hungers! It is as Zhoonali has told you. The wanawut has come to feed upon the flesh of the band as punishment for the arrogance of Torka and Lonit!"

Torka could feel the sudden change in his people, a gale of apprehension, distrust, and fear of the unknown. They had lost their faith in him. The wanawut lived, and Manaravak was dead. But he had another son—another feeding to be given to the beast of the cold, gray mountain mists for the good of the band.

"No . . ." he said, shaking his head, aware of Karana's standing apart from the others, his face set, his eyes hollow. Why did the magic man not speak?

Cheanah spoke for him. "Zhoonali is old, but she is wise. And she is right! Too long has this man bent himself to the will of Torka! Now Torka must bend to Cheanah . . . to the will of the band."

"I will not consent to the killing of my son!"

"It is not for you to consent. That which affects us all must be decided by us all! So it has always been, since the time beyond beginning."

Torka knew the truth when he heard it. The people knew it, too. There was not a man or woman who did not murmur in affirmation of Cheanah's words.

But this was a truth to which Torka would not yield. He stood firm, feeling the eyes of everyone in the encampment on him. Eyes of friends—of men and women who had chosen to walk with him, who had prospered under his leadership. But now they were afraid, and because of their fear, they were his enemies. They would kill him if he did not yield. And then they would kill his child.

Anger flared within him, then bled away into a terrible sense of betrayal. How quickly they had forgotten all the good days, the fine hunting, the dangers shared and overcome in this new land.

The tension in the air was palpable as Cheanah moved to stand between Torka and the hut of blood. His sons were at his sides—his bright-eyed, adoring, avaricious sons. They fairly exploded with pride as, with a nod of his head, Cheanah commanded evenly, "Go with your grandmother. Take the suckling meat that Torka names Son from its mother and bring it here."

They would have scampered off, but Torka feinted quickly to one side and then to the other, tripping all three of them. "I have warned you before, Cheanah, that I will make meat out of any man who would harm my son."

Cheanah nodded. "But how long will it live, Torka, after I have made meat of you?"

2

As the band watched in stunned silence, Cheanah lunged at Torka. They went at one another as if they were stag elk in rut, butting hard, pressing harder, grappling until they were huffing and groaning and wrestling on the ground, locked in a combat from which neither intended to allow the other to retreat alive.

But even as Cheanah took the first step of aggression against Torka, Zhoonali knew that his timing was wrong. She saw the black, bottomless sheen of resolve shining out of Torka's eyes and feared for the life of her son.

Cheanah was headman again at last. She *knew* it. She *sensed* it. There had been no need for him to come to blows with Torka. All he had had to do was stand back and watch the authority of Man of the West continue to wither away to nothing while the omens, and one old woman, continued to conspire against him.

She had succeeded in riling the bear in Cheanah's spirit, but she had failed to foresee the full consequences of her manipulations. He was thinking like a bear, not like a man. He was reacting, not reasoning. Could he not see that the outcome of this wrestling match with Torka would accomplish nothing except to grease his male pride? And what if Torka proved the better combatant? She and Cheanah could lose everything.

And so, when Torka's totem appeared on the ridge and suddenly trumpeted and turned eastward into the far hills, Zhoonali knew what she must do. She assumed the posture of a seeress and shouted for all to hear:

"No! Stop this battling! There is another way! *Look!* The mammoth turns eastward, out of this valley and away from the hunting grounds of the people! The forces of Creation have spoken! They have shown us another way!"

Her words struck Karana, stunning him. As magic man, he knew that he should have been the one to stop the confrontation between Torka and Cheanah before it had come to blows. As Torka's son, he should have stepped into the fray, as Cheanah's sons had been eager to do. But there was no voice in him. The forces of Creation had taken it from him and given it to Zhoonali. He stared eastward and saw the mammoth turn its back as the world seemed to give way beneath his feet.

The old woman pointed off and shouted in the voice of a seeress: "Behold, Thunder Speaker! Behold, Life Giver! It is a sign unto the people!"

Her pronouncement was a wedge that deepened the crack in the earth beneath Karana's feet. The mouth of Mother Below opened to swallow him. He heard the mammoth trumpet once again as, arms up, he fell straight through the earth—not into it but through it, into absolute blackness. All around him the spirit wind wailed, and the cold, stony flesh of Mother Below writhed and groaned, then grew hot and molten, burning him, threatening to close in on him, to melt him and grind him into a part of herself.

As suddenly as he had fallen, Karana emerged through the scorching heat into cold darkness once again. He kept on falling . . . falling . . . until he hurtled through the bottom of the world. There was a great roaring and an explosion of light, then the sudden sensation of weightlessness as the spirit wind bore him up.

As a fish is caught in the flow of a river, Karana felt himself swept up and away, around the world. He went higher and higher, into the domain of Father Above, a vast, star-filled vault of space that was filled with the invisible presence of the dead.

Terror struck him. He could feel them touching him, reaching for him, trying to hold him captive in their world. He wrenched free of their grasping hands. He heard their voices whispering, calling, entangled one within

another as he had often seen clouds mesh and skein together when driven by a strong wind. But then one unmistakable voice rose above the others—the voice of
Navahk, his father.

*Beware, Karana. I have seen your death and Torka's in
the face of the rising sun, beyond an endless corridor of
ice and storm. . . .*

"We will all die someday!" It was his own voice, defiant
and angry, but he had not spoken. The words belonged to
the ghost of his youth. It was swept away, along with
Navahk and all the other ghosts until, at last, Karana was
alone with the wind and the sky, weightless in the black,
star-freckled arms of Father Above. The moon shone to
his left and the sun to his right.

Look down, Magic Man! demanded Father Above.

Behold! commanded the spirit wind.

Karana looked down. In amazement, he beheld the
world. He saw all of it—not a foreverness of land and sky
as he had always perceived it, but a blue-and-white orb
magically floating within the substance of space, half in
night's darkness, half in day's light, spinning . . . spinning
. . . its landmasses buried under mile-high skins of ice.

He zoomed breathlessly closer, to view a valley between great, glaciated mountain ranges. He saw the encampment of his people—a tiny cluster of shaggy blisters
made of hides, with meat and skins drying in the wind,
and people gathered around while two men, Torka and
Cheanah, grappled on the ground, and Zhoonali, from this
height a mere ant of a woman in a robe of dirty white,
pointed at a man who stood with a dog at his side, apart
from the others . . . at a man who looked disconcertingly
like himself.

Disoriented, Karana looked down, wondering how he
could be in the sky and in the world at the same time.

Magic, he decided. It was the Seeing gift! The spirit
wind had caught him up in its supernatural tide, and he
was not being swept away; he was being given the gift of
Seeing as he had never experienced it before! A sense of
wonder filled him. Soon the vision would fade, and his
spirit would be captive inside his skin again. And so he
looked down upon the world and drew into himself all that

he could see of it. It was breathtakingly, awe-inspiringly beautiful.

Suddenly he was a bird, a hawk, an eagle, a great teratorn with mighty wings capable of taking him straight into the watching faces of the moon and sun. The wings of his vision veered over the familiar contours of high, cloud-shrouded hills, and his eyes penetrated the clouds, allowing him to see through the hills, into the dark, low-ceilinged, fire-charred interior of a cave. And there he saw the wanawut. She was sleeping, with *two* cubs dreaming contentedly at her hideous breasts!

The child lived! Manaravak lived! The beast had not consumed it.

The spirits of Creation had taken pity on Torka and allowed the child to live.

They had also taken pity on a magic man whose powers had failed him, summoning up the spirit wind and leading Karana to this truth. They had allowed him this one chance to redeem his earlier betrayal of Torka. He *knew* where the child was! He *knew* that it lived. He could lead Torka to his son!

Excitement filled him. Well-armed and unafraid, they could wrest the baby from the beast! The forces of Creation would help them to slay the wanawut. The people would know that the forces of Creation still favored their headman. They would accept Torka and his twins without reservation. All would be well within the band again.

And Karana would be a magic man, a mystic, a shaman such as the world had never known! How proud Mahnie and Lonit would be of him!

His excitement cooled. What man would continue to name as son the one who had wantonly lied about the death of a child when, with only a word, he might have led others to save it from the jaws of the wanawut? Karana shook his head. Not even Torka would do that. Nor could he blame him.

Karana exhaled with grim resignation. By deliberately misleading Torka into thinking that the second-born twin was dead, he had committed himself to a lie from which he could see no retreat. Torka had managed to save the life of one of his twins and was resigned to the loss of the other. Why upset him with the truth when he needed his wits about him—as well as his trust in the advice of his magic man and his eldest . . . *son*.

Bitterness soured his mouth. Let the wind of vision try to lead him; he would not follow.

The wind sighed as though in disappointment, and the wings that held Karana skybound began to melt away. He felt himself falling, sliding toward earth past a moon that turned into darkness as he passed, through cold rivers of stars upon a waning tide of the Seeing wind. Would it hurl him to his death now that he had decided not to heed the vision it had offered?

Let it try! He straddled it, gripped it with his arms and thighs, and rode it as he had once imagined how it might be to ride the stallions of the tundral steppe. The earth was rushing up to meet him. He was certain that he was going to crash and die until, beyond the camp, he saw the great mammoth plodding into the face of the rising sun, into a wide, open corridor of grassland that stretched between huge, tumbled, ice-ridden ranges. It was a wondrous ribbon of tundra that flowed on and on before veering southward into the mists of distance and the unknown reaches of the Forbidden Land, eastward out of the land of the wanawut!

Beware, Karana. I have seen your death . . . and Torka's in the face of the rising sun, beyond an endless corridor of ice and storm. . . .

Once again the haunting, threatening voice of Navahk sliced through his consciousness as he slid unseen into his own body and stood glassy-eyed beside those who had no idea that he had been away.

Only seconds had passed since Zhoonali had called out to Torka and Cheanah, but in that time Karana saw Torka release an armlock that had pinned Cheanah flat on his belly. Staring at his adopted son out of stern and steady eyes, Torka knelt back from his opponent, then stood, allowing Cheanah to sit up, scowling belligerently.

"We must all die someday." Karana's reply to the ghost of his father made no sense to anyone who heard it, except as a frightening, disconnected threat.

The power was leaving him. He could feel it. He had betrayed the gift of Seeing. He had turned from the path through which he might have saved the life of a child, because he feared losing the love of one who had raised him and named him Son. With the departure of the great tusker, Karana knew what would be—what *must* be—and managed to convince himself that this would be best for all.

With the eyes of every member of the band on him, Karana consciously drew himself to his full height and continued to stand with his arms raised. He was aware of Mahnie's troubled gaze but more aware of Zhoonali's glaring at him as if fighting for control of the moment; he could not allow her challenge to continue. He slowly lowered one arm as if it were a lance. With his hand curled and his index finger extended, he pointed violently at the old woman. The invisible power of his intent flew from his fingertip, striking the old woman like a projectile.

Startled, her own pointing arm fell to her side; she grasped it with the other and cradled it protectively against her torso. Karana could not tell if he had caused her actual pain, nor did he know why she had been pointing at him in the first place. But Zhoonali was visibly frightened by the change in the magic man whose powers she had openly doubted until now, and she nearly choked on the words that she had been about to speak. They croaked and went leaping down her throat like frightened toads.

"As all men must die . . ." Karana said, altering his statement slightly to strengthen the following words, "so must all things change." He looked directly and confidently into the eyes of the old woman, and to the astonishment of all who watched, she shrank visibly within the skin of the great white cloak that covered her from the top of her greasy head to the tips of her booted toes.

Karana did not miss the low, awestruck murmurs of his people and the expression of bewilderment that replaced Cheanah's belligerence as the big man climbed to his feet.

He had them now! He would bend them to his will! Torka's firstborn twin would live whether or not Torka bested Cheanah in hand-to-hand combat . . . and although the second-born twin would live or die at the whim of the wanawut, what matter? Torka would never know. It was only one tiny son. Torka had another.

Beware! Karana's belly tightened at the sudden inner sting of warning. Memories flared within him—he himself had been abandoned at Navahk's command with so many other little ones of his band . . . for the "good" of the people. It was so long ago, in a land so far away, in starving times, in the depth of a winter that had eventually claimed all but him. A mere stripling, he had risked his life time and again to save the smaller children against the deadly cold, starvation, and the wolves that won against him in the end.

The memory still scalded: He had lived; they had died. But somehow they lived on within him, those sad-eyed, abandoned little children whose mittened, fur-clad bodies he had placed with his own hands to look upon the sky forever, before the wolves had come at last and he had barely managed to escape with his own life.

Had their mothers and fathers mourned them less because most of them had the consolation of other children, or because their deaths allowed others to survive on the scant rations that they might otherwise have consumed? No.

But now he understood, as he had not understood then, that decisions that went against the grain of compassion must sometimes be made. Now, as then, was such a time.

Beware! The warning was more intense than before, as was the recollection. This time it was of Sondahr, magnificent seeress of the Great Gathering. Teacher, lover, and true mystic, she had perceived the gifts of Seeing and Calling in him and had singled him out to become a recipient of her passion and wisdom. She had spoken to him of the differences between men of mere flesh and men of transcendent spirit. The latter were rare, she had said, assuring him that he was such a one. And she had warned him to be true to his gift, lest his magic become false, distorted, and a thing of darkness that, in the end, could serve neither itself nor the one who perverted it.

Sondahr's warning filled him, but he would have no part of it, not now! She was dead—murdered. He was alive, magic man in a camp where he had been silent for far too long. Decisions needed to be made, which would affect the lives of all. They *must* be made quickly, for the sake of the future.

"Heed now the words of Karana, for they are the words of the spirit wind!" he cried, and for an instant, he wondered if the forces of Creation were going to strike him deaf, mute, or blind as punishment for this outright lie. But the moment passed, and he was not struck down. "Zhoonali is right—there *is* another way for Torka and Cheanah to settle their differences! The great mammoth Life Giver walks eastward out of the land of this people! It *is* an omen. Let there be no further hostility between us. The traditions that bind Zhoonali's people and Torka's are not the same. If Torka would have his son Umak at his side, then Torka must do as he has always done: Let him take his women and children and follow that which is totem to him. Let him take his son and go out from among this people."

And out of the land of the wanawut, he thought guiltily. *Far from the truth of Karana's betrayal—a truth that must now live or die in the arms of the beast—as a beast . . . forever.*

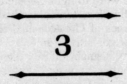

3

And so it was that Torka found himself cast out of the encampment to which he had brought his people. They were his people no more, and now he knew without a shadow of a doubt that they had never been.

"Go!" demanded Teean.

"Go!" urged the sons of Cheanah.

"Go!" cried Ekoh and Ram, Kap and Nuvik and Buhl, while their women and children took up the cry and shook their fists and stamped their feet. The word became an echo that reverberated wildly through the gathering. And of all the people, only Simu and Eneela, and old Grek and Wallah, and their daughter, Mahnie, woman of Karana, remained silent.

"Go!" pressed Cheanah with an air of newfound authority as he basked in the open adoration of his sons and of his women.

Torka eyed him angrily. Looking at Cheanah, no one would have guessed that only moments ago the son of Zhoonali had been flat on his belly with his legs kicking helplessly and his right arm twisted back into a hold that was about to have him howling for mercy had Zhoonali and Karana not broken Torka's concentration. Cheanah was a broader, heavier man, but Torka had known that he was also slow and clumsy, with a temper that cooled as quickly as his resolve. Once Cheanah was prone and straddled, Torka had felt the man's anger ebb, along with his desire to deal with what he apparently considered to be unnecessary pain and possibly even death.

But now there was no way for Torka to take back the moment or to prove to the people that he was the better leader. Even if he were to fight Cheanah again and win, it would make no difference, for Karana had spoken. Through his mouth the forces of Creation had decreed who must stay and who must go.

Torka glared at Cheanah. "If any man should leave this valley, it should be you, not me," he declared.

The guarded look in Cheanah's eyes indicated that the son of Zhoonali recognized the truth. But truth in this camp had nothing to do with right or wrong, with justice or injustice; it had to do with the number of spear-carrying hunters who now stood with Cheanah against Torka.

They were many. Torka was alone. He felt the eyes of the people watching him, waiting to see what he would do. He did not do anything. He stood his ground and moved his gaze coolly from Cheanah to Karana.

The younger man's face was set, his eyes steady and unreadable. Suddenly infuriated by the troubling and perplexing change in the magic man, Torka could not understand why one who had been as a son to him had become an adversary. With only a word or gesture on Torka's behalf, the magic man could have turned the tide of events in Torka's favor; but Karana had chosen to do just the opposite. *Why?*

"The time of the long dark has not yet ended," Torka pointed out, desperately attempting to establish a way by which the magic man might rethink his position. "The days are short, and the great herds have not yet returned to this country out of the face of the rising sun. Has the spirit wind *truly* commanded you to ask one whom you name Father to abandon his newborn son to certain death or take his women and children to walk the frozen world alone, without the protection of a band?"

Karana hesitated for a moment. "The spirit wind *has* spoken. No twin may be suffered to live among these people. It is for them that the sky burns in anger, the earth trembles, and the wanawut howls. But for Torka there is no proscription speaking against the lives of twins. It is for him that the new star rises and the mammoth walks eastward into the new day."

Confusion swept through Torka. Could the magic man be right? No! Lonit was too weak to travel, and they might be forced to go far before they found another hunting ground as fine as this one.

He was glad to overhear Iana, standing to the lee of their pit hut. She reached down and laid strong, comforting hands on the shoulders of Summer Moon and Demmi. "Do not be afraid," she said boldly to the trembling little girls. "We will go with Torka from this camp, and it will be a good thing. As long as Torka is headman of this family, we will need no band to protect us!"

The wind took her statement around the camp. All heard it, and it made Torka proud. She was voicing her explicit faith not only in his leadership abilities but in Karana's powers of revelation; unfortunately, Torka could not share the latter.

Cheanah saw the concern and indecision in Torka's expression, as did every man, woman, and child in the band. Emboldened, the son of Zhoonali folded his arms across his chest in the manner of a man who has maneuvered a superior into a losing situation and knows that he is in control, even if he is undeserving of it. "Reconsider then and stay in the band of Cheanah!"

The band of Cheanah. The statement hung in the air, and no one disputed it.

Cheanah should have been more patient about claiming the band as his own. Given time, the idea might have become palatable to Torka; but Cheanah was enjoying himself far too much to think the situation through. It was good to be in a position of leadership again. He liked the way the other hunters and his women and sons were looking at him. And it was pure exhilaration to force Torka to yield to him for a change. He was Cheanah, and it was in his blood to lead.

It was also in his blood to be petty, perverse, and unforgiving. And so now, as he looked at Torka and made what he sincerely believed to be a generous offer, he smugly asserted his newly won authority and humiliated one who—although Cheanah might vociferously deny it even to himself—had come all too close to belittling him.

The sneer on his lips and the underlying nastiness to his magnanimous grandiloquence raised the hackles on Torka's neck.

"Yes," said Cheanah. "Torka *should* reconsider. Torka is welcome to stay in this good camp among those who have chosen Cheanah to lead them. But as Cheanah has sacrificed twins for the good of his people, so must Torka. Our women can always make more babies, yes? Unless, of course, Torka's women are different or Torka fears that he cannot make more sons. In this case, gladly would Cheanah make them for him out of Torka's women."

He enjoyed Torka's stunned reaction and listened as his sons snickered and his fellow hunters offered appreciative grunts. If Torka moved against him, the others would intercept him, so Cheanah could not control the irresistible urge to push Man of the West to the limit.

With a smile that was anything but affable, he raised a conciliatory hand that belied his words. "Let it not be said that Cheanah was not loyal to one who was once headman of this band. Iana, second woman of Torka, may say that she is not afraid to walk from this camp, but Cheanah tells her now that if Torka insists upon keeping the son that is forbidden to him, she is welcome to stay and join Cheanah at his fire circle."

The son of Zhoonali had entertained the idea before; it had been, and was now, an intriguing and erotic fantasy. Fully aware that Xhan and Kimm were scowling at him as they stood with the other women, he directed his next words specifically to Iana. "If Torka goes from this camp, Iana might be better served by this man. There is always room for another female at a hunter's fire, to work skins, to make meat. . . ."

Torka stiffened. No man could offer greater insult than to speak to another's woman without his permission, but the son of Zhoonali had done that and more; he had actually dared to impugn Torka's manhood. The insult was too great to overlook.

Torka took a step toward him that would surely have resulted in another confrontation, but Cheanah smirked with satisfaction as hunters Ram, Buhl, and Teean placed themselves belligerently between Torka and him. Even little Ank scurried forward like an aggressive baby badger.

Cheanah beamed. He had not felt better in years. He would thank Zhoonali later for her prodding by presenting her with a new bed fur and having Xhan and Kimm prepare a special meal for her. But now he eyed Iana with undisguised lechery.

"Come," he invited, gesturing her forward, knowing that by the customs of his people and Torka's, the choice to accept or refuse was Torka's to make for her. Should Iana accept Cheanah without Torka's permission, it was his right to come after her and kill her if he could, along with the man who seduced her into shaming him. But Cheanah was certain that Torka was no longer in a position to do this. And deep within his inherently promiscuous, woman-hungry core, the son of Zhoonali assumed that the lovely Iana would accept him rather than walk off into almost certain death with Torka. After all, she had been the second woman of Man of the West for some time now but had borne no children. Cheanah assumed that she would be eager to try her luck with another man—especially if that man was headman now.

But Iana replied with open disdain. "As long as Torka would have Iana by his side, there she will be—a sister for Lonit, a second mother for Torka's children!"

"Why should Iana be content to be second mother to any woman's children?" Cheanah was certain she would change her mind with a little coaxing. "Torka is no longer headman. Torka has yet to give Iana a child of her own. Yet now he would ask her to risk her life for the sake of the infant of a woman he favors more! How little Iana means to him! And how warm and sheltering and full of meat is the camp of Cheanah!"

Iana tensed. "This camp is full of meat because Torka has led us to it. For Iana, no camp would be warm enough or be suitable as shelter without Torka at her side."

The woman's reply stung Cheanah before his people, before his women and sons and mother. For the first time, he was infused with anger. He glared at Iana, Torka's little girls, and then Lonit as he sought to hurt Torka through them.

"Ask your daughters if they are not afraid," he drawled maliciously, fixing the little ones with his eyes, trying to frighten them even as he smiled benignly and offered them safety in his care. "Yes. Torka would lead you alone into the unknown vastness of the Forbidden Land, where wolves and lions dream of eating the soft flesh of little girls! And why does Torka do this? Because he has made the people angry for the sake of an infant brother whose life causes the sky to catch fire and the earth to shake and the wanawut to howl!"

Wide-eyed, the little girls stared at him. How pretty they were, especially the older. In a few years' time . . . He allowed the speculation to continue but without disrupting his thoughts: "In order to save the life of a suckling, Torka would risk his daughters. They are welcome in this band, whether Torka chooses to stay or go. Cheanah will raise them as his own, for himself and for his sons, who will be men for them when they are grown."

Torka stared at him with cold contempt for a moment before seeming to come to a decision. "Is that an invitation or a threat? Or can you tell the difference, Cheanah?"

Cheanah hated him now; he had failed to humiliate Torka, and in that failure, he knew that he himself had been diminished. "May the spirits of the angry sky fall and break upon your head, Torka. I am headman now, and for the good of the people, I tell you to take your suckling and leave this band, or expose him and stay within it. The forces of Creation have spoken through the mouth of Karana, your own son! Before you go, so the people may know you for what you really are, I ask Lonit, who is weary from enduring the mysterious suffering within the hut of blood, if she is not afraid to walk the world alone, without the protection of a band, for the sake of a suckling that should never have been born."

"Yes! It *is* time that someone asked Lonit!"

Startled by the hostility and unexpected strength in her voice, everyone looked at her. Torka turned and saw his beloved first woman standing with Wallah at the entrance to the hut of blood. Still holding tiny Umak protectively within the bed furs that she had wrapped around herself, her posture revealed the extent of her exhaustion. The morning sun illuminated her face and the dark-blue circles beneath her eyes. Nevertheless, she held her head erect, and her voice was clear and emphatic. She spoke loudly, so all could hear her words, as well as her contempt for Cheanah.

"Lonit is *Torka's* woman, always and forever. Where Torka walks, there will Lonit walk also, gladly and without question or fear. Lonit is the mother of Torka's daughters and son! Yes, this woman is weary from her ordeal, but more draining is her grief for her stolen baby, whom Zhoonali has seen fit to feed to the wanawut! No, Cheanah, Lonit is *not* afraid to walk out of this camp alone with Torka and her little ones. But truly she would be afraid to *stay*, for what trust may be placed in a headman who cannot be moved to action except at the prodding of his mother and with strongmen at his side to protect him from the consequences of his actions? And what loyalty may be expected from people who turn so easily against their friends, feed their babies to beasts, and gladly throw away the lives of healthy children because they would rather bend to their fear than learn new ways in this new land?"

Cheanah's eyes widened. He was stunned by the woman's audacity and open disdain. "No woman speaks so to a man in the camp of Cheanah!"

Lonit did not flinch. Her shadowed, weary eyes sought Torka. "Then it is time for us to leave it."

Torka could have kissed her right then and there, before the entire gathering. Instead, he nodded. For the first time, as he appraised the avaricious faces of those who had professed unending loyalty to him only days before, he had no doubts about the way he had chosen. He would not abandon Umak to ease the fear of such people as these!

For Cheanah and his followers, the omens would always be bad; Torka needed no magic to tell him this. Nevertheless, he waited for Karana to speak, to say words that would ease the way for him or even turn the flow of events against Cheanah and put Torka back into authority.

But Karana stood aloof, impassive, as though watching with the eyes of a blind man. Whatever the young man felt, thought, could or could not do, he was deliberately standing aside, not at all like a son but like an uncaring stranger who had inexplicably determined the way that Torka and his little family must follow and felt neither concern nor responsibility for the consequences.

"Torka and his females and his bad-luck baby will not survive!" Cheanah portended sullenly.

Torka waited for Karana to speak in his defense. When he did not, a small portion of Torka's heart seemed to bleed, as a man's heart will always bleed when he knows that a son has turned against him. He pivoted, heart blood congealing into a bitter anger that strengthened his resolve as he eyed Cheanah coldly. He felt stronger now, almost as though he had eaten. "But we *must* survive, Cheanah, and not only for our own sake. Because when at last Zhoonali is no longer at your side to tell you what to do, when Cheanah withers and breaks under the inflexible burdens of the old ways, *someone* will have to come and show him how to survive in this new land."

Cheanah reacted as though Torka had struck him. Standing in the shadow of her son, Zhoonali was bristling, waiting for him to react. And so, chafing against Torka's insults as well as against Lonit's slurs about his inability to act without his mother's prodding, Cheanah stood tall, impressively, he thought, in command of the moment.

"Go! There will be no more words between us. The spirits of the angry sky and the trembling earth have spoken against you. Walk out of this camp. Take your women, your children, and your suckling with you! But should you return into this land, know that Cheanah will kill you!"

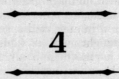

4

Night was upon them by the time they were ready to travel, and although Torka would have preferred to wait until first light before moving on, he was not allowed that choice.

His spear hurler and whalebone bludgeon were in hand, and his spears were thrust laterally through his heavily loaded pack frame of crossed caribou antlers. He silently led his women and children eastward under a rising moon, across a blue world, beneath a sky from which the fires of heaven had faded.

Close to him, bent forward under a pack frame that was much lighter than she normally would have carried, Lonit walked with a slow but resolute step while baby Umak snuggled to her breast. She looked at the sky but did not speak; she was too weary, although time and again since leaving the encampment she had sworn that she was not.

"A good sign . . ." Iana remarked, also looking at the sky as she walked beside Torka.

"Perhaps," he assented, knowing that the people in Cheanah's encampment would certainly view it as such. But he did not want to think of signs, omens, or Cheanah's encampment, for such thoughts brought memories of the magic man, and Torka did not want to think of Karana.

"I will come with you," the young man had volunteered, coming to stand beside him as Torka had hunkered outside his pit hut, assembling his knapping tools for the journey.

Torka had looked up at him and had shaken his head.

"No. I think not. I am the grandson of Umak, and the blood of many generations of spirit masters flows within me. Torka will need no magic man on the journey that he is now forced to make."

"But I am also a hunter, and a good one! You should know! You have taught me everything!"

"It is difficult for me to remember when you yourself forget so easily. I see you not as a hunter but as a young man gone from my side when your magic was needed most, off wandering the misty hills, unable to use your powers to save my infant from the wanawut. And then you stood against me, looking on in silence when, with only a word, you might have turned the fears of the people in my favor. Oh, yes, Karana, you *are* a magic man. But a magic man needs a band to impress with his magic. Now, thanks to you, I am headman of a handful of women and children and am not impressed. Your magic has nothing to offer me or mine but danger and the threat of death. So go. You have chosen the path to follow and those with whom you would walk it."

Karana had stared with disbelief. "But the spirits . . . the forces of Creation—"

"Have spoken through your mouth to deny Torka, his women, and his children a place within this band!"

"But the mammoth walks to the east. Surely you have seen it! Surely you know that we must follow Life Giver together! We share the same totem! Wherever Torka walks, whatever dangers Torka faces, these things Karana always shares! I am your son!"

Even now Torka could feel the way his anger had moved in him—slowly, painfully, like the tip of a spearhead probing a wound. He could still hear himself saying coldly: "No, Karana. A son stands with his father when he is needed. He does not choose to stand apart. You have shown Torka that he has only *one* son, an infant named *Umak*. Karana is a man now, no longer in need of a father—especially a father against who he has spoken before the assembled people of the band."

"But I did not mean— I— You do not understand."

He had waited, *wanting* to understand. But in that moment, from within the pit hut he was about to disassemble, the sounds of little Umak fussing hungrily at Lonit's breast reached him. And so he had said: "No, Karana, you are no longer my son. Sons do not speak against their fathers. You have a woman in this camp. Stay here with Mahnie, within this band over which Torka would still be headman if you had kept the spirit voices captive within your own mouth! Because of your so-called vision, my life and the life of my family is at risk. Torka has survived *without* you. And now, *because* of you, he shall do so again!"

Now, as he led his women and little girls slowly upward through rough and stony country, he regretted those words as much as he regretted his uncharacteristically impetuous decision to leave Karana behind. If the spirits had spoken through Karana's mouth, how could Karana be held responsible for their words? He had not chosen his gift; the forces of Creation had made him what he was. How could Torka have turned his back upon one who had been a son to him, who was and would always be a son to him? But he had done just that. Karana had remained in the encampment of Cheanah, and Torka had left it. It was impossible to go back now, and even if he could, he doubted that the young man could ever forgive him for the anger and coldness with which he had left him.

Although he heard no words of complaint from them, Torka walked slowly for the sake of Lonit and the little girls as they crossed the valley that Cheanah had taken to calling the Place of Endless Meat. He created opportunities to rest without conveying to his family how much they were slowing a journey that he could easily have made at a lope, traversing the ground in the great strides that a hunter takes when he has great distances to travel and no reason to look back. Now and again he would find the women covertly watching him. Both had traveled with him before and had seen him on the hunt, so they recognized what he was doing. He knew they were grateful.

As they began the gradual ascent into the hills, Demmi took pride in riding much of the way on her father's hip, until a petulant Summer Moon called her Baby Feet. Stung by the insult, Demmi insisted on walking.

It soon became apparent that, try as she might to prove otherwise, she was a baby—a proud little three-year-old who could not go far without becoming distracted by the unfamiliar landscape or sitting on the moonlit stones when her feet began to hurt.

The second time this happened, Summer Moon tugged at Torka's leggings to alert him, rolling her eyes in the way that children have when they are trying very hard to behave like an adult.

Torka turned. As the first time that Demmi had lagged behind, Lonit, despite her increasing fatigue, was already hovering over the little one, softly insisting that she must keep up or be carried.

"I think it is time for Iana to carry this one," said Torka's second woman, reaching for Demmi. "She will be no burden for me. Even though my pack is heavy, I have no other baby to carry."

"Demmi is not a baby!" protested the little girl.

Summer Moon, feeling the need to vie with her sibling, was delighted. "You *are* a baby! Babies fall behind and—"

Lonit put loving but firm fingers across Summer Moon's mouth to silence her.

Demmi's misery was clear in the moonlight. To ease the hurt pride of the little girl and to eradicate Summer Moon's obvious feelings of being overshadowed, Torka knelt and made both daughters face him, gesturing them close in the manner of a conspirator. "Listen now, Daughters, and keep what I will say secret in your hearts forever."

They listened, enthralled and enraptured.

"This man must admit that now and again it would be a great help if he could carry at least one of you—both would be better—to balance the load of his pack frame. If Mother or Second Woman see that Torka's pack needs balancing, they might ask him to carry *them,* and as you can see, they are much too big and too heavy for a man who is not as young as he used to be. But with one of you on each hip, you are the perfect size to balance this man's pack frame."

Much too young to know a ruse when they heard one, they were instantly eager to assist. They raised their arms and competed for the honor of being the first to help their father.

Lonit and Iana, realizing at once what Torka must have said to the girls, turned away and avoided each other's glance so that the children would not see them smile.

Lonit observed her little family from her encircling ruff of wolf tails. Her hooded winter traveling coat was of dark, shaggy bearskin, its well-fitted slee∕es cut from the hides of winter-killed caribou and worn with the fur side in. Deep within that warm shelter, tiny Umak wiggled in the binding that held him snug against Lonit's breast. Invisible to all except his mother, he could nurse whenever he hungered without causing her to stop.

He was feeding now, drawing deeply with his little gums clamped together hard and hurtfully, allowing her to feel the nubbins of tiny teeth that had yet to protrude. By the time they did, her nipples would be ready for them. Now they were tender, as was her heart as she looked at Torka and her daughters and longed for the lost son who would never know the comfort of her arms.

Manaravak. She almost spoke his name aloud. Her mouth was set, but a sad, bittersweet smile was shining in her eyes; Torka had risked everything to keep the vow that he had made so long ago in a land so far away: He would never abandon the children or babies of his band, because they were the future of the people; if a people were careless of the future, there might come a day when they would have no place within it.

In the clear, blue light of the moon, she observed Torka's behavior with Summer Moon and Demmi. It was exactly as she had expected: gentle, patient, loving, and wise. As he hefted the two little girls and walked on as though their combined weight were no more than that of the moonlight, her love for him was so great that her terrible fatigue and the soreness, natural after childbirth, fell away.

"Come," said Iana, slipping an arm through the crook of Lonit's elbow. "Lean on me. Together we will both feel stronger. Perhaps your pack is too heavy? I can carry more, if it would ease the way for you."

Lonit's affection for Iana was deeper than words could have expressed. What a fine band this was! Small and vulnerable, yes—but soon she would be strong and could hunt beside Torka. She was not sorry at all that they had put the encampment of Cheanah and the others behind them, although she would miss Wallah and Mahnie and gruff but lovable old Grek. Briefly and fiercely she missed Karana. But Torka was right; Karana had chosen to act like a stranger—even an enemy. It was best to release him from her thoughts, with the hope that the forces of Creation would be good to him, and that with loyal Brother Dog ever at his side, he would find the happiness with Mahnie that Lonit would always wish for him.

With a sigh of acquiescence, she began to walk with Iana, assuring the sister of her fire circle that she was in need of no support.

"Truly, I can carry the weight of my own pack, and your presence at my side is enough to ease the way for me, Iana, as it has always been!" She felt strong and renewed as they climbed to follow the tracks of the great mammoth from the valley and along the spine of the ridge over which it had disappeared.

Here, at Torka's insistence, they rested, eating together as they watched the moon slip lower in the broad, black, star-flecked lake of the long, long night. Sated on strips of cured bison meat and sweet wedges of fat into which dried cloudberries had been pounded, Summer Moon and Demmi slept close to Iana while Lonit joined Torka.

He sat alone upon the ridge, looking back, observing the flickering, golden glint of a fire in the encampment over which Cheanah was now headman.

"Listen . . ." he said, inviting her to sit beside him.

She could just make out the distant sound of chanting and drumbeat as she knelt. Was Karana making the magic smokes and singing the spirit songs for Cheanah's people? Or was he making them for Torka's family . . . or against them?

Far away, the barking of a dog could be heard echoing in the hills. Aar, Brother Dog!

"Will we ever see them again?"

He shrugged, miserable. "Only the spirits of the world beyond this one may know the answer to that."

She nodded and, sensing his sadness, moved closer and laid her head upon his shoulder. "They will live always in this woman's heart."

"And in mine," he admitted, sighing as he drew her close and wrapped her in the sweep of his own wide, warm traveling robe so that they, and the sleeping infant, huddled together within it as though within a tent.

She felt him relax into sleep. In the valley far below, the glittering light of the fire blinked out like a little red eye that fought against sleep. The thought made her smile. The moon was setting, taking the blue light with it. Gradually, darkness filled the world below, and the world above.

Lonit dozed. The sound of a barking dog awakened her. This barking seemed closer than Aar's had earlier—one dog, not a pack. No danger in one dog. Was he also an outcast, wandering the world as she and her little family wandered it?

Sleepiness took her briefly into shallow dreams of happy, long-gone days that would never come again. She drifted in memories of the past until Umak stirred sleepily against her breast and she awoke to lie silently in Torka's embrace, knowing that two infants should be suckling within her arms.

"Manaravak . . ." She whispered the name of the one who had been taken from her, mourning the loss of a baby whose warmth and sweetness she had never known, hating the old woman who had taken him to his cold, compassionless death without ever having allowed him to know the touch or the kiss of his mother.

Suddenly bereft, she sat up, her grief so intense that it was choking her. Careful not to disturb Torka, she rose and stood facing into the wind. Far across the benighted world, something—not a dog or wolf—howled. It was something almost human. The *wanawut*? She trembled violently. "Manaravak . . ." She exhaled the name of her son and tried not to think of the way in which he must have died or how much he had looked like her beloved Torka.

Umak's tiny fingers clenched and unclenched, pinching her. She winced, drawn forcibly from her dark reflections. The wind trespassed into her ruff to touch her face. She looked up. The new star was high in the sky, bright and clear without the moon to rob it of its light.

Startled, she felt the presence of her lost son, of his spirit. Was he alive in the sky, watching her from above the world and soothing her in the cool, constant breath of the wind? Yes! In that moment, the terrible anguish somehow passed from Lonit.

She knew that Manaravak would live in her heart forever, just as Karana and Brother Dog, Simu, Eneela, and Dak, and Mahnie, Wallah, and Grek would forever be a part of her band.

For even in the darkness she could see them moving up from the valley. She knew them by the varying styles of their heavy furs as they trudged on, silhouetted against the stars, bent almost double under heavy pack frames while a great, barking, broad-shouldered dog ran ahead of them, following the way that Torka and his family had taken into the Forbidden Land.

PART III

THE FORBIDDEN
LAND

1

They followed the mammoth eastward into the face of the rising sun, but before that first day Torka and Karana lay their hands upon each other's shoulders and affirmed the bond between them.

"Karana *is* this man's son," Torka assured him. "That which we have shared and endured makes this so. No words spoken in anger can change it."

For a moment, Karana looked as though he were about to weep. He started to speak but sucked in his thoughts and ground them into silence between his teeth. Whatever was in his mind remained unspoken as he embraced the hunter who had raised him to manhood. "Never again will Karana speak words that will hurt Torka or cause his father to turn away from him in anger. *Never*."

The women nodded in approval, and the dog wagged its tail. When the two men stepped back from one another, Torka looked slowly from Karana to Mahnie, the magic man's girl-woman, and then to Grek and Wallah, her parents. Grek had proved his loyalty as a friend in the past, and Torka was not surprised that he was doing so again. But the presence of Simu and Eneela puzzled him. He knew it would have been difficult for Eneela to say good-bye to her sister, Bili, who was Ekoh's woman. And he had not forgotten Simu's open hostility toward him.

"Why has Simu taken his woman and infant from a meat-rich camp to follow me?"

The young man looked embarrassed. His woman did

not. Her head was high as she rocked her yearling boy and stared at her man, her eyes prodding him to reply.

Simu swallowed, then spoke softly but defensively. "For her I follow! For *Eneela*. I would not have her stay in a camp with a headman who looks at her all the time with hungry eyes, or who makes good hunters walk the world alone because they are unwilling to abandon their babies."

Torka leveled a thoughtful gaze at him. "Does Simu no longer believe that twins bring back luck?"

The young man thought long and hard. "Maybe what brings luck *is* different from one band to the next. Since following Torka, Simu's luck has always been good. And Simu has a baby, too! A *son!* Eneela has said to this man that if we stay in the camp of Cheanah, maybe the sky will catch fire again, or maybe starving times will come, and then maybe Zhoonali will point a finger at our son and say that for the good of all little Dak must become meat for beasts. And so, since it was Torka and not Cheanah whom Simu chose to follow out of the far country, he thought that maybe Torka would not mind if he came along."

Old Grek chortled like a musk-ox with a foxtail up its nose. "And why would Torka mind?" he queried, looking at Simu as though the young man had just posed the most stupid question that he had ever heard.

Before the younger man could speak, Wallah jabbed Grek sharply with her thickly sleeved elbow. "Simu has not spoken to you! He has spoken to Torka!" she said, admonishing her man with stern eyes and puckered lips.

Torka expected to see Grek react strongly to his woman's shaming reprimand; but they had been together for a lifetime of seasons. Instead of castigating Wallah, Grek drew her close. "A man cannot have too many women," he teased.

"Grek has but one!" she snapped.

"And she is more than enough for me!" He squeezed her hard, deliberately teasing his flustered mate as she spluttered and demanded that Grek unhand her.

He obliged, winking at Simu, then at Karana and Torka. "And a man can stay too long even in the best of camps! Wallah will tell you. Look at her. See how she has grown fat—and I do not mean glossy fat as all must strive to become before the rising of the starving moon . . . but bear fat, rodent fat, *fat* fat."

Wallah glowered. "This woman has not heard Grek complain before!"

"It is time," he declared, pulling her close again.

Torka watched the matron squirm to free herself from her man's embrace, but Grek only hugged her harder while Mahnie, standing proudly beside Karana, clamped a mittened hand across her mouth lest others see her grin at the antics of her parents.

"So I say that it is good that we leave the Place of Endless Meat!" the old hunter proclaimed. "Grek, like Torka, is a *hunter*, a *nomad*, always following the herds, seeking the caribou, the horse, the musk-ox—"

Torka felt obliged to interrupt him. "In this new land there may be lean times ahead of us."

"Good!" Grek stated emphatically, and pinched Wallah's bounteous backside. Although she could not have felt pain through the many-layered furs of her traveling robe, winter tunic, trousers, and undergarments, for the benefit of those gathered round, she winced and reached back with both hands to rub the spot.

Torka tried hard not to smile, but his effort was in vain.

Grek continued: "Let Cheanah live his life in one denning site, content to eat of whatever comes. He is a rodent, not a man! Grek has chosen to walk with Torka once more, to follow the great mammoth spirit into the face of the rising sun. Grek thinks that Torka will be glad to welcome others to his little band, for even such a great hunter as he might be able to use an extra throwing arm or two, or even three!"

Torka nodded and laughed aloud with joy as he reached to lay a hand upon the old hunter's shoulder, and another on Simu's. And since he did not possess a third arm, he looked directly into Karana's eyes as he replied: "I think that I can learn to put up with the lot of you!" He was no longer alone. He had a band again! And no headman could have asked for finer hunters than Grek, Simu, and Karana, or for stronger and more agreeable women than those who boldly shadowed these fine men.

*   *   *

And so they traveled on, resting often but making no encampments in which they stayed for more than a single night until the hills that would forevermore form a wall between Cheanah's people and them lay at their backs.

Now they stood at last at the edge of unknown country, deeper into the Forbidden Land than any of them had ever gone before.

"Why is this called the Forbidden Land?" asked Summer Moon, walking close to Torka's legging and wrapping her mittened hand around its shell-beaded fringes.

He paused, knelt, and put an arm around the child as he stared ahead. "No man may say. No man may know. It is said that no man has walked into this far country. It may be forbidden because men fear what they do not understand."

The little girl thought about his words. She sighed and leaned her head upon his shoulder. "Life Giver does not fear it. He walks on as if he knows where he is going."

Torka rose and hefted his daughter onto his shoulders. "Perhaps he does, my little one . . . perhaps he does," he said as he began to walk again.

Behind lay the past. Ahead lay the future. Torka led his people on and did not look back.

2

The land opened wide before them. It was a high, wind-ripped, shaggy steppeland that plunged eastward along the course of a great frozen river, which cut its way between broad, shouldering, unglaciated mountain ranges. On the far horizon, the sun rose over massive, snow-mantled peaks so high that it seemed that birds would not be able to fly over them. But they did, and sometimes in numbers so great that they took most of the day to pass overhead.

"Where do they come from, Father?" asked Summer Moon, always full of questions.

"From out of the face of the rising sun," he told her.

"And where do they go?"

"Into the face of the north wind, seeking good feeding grounds in the land from which we have come."

"But the lakes are still frozen, and there is little grass," said Simu.

"Not for long," replied Torka, eyeing the ever-widening arc of the sun.

Following the mammoth, he led his people on and on. The land was hard, the way difficult, and game scarce. Although Grek had spoken with disdain about the prolonged comforts that had softened them all within the Place of Endless Meat, even he began to long for another wide, wind-sheltered, meat-rich valley such as the one Cheanah and his followers had usurped from Torka.

"You see, we have all gone soft, like old meat," Grek grumbled.

"Speak for yourself," suggested Simu, and smiled when the older hunter glowered at him and showed his teeth in a most impressive snarl.

With Brother Dog leading the way, Karana walked at Torka's side. As the distances slipped away beneath their feet, the magic man began to wonder if they would ever find good hunting again, let alone a wonderful haven such as the Place of Endless Meat.

As the days wore on, Karana watched weariness grow within the women and children, and by the silence of the hunters, he knew that they might be wondering if they had done the right thing.

"What does my magic man see ahead of us?" whispered Mahnie, bundling close beside him in the night beneath their traveling lean-to of bison skin.

Her words startled him. His reverie exploded into pain within his head.

Nothing. Karana saw nothing except haunted visions of the past and his own guilt-ridden fears. But he could not tell her that. Instead he told Mahnie that he saw good things ahead for them. And in the days and nights that followed, he began to speak of that which he and the others longed to see . . . to keep them plodding on and on. It did not occur to him that he was lying as he began to conjure stories of a wonderful valley ahead of them.

In a way he did see it, as any storyteller sees the images that he creates and sets to life through words. Somewhere beyond the country of the big river, beyond a broad, blue lake, beyond the white arm of a great glacier, protected from the wind by the sheltering heights of tall peaks, such a valley *must* exist. Whether or not they would find it, or whether or not it would be rich in game, he could not say. He only knew that in this land of many rivers and glaciers and lakes and peaks, there was the likelihood of their stumbling upon the place of his conjuring.

So it was that with the passing of each day, the story of the wonderful valley grew. By night it was like an owl winging across the moon, casting a giant shadow, its song of hope and good hunting embellished by the wind and stars.

Thus, on this bleak, overcast, snowy day, when Torka bade his people rest lest the footsteps of Lonit or the children begin to lag, the magic man raised their flagging spirits with visions of the wondrous new home waiting for them in the east.

"Behold . . ." he said as, bending to rummage amid a snowy clump of cold-brittled dry grasses, he plucked up a quivering longspur. Exhausted from its long overland flight, the tiny, sparrowlike bird had plummeted to earth and, with pounding breast and quivering wings, had hidden unsuccessfully. While the other members of the band looked on, Karana held the trembling creature captive in his hands, blew the warmth of his breath upon it, then held it to his ear for a moment before allowing a delighted Summer Moon and Demmi to peek at it through his gently closed fingers.

"You see? The longspur knows," he told them.

"What does it know?" pressed Summer Moon, looking at Karana out of tired but ever-adoring eyes.

"That it *is* spring, even though it seems as if winter will last forever. If it could speak, the longspur would tell you its secret—as it has just shared it with me. It has seen the sweet, sheltering valley that awaits this people, a valley where the great herds winter, where rivers will soon churn with leaping fish, where ponds await the gathering of cranes and herons and geese and swans, where warm pools bubble from the earth amid groves of fragrant spruce . . . and where children will have to be very, very careful."

He waited until he saw the question in their eyes, and then went on: "Because they will not be able to take a single step in springtime without staining their legs with the purple blood of blueberries. And in autumn, it will be the same as they go with their mother into the mountains to gather craneberries."

"We will be careful!" promised Summer Moon eagerly, her imagination already having placed her well within reach of the yearned-for fruits of summer.

"Demmi does not like craneberries," informed the littler, her round, chapped face set and serious within her ruff of foxtails. "Demmi would eat *blueberries*." She sighed, creating a cloud of condensation before her ruff. She was tired and sat down. "Longspur is lucky. Wings are better than feet, Demmi thinks." She looked at Karana, cocking her head. "Has Longspur really told the magic man about the valley?"

Summer Moon flushed with anger. "Would the magic man lie to us?"

The girl's words stung Karana. He rose, still holding the bird. He turned and walked away, with Brother Dog following. When he reached the lean-to that Mahnie was raising for the two of them, she ruffled the thick fur of the dog's shoulder with one hand and reached out to Karana with the other.

"Come," she invited. "Rest beside me."

He refused the offer of her comforting arms, oblivious to her hurt expression as she turned away and began to rummage through their larder of traveling rations for something to please him. He sat beside her in silence, arms wrapped around his knees, as memories of the wanawut filled him.

Yes, the magic man would lie. Yes. He has lied.

And he was prepared to lie again. Karana felt his lies settle and harden within his chest as he gruffly waved aside an offering of food from Mahnie.

She shrank back from him, her eyes full of hurt and confusion. "Why is my magic man angry with this woman?"

"He is not angry!" he retorted sharply. He made no move to stop her as she hung her head and left him to brood.

He was glad. He did not want her company. Mahnie tried too hard to make him happy. He did not deserve to be happy. He was no magic man. He was a liar.

He looked down and slowly uncurled his fist. The little longspur lay dead in his hand.

The days passed.

If there was another wonderful valley such as the Place of Endless Meat, Torka and his people could not find it. They continued on, sleeping under lean-tos, camping only when their traveling rations were gone or when the weather was bad, which was often. The duration of their stay in any one place was determined by the amount of game available, the weather, and Life Giver's own migration.

While the men hunted with Aar, the women and girls set snares and marveled at Lonit's skill with a bola. It was a simple enough contrivance—four long, harmless-looking braids of thong were brought together at one end and secured by another neatly wrapped thong; two condor feathers attached to the united end lent stability in flight; four round, perfectly matched stones weighted the tips of each of the four loose ends—but in Lonit's skilled hands, the bola took life! Now that she was strong and well again, even with baby Umak bundled and bound to her breast, she could whirl the hunting device in circles of deadly speed. When the thong found the prey, it snaked around the neck or limb of the hapless bird or animal.

"Someday I would love to be able to use a bola like that," confided Mahnie, striding out with Lonit to pick up a felled ptarmigan.

"It is learned through practice. I would be proud to teach the woman of Karana! After all, our magic man is as a brother to me, and so you are my sister!"

Mahnie looked up at the lovely, much taller woman. "I have often wished to have a sister, Woman of the West." She paused, gathering courage. "And as your sister, I would ask why our brother hates me so."

Lonit should have been surprised by the question, but she was not. Karana troubled her. He was so sad, so moody, not the same person she had known and loved. He had been a wild, savage little boy, whom Torka and old Umak and she had discovered abandoned and surviving by his wits in a cave high on the Mountain of Power in a distant land. They had tamed the child and come to love him. He had matured into a brave, handsome, laughing youth, who had come to his manhood in the Corridor of Storms, in the arms of the mystic Sondahr.

Lonit sighed. *Sondahr.* Perhaps Karana had not forgotten her after all? It was said that one never forgot a first love. She would never know, for Torka had been her *only* love, first and last and forever. It was not the same for Karana. Sondahr was not a woman that a man could forget. A shadow of lost love would haunt Karana forever, even

as Lonit's hatred for his father, Navahk, still shadowed
her. She cringed, unable to bear the thought of him—of
his hands on her, of his body forcing her, hurting her,
entering her. . . .

And yet she could not help herself. Deep within her
mind, the threatening specter of Navahk rose from her
memories. She tried to focus her thoughts on Mahnie as
she willed the past away . . . away . . . forever away . . .
back across the bloodied miles . . . back into a far land
where it could not touch her again.

"What is it, Woman of the West? You look so strange
and pale. Here, I'll carry the bird. Lean on me. I am
small, but I am strong. We will go back to the fire and sit
together."

Lonit drew in a deep breath. It steadied her, as did the
consoling sweetness of the girl. How could Karana be so
cold to Mahnie? In all her days, Lonit had never known a
more caring, more affectionate girl. Karana had led a sad
life, but the forces of Creation had rewarded him when
they had put Torka in his path and had given Mahnie to
him as his woman.

"Be patient with Karana, my sister. There is a terrible
sorrow in him. He wears it night and day, like an invisible
robe, but one of these nights, warm in your arms and sure
of your love for him, he will cast it aside."

"Do you truly think so?"

"Yes, I truly do," assured Lonit, but in her heart she
wondered.

They ate well that night, and on all the nights that
followed—usually the meat of winter-lean steppe antelope, stringy, pink-fleshed hare, crunchy-boned voles and
ground squirrels, or ptarmigan, the plump little grouse of
the Arctic. Although they suffered no hunger, Torka's
people dreamed of a settled life in the promised valley and
of real meat—haunches and humps and flanks, livers and
tongues, sweet, juicy eyeballs, and intestines packed tight
with partially digested grasses and lichens, made delecta-
bly sour by the stomach acids of grazing animals. *Meat*.

The time of the great spring migrations was at hand, but
the frozen, wind-scoured, and often snow-covered grass-

land between the mountains offered only small game: wintering birds, the occasional fox or hare, and burrowing animals. Woman meat, the men called it, but in a land that was devoid of big game, it was better than no meat at all.

When their traveling rations had been renewed and the area around a given camp was depleted of a ready food supply, the little band moved on. Traveling ever eastward, following in the tracks of Life Giver, they sought the herds of large grazing animals. And as they walked, the hunters offered up the time-honored chants that men of all bands made when they wished to call the great game that had been sustenance for the People since time beyond beginning.

For Torka, the chant was a calling to the caribou, for, to him, that meat was the sweetest, its skin the softest, its fur the warmest, its sinews and bones the most malleable, and its blood the lifeblood of his people. Grek hungered for bison and longed for the sweet taste of horse. His chant was of horns and dust, of flying hooves and manes. Simu sang of blood-rare steaks skewered on the sharpened bones of any big game animal that would deign to honor him by coming to die upon his spear.

And so, with their magic man echoing their chants, the hunters sang of meat while their women sang of the good, shared work that would come with the flaying of skins, the making of oil, the stretching of sinew, and the cutting and sewing of furs.

Days and nights passed for them—in wind and in storm or under clear, cold skies. The new star was still in the sky, its tail seeming longer now. It was almost transparent, as if the winds of earth also ripped across the sky and, like the mammoth, chose to point the way into the face of the rising sun.

At the confluence of two major rivers they kept to the wider, more easterly course, following the mammoth into an enormously broad, beautiful, river-cut valley in which floodplains stretched for miles. Great grassy dunes banked frozen lakes that glistened in the cold, thin light.

"Is this the wonderful valley?" asked Demmi.

Torka scanned the land. "No, Little One. This is no wonderful valley. The dunes tell us that there is too much wind. The land may be firm now, but all signs point to its being a fly-eaten bog during the days of light. We will rest in this valley and hunt in it. Then we will go on—as Life Giver goes on. Look, even now he walks ahead of us. He will not stay in this land where we have found no sign of his kind."

"Or of ours, either," Grek said, his voice low and troubled.

The wind took the older hunter's words and blew them fast and far. Nevertheless, they stayed to burden the hearts of those who heard them.

Before darkness fell, they tracked and took a moose in one of the nearby sparsely forested stream canyons. It was an old bull, so far gone from lack of adequate winter browse that when Simu's spear brought it down, it seemed to sigh with relief. They butchered it, feasted off its carcass, and prepared steaks for travel rations. But the wind in this valley was cold and brutal, and in less than a day it not only sealed and dried the moose steaks, it so pitted them with dust and grit that they became unfit for eating.

The people broke camp and moved on. The mammoth walked ahead of them, its shaggy, mountainous form barely visible in a thin, dry snow that blew horizontally in the low, constant whistling of the wind.

Now, at last, they began to find sign of past migrations of great herds of bison, caribou, horse, camel, musk-ox, elk, and the fleet, big-footed, hook-nosed little antelope of the grasslands. But it was old sign, so old that the hunters knew that their grandfathers had been boys when game had walked across this land. Nevertheless, it *was* sign, and it gave them hope that newer game trails would lie ahead. But nowhere did they find a single sign that any man, woman, or child had ever passed this way before.

With her arms wrapped about Torka's neck, Summer Moon looked around and frowned. "Will there be no children for us to play with in this new land, Father?"

"It is lonely country," observed Simu.

"No longer," said Torka. "We are in it now, and we will fill it with our songs!"

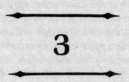

3

The great mammoth foraged on dried sedges and cotton grass or feasted upon entire groves of spruce trees and bare, stunted, miniature hardwoods such as larch and willow. Whenever the mammoth stopped, Torka and his followers made temporary camps on south-facing slopes, dreamed of the great migrating herds that must soon return, and continued to hunt small game and set snares.

The bolas of Lonit and Iana, and novices Mahnie and Eneela, whirled and hissed in the brief light of day. The people sang songs of hope.

They found nourishment, if not satisfaction, in their way of life, and as they rested in the long, cold nights of an Arctic spring that had yet to hint at a thaw, the wind was a constant companion, filling their huts with a song of its own and plucking at the thong lines that secured their lean-tos. Often they lay awake, trying to understand its meaning. They pulled their sleeping robes over their heads and tried not to listen, for the wind sang of emptiness, of endless, rolling steppe and towering snow-clad peaks, of glistening glaciers extruding through distant passes, rivers of frozen water, and grass that lay waiting for herds that had yet to come.

While the others slept bundled tight against the song of the wind, on this night Torka rose, wrapped himself in his sleeping furs, and left his lean-to, to stand alone beneath the stars.

The wind keened all around him. It was a dry, subfreez-

ing, dust-laden wind, which bore the scent of primordial
seas and the ancient ice of eternal winter as it moved out
of northern wastes and blew downward across the world.

Will this winter never end? he wondered. *Will this wind
never cease? Will the rivers never grind and roar with the
great, joyful birthing of spring? Will caribou, bison, horse,
and elk never come to feed my people and bring the songs
of happiness and good hunting to their lips?*

The great herds may never come, taunted the wind in
reply. *The spring migration routes may be blocked. You
have experienced that before, in the far land. You have
survived bitter winters that bled their unnatural coldness
into springs and summers, so the snowpacks in the passes
grew and rose like living beasts to walk out of the mountains and flow like rivers of ice across the land.*

"Yes . . ." Torka exhaled the word, troubled by memories that confirmed the whispering warning of the wind—or
was the warning from his own heart? "I have seen this. . . ."

The wind rose. It slammed against him. *When the ice
mountains walk, old migration routes are cut off, and as
the grazing animals come westward they must seek new
ways through the mountains toward ancient calving
grounds. And if this is so, then to what has Torka boldly
led his people? How long will Torka's hunters be content
to eat woman meat? Perhaps it is time to go back where
you belong, Torka, Man of the West . . . return to the
land of your ancestors . . . to the fine, fat encampment
that you have allowed Cheanah to steal from you.*

And give up the life of my son? A muscle throbbed high
at Torka's jawline. "Never!" he vowed.

The wind, hissing, seemed to veer up and away. His
eyes followed. Above, among uncounted and uncountable
stars, the new star shone. How bright it was, with its
golden, upturned tail! How beautiful!

Umak's star! He smiled at the thought. It was comforting, as was the star. It *was* a good omen; he knew it in his
heart. He drew in a breath and held it, then exhaled it
along with his doubts.

Let the wind wail and whisper! Torka would not listen.
He set himself against the marauding, confidence-consuming
sedition of the wind, certain that it was only the voice of

his own fears. The mammoth was his totem. When Life Giver had left the Place of Endless Meat, he had no choice but to follow into the Forbidden Land. He was a fool if he allowed himself to worry over his decision.

He was about to return to the warmth of his lean-to when he saw a figure emerge from Karana's shelter. Beneath the stars, the dog rose to stand silhouetted against the night beside the magic man. For a moment Torka assumed that Karana had come out into the night to relieve himself, but the young man stood very still, unmoving, head back as though in a trance.

Slowly and quietly Torka went to him. "The wind speaks to us both this night, it seems," the older man said.

In the darkness, the magic man was a motionless shadow against the stars, standing stiffly, as if made of stone. "The wind always speaks."

"And what does it say to a magic man that it might not reveal to one who is only a hunter?"

There was no reply. Even with the wind rivering all around, Torka could hear Karana's tense, measured breathing. Was the young man listening to the wind, attempting to translate its song? Or was he merely thinking, as a troubled man would think, trying to come up with a reply that would satisfy the moment?

"The wind . . . says that it is with us . . . always."

Torka frowned, sensing Karana's evasiveness. "Tell me something that I do not know."

Karana told him nothing; he neither spoke nor moved, but at his side, the dog lowered its head, reacting to the magic man's tension.

"What is it that troubles you?" Torka pressed.

Karana remained silent.

Miles away, within the distant ranges to the east, an avalanche roared and echoed like the exhalation of a dying giant. The mammoth answered. Giant to giant. Life to death.

Karana gasped. There was fear in the sound.

Even though he was naked within his sleeping robe, Torka had not been cold until now. With a wide, powerful hand he reached out and touched Karana's shoulder. "The wind speaks to men in the night. A mountain calls, the mammoth answers. What does this mean?"

Karana hesitated. Then: "That we must follow."

"To the valley of which you have spoken?"

Again hesitation was unmistakable. "Yes. To the valley."

"You have seen it? *Truly* seen it?"

Yet again Karana hesitated. Then, in a tone so brittle that had the wind turned in that moment, his voice would have cracked and fallen back into his mouth to choke him: "Of course I have seen it! I am a magic man, am I not? Beyond this place, in the tracks of the wind and the great mammoth spirit, I have seen it. Life Giver walks before us. We *must* follow. Has our totem ever led us wrongly before?"

They stood together in silence for a long while before, at last, Torka turned and walked away.

Karana watched him go as his conscience screamed: *Do not turn your back on me! I am not to be trusted! I am no magic man! I follow our totem as blindly as you do! The Seeing wind has not risen in me this night! I have come out into the dark to escape the wailing of the wanawut, which prowls in my dreams. . . . And in those dreams I have heard your Manaravak crying . . . and I have seen him—a man grown, with your face and your form, clad in the raw, white skins of beasts . . . following . . . calling his name in the voice of a beast.*

But was it dream or vision? I do not know! I only know that this night I have seen you dead in my dreams—you and Lonit and all those who trust in you. I have seen you drowned in great, roaring tides of blackness, which fill the wonderful valley that I have caused you to seek. But have I seen the truth, or have I only glimpsed the black, ugly heart of my own fear?

I do not know! I only know that long ago Navahk foretold death for us within the Forbidden Land.

But all men must die someday, somewhere, and so I will remain silent; I am Karana, and I will be your son! I will follow your totem! And if my dark dreams are true, I will beg the forces of Creation to bring wisdom to me, so I may see the dangers that lie ahead and guide the father of my heart, Torka, to all good things!

4

The steppe narrowed ahead of them. They walked between jagged, stony hills until, at last, they found themselves once again within a broad, river-cut, dune-channeled valley.

It was a gray, bleak day. The air felt thick, and the wind was pouring out of distant passes and surging down across the world in a great, whistling, dust-and-snow-laden tide. Gathering clouds, plummeting temperatures, and Wallah's aching bones told them that a storm was coming.

"This bad weather will last awhile," she declared. "This woman's bones are never wrong!"

The people of the band observed the sky. It was a sobering sight. High banks of wind-ripped clouds raced toward them like maddened herd animals running ahead of a summer firestorm. This storm would freeze them where they stood if they did not have adequate protection.

Without a word, the men set to work hacking out a broad, foot-deep circle within the frozen skin of the steppe. Using sharpened caribou antlers and stone wedges, they cut away thick sods of grass and earth, which would later be piled high around the peripheries of the circular shelter to help anchor it to the ground and secure the entry against wind, snow, and dust.

The materials that would ordinarily have gone into the construction of individual family huts were consolidated by the women and girls, who worked together to lay out the bone-and-antler framework for a large communal round-house. The long bones and ribs of large animals were carried solely for this purpose by the men, wedged in their heavily loaded pack frames next to their spears.

"Why do we build one big hut?" Summer Moon asked.

"Because this storm comes on fast and may last long," replied Lonit, removing her neatly rolled travel pack, while, at her breast, an ever-hungry little Umak sucked happily. "The storm will be on us before we can each make a separate shelter against it. And in one big hut, we will be warmer and enjoy the passing of time more. Soon you will see!"

Despite the lightness of Lonit's tone, Summer Moon sensed her mother's worry. "Is Mother afraid of this storm?"

"Mother is *not* 'fraid!" retorted Demmi in quick defense. "Not *ever*! Mother Mine is brave!"

"It is always wise to fear a storm," said Lonit soothingly. "And it is always wise to prepare for the worst, so that if it comes, you will be ready for it."

The worst. Summer Moon did not like the sound of the words or the way Demmi was making a nuisance of herself.

"Demmi is too small to help!" Summer Moon complained.

"Am *not*!" Demmi whined.

"Hush!" Lonit insisted. "We must work together, First Daughter. If Demmi does not try to do her share, she will never learn how to be of help to anyone."

Summer Moon hunkered back on her heels and sighed wistfully, wishing that she were Only Daughter instead of First Daughter.

"Come now, do not pout," Lonit admonished. "See? Iana has already unrolled her pack and has taken her skins to be placed atop the big hut. Here, help me to free your sister's mitten from the thong."

Summer Moon watched the others hurriedly laboring together to raise the big hut. It seemed to be a great deal of work. She felt guilty. She *should* be doing her share. But how could she, with Demmi always in her way? Within her ruff, her eyes turned skyward. The storm clouds were beautiful as they raced like wild gray horses, away, away.

"Magic Man could catch the clouds," she said, and smiled with pleasure. Just thinking of Karana made her forget Demmi. He was so handsome! And his eyes were so sad and kind! "Karana could catch the clouds with snares of magic and whisk them away!" she declared. "Why does Father not ask Magic Man to make the storm go away?"

"Perhaps he already has," said Lonit with an unmistakable edge to her voice. "But now the clouds continue toward us, and every hand—including Karana's and *yours*, Daughter—is needed to build a shelter! Hurry now. There is no more time for talk!"

Demmi felt hot with shame. The hides had been unpacked, but the fringes of her mitten had become entangled in the pack-frame thong. She watched as long, fitful gusts forced Lonit to lean forward and slowed her progress toward the other women. The wind grabbed the heavy hides from her arms and filled them with air. Demmi's eyes widened as Lonit turned her back to the wind and tried to gather the hides into a neat, controllable bundle. But with little Umak bound to her bosom, her arms would only reach so far. The hides billowed out like wings, pulling Lonit back and around and throwing her down on her side.

Demmi cried out, but Lonit was on her hands and knees now, with her back to the wind, grappling with the hides, as Wallah, Iana, and Eneela helped her to stand. Together the women dragged the skins to the place where the men were struggling to raise the hut frame.

"Sit still! Look what you have done! No one will ever be able to untangle this!" fumed Summer Moon, trying to unsnarl the mitten from the thong. "You little baby!"

"You are not so *big*!" declared Demmi.

"Bigger than you!" The older girl gave Demmi's mittened hand a nasty jerk. "Soon I will see the passing of six times of light! That is almost grown!"

"Three summers has this girl see'd. That is old, too!"

"Three is nothing!"

The wind was whistling madly now. It was angry, ferocious, and Demmi felt angry and ferocious, too. She preferred to leave her mitten snarled in her mother's pack-frame thong rather than suffer another moment of her sister's meanness. She felt like crying; but that would only be one more reason for Summer Moon to call her a baby. She pulled her hand as hard as she could, and to her surprise, although the thong still held the mitten captive, her hand was free. She waved it triumphantly. "Now I go and tell Mother what a mean girl you are!"

"Oh, no you don't! Come back here before your hand freezes off!"

"Will *not!*" cried the child.

Propelled forward and half off her feet by the wind, she ran to her mother for sympathy. The women were hunkered in a small circle, hurriedly stitching the hides together and checking to make certain they had the necessary number of extra-heavy leather thongs, which would be used to lash the assembled skins to the bone framework of the hut. They obviously had no wish to be drawn from the task at hand, so the little girl was berated by Lonit, Iana, Wallah, Mahnie, and Eneela, not only for disobeying her mother and distracting them from their work but for leaving her mitten behind and risking frostbite.

"Told you so!" Summer Moon shouted to be heard above the wind as she came to stand beside Demmi. The older girl turned to her mother. "Please, Mother, I am big. I can help."

"Fetch your mitten, Demmi, and put it on," Lonit said shortly. "Summer Moon, give us what assistance you can here."

Tears stung Demmi's eyes. Lest anyone see them she pulled her ruff forward and stuffed her bare hand deep into the warm fur that protected her face as she stalked back to the place where she had left her mitten.

But Aar was there, eating her mitten! Brother Dog was as big as a wolf, and his teeth were just as sharp. What could she do to stop him?

"Brother Dog eats meat, *not* mittens!" she shouted, pointing a finger at him, then she quickly put the finger into her mouth and sucked it. It was already so cold that it hurt!

The dog cocked his head. His eyes were slitted against the wind that was combing viciously through his fur. He spat out what was left of the mitten, hacked a few times, and made no move to stop her as she snatched the remnants of what had, only moments before, been a very nicely sewn object.

It was in shreds and wet from the dog's saliva, but Demmi put it on anyway, dismayed to discover that the fringes had been chewed off and that her mother's pack thong was missing. Bending low, she began to look for it, but a gust rose and slapped her so hard that her knees buckled and she sat down heavily next to the dog.

This girl does not like all this blowing, she thought, hoping the wind could not hear her.

The dog was big and warm, and his body broke the wind. Demmi looked up at his broad, grizzled, black-masked face, and to her surprise, the animal looked down at her. His long, wet tongue landed a sloppy lick inside her ruff on her cheek. The lick tickled; it took away her fear.

Demmi giggled and pressed closer to the dog. She liked him. He was nicer than Summer Moon. At least he was not angry with her.

"You stay, Aar. Help Demmi to find the pack thong." She sat with one arm wrapped about the dog's forelimb.

Aar stayed, but not because of the child's request; something bad was in this wind, something dangerous and terrible. The girl and the dog knew it. Demmi could feel his heartbeat, fast, pounding. The child could sense his nervousness as he lowered his head, pointed his snout into the rising storm, and stared toward where the men were battling to raise the framework of the hut.

Through a rising haze of wind-driven dust and ground snow, Demmi could see that they were not doing very well. The hut was going to be very large—if they ever managed to raise it. They had already hacked out the post holes and were inserting the long, multibranched caribou antlers and the rib and long bones of large grazing animals that had formed the support frames of their packs. But no sooner was a long bone lodged into a hole and steadied to be cross-braced with sinew against another than the wind rose, eddied violently, and toppled the bone posts that were already secured. Shouts of frustration from the men joined the groans of dismay from the women.

Demmi was worried. She knew that the bones would

not hold steady until the skin covering was laid across them, lashed tight, staked deep into the earth, and weighted down with sods. She also knew that since time beyond beginning men and women were forbidden to work together on tent raising. The erection of the bone framework was men's work, while the spreading of the skin covering was women's work. But if the men and women did not work together at these tasks, neither chore was going to be accomplished and the storm would be upon them before they had raised a shelter.

Shelter. Suddenly the reality of that word took on a totally new meaning. As she watched in terror and amazement, a great gust of wind blasted the earth so hard that she and the dog were both knocked backward.

It was a cold, black wind that roared like a thousand lions gone mad with hunger. Demmi had to wrap her arms around Aar's neck in order not to be blown away. But she *was* being blown away, the dog with her! Head over heels Aar and she went. She could feel him grappling for footing. He snarled, not at her but at the wind, as he fought to right himself. Then he deliberately positioned himself between her and the wind.

"Aar!" she cried his name in terror as she buried her face in his neck and fought at the dog's side to help him to hold his footing, and her own, against the wind. Although she tried to dig into the frozen surface of the tundra with her heels, she was still being shoved backward. Try as she might, she could neither get to her feet nor stop her backward motion.

The hand slung around Aar's neck was the one with the shredded mitten. She could no longer feel her fingers, but she knew that she was losing her grip. Looking back toward her people again, she saw Simu knocked flat on his face while Grek, Torka, and Karana fell to their knees amid collapsing bones. As Wallah, Eneela, and Iana clung to one another, Lonit reached for Summer Moon just as several of the larger hides went flying. One hit Lonit hard, causing her to fall, as a screaming Summer Moon was swept away . . . away across the world toward Demmi.

Disbelieving, Demmi stared wide-eyed as her sister's fur-clad form rolled along the ground toward her, until they collided. Together with the dog, they rolled over and over in the black, choking wind, off the edge of the world. . . .

Torka did not know that it was possible for a man to fly, but the wind had taken control of his children, and so, on the stroking power of fringed, featherless arms, he flew. No wings could have served him better. With the wind howling at his back and attempting to beat him into the ground, he launched himself upward from his knees into a run.

"Demmi! Summer Moon!" he cried.

Bending low, he felt the power of pure strength of will surging through his limbs as he ran forward. But the power of the wind was greater. It knocked him down and sent the children and the dog tumbling beyond his reach.

Pain flared in his knees and across the palms of his hands as he stumbled forward, barely managing to break his fall; but the ache in his heart was a deeper discomfort when he thought of his little ones helpless in the invisible, malevolent grip of this monstrous gale. The pain quickly became anger, and that anger was fed by the dark fire of resolve.

And so again, Torka launched himself into a run, this time with so much power that he closed rapidly on the tumbling, jumbled clot of tangled arms, legs, and fur.

The wind rose and shrieked as though in anger. It poured over him, pressed and pummeled and would have struck him down had he not in that moment uttered a defiant shriek of his own, hurling himself up and out and onto its back.

He felt himself being thrust forward in an arc of pure intent like a well-aimed spear, and for an instant, he thought with amazement, *This is what it is like to soar . . . as an eagle . . . as a hawk . . . as a teratorn!*

As he lifted, the wind tried to smash him down and break him. When at last he fell, he landed lightly, as though his bones were as hollow as an eagle's, and his wings as broad. He came down splayed wide across his little ones and the dog. He held them fast beneath the

protective span of his body while the wind suddenly veered
and stopped.

"It will rise again," portended Wallah. "Look! Even
now the clouds grow darker and thicker!"

Lonit embraced her little ones within a protective circle
of women and checked for bruises and broken bones.

"The shelter must be raised now! Come! It will take all
hands—men and women working together," Torka said.

Lonit looked up. Torka stood between the women and
the men, with Karana kneeling at his side, examining
Brother Dog for injury.

"Yes! We must hurry!" Grek agreed, scanning the sky,
noting that the wind was already rising. "You are the most
experienced of the females," he said to Wallah. "Lead the
others in the assembling of the skins, and when we men
have raised and secured the bones, you will work together—"

"No!" Torka interrupted. "The bone framework must go
up *as* the hides are stretched over it. Male and female
must work *together*, for every hand will be needed to
secure the lashings as we—"

Lonit saw young Simu stiffen. "The women cannot touch
the bones before they are fully secured into the post holes
and cross-braced at the right of the—"

"They will be secured from *under* the hides," Torka cut
in. "The skins will break the wind and keep the bone
framework stable until the final knots are tied."

"It is forbidden!" protested the younger hunter.

Grek nodded and lowered his head. "It is forbidden in
the far country. Among the bands it was—"

"This is not the far country!" Torka retorted sharply.
"This is a new and unknown land! And in new and unknown situations, if men are to survive, they must learn
new ways!"

Lonit felt her heart beating very fast. Little Umak was
stirring at her breast, stretching and making unhappy
sounds as both Summer Moon and Demmi pressed close
inside the protective curl of her arms. Her eyes took in
the faces of the hunters and their women. How lost they
looked, and how frightened.

But a great storm was coming, and Lonit knew, as did

everyone else, that the little band had no hope of surviving without shelter. Slowly and with great determination she rose and stood tall. With a hand on the head of each of her daughters, she looked at her man, and then at her people.

"Come. All of you," she said evenly, as if standing before a fully assembled pit hut beneath a calm sky and a sweet sun. "You have chosen to walk with Torka as the forces of Creation have led us into this new land. The great mammoth spirit walks ahead of us. If we must work together in new ways, then it must be because the spirits wish it. This black wind is a predator, and we will be its prey if we cannot raise a shelter. Come. We are people of the open tundra and have seen our share of storms. Lonit will work with Torka, side by side, woman with man. At his side, in his way, always and forever, Lonit is not afraid."

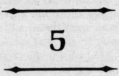

5

They worked together to raise the pit hut. Before the last of the bones were raised and the hides lashed down, the wind was screaming again, and dust and blowing ground snow whirled in the air.

"Brother Dog kept this girl warm," said Demmi, calling out from the hut to Torka as he worked frantically with the other members of the band to make certain that no belongings were inadvertently left outside. "May Aar share our big new hut?"

No one objected to the girl's request—except the dog.

Karana called to him, "Come, my brother. You are welcome to share the shelter of your man pack during this storm."

The dog looked at him long and hard before disdaining the invitation and trotting off to curl up out of the wind at the base of a tall, age-old pyramid of tussock grass.

"Not exactly a vote of confidence in our hut-raising practices," Grek remarked drolly.

No one was amused by the older man's attempt at humor. They had all endured storms before, and not one of them had ever lost the protection of a well-secured hut. But there were storms and there were storms, and they all had heard tales of winds that had blown so hard that entire bands of people were swept over the edge of the world . . . as the rising winds of this storm had very nearly swept away the girls and Aar.

They huddled together in silence, listening to the growing power of the storm. All knew that they had broken the

142

traditions of their ancestors when they had elected to raise
the hut, men and women working together. And all knew
that at the breast of Lonit was a child who had been born
beneath a burning sky and upon a trembling earth. . . .

But the storm was upon them, and it would do no good
to think of that now.

"Chant!" commanded Torka. "Chant loudly and boldly
and with great respect! The people need a magic man to
drive back their fears of this storm!"

Karana winced. Brooding pensively on the men's side of
the fire pit, which the women had just completed digging
in the center of the floor, the magic man looked up with
sad and speculative eyes. Torka's tone had been imperative, but the sound of the storm all but drowned out his
words.

"Chant!" commanded Torka again.

Karana turned his eyes back to the fire pit. Wallah's
bow drill whirled amid grasses and carefully arranged
pieces of dung, which now began to crackle and spit
sparks. Lined with small stones and banked with sods cut
from the surface of the permafrost, the pit was a shallow
well in which light and heat were being meticulously
kindled as Wallah worked to nurture a fire that was already sending back the shadows of the storm's gathering
darkness.

Beyond the walls of the hut, the shrieking wind was
rising to the same force that had nearly blown Brother
Dog and the daughters of Torka away. Karana did not
want to hear it or think of it, for when Torka had leaped
into the storm to save his young ones, Karana had crawled
to his beloved Mahnie. He had held her close as she had
begged him to will the wind away. He had tried. He had
honestly tried. He had hurled his voice into the gale,
imploring it to pity his people. But the storm wind had
blown on, and only Torka's daring selflessness had stunned
it into momentary breathlessness.

Bitterness and contempt filled him. *Why does Torka ask
me to chant? It is his magic that has driven back the
spirits of this storm. Surely he must realize this!*

Karana deliberately kept his gaze focused on Wallah's

ritual movements as, kneeling close to the circular embankment of sods cut from the permafrost, she added small bones one at a time, one across the other, while shielding herself from rising sparks with a hide apron. After her bow drill gave birth to the fire, the kindling grasses were quickly spent. Reduced almost instantly to white-hot filaments, they settled into ash over the glowing dung and stones, but not before igniting the bones. When the fire began to smoke, Wallah wafted the apron skin gently back and forth; then suddenly, as she drew the skin away and let it settle onto her broad lap, the dung and bones exploded into bright, hot, cleanly burning little flames. The corners of her mouth betrayed the pleasure she found in her success. She was the eldest female in the band; the spirits of fire could not trick Wallah.

Behind her, the women and girls murmured their appreciation of her skill as they worked to arrange their belongings along the inside radius of the hut to further baffle the intensifying cold of the storm. From the men's side of the fire, Grek made a sound of approval, and Wallah, reacting to it, settled back on her heels and beamed at him with pride.

Karana saw their look of pleasure vanish. Beyond the hut, the shrieking wind was hurling snow against the layered outer skins with such ferocity that it sounded as if a large predator were throwing itself against the walls. The thong lashes tugged at the stakes, and their untied ends flapped madly. A vicious gust struck the shelter, and the entire dome leaned away from the wind. It shook so violently that for a moment Karana was certain that the stakes were going to wrench from the earth and the entire hut was going to fly away into the storm, taking the band off the edge of the world.

Then the moment passed. The stakes held. The hide covering remained in place. The sinew joinings creaked and rubbed, but although the bone framework trembled, it stayed intact. The wind stopped.

Karana listened, waiting. On the women's side of the fire pit, no one moved. The little girls, gathered into Lonit's embrace, were crying. On the men's side, Grek and Simu were holding their breath; Torka was sitting cross-legged, his face and body tense. Then, slowly, the wind began to rise again, as if the clouds were drawing in a great breath.

"Make it stop!" sobbed Summer Moon, her face buried in her mother's lap.

But it did not stop. Karana could feel the air being sucked from the hut. Outside there were strange snapping sounds as the fire guttered, then flared. Beyond the hut, the wind rushed forward . . . out of the belly of the storm.

The people cried out as air again filled their lungs, and the wind struck the hut harder than before, screaming like a monstrous, invisible beast that raged above the world, spitting snow and dust, hungry to make meat of all the earth's living children, whether they were men huddling in tents or animals sheltering in burrows. Karana had never heard such a wind as this. Never.

Something went crashing and tumbling by outside, close to the hut, and suddenly a snow-encrusted Aar forced his way inside by nosing and shouldering through the entry flap. Karana welcomed the dog, reached to close the flap, and then urged Aar to lie by his side. He felt a stab of guilt, for until this moment, he had all but forgotten the animal's existence. Brother Dog shook himself, and snow flew, but no one objected. Then their brother whined and lay close to Karana, snout tucked deep beneath the magic man's thigh, as if ashamed to admit that a brave, weather-spurning animal had been forced to take shelter with his not-so-weather-resistant man pack.

Karana's fingers curled into the moist, thick neck fur of the shivering dog. He knew that although the animal was seeking comfort from him, it had come to the wrong man. And although his people looked to him as their magic man, he felt vulnerable and afraid.

It was not Karana who leaped to save you from the killing wind, my friend. It was Torka. And it is because of Karana's lies that Torka and his followers are here, in this hostile far land, walking toward a watery death.

But he could not bring himself to speak his thoughts. He observed the terror in the eyes of his people, heard the sobbing of the children, and saw Eneela, Simu's woman, cradling her yearling boy as she buried her face in her furs and in the soft thatch of Dak's little head. Beside her, Wallah had scooted back from the fire pit to draw her grown daughter into a protective embrace.

Mahnie! Karana almost called out her name. As his gaze met hers, he saw terror leaping in her eyes like frightened caribou racing across a darkened plain. How young she looked! How young she *was!* How he loathed the custom of their ancestors, preventing men and women from mingling within a communal hut as long as the spirit of life leaped within the central fire pit. He longed to go to her, to draw her into his arms and hold her close; but he was as frightened as she, and with the storm menacing them, this was no time to risk breaking a taboo.

"Karana!" Mahnie spoke his name as a tremulous sigh of love and longing, then clung to her mother as if she were a child again and all of the problems of the world might disappear if only she could burrow deep enough into her mother's arms and breasts.

Across from him, Lonit and Iana cleaved with the little girls as, in a voice no louder than the peep of a tiny bird, Summer Moon piped a query that struck all who heard it with a power somehow greater and more threatening than the storm's.

"Are the sky spirits angry with baby Umak again, Magic Man?"

"No!" cried Lonit before Karana could respond, as though her denial could erase the question.

The eyes of the people focused upon her and the infant that lay hidden within her fur.

"Chant *now*, Magic Man!"

This time Torka's command could be neither ignored nor denied. The young man obeyed, although he did not know the time-honored words and was certain that even if he did, it would not matter. He sat cross-legged, his hands resting upon his knees, his back perfectly straight, and his eyes closed as, through his chant, he implored the forces of Creation to hear him . . . not for his sake, for he was surely undeserving of anything but contempt, but for the sake of his people.

He did not know when the trance came over him, or

when the storm began to ebb, or when the dog looked up at him and began to nudge his hand. He knew only that his eyes were open, and although he could see his breath hovering as a cloud before his face, it was no longer cold under the broad, antlered dome of the communal hut. The burning dung and bones had yielded their substance and warmth to the glowing stones beneath them. Outside, the dry, subfreezing wind still howled across the world like an invisible horde of ravening wolves, but somewhere along the way the wind wolves had eaten, and the worst of their bite was gone. Around him, the hut smelled of warmth and life, and in the soft, pulsing glow that emanated from the stones in the fire pit, the faces of the members of Torka's little band seemed to float in the darkness as they all stared at him in wonderment.

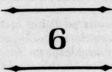

6

Was it Karana's magic that turned the tide of the storm in favor of Torka and his little band? Perhaps, but Karana could not be certain. The wind had definitely died down. And something had happened to him—he felt as if he had been wounded and weakened by the loss of blood . . . as if his spirit had drained from his body, leaving him cold and mysteriously detached from himself. Now, slowly, his spirit was flowing back into his body, along with warmth and consciousness.

Mahnie was kneeling before him, lovingly touching his face and shoulders and arms as though she were not certain if he was alive. "Karana?" She whispered his name as though intoning a prayer.

He could not summon the energy for a response.

Peeking around Mahnie's side, Summer Moon came forward and smiled. She was such a pretty little thing, with her oval face and great antelope eyes, which always followed him with adoration. "This girl told her mother that Magic Man could send the storm away if he wanted to! For Magic Man . . . from Summer Moon, who is glad that Karana did not let the storm eat her up."

Her upturned palms were pale hollows in which lay two gifts: a fluff of downy owl feathers and a greenish, unusually smooth pebble. Tiny things, meaningless souvenirs gleaned here and there on the trek eastward across the Forbidden Land . . . insignificant objects that would have no importance to the man except that he knew them to be precious to the child. For her sake, he smiled back at her, and for her sake, although he had not bothered to summon the energy to speak a single word to his adoring Mahnie, he managed to raise a hand and accept the gifts from Summer Moon.

He held them close as he drifted back to sleep. And for the first time in more days than he could remember, it was a sound, untroubled sleep, for Summer Moon's confidence in him permeated his dreams: Magic Man had sent the storm away.

The worst of the storm passed quickly. The wind had blown itself out, and the weather settled. It was cold but not bitter. Snow fell softly, in absolute silence, to settle upon the world. It *became* the world. There was no earth; there was no sky; there was no horizon. There was only snow. Traveling would be impossible.

Aar resumed his usual disdainful position of independence outside the hut. Now and again, the trumpeting of the great mammoth was heard. Life Giver was near. Within the communal shelter, the people huddled in comfort. They had food, warmth, and a magic man who had saved them. They had endured bad weather before and had no doubt that they would do so again.

They passed the snowy days and ever-dwindling nights in the ways of their ancestors. The women ventured out to set snares, and the men made brief hunting forays. They did not catch or kill much, but their traveling rations were far from being exhausted, and they knew how to discipline their appetites.

The snowfall became fitful. Nevertheless, the weather still warned against travel. They ate sparingly, slept a great deal, and spent lazy hours at games of chance or at the simple tasks of everyday camp life. The men worked at the maintenance of their hunting weapons. The women sewed and patched clothing and hides with bone needles and thread of sinew and musk-ox hair and enjoyed teaching the girls to work skins by instructing them to construct dolls from pieced bits of remnant hides taken from the few kills that the men made. Lonit made a new mitten for her younger daughter, and Torka made etchings on his whalebone bludgeon.

And so the good and restful days passed for them. They still dreamed of "real" meat, however; slowly their dreams began to fill their waking hours as well, for they knew by the subtle changes in the pelage and plumage of the hunters' kills and the ever-shortening nights that spring was indeed becoming a reality. Furthermore, the days were growing noticeably longer, and the falling snow had a different texture. Soon, with the final banishment of winter from the high passes, the long-awaited big game animals would walk toward them out of the face of the rising sun.

More days passed, full of laughter and loving, of the joyful sounds of infants and children, and of the constant anticipation of even better days to come. When Torka found himself unsettled by recollections of that night when the wind had spoken to him of mountains of ice, closed passes, and snow-blocked migration routes, he willed himself to think of the sun—of melting snow, of racing rivers, and of the great mammoth Life Giver, plodding on amid a living flood of hooves and hide and horn and antlers. He would stare at Karana and remember the words of the magic man: "Has our totem ever led us wrongly before?"

And then he would look at Lonit. She would look back at him in the golden glow of firelight and smile. After the fire had lost its strength, the men of the band crossed to the women's side of the circle so that they might share the time of tale-telling and later sleep together with their women. Torka sought Lonit's arms, and she welcomed his embrace.

"It is good for us in this new land," she unfailingly whispered.

"Yes," he agreed, and lost himself in the fragrance of her hair and skin and the softness of her body. "It is good."

They sat close as the children bundled together in a single, furred mound of tangled arms and legs and sleepy, watching eyes. While their women lounged beside them, the men took turns lulling the little ones to sleep with story chants of their people, with wonder tales that had been born in the misted lore that their ancient ones had passed down through the generations since time beyond beginning.

The droning chants of Grek and Simu recounted tales of high adventure—real and imagined—until, at last, both were yawning. To Torka's surprise, Summer Moon urged Karana to tell the stories that he had learned as a magic man among the shamans at the Great Gathering far to the west.

"It grows late," Karana protested.

"This girl is not sleepy!" responded Summer Moon.

Torka saw Mahnie rest a small hand upon Karana's forearm. "Speak to us as the shamans have taught you." Mahnie's entreaty was soft, redolent with love and pride.

Karana acquiesced. He spoke slowly, hesitantly, as if he would prefer to leave the past behind. Torka saw him gradually relax as he gave himself to the most magical tales of all. Not only did he chant them in the manner of a true story-singer, he enriched them with the cosmologies and adventure tales of all the bands that had convened at the Great Gathering of mammoth hunters in the far country.

Torka observed the rapt faces of the enthralled listeners as the imagery of Karana's words swept his listeners away . . . out of the hut, beyond the monotonously snowy skies, and back through the legends of the People to the days when the great mammoth spirit Thunder Speaker shook the sky in anger. "Never," said Karana, "since time beyond beginning to this day, has there been a bigger mammoth. When he walked, the mountains trembled, as did the men and women and children who died beneath his feet while they called out his name—Destroyer!"

Torka leaned forward. In his arms, Lonit's heartbeat quickened as Karana spoke of how many mammoth-eating bands had died beneath the weight of Destroyer's anger until only one man, one woman, one spirit master, and one wild dog survived his wrath to stand against him.

"Were they not afraid?" pressed Summer Moon, so engrossed that she forgot that as a child it was not her place to interrupt.

Torka saw Karana smile indulgently. "Oh, yes, great was their fear. But even greater was their understanding. They knew that the wrath of the mammoth was born of pain and anguish over the death of his children at the hands of Man. And so a covenant was made between them: Never again would the man eat of the flesh of the mammoth's children. And so, from that day to this, the magnificent creature is totem to that man, and from that day to this his people walk safely in the mammoth's great, life-giving shadow." Karana raised his voice, and his eyes sparkled. "And the wondrous mammoth spirit was Life Giver! And the dog was Aar, the first dog ever to walk as one with the People! And the woman was Lonit, first woman of Torka and mother of Summer Moon and Demmi and little Umak. And the spirit master was old Umak, father of the great hunter Manaravak and grandfather of Torka, headman of this new people in this new land."

The people of the band murmured with appreciation and pleasure.

Torka sighed. Karana had a way of squeezing the pain from a story. Old Umak had been able to do that; but then, Umak had been Karana's mentor. Now the old man would live forever in the flesh and blood of the great-grandson who bore his name. Torka reached to touch a finger gently to the sleeping infant as it lay naked, except for its moss swaddling, across Lonit's lap.

Such a handsome baby, thought Torka proudly, yet his brow wrinkled, for there was something in that finely shaped little face that was disturbing, vaguely reminiscent of . . . The howling of wolves in the snowy distances caused his thoughts to drift. He was glad to let them go.

Karana was telling a new story, one that captured the rapt attention of his listeners:

"In the beginning, when the land was one land, when the People were one people, before Father Above made the darkness that ate the sun, before Mother Below gave birth to the ice spirits that grew to cover the mountains—"

"No. That is not the tale of the first beginning." Grek was amicable enough but stern. "You are wrong, so perhaps you do not remember. First there was only Mother Below—no land, no people, not even spirits. And in this time beyond beginning, Mother Below had no shape, for she was only darkness . . . a great darkness all around. And then, from exactly where no one can say, First Man came sneaking into the darkness with First Fox, First Hare, and the seeds of First Grass."

"No, no," interrupted Simu, thoughtfully using a finger as a pointer to emphasize his words. "*You* have it wrong, Grek. You are of the people of Supnah. I, Simu, of the people of Zinkh, will tell you how it goes: First there was Mother Below, yes, but she was not the darkness; she was *in* the darkness, floating like a big, black cloud, pregnant with rain to water the children of First Grass."

"No. That is *not* how it goes." Grek grunted with open annoyance as, beside him, Wallah, obviously concerned by the growing tension, looked from him to Simu.

"Perhaps among Simu's people, it was told so," the old hunter went on. "But in the days when Supnah lived and we were a great band of many hunters, it was told like this: *first* Mother Below, and *then* Father Above."

Simu and Grek both lowered their eyebrows and tucked their chins like two bull musk-oxen about to butt horns. But it was the older man who snorted and challenged: "And how do Simu's people say that light came into the world?"

The young man sighed through his teeth as though he had been posed a question that only a child should be asked. "Everyone knows that! First Fox cried out, and from his mouth came the first word ever heard in the world, and that word was *darkness*, because the fox has always loved the dark, wherein he and his kind can sneak around and steal the caches of the hunters of this world!"

Grek's head swung back and forth. Impatience made him snarl. "Yes, yes. This is so. And so all men call the fox a thief. But First Fox cried the first word *three* times, not once. And you have still not told me how light came into the world!"

Simu looked at Grek with strained patience. "Once, twice, three times, what does it matter? What *does* matter is that the first word was great magic! *Stolen* magic! Stolen from Mother Below and Father Above. And it was because of this theft of magic that light came into the world."

"How?" Grek persisted.

Simu was riled but still in control of his temper. "I will tell you how, if you do not know the story!"

"I know it! The question is: Do *you* know it?"

"Since before I was born, my mother told me this story!"

"What good little baby ears you must have had to have heard it through the skin of her belly."

Torka almost intervened, but Simu waved him to silence and drew in a calming breath as he glared at Grek. "Yes. Always has this man had good ears . . . and a sharp memory—sharper than *some*, it seems. But then Grek is not as young as he used to be."

Grek gritted his teeth, as was his habit when he was on the brink of losing his temper. Beside him, Wallah heard the noise of his grinding molars and nudged him sharply; it was a habit that had always disturbed her. Let her be disturbed! His teeth were still sound. He would be willing to wager that even brash young Simu did not have such strong teeth.

"I think that you are wrong," the young hunter continued. "Light came into the world when Mother Below heard the power of that first stolen word. So surprised was she that she curled herself into a knot, with the bulges in her skin making the mountains and the valleys. And as Mother Below moaned and shook against the stolen magic of First Fox, Father Above flew up in anger. In that moment the First Bird was born out of the feathered armpits of the sky as Father Above stretched. Father Above stretched until he became so thin that little bits of twilight bled into the darkness through his skin. In that very moment, First Hare seized the power of word magic for himself and cried out, 'Light!'—because hares like the brightness of day in which to find good places to feed. And so, with this one cry of word magic from First Hare, the sun was born, and then the moon, and from that time to this, there has been day and night, light *and* darkness."

Grek was disappointed that the young man knew the story after all. "*Hmmm*," he grumbled, not willing to concede a victory to Simu. "But three times, not once, did First Hare cry out."

Simu rolled his eyes. "If that is the way that your people tell it, then for you it will be three times. For me, it is once!"

"Then the people of Simu know nothing! Because if it were not for the calling out of the magic words *three* times, wolves and dogs would not always walk three times in a circle before lying down. Karana, you are a magic man who has learned the tales from the shamans. You tell Simu that this is so!"

But it was not Karana who replied.

"There is no 'proper' way to tell the tale," said Torka sharply. "This man tells you now that he has lived long and dwelled in many camps among many bands, and he has heard the Creation story told so many times, among so many peoples, that he has come to understand this—the tale of the Creation is like a haunch of meat that must be divided and consumed by many if all are to survive. All have eaten a different portion, and yet all have been nourished upon the same meat." He paused.

All eyes were on him.

He nodded, satisfied. They must heed what he would say to them now. "I have listened in silence as Grek and Simu have argued. As they have argued, I have felt the anger of each man growing toward the other. Soon, if their words were allowed to continue, they would no longer think of themselves as brothers within this band."

"We are not brothers!" Grek snorted.

"No!" affirmed Simu. "In this new land we must respect each other's ways and differences. Grek has no right to say that Simu's tale is wrong and that Grek's tale is the *only* tale! We must remember that we are not originally of the same band. We have different customs, different beliefs, different—"

"But we *are* one band now!" Torka was emphatic. "One very *small* band. We must never forget that there is no greater magic, be it for good or bad, than the power of words. And so, since you have chosen to name me headman, now will you listen as I speak words that will be a magic that will make us strong together!"

Simu stared, obviously taken aback by the power and strength of purpose in Torka's tone. "This man will listen."

Grek clenched his teeth and nodded.

"Good. Hear me well, both of you. There will be no more words of anger among us as to who is right or who is

wrong in matters that no man or woman can prove. Among
the ancestors of Torka, neither Father Above nor Mother
Below was first to be born. Rather was it said that male
and female, earth and sky, together they were *one* beginning. And so I tell you now that *we* are one people who
have shared the *same* beginning."

He allowed the words to settle. The concept disturbed
his listeners; they shifted uncomfortably in their bed furs.

Torka continued, "Just as the great herds that walk out
of the face of the rising sun were once one herd, so were
the People once one people, one band splitting into many,
and the many dividing into many more until not one can
remember the truth of the beginning. And so it must be
for us now in this new land. This band must be *one* band,
or it will be no band at all. No longer are you the people
of Zinkh or the people of Supnah. Nor will you be the
people of Torka, for someday this man will join Zinkh and
Supnah to walk the wind forever, and in time no living
men will remember our names."

Within the hut there was silence. Outside, the wind
moaned, wolves howled, and to the east, a mammoth
trumpeted. Torka knew that Life Giver was near. The
mammoth gave strength to the words that followed, and
for all who heard them in the shadowed confines of the
communal hut, they *were* magic.

"Here, in this Forbidden Land, from our combined
pasts we will make *one* past. From our combined customs
and laws, we will now set ourselves to find agreement
upon *one* body of tradition by which we will live and by
which we will grow strong. In the future, when differences arise, all will gather to reason them out until those
concerned are satisfied. Never again will the men of this
band lock horns like beasts, to fight as Cheanah and Torka
once fought in the far land. From this day until days
beyond our knowing, our children and our children's children will sing the songs that our magic man shall create in
honor of this new beginning! In this new land, in this
dawn of our new beginning, no longer are we the men and
women of Zinkh and Supnah and Torka. We are those who
dare to walk into the face of the rising sun, and from this
moment until the last moment of the world, we are *one*!"

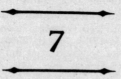

7

Three days later, little Demmi awoke in the dawn crying: "Mother Below is waking up! Her skin moves! Her belly growls!"

In the thin light of a cold, cloudless morning, the naked child leaped to her feet, certain that the earth was about to swallow her and her people. The moments passed, and no one was eaten. But the people sat up as though a single sinew rope had jerked them from their dreams. No one seemed to be breathing as they leaned forward, their splayed hands pressing down upon the leather-and-fur-covered floor of the hut. No one moved. No one blinked. Everyone was staring at Demmi.

She stared back. What was wrong? The men suddenly knelt and, bare backsides up, rested their ears against the floor while the women remained motionless, breathless.

Demmi, shivering now, was confused and frightened. "Is M-mother Be—"

"Shh!" Lonit silenced her.

And then, as one, Grek and Simu and Karana and Torka raised their heads and looked from one to another, and then to their women. As from one mouth, the hunters suddenly let out a hoot of pure joy. "Aieeay!"

The women clapped their hands and answered with little squeals of their own, and then everyone was hugging everyone else. Everybody scrambled to pull on their boots and shove themselves into their clothes.

"For Demmi will the first tongue be cut!" declared Torka, bundling her in his robe of lion skins, kissing her

157

round little cheeks, and nearly smothering her with his hugs.

"Whose tongue?" queried Summer Moon, peeking up from where she still lay buried fearfully beneath her bed furs.

Laughter filled the hut, and Demmi found herself carried high on Torka's shoulder as he took her outside, swathed in his own winter furs. His shoulder was warm and broad and firm beneath her bottom. The wonderful smell of his hair and skin enveloped her as he held her tightly with one big hand braced around the small of her back. Her little arms wrapped around the top of his head. She felt as if she rode upon the shoulder of Life Giver himself. "Look, Daughter! Look, everyone!"

Demmi frowned. All she could see was a great blur of dust on the eastern horizon. Then all the adults but Karana were whirling around and around, jumping up and down like excited children as they waved their arms toward the blur of dust.

The magic man stood apart from the rest, stark naked with Brother Dog at his right hand and Mahnie behind him. His handsome face was taut with cold; but his eyes were afire with pleasure.

"Behold and rejoice! When the wind comes to us from the east, the people will know what we will hunt in the days to come!" he cried.

Puzzled, Demmi nestled close to Torka. Viewing only the distant cloud of dust, she saw no reason to rejoice. "We will eat *dust*?"

He laughed and shifted his weight. "No, my little one! Beneath the dust cloud to the east walk the great herds for which we have so long hungered. Soon we will eat meat— *real* meat—and Demmi shall feast upon the first tongue cut from our kills because she was the first to feel the herds moving upon the earth!"

The warmth of intense pleasure filled the little girl. "A baby could not do that!" she announced to all.

Far below her, in the tumbled, downwardly cascading canyons of the furs of Torka's winter robe, Summer Moon looked up with envy as he said: "No, Daughter, a baby could *not* do that!"

By midmorning, the dust cloud was still far away on the high, mountain-toothed horizon. The wind had turned, and the overpowering stench of the herd was on the land—the smell of hide and antler, of slobbering muzzles nuzzling deep into the brittle remnants of the previous summer's grasses, of urine and feces that reeked of chewed and digested lichens and mosses. The wind named the prey. *Caribou!*

Nevertheless, no one spoke the word. No one would *dare* to speak it until they had first praised it. To do otherwise would be an affront to the life spirit of the herd, and the animals might transform themselves into crooked spirits and become the hunters of men. Or they might turn away, and not even the oldest cow or weakest calf would consent to die upon the band's spears.

Torka was the first to raise his arms. "Come now to the People!" he cried, offering to the forces of Creation a calling-forth chant that had been spoken by his people since time beyond beginning:

"Great bull,
Eater of moss,
Father of caribou children,
Feeder of the People since time beyond beginning,
Come now, come again to those who wait!
Follow the great cow,
Follow the caribou children,
Come now to feed the People!"

"I know this chant!" enthused Grek.

"And I know it," Simu put in, as, together, the young hunter joined the old in the litany while Karana and the women and children listened in wide-eyed amazement. The chant was one chant, and their shared knowledge of it proved that Torka had been right. In time beyond beginning the People had been one.

"Come, come now to feed the People!" the hunters

chanted together, standing with Torka with their arms raised high.

Karana joined them: "Come now to feed the People!"

And now all four men of the band chanted as one:

"Great bull,
Great cow,
Little caribou children,
Lichen and moss eaters,
Come and we will share your spirit,
Come and we will be the wolves that make you strong!
Our spears are sharp
Our children are hungry.
Come!
That we may sing
Of your brave deaths
That will give life to this People!"

The chant ended. The days passed, spent in preparation for the hunt. The cloud was far away across miles of open country, beyond high hills and on the other side of a mountain pass.

"When will they come, Mother?" Summer Moon asked Lonit.

"Only they may know that, Daughter. They and the wind and the forces of Creation."

By the dawn of the third day, although the rumbling in the earth continued, the dust cloud was no closer. The hunters, meanwhile, could find no fresh mammoth sign in the vicinity of the encampment. It was Karana, with Aar at his side as he sought a place of solitary meditation away from his people's fires, who found Life Giver's spoor far to the east.

"Life Giver walks ahead of us, out of this country, into the country of the caribou, it seems," he advised upon returning to camp.

Torka nodded. Somehow he had known that it would be so. "Then it is time for us to leave it, too."

And so at last they broke camp and, following the mammoth, walked eastward into the dawn as they sought to intercept and hunt the caribou.

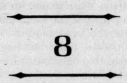

8

They walked through softly blowing ground snow, across a world that seemed textureless, substanceless, as though composed only of color and space: white land, gray mountains, blue sky. As they looked ahead the colors moved, shifted, and merged. Sometimes the sky was white; sometimes the earth was gray; sometimes the mountains were blue. Sometimes clouds touched the horizon. Sometimes, through the wind-churned, ephemeral cloudscapes, the land and the mountains appeared to float, disconnected from the world.

The days of storm had blanketed the steppe in snow. Thanks to the return of the wind, it was no more than two fingers deep in most places. But this had been a spring snowfall, so the huge, sloppy flakes that had managed to stick to the earth had frozen into solid ice when the bitter wind returned to blow across it. Travel was difficult, slippery, and slow despite the bone ice-creepers that they fastened securely with rawhide thongs across their boot soles.

Only the movement of the mammoth convinced them to go on—that and their dreams of sweet caribou steaks dripping over open fires; of thick, treasured winter pelts stretched on drying frames . . . and the fears that those steaks and pelts might disappear on the hoof before their little band reached the faraway hunting grounds.

The men steadied their steps with their spears, but when Torka suggested that the women do the same, everyone was appalled.

"It cannot be!" protested Simu.

"It has been forbidden for females to touch the hunting spears of men lest the male magic be sapped from them and they go limp!" Grek added, looking at Torka as though he could not believe the headman was unaware of this.

Torka was not unaware; there had been a time when he would have defended this belief with his life. "Did we not work together, man beside woman, to raise a shelter against the great storm even though the customs of our ancestors forbade this? And did the forces of Creation not smile upon our efforts and turn the wrath of the terrible wind away from us? Yes! And long ago, in the far country, when this man was alone on the winter tundra with Lonit and old Umak, it was Umak who, for the sake of our survival, put a spear in Lonit's hand. It was Umak, a spirit master whom not even the most revered of shamans could equal, who taught Torka that when men are alone and faced with new situations, it is a good thing for them to learn new ways."

Simu and Grek chewed the words as though they shared a cut of meat of questionable palatability.

By their reticence Torka knew they were not convinced. He nodded. The day was young, there were many miles to travel before nightfall, and there was game ahead for the taking. With these prospects before them, he would respect their hesitancy to break with the old ways. For now.

They walked until the day was nearly done. While the women and girls worked to dismantle the sledges and set up the night's shelters, the men took up their weapons and spear hurlers and, with the dog bounding ahead of them, went out from camp.

They found nothing until Karana, walking with the dog well ahead of the others, pointed to a half-starved antelope, which lay quivering and panting in the cover of a broad span of tussocks. Well-hidden in the snow-dusted grasses, it was not much more than a sack of hide stretched over heaving bones. It must have been lying in the tussocks since before the last snowfall; no tracks had betrayed its hiding place.

The dog lunged in to harry it, and Karana saw the antelope's head go up. The animal made pitiful "yuk-yuk" noises as it fought its way to its feet and stood on quivering stick legs. Its bowels went loose with terror, and it lowered its head and stared at the dog out of bulging eyes already clouded with approaching death.

Karana froze. Its gray eyes made him think of another animal . . . of the gray-furred beast with eyes the color of mist—the wanawut—and in its arms he saw a human child and a half-human *thing* that called to him across the haunted miles. *Brother! Do not abandon me! Brother! Do not forget me!*

Immobilized by the vision, he was unaware of the others moving in for the kill until they were on either side of him, hurling their spears. The bone shafts hissed to their mark, and Karana came to his senses in time to praise the life spirit of the animal as it died, struck through the heart, belly, and throat by the spears of Torka, Simu, and Grek.

He felt foolish as he stood with his own spears still in hand while the others retrieved their weapons and sought to determine which spear had struck the killing blow.

"Torka!" announced Grek. "Torka has made the heart wound!"

Karana was aware of Torka eyeing him, asking him if he was well. "I . . ." He hesitated, not really sure. The others were already working at the carcass, gouging out the eyes, opening the throat, cutting out the tongue. His stomach lurched—a loud, undignified growl that did not at all befit his status as magic man.

Torka made no pretense of not hearing it. "Come," he invited. "We will share the eyes. Simu and Grek will take one, you and I will suck out the juices of the other. After all, you led us to this meat. It is as much yours as ours."

Karana appraised the little animal. He was glad that Simu and Grek had removed the eyes—the gray eyes . . . the haunting eyes . . . the eyes that somehow spoke to name him Brother. Nevertheless, the sight of the carcass sickened him. "There is not much meat," he said, feeling that he had to say something.

"Much or not much, meat is meat!" replied Torka.

"It is so!" affirmed Grek.

"And we'd be sucking bird bones from our women's

snares were it not for the magic power of your skill as a tracker, Karana," added Simu. "Your eyes are quicker than this man's spear, and a true thing it is when Simu says that it was our magic man's Seeing gift that led us to this night's feast!"

Feast? Karana allowed the word to pass without argument, although he knew that even under the most benevolent scrutiny, the little antelope would barely make a meal for twelve people at the encampment. Nevertheless, Simu's praise made him feel better. He accepted it in silence, acknowledging it with a nod even though he knew that it was not through any magic gift of Seeing that he had sighted the antelope. Brother Dog had led him straight to it.

They gutted the little animal, shared its liver and eyes immediately, then stuffed its intestines back into its body cavity. Although the kill had not been from the herd of caribou, at Torka's urging, they saved the tongue for Demmi, and the intestines, he had decided, would go to the other females.

"They have walked far this day," the headman pointed out. Since his spear had inflicted the killing wound, he slung the limp carcass over his shoulder and, insisting that Karana walk at his side, led the others back to the encampment.

"And two of them with babies at breast!" added Simu with paternal and husbandly pride.

Grek nodded in stolid approval. "This man can tell that his woman's hip aches. She deserves a special treat, and there is not much better than a sampling of fresh-taken gut to make a woman smile!"

They all agreed. The day had been long. They were tired. It was nearly dark, and the wind was bringing the scent of a cooking fire, which the women had raised in their absence, and of roasting ptarmigan and hare.

The females praised the kill and were kind enough not to remark that it was the *only* kill. Their men stood back with pleasure as the women and girls rejoiced in the intestines that the hunters had so unexpectedly elected to share with them. Demmi, whose pride shone brightly in her dark eyes, was given the tongue with a great show of ceremony by her father.

"And this most special portion of our kill is for Demmi, to honor her for being first to sense that which lies ahead of us, and thus to make this feast possible. Eat well and share of it what you will, for from this day you are no longer a baby in the eyes of this band!"

The girl, after eating the first sliver of flesh, shared her prize with Summer Moon, then the women.

Karana, watching them as they crouched together in a circle to divide these precious portions, was taken aback by the adoring look on Mahnie's lovely face as she paused and looked up at him. Her eyes shone with pride. "My magic man has led the others to this kill!"

Karana looked down at her coldly, as if neither she nor her words meant a thing to him. If he allowed her to see his true feelings, she would know him for the deceiver he was; so he turned away, but not before seeing her face fall. Tonight he would seek solitude at the fringes of the traveling camp. He had walked as far as any man this day and had pulled his share of the weight of the sledges, but for reasons he could share with no one, he had failed to help his fellow hunters with the kill.

He had no appetite for this antelope. Mahnie would save his portion for him. Later he would feed it to the one member of the hunting team who had not received his full share of the credit for the kill. Brother Dog would be grateful.

As darkness settled upon the world, the people feasted, roasting the muscle meat of the antelope and picking clean the bones of the ptarmigan and hare. Later they would feed the remnants to the flames and lay the head of the antelope to singe upon the coals, then bury it in the ashes; by morning it would make a tasty meal.

It was a moonless night, but a night alive and shivering with stars. Their positions were changing with the season, but the new star was still there, always watching them.

Lonit watched it back. She sat with the other females at the women's side of the fire, using her special tiny scoop of bone to scrape the last oily, precious bits of blood-rich marrow from a leg joint that Torka had cracked and presented to her. Both Eneela and she, as nursing females, had been given generous and coveted portions because their men were thoughtful.

She smiled to herself. Had Torka ever been anything else? Her smile faded. *If only Karana would be half so considerate of Mahnie! Poor girl. Look at her sitting by herself, eating nothing. She loves him so. This woman will talk to him. Magic man he may be, but he is so young! It is time that this woman explained to him that his woman needs more than the meat of his kills to be nourished. She must have her man's affection, as well.*

She looked off to where Karana sat on a stony rise, silhouetted against the night with Brother Dog. Man and dog, almost always apart from the band these days. Why? What troubled him so?

She would have risen and gone to him, but in that moment little Umak made a happy, smacking sound and distracted her from her purpose. Her son's swaddling moss had been changed, his bottom cleansed, and now he was hungrily at her bosom again. What a fine, healthy, ever-hungry son he was! She looked down at him. Her nursing tunic lay partially open. Beneath the shining light of the stars, Umak's little face shone of oil and good care and satisfaction.

Contentment suffused her as she turned her eyes to the heavens and focused on the new star. But gradually, as she watched it, her happiness faded. *Two sons. Lonit has two sons! One is lost and far away, abandoned to—*

No! She would *not* long for him! She would *not* allow her breasts and arms and heart to ache for him. She would not think of him. Manaravak was dead. Why, then, knowing this, did her spirit continue to plague her with the agony of feeling that somehow he was alive, crying for his mother's love?

Her longing nearly choked her. What an ungrateful creature she must seem to the forces of Creation to grieve so long for a lost child when she had Summer Moon, Demmi, and tiny Umak to comfort her.

With a sigh, she turned her gaze upward again and tried to concentrate on the star. "Umak's star"—that was what Torka had come to call it, and if she squinted, its light filtered through her lashes and looked just like . . . a maned, leaping lion with a pelt of white-hot fire.

Lonit felt suddenly cold. The star looked like the lion that had roared within her as she had labored to give birth to Umak. Why did it seem to threaten her? Why did she fear it? Why did she instinctively draw her infant close whenever she thought of it?

Could it be because she saw not the image of a lion but of a man in its wild, savage beauty—a savage, magnificent man dressed entirely in the white skins of winter-killed caribou, with the white feathers of an Arctic owl shimmering in his mane of raven-black, knee-length hair . . . a magic man who showed the bone-white, serrated teeth of a beast when he laughed and danced and whirled maniacally in the starlight of her memories, roaring in defiance of the traditions of his ancestors as his chanting set fire to the night . . . and to her body before he raped her.

Navahk. Navahk was the lion that haunted her dreams! Navahk was the lion in the sky! Navahk was . . . the father of her son?

"No!" she cried out just as Umak's nubbin teeth bit deep. She was so distraught that her fist curled around the marrow scoop and snapped it in two.

Beside her, Iana smiled benignly, assuming that Lonit's exclamation had been the result of little Umak's excessively zealous nursing.

In the distant ranges wolves and wild dogs began to bark and yip in excitement and anticipation of the coming hunt. At the edge of the camp, Brother Dog howled as if in answer to his kindred.

"Listen," urged Torka from the men's side of the fire. His strong, even features were defined by the flames, and his eyes rested steadily on Lonit's face, as if he spoke to her alone. "Wolves and dogs are leaving their winter denning sites to gather into packs. They know that the herds are returning to feed them and their children, as they will also feed us and ours."

Lonit stared at him. *Ours.* Our daughters. Our son.

"Yes!" Her affirmation was as bold as the sound of the wolves. *Our son. Torka and Lonit's son! Not Navahk's. It can be no other way!*

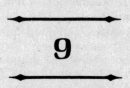

9

They walked on and on. Ice crystals danced in the light of day, and although it was spring, with days that were gradually warming, the mammoth crossed a still-frozen river. The people followed.

Now the mountains loomed ahead. Awestruck and intimidated, the band stopped and stared. Before them, the familiar tundral steppeland yielded to bare, scabrous foothills bisected by outwash streams thick with willow scrub. It was not the hills that held their gaze, however. Beyond the hills, encircling the entire eastern horizon, the mountains were ice-ridden walls that seemed to hold up the sky.

They had walked silently for days now in the presence of these great peaks, drawn ever eastward by the mammoth and the tantalizing game-rich stink of the wind. Yet although the stench of game grew stronger the closer they came to the mountains, they found no sign upon the land that the caribou had ever passed this way. And still the mammoth plodded on, without stopping to graze, across the hills and into the shadowy depths of a great pass.

The smell of glaciers—ice and rotten rock—was strong. Beyond the pass lay a big glacier, big enough to block the pass and prevent the caribou from coming through. Torka did not mention the fact; he did not have to—the others were reacting to it as well, as the smell of the still-distant herd mingled in the wind with that of the unseen river of ice.

"So high!" Summer Moon exclaimed, distracting him for

a moment. His elder daughter was close by his side, pointing ahead. Never had Summer Moon seen such peaks as these.

"When will the animals come to die upon our spears, Father?" Demmi asked, riding on his hip. "This girl is tired of walking."

"Demmi does not walk at all!" snapped Summer Moon, looking up at her sister with disgust. "When she is not riding on a sledge, Father carries her!"

Lonit, standing beside Torka, hushed the girls, and Torka was grateful. He was weary, and their bickering was irritating. He, like Demmi, was tired of walking, and it was clear that high, rough, and broken country lay ahead. Unfortunately, if a massive glacier blocked the pass, the people would have to go to the caribou—not only through the pass but across the glacier.

This was a grim prospect, for glaciers were living beasts that ate people and animals and never gave back their bones.

"Perhaps this herd is not for us after all?" Simu suggested. "Shall we go back into the country where we first lost sign of the old game trails and—"

"Into Cheanah's hunting ground? Never!" Karana actually shouted at him. "We cannot go back! The great mammoth walks ahead. We *will* follow."

Simu stiffened, resentful of the magic man's admonishment, which shamed him before the others. "This is odd, hungry country for a mammoth. It promises to be hard, dangerous country for our women and children."

"Life Giver leads us to the herds!" Karana responded hotly. "Life Giver knows the needs of our women and children! There is good browse beyond these mountains, and where there is good browse, there is good hunting!"

"In the wonderful valley?" asked Summer Moon.

"Yes," replied the magic man. "Of course. In the wonderful valley."

Torka's brow creased. Karana seemed so sure, as if he had already been over the mountains and back again. And yet, as on the night when they had stood beneath the stars and listened to the wind, there had been a hesitancy and a sound of regret in his voice.

"But so black are these mountains and so big on either side of the pass!" Wallah grimaced as she rubbed her right hip and stared off, not liking the look of the mountains or the pass.

Grek came to stand beside Torka and looked him in the eyes. "These high passes and peaks may be the hunting grounds of wind spirits. There is ice enough upon these mountains to make me think that they will walk. They could fall upon careless travelers."

"We will not be careless," interjected Karana adamantly.

Torka saw Simu eye the magic man thoughtfully, then he eyed Karana, too. Karana's passion on the subject was unmistakable and somehow troubling.

"There are other herds," Simu pointed out quietly.

"No!" Karana's voice was sharp with warning. "No man can know where he will next find meat—of *if* he will find it. But the great mammoth spirit—my totem, Torka's totem—knows, and it has never led us wrongly before."

"*Before?*" Simu turned the word into a question of dark portent.

"Never!" Karana corrected himself.

Simu nodded, accepting the magic man's reply, but when he spoke, it was to Torka. "As this man thinks of the great distances across which we have come with no recent sign of big game, this man remembers that once, in the far country, under a starving moon, there was a tale told by the old men that—"

"This is not a time for the telling of tales!" Karana interrupted irritably, his tone sharper than before.

"Perhaps it is," replied Simu evenly. "For this tale is of the great tuskers, the ancient bull mammoths, and of how, at the dusk of their lives, they wander off to die alone in a far place that lies beyond the Forbidden Land, somewhere beyond the edge of the world, where no man or beast can ever hope to find their bones."

The little band murmured with apprehension.

Torka's heart went cold as he thought again of the glacier that lay ahead of them. He would never forget the great living glaciers that he had seen in his lifetime—not minor ice fields but mile-thick rivers of surging ice so wide that a man could barely see across them.

"Is this what Simu has come to believe?" Torka asked. "That the great mammoth spirit is not leading us to better hunting grounds but is instead leading us off the edge of the world to die?"

Simu drew in a breath. Everyone in the band did exactly the same thing as they all stared at the young hunter. Simu gulped and seemed to shrink within his furs as he shook his head and looked at Torka with an expression that clearly showed that he had no desire to be the focus of attention or the cause of dissension.

"This man *believes* nothing," he said in a tone that was earnest in its need to be understood. "But this man *fears*— for his woman and for his son."

"The mammoth will lead us safely through the mountains to the herds!" Karana vowed.

Simu stood tall again. "You have seen this?"

"I have seen this!"

How sure he is, thought Torka, more troubled now than before. Not even the legendary Sondahr or his grandfather Umak had ever been so sure. He looked at Karana, and to his shock, the magic man deliberately averted his eyes. Warning flared within Torka. *Something is wrong! He is lying! He has seen nothing. He is afraid to go back!*

No! It could not be. In all of the time they had been together as father and son, Torka had never known Karana to be afraid of anything. Yet he was acting so strangely. But then, they were all tired and irritable.

"No more words!" the headman decided. "We will stop in this place. We will eat and rest. Tomorrow two of our number will follow the mammoth into the pass and see what lies ahead."

"And if a glacier does lie between us and the herds?" Simu wanted to know.

Before Torka could speak, Karana replied emphatically: "The mammoth would not lead us into country that we cannot cross! We *must* follow. We dare not linger here. We must go *now*! We *cannot* go back!"

Torka's brows expanded across his forehead. There had been unmistakable panic in Karana's voice. The magic man *was* afraid, but what did he fear? Surely his terror could not be of Cheanah; in Karana's short lifetime, he had fought against his own kind before, and whether with spear or dagger, barehanded or with the use of his extraordinary wits, he had always come away the victor. With Torka he had faced lions and wolves, and had even dared to stand against charging mammoths and woolly rhinos.

What could be so terrible to Karana that he would risk not only himself but his entire band to the perils of a glacier crossing rather than return to face it?

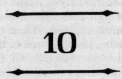

10

No one was certain who heard the lions first, but once they did, all talking stopped. They were on their feet in an instant, drawing their little ones into their arms as their men took up their weapons. Everyone stood with backs to the flames, facing out and listening. The fire spat and crackled as skewered wedges of fat dripped and flamed, consuming themselves as well as their bone skewers because the women who cooked them had lost all interest in food.

"What is the matter?" asked Summer Moon, refusing to be held.

"We are not the only ones who hunger in this land," explained Torka.

"But we have seen no sign of lion," whispered Eneela, hugging Dak close.

Grek responded to Simu's woman. "Perhaps as we have been following the herd, the lions have been following us?"

"We are people!" Summer Moon protested, again forgetting that she was only a female child. "People are not *meat!*"

Lonit hushed her while Demmi, balanced on her mother's hip, begged in vain to be put down.

Torka appraised his little ones. What bold little creatures they were! But with Lonit as their mother, how could they be otherwise? He would talk to Summer Moon later about remembering her place; but now, in the growing darkness as lions bellowed like booming thunderclaps in the scrub growth between the band and the river, the girl deserved an answer.

"The forces of Creation have made us—man, woman, and child—predator *and* prey. The lions are hungry, just like you, and they must eat, too. When we eat of the flesh that is the prey of lions, the life force of the animals we eat is in our blood and flesh. And so yes, Daughter, we *are* meat. Because the forces of Creation have set us to live upon this earth with neither the fleetness of foot of the grazing animals nor the claws and fangs of the flesh eaters, they have made us as wise as we are weak, so that we may have the wisdom to form a circle close to a fire, against which no lion will come."

They built their fire high and hot that night, lining the little pit with stones to keep the base of the flames well heated, then feeding the fire with all the grasses and scrub growth they could find, plus dried bones saved from many a meal and all the dung the women had gathered across the long miles. The precious fuel should have lasted for many fires to come, but this was a blaze that held the heat of many fires. As sparks rose and flames crackled, the men, at Torka's direction, stayed vigilant and at the ready with their spears. The people sang bold songs so that the lions would hear their voices and know that those who held fire captive and caused it to leap at their command were strong and unafraid.

Perhaps they sang too boldly. Perhaps their fire leaped too high. Sometime in the night, long after the lions fell silent, the wind turned and the air warmed. In that soft, mellow hour just after dawn has begun to leach the color from the horizon, a great and terrible sound had the people on their feet and staring back at the way they had come.

The ice was breaking up on the river. The spring thaw had come at last. With tumultuous, horrendous force it came, as, from out of a thousand canyons, long-frozen water began to flow.

For days now the melt had been going on—deep in the earth, deep in the mountain snowpack, and deep in the river. It was unseen and unperceived except perhaps by bottom-dwelling fish or by pikas peeking from crevices on south-facing mountain slopes, where mosses had begun to swell and soften. Sheep, ears back, their senses disturbed by the sound of water running deep and fast within the core of the glacial mass, crossed high on glacier-clad mountain walls, stepping cautiously over slush that had been solid ice only days before.

It began with a drop of water . . . a single drop, as clear as air, sweet and swollen from the ice and snow . . . a single tear of moisture, weeping with sadness for the winter's passing, or with joy in hope of the spring to come. It was only one drop, one minute drop, but soon there were two, and then a thousand, and then uncounted thousands, and soon that single bead of moisture was a roaring, erosive force draining from a thousand ice fields, glaciers, and banks of snow until every stream and river in the land was alive with rushing water beneath its skin of winter ice. The frozen river that Torka and his people had crossed with ease was now a living force that grew and grew until its surface ice broke wide and shattered screaming. The foaming waters screamed back beneath broken, crashing, overriding slabs of ice. The floes groaned and whirled and heaved to the surface, only to disappear in clashing, dying tumult as they were swept away by raging waters. The sound of the newly reborn river filled the world and sky, echoing up into the highest passes as winter died.

Karana, standing rigid beside Torka, looked westward across the river and the great distance that lay between him and the far country of Cheanah, where a human child suckled at the breast of a beast, beside a half-human infant that would someday grow to name him Brother.

"We cannot go back," he said, as if emerging from a dream.

"No," assented Torka as the others came to stand at his side. "The forces of Creation have spoken. We cannot go back. It seems that the mammoth has led us truly, after all."

And it was so, for as the river swelled and began to overrun its banks, they followed the mammoth into the pass. It was high and broad, with good footing and grass well above the river. Although the high ice peaks talked back to the wind and the sound of spring thaw filled the world below, they felt no danger in this place, for they saw no sign that they were reaching the edge of the world. By day, teratorns, which had always been a sign of good luck for the People, circled in the sky far ahead of them. Wherever the giant condorlike scavenger flew, always there was game ahead.

At the end of the third day's journey from the river-bank, after skirting the stony bank of a broad, iceberg-ridden lake whose northeastern shore was rimmed by soaring cliffs of ice, they came to pause atop a long, flat-topped ridge at the far end of the pass.

"The wonderful valley!" cried Summer Moon.

No one argued with her. The mountains fell steeply away before them. Two broad, river-cut canyons cleft the tumbled mass of the stony range. One canyon opened directly east and south, offering a clear route down into the enormous valley below; the other was aligned toward the north and was blocked by the glacier that they had feared. Now, for the first time, they could see it clearly: It was a vast, vertically aligned alpine glacier. Its upper reaches extruded onto the far side of the ridge to form the high, crenellated white cliffs that they had seen walling the northeastern shore of the highland lake. Its lower reaches were like a vast white scab wedged between the precipitous stone walls of the north-facing slopes.

Brother Dog whined at the treacherous prospects that it offered to his fellow travelers as he looked down and across its bleak, crevasse-scarred surface into the perpetually shadowed, ice-ridden gorge that held it captive.

The band had already turned away to look to the south-east now, scanning the depths of the second, much less precipitous canyon that tumbled downward into the val-ley. It was ice-free and thick with mixed hardwoods and fragrant spruce.

"Mammoths . . . many mammoths!" exclaimed Grek, for as they stared down, the trumpeting of the tuskers came up to them out of the shadowed, wind-sheltered forests. "It seems that our great mammoth spirit is not wandering off the edge of the world to die alone," he said, winking broadly at Simu. "You may put aside your fears, my brother, for our Life Giver knows where he is going. Listen! His women and children are waiting for him, as the game awaits us in that fine, good valley that lies ahead!"

And fine and good it was. Surrounded by hills and mountains all around, it was breathtakingly beautiful, and game was everywhere they looked. Not just caribou—thousands of caribou, so many that the smell of them had masked the smell of other game—but bison and horse, camel and elk, all feeding on new grass and drinking from willow-choked outwash streams and marshes along the shores of dozens of small lakes that lay along the curves of a great oxbowed river.

The people stood in silence, enthralled, until Grek finally said: "We must thank Father Above and Mother Below for allowing us to come safely to this place."

"And all the forces of Creation for allowing Life Giver to lead us," added Simu.

"And our magic man!" piped Summer Moon. "He promised us that the wonderful valley lay ahead!"

Thanks were offered, and praises were sung to Father Above and Mother Below, to Life Giver and Magic Man and all of the forces of Creation. And when the last chant was done, Torka nodded, grinning.

"There is one whom we have forgotten," he told them. Although his tone was low and serious and full of respect for his intent, amusement sparkled in his eyes. "We must thank the son of Zhoonali, for if Cheanah had not forced us to move on, we would never have left the far country and found this valley in the Forbidden Land . . . this wonderful valley . . . that he will never see or know. . . ."

PART IV

SPIRIT WIND

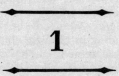

1

Now was the time when the people of Cheanah celebrated the rebirth of the time of light. The wind was soft with spring, and the far country sang the song of the awakening land. Rivers roared, and lions answered. Leaping cats ventured from the willow scrub to hunt within marshes, where grazing animals ventured from the ever-greening steppe to drink. It was the time his people called the Moon of the Green Grass Growing.

It was the time for hunting, for renewed joy in the chase and in the kill, for men and women to come together with new enthusiasm—the males sharing one another's females until at last they were sated—while young boys, watching and learning, wondered how they themselves would claim a woman when they were grown. For in all of the fire circles of the encampment of Cheanah, only Honee, the fat, homely little daughter of the headman, was a female child.

"She will have her pick of the best, and I will teach her how to please them!" declared Zhoonali as she came to stand before her son.

Seated on a lichen-stuffed pillow of horsehide, with his wide back supported by a fur-softened bone backrest, Cheanah was lost in thought. He was taking his ease in the full light of the sun.

"Cheanah, have you heard your mother?" the old woman pressed him soberly. Her tone indicated that she had long been preparing to make this speech and was irked that her intended audience obviously was not interested. "From this time until a time yet to be determined, the people of Cheanah must allow all fit and strong girl babies to live . . . whether or not their fathers and mothers want them."

Cheanah frowned. Annoyed, he looked up at her. Zhoonali was standing in his light, but this was not what irritated him. Her statement emphasized the concern that had brought him to sit here alone before his hut, moodily reflecting that he had sated himself on every woman in the camp—with the exception of his mother, of course, and old Frahn, who was beyond the interest of even her own man. The hunters had not objected to the woman swapping; indeed, they had welcomed his suggestion. The ancestors of Cheanah's people contended that such sharing made a band a closer, stronger unit.

All had enthusiastically taken up the old custom of *plaku* now that Torka was no longer here to frown upon it. Mano, his eldest boy, had laughed with pleasure to hear him speak derisively of Man Who Walks With Dogs, and old Frahn, Teean's woman, had been the first to strip, grease her naked body, and festoon herself with feathers and beads. She had stomped and sung. She had rolled her hips and flicked her brown-nippled, bladder-skin breasts at potential partners. But in the end she had seated herself on the perimeter of the gathering, sucking her gums and slapping her thighs, destined only to watch the others couple—even her own man.

Of the adult females, only Zhoonali had elected to remain aloof from the enthusiastic ruttings of her people. Cheanah had respected her wishes. It was Zhoonali's right to stand apart, not only because of her advanced years but because she was the mother of the headman. He knew his mother well enough to understand that she would never put herself in the position of Frahn, who had allowed herself to be humiliated by rejection.

As though any man would want to mount and pound such old, dry bones when there are young, moist women for the taking! he thought.

Now, nearby, a woman scolded a child sharply. Cheanah's eyes sought the source of the sound. It was Bili, Ekoh's woman. Her boy, Seteena, had evidently snatched a skewer of meat from the fire and burned his hand.

Cheanah's glance lingered on Bili, whose narrow back was to him as she bent over her little son, no doubt rubbing fat into his pudgy fingers. As Bili worked and scolded, she turned just enough so that Cheanah could make out the side of her ample left breast as it quivered against the soft doeskin of her tunic.

Someone called out to her, taunting her about Seteena's clumsiness. Cheanah, realizing it was Mano, felt a surge of pride in his son. The boy had not yet seen the passing of thirteen summers, but already he was displaying a restless and intensifying virility that endeared him to his father. The women of the band were always here for Mano whenever he felt the need for release. All except Ekoh's woman. Bili did not seem to like the boy. Now, as she turned and taunted him back, Cheanah knew that the anger flashing in her dark eyes would only incite Mano to further teasing, which would not end until Ekoh ordered the youth to find another female to annoy.

Cheanah's predictions were soon proved correct.

But since there was no woman or girl nearby to harass, Mano turned to his favorite leisure pastime: teasing his little brother, Ank. Cheanah watched his youngest son jump to his feet and, braced on skinny, knob-kneed legs, hotly demand that Mano leave him alone.

Ank rose to the baiting of his brother much too easily, the headman observed. The boy would have to learn control, or when he was grown he would be useless as a hunter.

The headman's gaze drifted across the encampment. The other hunters and boys were lounging in front of their huts, dozing, working at weapons, gnawing at bones, or playing at games of bone toss. The women worked together over the newly taken skin of a camel. They had feasted upon the prime portions of that fatty-humped animal the night before, leaving the bulk of the meat and bones for the carrion, as they often did in times of plenty. Although camel skin was not of much practical merit when compared to the hides of more thickly pelaged animals, the dull-ocher fur had a vaguely spotted appearance that the women fancied; thus, the hunters had taken it. Now the hide was stretched and secured to the ground with bone pegs as the women fleshed it.

He watched them as they knelt, leaning forward and then pulling back again and again, drawing the wide-bladed scrapers rhythmically across the hide. Their backsides moved in a way that would have been erotic to him once—but no more. He sighed. With the exception of Frahn, his mother, and Honee, his own little daughter, he had lain with them all. He thought of his own women, Xhan, whom he suspected was pregnant, and Kimm. Used meat and, in Kimm's case, boring meat and much too much of it.

It was a sad thing for a man to realize that the challenge of future seductions was gone for him, at least until new females were raised up from among his own people to an age when they might become sexually interesting.

That won't be for a long time, he thought. *A very long time, at least nine years. Maybe less, but not much less.*

Again he sighed. Only Bili could still rouse much interest in him. Perhaps this was because she made very little effort to hide the fact that she did not want him. A smile pulled at Cheanah's mouth. There was still a bit of challenge left with her.

"Cheanah! Listen to Zhoonali! When the boys of this band become men, they will fight over who is to take Honee, our beautiful, beloved child, to his fire. Share her they will have to do, but although she is strong and good to look upon, she cannot be expected to satisfy all of the men of this encampment in future days, and it will be forbidden for her to go to her brothers."

Cheanah's brow expanded across his forehead. Zhoonali was blind in both eyes when it came to Honee. The girl *was* strong, but she was no beauty, and he doubted if any man would ever fight over her.

Zhoonali continued emphatically: "As the women in this camp grow older, Honee must have band sisters to help her. It would be a bad thing for her to grow old in a camp with no younger women."

He stared up at her, annoyed. Since Man Who Walks With Dogs had been sent away, his mother seemed to be growing stronger, nourished from the pride that one of her own was headman again. She nagged him constantly, and he did not like being nagged.

"Cheanah, *are* you listening?"

"All of the encampment will listen if only my mother will nag a little louder!"

Her eyes flashed, but she lowered her voice. "Someone must nag at you! I have come from your hut, where Xhan is grumbling that if she bears a girl child, she will kill it!"

So his first woman *was* pregnant. "Xhan will do as she is told. Male or female, she will be glad for whatever life I put into her belly."

The wind that gusted quietly through the encampment at that moment was warm and sweet with the promise of ever-lengthening days of light. Cheanah breathed it in and found it as rich and sweet as raw meat.

"Cheanah, we must kill no more of our girl babies until the number of females among us is sufficient to assure the future of our people!"

Cheanah, however, was thinking of the past, remembering the women and girls of Torka's band. The tall, antelope-eyed Lonit; the lovely, gentle Iana; the adorable girl-woman Mahnie; the pretty, bounteously bosomed Eneela; and the little ones . . . the strong and beautiful little ones . . . Demmi and Summer Moon.

Summer Moon. Now *there* was a child who would one day set a man's loins pounding. And in the meantime, a man could be teaching her, guiding her, opening her body gradually to— He stopped. Just thinking of the girl's potential made him restless and hard with need.

If only the women of Torka were here now, he would begin to work with Summer Moon. But first he would take the mother, and then Iana, and then Mahnie, and then suckle the milk-swollen, wondrously copious breasts of Eneela and—

"Cheanah!" Zhoonali's tone was sharp with impatience, and Cheanah was cut by it.

He snapped to his feet, uncaring that his mother stared at that which was now thrusting boldly upward beneath his lightweight tunic, moving with reawakened need. "This man should not have permitted the women of Man Who

Walks With Dogs to leave this camp. Or his girl-children. Were they here, your tongue could take a rest!"

Her face twisted with anger toward him as her eyes met his. "Forget them! We have women of our own. The sky has not burned, the earth has not shaken, and since Torka was driven from this land, the voice of the wanawut is far away." Her expression suddenly changed, becoming as avaricious as a hunting bird's as she boldly stared at the erected column of his manhood. "Look at you! You do an old woman proud! If I were not old and dry and beyond the making of life, and were it not forbidden by the custom of our ancestors, I would open *myself* to you. Ah, the children we would make together!"

He stared, appalled, because before he could turn away, she grasped him, her old, bony, high-veined fingers fastening around him right over his distended tunic.

She laughed aloud at the look on his face as she worked him with firm, sure, experienced fingers and then, feeling his response, stepped quickly away, releasing him. "What need of Torka's women has Cheanah? Go! Go now, I say! We have women enough in this camp. Do not waste the man fire! It will make new females for this band!"

And in the days and nights that followed, when he lay on the women of his band, he knew that they were good women and, all except Bili, willing. But they were not Torka's women. Nor would they ever be.

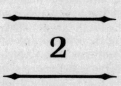

2

Leaning forward on her knuckles, the wanawut looked on the world that lay far below her fine new aerie and shook her head, huffing low and growling. Since the weather had cleared and the bright, eye-hurting hole in the sky had begun to stay longer overhead, the beasts had been venturing ever closer to the base of her mountain, far from the distant place where they gathered in a pack before skin nests close to fires that tainted the wind with the stink of burning flesh and bones and dung.

For many comings and goings of the bright hole in the sky, the wanawut had been content to remain on the misted heights, snatching and eating unwary marmots and voles and nursing her cubs while the dog bite on her shoulder festered and made her ill and then slowly healed as she listened to the song of the ever-constant wind. She had gradually regained her strength, comfortable with the knowledge that the beasts with their attacking dogs and throwing sticks were far away.

But now the wanawut watched them from high on the cliffs that overlooked a broad steppeland and the northernmost edge of the beasts' valley. Salivating with hunger, the wanawut frowned. The beasts were being greedy and wasteful. As always. They were now abandoning the carcass of a giant ground sloth, just as they had abandoned the bulk of a camel only days before. Why had the beasts killed the great, shaggy, lumbering sloth if they were not going to feed on it or at least hack it up and carry away the best parts, as they had done with the camel, back to their fires?

She squinted down. Distance and altitude made the
beasts appear to be no larger than the tiny winged things
that had begun to swarm since the rocky face of her
south-facing cliff had warmed just enough to transform
ice-filled crevices into pools of algae-thick water. The
wanawut did not like the winged things any more than she
liked the beasts. Even now they were buzzing around her
eyes and trying to bury themselves in her nostrils and
ears. She swatted at them, smashed them flat against her
massively muscled forearm and thigh, then picked them
up on the tip of a moistened finger and ate them as she
continued to watch the distant movement of the beasts,
scowling at their odd noises and their wastefulness.

Yesterday she had not felt quite strong enough to leave
the aerie to compete with other carrion eaters for the
remains of the camel. Nor had she wanted to leave her
cubs unguarded, although here, high on the mountain
wall, she could perceive no threat to them. They were not
yet crawling, let alone walking. Were they growing as
weak with hunger as she? Though her milk still flowed, it
was thin and no longer as rich with the smell of fat as it
had once been. For days now there had been no close-
flying birds to catch, or rodents of any kind. She had
probably eaten them all.

She turned and went inside the cave. At the rear,
where the light never quite penetrated, the bald little
beast cub stirred fitfully beside her own offspring in their
shared nest of twigs, lichens, and bones. The beast baby
was almost always fussing. It was cool here in the gray
shadows; the wanawut could see her breath. She looked
down to see that her own cub had kicked away its covering
of dried leaves, feathers, and scraps of skins. Warm within
its coat of thick gray fur, the strong, compact little form
lay curled fast asleep on her side. Beside her, the beast
baby lay on his back, shaking his little fists and squirming
against the cold, his body as bald and pale as a newly
hatched bird.

The wanawut was troubled. The beastling was always
cold and crying unless buried under a thick layer of insulating feathers and leaves within his nest or cuddled close
in the thick fur of her arms. He was shivering violently

now, and his skin was turning blue and was covered with tiny bumps. He was growing quickly, but compared to her own cub, he was still small. With the exception of the thick tuft of black fur on his head, he was as hairless as the day she had found him. Several of the tiny multilegged winged things were crawling on him. Snarling angrily, the wanawut waved them off, then bent over, close to the beast cub.

She cocked her head, concerned. Specks of blood dotted his cheeks, arms, belly, and legs. Without fur, the winged things would suck his blood as voraciously as they sucked it from the muzzles and ears of grazing animals—or as voraciously as she sucked it from the throat wounds of her own prey.

But she could not hold him all the time to keep him warm! She could not maintain a constant vigil against the winged biting things! She must leave the cave to hunt before they all starved!

She picked him up and licked the blood from his bites. Holding him close, she went to sit at the edge of her aerie in the warmth of the hole in the sky. Her shoulder ached high on her back, where the ripping, slashing teeth of the dog had done their worst. The beast cub rooted hungrily at her breast. She let him suckle and felt relieved when he stopped shivering. If he was to survive, this hairless little one would soon need more than mother's milk and masticated meat. He would need a new, thick, furry skin.

What strange, weak creatures these beasts were! Without fangs, fur, or claws, they were so puny, she wondered how they managed to make kills at all.

But as she watched them cavorting around the carcass of the fallen sloth like young, fractious colts, she knew that they were clever. She had seen the way they mastered fire, the way they maneuvered prey, and the way they used throwing sticks and somehow persuaded wild dogs to leap to their defense.

She frowned again when a new understanding dawned within her. As a pair of the beasts bent to hack off the huge clawed feet of the sloth and then wave them exuberantly, she realized that they all were covered from neck to toe in the skins of dead animals. This was how the beasts managed to survive! Now she knew how to keep her beast cub warm and free of bites!

He was asleep now, with one little hand curled about her breast. Ugly and tiny though he was, a mother's tender love for him warmed her. She rocked him, hunkering low, staring into the distance.

The beast pack was leaving the kill site now, and she watched as they disappeared toward the hills. Never had she seen beasts return to a kill site once they left it. Sniffing the wind, she smelled warm blood and freshly killed flesh. Birds were winging in on the scents. Her belly groaned and ached with need.

The wanawut circled in great agitation and frustration before returning the sleeping beast baby to the nest. Quickly covering him with a thick, insulating matting of leaves, feathers, and tattered fragments of skins, she went back to the edge of her aerie to scream the warning of the wanawut at the animals that were now feasting on the sloth. It was a resonant roaring, which filled the sky and sent birds screaming in all directions. Not without satisfaction, she saw the carrion eaters pause; some scattered while others turned back to their feeding.

She made a series of deep, warning grunts. She would drive them off soon enough, for on this day she would take up her man stone and leave her cubs sleeping unprotected in their aerie for the first time since she had brought them here. On this day, although her shoulder was not fully restored to its power, she would hunt again and kill any animal that stood between her and the sloth. On this day she would move quickly on the carcass, or the predators already feeding would not leave enough meat to satisfy her or enough of its long, thick fur to cover her beast cub. On this day she left the cave and began the descent of the mountain wall.

"Did you hear it?" Xhan's question trembled with fear.

No one spoke, although all had heard it. No one wanted to name the source of the sound.

"It was . . . far away. Very far," Zhoonali said at last, standing motionless as the other women gathered around her with their little ones.

"To the north," whispered old Teean, the one man in camp. "And not so far as before, I think."

The hunting party was still out from the encampment. Although Teean was a small man and as thin as a winter-starved running animal, he was flexible and stouthearted. He held his spears, and from the way he stood, no one would have doubted that despite his age and leanness he could use his weapons—and use them well.

For what seemed forever, the old man stood a cautious vigil, listening for the cry of the wanawut. He circled the encampment like a wary old wolf, shaking his spears and making his terrible faces. But the beast was not heard again, and at last the hunters returned.

"Did you hear the howling?" The question came from Mano. The youth was flushed with excitement. His spear had been the first to strike the bear-sized sloth, and now its claws—except for the two he offered as gifts to his mother and grandmother—hung around his neck on a length of thong.

Xhan and Zhoonali beamed with pride as they accepted these still-bloodied offerings from him, for the strong, curling claws of the giant sloth were coveted digging tools.

"We heard it scream from the far cliffs above the place where we took the camel under yesterday's sun," he went on. "This one boy wanted to go back, maybe track it down and kill it, but the others—"

"Men do not seek out or dare to look upon that which howled from the mountain!" Ram was a hunter in his prime, short, thick thighed, and broad across the neck. His wide, bony face held a scowl that would have warned any circumspect youth to silence.

Mano, however, was not circumspect; he was bold and antagonistic by nature. "The magic man Navahk wore the skin of a wind spirit on his back!" he reminded Ram.

"And Navahk's life spirit walks the wind as reward for that bit of arrogance!" Ram hurled back.

The hunters and women murmured agreement.

Yanehva, the headman's middle son, stepped forward to have his say. "The wind spirit was not the only meat eater drawn to our kill. We saw lions, leaping cats, and many birds when we looked back. Other animals will come to that place now—foxes, wolves, lynx, even the great bear with the shovel-nosed snout. It is not a good thing to leave so much meat at a killing site . . . unless it is intended to draw predators. Torka was right about that." Even before he finished speaking, he drew back from the others, because all were glowering at him, even his father. He had said the wrong thing. No one ever spoke well of Man of the West. Yanehva bit his lip and hung his head, ashamed.

"Torka is gone!" The headman's face was congested with anger. "Why does a son of mine speak of Torka or care what he has said or has not said?"

"I—"

"And with Torka have gone the burning sky and the trembling earth! With Torka have gone the last of the storms and the dark clouds that eat the sun! With Torka have gone his wom—" Cheanah stopped, shook his head, then went on just as hotly. "This Place of Endless Meat is ours now, and in it we will hunt as our ancestors have always hunted! We cannot take all the meat of every animal that we kill! Our young men must learn the way of the kill even though they dwell in a camp full of meat. *Torka!*" Cheanah spat the name as though it were a foul thing. "The wind spirit is far away to the north. We do not have to hunt there again. This Place of Endless Meat is rich with game! To the south, east, and west will our people go for meat if the wind-spirit wanawut claims the north country! Cheanah says that this is a good thing! We have found only sloths and camels in that open country. We will hunt there no more!"

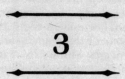

3

The wanawut gorged herself. She cracked the sloth's bones with her massive, crushing jaws and molars, sucked its blood, and gulped its meat. She had no trouble driving away other carrion-eating mammals and birds if they came too close, although most had retreated the moment she had emerged from the scrub growth, snarling and waving her fists.

The carcass was ripe with the stink of the beasts and of their flying sticks. She kept an eye out for them as she ate and made certain that her other senses were alert for any sign or sound of their return. There was still so much good meat on this sloth. How could the beasts be so wasteful?

The wanawut purred as she ate, thinking of her waiting cubs. She clutched the hollow tube of shaggy, bloodied sloth skin that she had peeled back from the arm of the carcass. It was a good, thick skin and would keep the beast cub warm.

It was time to go back to the safety of her mountain aerie, but first, before the long climb, she would take one more chew of meat, one more—

Birds suddenly flew skyward somewhere within the high scrub growth of the plain, and several antelope broke from cover to leap away toward the river.

The wanawut stopped eating, rose, leaned into the wind, and smelled . . . lion! She saw the old male emerge from the willows to stand looking at her out of eyes that were the color of the hole in the sky but without its warmth. Her head cocked to one side. His kind usually fed by day.

The lion's head went down; so did the wanawut's. She saw his yellow eyes half close, yet somehow she sensed that they were observing her more sharply than before. She had never seen such a big lion, or one with such a pale pelt. Had it not been encrusted with mud from a roll in the shallows of one of the many nearby pools, the coat would have been nearly white. His mane, however, was black—as black as his intention for her as he stood between her and the way back to her cave.

She moved to his right, to walk past him.

He blocked her.

She moved again, to his left.

He circled to intercept her, then stopped dead, roaring, shaking his great maned head to tell her that she could not pass . . . that she, not the mutilated carcass of the sloth, was to be his meal this night.

The wanawut screamed in outrage and bared her teeth. She stomped and waved her arms, flailing her fists and displaying her man stone.

The lion was not impressed.

She stomped again, hard on both feet, then gestured menacingly and showed her teeth once more.

The great cat merely lowered his head, flicked his tail, and came toward her, crouching now, pacing himself. When he was close enough, he would spring.

With her man stone in one hand and the cub covering in the other, she stood her ground, not believing that he would charge her if she faced him down. She was simply too big, too powerful, too agile, and too well armed. Her claws were bearlike, and her stabbing teeth could be equaled only by a leaping cat's. The lion's musculature was massive and designed for the kill, but hers was the same . . . only she walked upright, much like the beasts.

In a white arc of pure, black-maned power, the lion leaped at her. As he did, she ducked, then came up beneath him, shouldering him hard, knocking him off balance so that he fell onto his side. Stunned, he lay still, but only for a moment.

That was enough for the wanawut to perceive the weakness of her still-injured shoulder and to feel pain. Warm liquid ran down her leg. She looked: Somehow the lion had opened a long, deep gash on the outside of her right thigh—from hip to knee. She hooted low, concerned and confused, until, alerted by the lion's snarling, she looked up to see him coming at her again. This time he did not leap. He simply walked forward, smelling her blood, sensing her weakness and fear.

He was old and wise, this lion—but he was not wary. With an unexpected feint forward, she slashed his face hard with her man stone, then stabbed deep and quick. The lion's eye was ruined, and the entire left side of his face was laid open before he could turn away. She watched him circle madly, pawing at his face, before he turned and ran.

She waited for him to disappear into the cover of the willow scrub from which he had emerged to attack her. When she could no longer see him, she turned her back, and pressing the sloth skin into her thigh wound to ease the pain as well as to stanch the flow of blood, she began to limp home.

It was dark by the time she returned to her aerie. Hurting, weak, and in shock from loss of blood, the wanawut was nevertheless more concerned for her cubs than for herself. She went immediately to the nest and peered in to find the beastling uncovered.

He lay so still. His skin was so cold, she was certain that the breath had left his body. Her own cub was fussing with hunger; but it was warm and could wait for her attention.

She lifted the little beast and, cooing to him all the while, breathed the warmth of her own life onto his puckered skin and into his tiny nostrils, ears, and mouth. Still fearing that he was dead, she held him close and seated herself, cradling him in the fold of her thickly furred arms until he began to shiver.

He was alive! Relief nearly overwhelmed her. Exhausted, she leaned back against the cold, stony wall of the cave and listened to the cries of her own cub. The sound was strong with life. Despite her pain, her long, virtually lipless mouth turned downward into a smile. The hungry, healthy wails were almost as comforting as the pleasure that she found when the beastling stopped shivering and burrowed deep, searching for a nipple.

She let him suck for a while, then put him on the ground by her folded legs and, grimacing against the throbbing agony in her thigh, inserted him into the hollow casing of sloth skin. It was still wet and warm and softened with her blood. The beastling snuggled into it happily. When she rose to retrieve her own nursling and returned to sit against the wall, the tiny beast was fast asleep and as content as if she still held him in her arms.

Had the lion had his way, both she and her babes would be dead. Troubled, the wanawut blinked and tried to will the memory away. She was weary. Her shoulder ached. Her thigh hurt. She was weak . . . so weak. . . .

She fell asleep before she knew enough to wish for sleep and did not wake until the needs of her hungry cubs roused her. Her leg and shoulder were stiff and painful. She felt no stronger than when she had gone to her rest, but the sight of the cubs made her feel better.

She nursed and dreamed of Mother and of other strong, gray-furred creatures of her own kind. The beast cub, warm in his sleeve of sloth skin, slept again, too, until she felt the need to lift him and exhale breaths of affection onto him.

A wind was rising now, weaving among the clouds so that now and again the light of the hole in the sky turned the gray morning to gold. It illuminated the face of the beastling, and for the first time the wanawut recognized in the features of the babe those of the man, dressed in the skins of a golden lion, who had ventured into the far country in pursuit of the abandoned beastling.

Her clawed, hairy-backed fingers traced the delicate face of the tiny boy as she mouthed the beast's strange, never-to-be-forgotten lamentation: "Man-ara-vak."

And, to her amazement, the infant in her arms cooed, delighting in the sound of his own kind and of his own name.

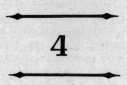

4

Manaravak!

Lonit almost cried out the name of her lost son, the feeling was *that* strong in her that he was alive, alive and calling out to his mother to come and take him into her arms, away from—

"Lonit?" Torka spoke her name.

She turned.

"Do not look back," he said, extending a hand to her. "Come. We must go on now, into the wonderful valley."

And it *was* wonderful. For several days and nights they had observed it as they rested on the high ridge that overlooked the valley. They raised individual lean-tos and consumed the last of their traveling rations. They recuperated from the long trek across the Forbidden Land.

Time passed quickly. By day the wind brought them the sweet scents and sounds of the world below. By night, when cold air swept downward from the mountain heights, they listened to the echoing voice of the spirits of the stony crags, to meltwater thickening and congealing into ice, to bergs colliding on the surface of the great gray lake that lay behind them, and to the restless shifting and grinding murmurs of the north-canyon glacier.

Now they donned their pack frames again. With the dog walking ahead, they strode on, under the warm sun or beneath gathering clouds, following the mammoth through upland groves that were strongly scented from pungent spruce wood and Life Giver's kind. They moved quietly, for although they walked in the tracks of their totem and were confident that no danger would come to them through him, they could not predict the reaction of the kindred of Life Giver. This was mammoth country. As strangers, they knew it was wise to tread respectfully through the land of the great tuskers. This they did, keeping their distance when Summer Moon and little Demmi pointed with delight at baby mammoths browsing in the woodlands with their huge, shaggy mothers, aunts, and grandmothers, while young bulls grazed in pairs, aloof from their females but wary and watchful of them all the same.

Downward the band traveled, through a wide, easily traversed, sunstruck defile, which bore neither scent nor sign of the vast glacial mass that lay on the other side of the mountain. Spruce trees and slender, greening hardwoods shadowed them as they descended. Never in all of their lives had they seen such tall trees.

Their progress was slowed by a gradual thickening of the undergrowth and by their wariness of what might lie lurking within it. Even the dog was intimidated.

"So much scrub! So many trees!" Wallah whispered, looking up as she paused and absently rubbed her hip.

Grek, hunching forward as though the shadows cast by the trees were pressing him down, prodded his woman on. He did not like this place. A man was at risk when he walked amid groves, where trees grew taller than his belly and undergrowth was higher than his knees.

Grek worked his jaw a little harder as he looked up and around, walking beside Wallah. Although these trees were twice his height, Grek could perceive no threat in them. They were widely spaced and full of sunlight. When he raised his head to draw in the scents of the defile, he could smell only the good aromas of sun-washed rock; the clear, cool meltwater cascading from the heights; the sweet, graceful, wind-stirred shadows redolent of plant life; the fragrant, sap-rich spruce needles; and the swelling leaves of hardwoods. Now and again he caught the acrid scent of mammoth . . . and the vaguely sour hint of fecal droppings left behind by various ground-dwelling creatures: rodents, foxes, badgers, lynx . . . a moose somewhere deep and far away within the trees, grazing by some upland pool—a cow, with young. Grek could smell an udder and milk clotting in the sunlight on the muzzle of a fawn.

Meat, he thought, and stood tall once again as, following Torka, he took a turn to the right and paused, sucking in his breath.

They had come out of the defile. The forest hills lay behind them, and the wonderful valley lay directly ahead. Now they could hear the herd again. Now they could smell it. Now, for the first time, they could *see* it.

Caribou! Long, broken rivers of hide and hoof and antler! So many caribou that the herd plodded under a great, vaporous cloud of steam, which condensed from the combined breath of thousands upon thousands of animals. Never before or again in the history of the world would so many animals of one kind walk together beneath the open, unspoiled sky. Out of the face of the rising sun, from unknown country far to the east, and through the high, wide, still ice-ridden passes the caribou approached the western ranges as they crossed the distant southeastern edge of the valley.

Torka and his little band stood in stunned silence. Not even in their most hopeful moments had they ever dared to imagine that the forces of Creation would allow the great mammoth to lead them to such a herd.

"As my magic man has promised, this *is* a wonderful valley!" Mahnie exclaimed as she stood close to Karana, looking at him with all her love shining in her eyes, and failing to note the petulant envy on the face of Summer Moon, who had been like a wayward little shadow to Karana these days.

He took no note of the child or Mahnie. He moved to stand slightly ahead of them and the others of the band and stared out across a world of light and beauty. Yet deep within the core of his being, the spirit wind was rising . . . whispering . . .

Go from this place. There is danger for you here. Go back into the track of the setting sun before it is too late . . . before the prophecy of Navahk is fulfilled for you all!

Karana stiffened against the warning. This was not what he wanted to hear! Not now, when the wonderful valley lay ahead, at last! Here was the real place—not a lie, not a conjuring of hopeful dreams, but real in every detail that he had described to the band. His words had given his people the determination and courage to find their way to this place of his promising.

A great hot lump lodged in his throat. The power of Seeing *was* his! Perhaps he had never truly lost it? Perhaps his lack of faith in his own shamanistic powers, his own guilt and indecisiveness, had dulled his Sight and blinded him? *Yes!* Surely this must be so.

Go back! warned the spirit wind. *Go back* now, *before it is too late!*

"Life Giver, the great mammoth spirit, has led my people to this good land. Never has our totem led us wrongly before!" he proclaimed loudly and defensively as he stood immobile and crossed his arms over his chest.

"And what does our magic man see for his people in this wonderful valley?" asked Torka, coming to stand beside him.

Truth snared his tongue. "Many things."

"And some of them are troubling to you?"

Karana was painfully aware of Torka's scrutiny. Torka had always been able to see into his heart—except on a day, long ago now, when the hunter had been too heartbroken to recognize the lies and the deception of one whom he called Son.

"Something *is* troubling you," Torka observed. "Something has been troubling you since before we left Cheanah's people in the Place of Endless Meat."

Their eyes met and held, then Karana looked away, lest Torka glimpse his spirit and see everything that Karana could never allow him to see: *Deceiver. Manipulator. Liar.* But Karana would not lie to him now, not as they stood together on the brink of a new world and a new life.

"Perhaps this valley is not all that it seems," he replied obliquely.

"Nothing in this world is ever all that it seems," responded Torka. "But it has been said by the ancients that a magic man sees the world more clearly than do others. I thought that you might tell me more than I already know."

Karana shook his head and choked back his reply: *No. We know much less, for we must see through mists thrown*

*before our eyes by the spirit wind, which always tries to
trick us, to confuse us, and to take back the power given
us.*

"It is no wonder that we heard the passing of these
animals even though we were so far away!" Iana whispered in awe.

"So *many* animals! So *much* meat!" Wallah sighed rap-
turously.

So many animals! Her words echoed in Torka's head.
Karana was being evasive, as usual, but the moment was
nevertheless one of supreme gladness. At last those who
had followed him were to be rewarded, and he could relax
momentarily and anticipate with joy the exhilaration to be
had in hunting and feasting.

As always happened when he was brought short with
amazement by the sight of the great herds returning out of
the face of the rising sun, Torka found himself intrigued
by questions that had haunted him since boyhood: *How
can there be so many animals? Where do they come from?
Where do they go to?*

"Torka? We will prepare to hunt now, yes?"

Grek's query sent the revery away. Torka nodded in
reply. This was not the time for questions. This was the
time to hunt. At last.

They unloaded their pack frames, raised temporary lean-
tos to shelter them against any unexpected change in the
weather, and quickly prepared for the kill and the butchering to follow.

"So many caribou . . . so few hunters," lamented Simu,
dressed for the hunt and looking off toward the herd. "It is
a sad thing that this band has fewer spearmen than this
man has fingers on one hand. With more men, think of
the meat with which we would fill the camp!"

"Then count on both hands, my brother!" Torka told
him, then called out the names of the women and girls,
summoning them forward.

"Females do not hunt with their men!" Simu protested,
shocked.

Torka took measure of the younger man. "Knowing that

it would offend the ways of your ancestors, I am not suggesting that our females pick up spears and hunt game. But I do have an idea that will involve them and should increase our take of meat."

"We have our spear hurlers," Grek pointed out. He was obviously uncomfortable with the concept of bringing females into the hunt. "With spear hurlers, four men can do what eight would be hard put to accomplish in any other band!" He hefted the hunting tool that Torka had invented long ago in the far land.

An elongated shaft of fire-hardened bone approximately the length of a man's forearm, the spear hurler seemed to be little more than a barb-ended bone with a sinew-wrapped handgrip at one end. But with the grip held tightly, the butt end of a spear braced against the barb, and the pointed end of the spear resting back over a hunter's shoulder, a spear hurler could double the speed, distance, and power of a hunter's thrust.

Torka watched Simu test the weight of his own spear hurler; the device was relatively new to the young hunter, and Torka knew that Simu was not as competent with it as he would like to be.

"This is not as good as having another strong man to hunt beside me," Simu muttered.

Grek, who found humor in virtually any situation, said, "But it *is* better and more trustworthy than any of the so-called hunters who follow that perpetually bone-loined, camp-stealing, say-yes-to-mother man Cheanah!"

Simu grinned. "Would it not be a good thing to see the look on that one's face if he saw this fine, sweet valley and the number of animals that wait to die upon the spears of this band's hunters!"

Grek guffawed. "It would be good! So good that it would almost be worth going back to see it!"

Torka was amused and pleased by the men's good-natured exchange and saw all the women blush and titter. Then the headman took the band into his confidence: "We will use our spear hurlers. Only males will use spears. But for the women, my idea is this. . . ."

*   *   *

In stalking cloaks of caribou skins brought from the far country, the hunters went out from among their women and children. Quietly they walked, with the antlered heads of long-dead animals balanced atop their own, and with their spears and spear hurlers at ready. Not a word or whisper was spoken. When the herd was close, the men stopped to gather the feces of their prey, rubbing it into their skin so the animals would detect no scent of the human intruders.

Now the hunters stalked the caribou in the manner of wolves, in silence, with cunning. And not until the caribou heard the song of the spears did the herd know that Death walked among them.

Now the hunters *were* wolves. With the great dog Aar working as a part of their pack, they deliberately set terror to the herd, howling, yipping, and running among the panicked animals like fire in dry grass.

The killing site had been chosen with care. A broad, open stretch of steppe, it lay directly between the herd and the western ranges and was bisected by a wide, shallow, stony-bedded stream. The area was far from marshes and lake beds into which the terrified caribou might plunge and disappear underwater before the hunters could retrieve the carcasses and precious spears.

Here, in the grasses bordering the stream, the women and girls hid with old Grek to protect them in case anything went wrong. Each was covered with the largest skin she could carry. When the herd came close, the females held up the skins and rose in unison, to screech and howl like wolves and wanawuts. The already panicked caribou broke and scattered, then old Grek and the females took after them, driving the caribou back toward the spears of the waiting hunters.

So much meat was taken, old Wallah was later inspired to predict that in generations to come, the children of the People would sing of the magic of the first hunt in the wonderful valley. Torka, however, insisted that there had been no magic.

"It was merely a good idea that worked well," he told her. "If you want magic, look to Karana."

But that night while Iana and the girls slept in a separate lean-to, when Torka and Lonit lay together beneath their sleeping skins, Lonit told her man that he had been wrong.

"What you did this day *was* magic," she said. "A greater magic than this woman has ever seen Karana work. This day, at Torka's command, the men and women of more than one band worked together as one people, men and women for the good of all. Once before, in the storm, you commanded the others to work together, despite their fear, to raise the hut. Surely this is a great and powerful magic."

Beneath their bed furs Lonit put little Umak to sleep close at her back. She turned and stirred softly against her man. Her bare skin was warm, then hot against his as she moved to lie atop him, balancing herself on her palms, slurring her breasts against him, opening herself to him as she looked down at him, then bent to kiss his mouth, to breathe her love into his nostrils. He caught fire from her intent, gasped, and pulled her down. Once more man and woman were one within the camp of Torka.

"Magic . . ." Lonit exhaled, trembling and arching to prolong their union. When the night caught fire and burned with the power of their joining, Torka knew that she had been right after all: When Lonit was in his arms, there would always be magic.

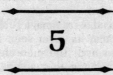

5

The days of endless light poured across life's surface as the people of Torka hunted and gathered beneath a never-setting sun. Hibernating creatures emerged from their dens and burrows; the coats of ptarmigan, owls, and rabbits changed from winter white to summer brown, and geese, swans, ducks, and other migratory birds came gliding from the skies to the south to mate and raise their young upon the ice-free lakes and ponds that jeweled the wonderful valley.

In the camp of Torka and his people, the cache pits were full, and the drying frames sagged from the weight of curing meat. Weary hunters had new tales of daring, bravery, and high adventure when it was time to rest from the kill and sit together with their women and children. And while the men hunted and explored the valley, the women and girls sang and laughed as they worked to butcher the meat, flesh the hides, and work the skins of caribou and horse and of moose and elk. Although Wallah confided that Grek still longed for steaks cut from the fatty hump of a bison, she had no doubt that sooner or later he was bound to have his longing sated, for it seemed that in the wonderful valley every good thing that men and women wished for came to pass.

"Magic Man?" Demmi's voice was soft on the warm wind.

Karana was startled by the appearance of the child, for he was well out from camp, seated on a lichen-stuffed pillow of bison hide. Aar sat at his side as he worked to bind a new spearhead to his favorite bone shaft. His brow furrowed. What was she doing here? It was pretty, adoring little Summer Moon who dogged his steps.

"Why has the second daughter of Torka come away from camp alone?" His question was a deliberate scolding.

Demmi hung her head. Only barely able to hold her own against the enthusiastic nuzzling of the dog, she wrapped her arms around Aar's neck lest he knock her down.

Karana called the dog. Aar obeyed and came close, seating himself with his tail and half a bony buttock on the magic man's right thigh.

Demmi followed, nestling herself on his left thigh, like a little bird wiggling into the comfort and security of its nest. "Where is Longspur, Magic Man? You said we would find him in our valley, but Demmi has looked. Demmi cannot find him."

Karana felt a quick sinking feeling as he remembered the tiny bird he had inadvertently crushed in his fist during their journey from the Place of Endless Meat.

"There are longspurs all around us in this good land," he told the child.

The young man was surprised by his reaction to her closeness; there was something calming in the minuscule weight and warmth of the tiny, serious little girl. He saw the look of trust on the child's face and knew that there was only one way to live up to it. He took a last turn on the sinew spear joining and secured it. "Come." With his spear held upright in one hand, he scooped her up in one lean, strong arm and rose. "Together we will find Longspur."

Eagerly she took his hand as he set her upon her feet and told the dog to stay. Disappointed, Aar whined and lay down, resting his head on his paws as the tiny girl walked at the magic man's side until, to her obvious delight, Karana bent and lifted her again.

"We will walk faster as one, Sister," he said, and to his amazement, the sober-faced little girl leaned close and kissed him on the cheek.

Sister! Karana smiled for the first time in many days. *Yes!*

It was good to think of her in that way. Demmi *was* his sister—not by blood but by a deeper, more heartfelt bonding than a mere happenstance of birth could ever make. The *thing*—the child of Navahk and the beast—was far away, in another world, in another life, and no longer a part of him unless he chose to journey back to seek it out. And that he would *never* do.

A sudden and wondrous euphoria nearly overcame him as, for the first time, he felt a sense of control over his true father. Navahk could not be reborn through a daughter, so the half-human cub offered no threat. The only piece left of that evil man was that small portion that lived on in Karana—never to be reproduced if he refused to couple with Mahnie—and the half-human cub that lay impotent, far away, in another world, in the arms of a beast.

And so now, with a lighter step and a joyful spirit, he carried his tiny sister Demmi to a broad space of tundra, where they both lay flat and peered through the grasses. The child saw only a relatively barren stretch of lichens and mosses until Karana whispered: "Look, my little sister. Listen and be very still."

Demmi chewed her lower lip and held her breath, straining to hear. Gradually, as she lay beside the magic man, she smiled. Her ears began to perceive the little sounds of insects, the larger sounds of the world above and beyond the grasses, and the quick, musical *teew-teew* and high, whistling *tick-tick-tick* of longspurs.

As the moments passed, Karana became aware of the child's controlled breathing. It was so soft and measured, he could barely feel her side moving against his. He could not hear her exhalations at all, for she blocked them within her tiny palm lest her breath betray her presence to the world of grasses. He raised an eyebrow. *This one is female, but she has the instincts of a hunter.*

Slowly, so slowly that even the magic man was not distracted by the movement until Demmi's finger was practically below his nose, the little girl pointed off. The subtlest tremor of pleasure shook her form as she saw

what he had brought her to see: hundreds of drab little
birds sitting on drab little nests.

He nodded. "Come now," he whispered, and together
they rose and went stalking amid an upward spray of
panicked, chittering longspurs. Karana knelt before an
indentation in the tundra no larger than the palm of his
hand. "Look."

The child knelt and gazed upon a minute, feather-lined
nest in which lay half a dozen pale, lichen-green eggs. Her
eyes went wide with amazement and joy. "For Demmi?"

"Just for Demmi. Your mother has told me that eggs are
one of Demmi's favorite things."

Her round face puckered with concern as she turned
back to stare at the magic man out of eyes that were so
much like Torka's: long and angled upward beneath the
brow. "Demmi will not eat Longspur's babies!"

"There are thousands of eggs here for the taking. Longspur will not mind."

"He has told you?"

"He . . . has told me."

"Has he asked his woman longspur if Demmi could eat
her children?"

"These are eggs, Little One, not children."

And so they sat and shared the eggs from several nests.
Sweet they were and slippery on the tongue, and as the
magic man watched the little girl happily suck the shells,
he was suffused with a warmth and contentment that he
had not felt in all too many moons.

There *was* magic in the world, he thought. The tender,
trusting magic of a little sister for an older brother. He
had decided never to have a child of his own, but he had
Demmi's love, and this was more than enough for him.

Suddenly, Demmi grimaced and spat and spewed a tiny
beak and half-formed clawed foot from her mouth. "Baby!"
she shrieked, snapping to her feet, shaking violently, waving her pudgy little hands in horror at having eaten one of
Longspur's children.

Karana was at a loss to ease the child. Why was she so
upset? In her brief lifetime she must have consumed
dozens of such nearly formed eggs. "Truly, it is all right!"

he assured her. "Longspur told me that it would be all right. Would Magic Man not speak the truth to his sister?"

She stared at him, her mouth quivering. "*Not* magic!" she accused, then turned and stamped back toward camp.

Karana followed, but neither he nor Demmi spoke when they returned to the encampment. In the days that followed, the child refused to eat the various eggs that her people gathered in the surrounding grass and marshlands. He alone understood. He did not ask why lest she publicly name him Liar.

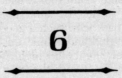

6

Summer gradually yielded to autumn. Beneath the returning skies of night, the people of Torka looked up, waiting
for the first glimpse of the new star that had appeared
when little Umak came into the world.

He was a strong baby now, crawling energetically around
the encampment. Wallah predicted that before the time of
the long dark was over, he would be walking and talking
nearly as well as Dak, Eneela and Simu's boy.

"Dak is much older!" reminded Eneela, indignant that
her offspring's excellent qualities were in danger of being
overshadowed by another's.

"They will be as brothers," Lonit enthused. Although
she felt the ever-present pang of longing for her lost twin,
she forced a smile at Eneela. "They will grow and learn
together in this wonderful valley!"

And it was so. Each day Lonit and Eneela fed their sons
together, and as Umak's serrate-edged little teeth began
to sprout and Lonit winced and frowned, secretly comparing them with the teeth of Navahk, Eneela assured her
that her own son once had had similar milk teeth.

"Dak had put more than a few holes in me before I
toughened up to him!" she recalled. "Many infants have
such teeth—especially boys. Little lions they are! Perhaps
they need a little blood in their milk to make them
strong!"

For a moment, the white lion growled within Lonit's
memories, but Eneela talked happily on and on, reminiscing with pride about her son. In spite of her longing for

her sister, Bili, Eneela was such a cheerful companion it
was impossible for Lonit not to be cheerful herself.

At each day's end, Lonit took Umak into her arms, held
him up, pointed to the sky, and spoke to him about the
new star, which had been such a good sign at the time of
his birth. He gurgled and mimicked her sounds and her
gestures. Together, night after night, while Torka engaged
in talk of the day's hunt with the men of his band, mother
and son sat with Demmi and Summer Moon outside their
pit hut, eagerly awaiting the return of "Umak's star." But
as the nights grew longer, only the old, familiar fires
burned in the black skin of the sky.

"Has Brother's star gone away forever?" Demmi asked.

"We will ask our magic man," Lonit suggested.

"Not ask *him*. Mother knows better than Magic Man
about Brother's star."

"This girl will ask him!" Summer Moon volunteered.

"No! Not ask about Brother's star! Not ask Magic Man
about anything!" countered Demmi.

Lonit did not fail to note that for unknown reasons
Karana had fallen out of favor with her little girl. And
secretly, as night followed lengthening night and the new
star did not reappear, Lonit decided to seek comfort in the
words of a seer.

"What does the absence of the new star mean?" she
asked the magic man as he sat alone outside his pit hut.

He was so withdrawn these days, so consistently sad.
And because of his aloof bearing he seemed so old. She
knew him to be young, but the look of the boy whom she
had raised to manhood was gone forever. And Mahnie had
been looking unhappy, too, these last few days.

Karana's face was a man's face now; and although he had
always strongly resembled his father, on this night, with
the starlight illuminating his handsome features and shining sparkling-blue upon his black hair, he looked . . .
identical to the man whom she would prefer to forget, and
yet could not: *Navahk*, the beautiful, whose outward perfection was equaled only by the inner hideousness that
was his soul. She almost spoke the name of the hated dead
man aloud.

"Perhaps the new star was a sign for only one time. . . ."
Karana was saying, staring at the sky, unaware of the
strange, strained expression that had tightened Lonit's
features as she looked at him, and then away. "The new
star," he went on thoughtfully, "was an omen, of course, a
sign from the forces of Creation that the birth of Umak,
son of Torka and Lonit, was a good thing. But once the
omen was given, the sign made, the star had no need to
come again."

Although she had the uneasy impression that he was
trying to justify himself, his reply satisfied her—in the way
that all things are satisfying when they gratify a need and
assuage a fear. Besides, she felt so distressed and disoriented from seeing the visage of his true father on Karana's
face that she was anxious to get away.

Later, watching Karana from the windbreak of her pit
hut, the resemblance to Navahk seemed less marked. She
chided herself for having reacted so intensely to it. If
Karana looked more like him now that the full maturation
of manhood was his, was this not only natural? After all,
he was Navahk's son. But he was also the brother of her
heart, and she would not turn away from him because it
was his misfortune to resemble one whose memory he
despised even more than she did.

Everywhere upon the steppe, animals were changing
back from summer brown to winter white; man-tall stalks
of fireweed crisped in the cold, dry air and turned the
land red with the color of fading blossoms and setting
seeds; and the softest dusting of snow fell but was gone on
the back of the wind practically before it had a chance to
settle.

The days were still long and full. The women gathered
and gleaned, using their digging claws and sticks to root
up succulent tubers and sweet, albeit fibrous, roots.
Craneberries were ripe in the hills now, and although
picking them was woman's work, even the men joined in.
All gorged themselves except Demmi, whose mouth puckered against their sourness, and helped to pile skins high
with them as they set them to dry in the now-oblique light
of the sun.

It rained several times. The skies grew thick with clouds, then cleared. Vast wedges of migrating birds headed south-eastward, into the face of the rising sun.

"Where do they go?" Lonit asked Torka, her eyes locked upon a pair of black swans as they rose from the earth together and took wing into the dawn.

He smiled tenderly to hear her phrase the question that he had asked himself so many times. "To a place far away, where, perhaps, the sun never sets and the world never grows cold."

Grek, within earshot, looked up from the bone stave that he was hardening in a fire pit made for that purpose. Smoke and steam were rising. He peered through the fog at his headman and his headman's woman as Wallah emerged from their pit hut to stand behind him. "We could go there," he suggested. "Then, when the time of the long dark is over, we could follow the winged ones back to our valley, into the face of the setting sun."

"With my bad hip, I hope that we will fly, as they do," said Wallah sourly.

"Restless as always, old friend?" Torka teased, ignoring Wallah's uncharacteristic dourness. "Always the nomad. Grek, even in such hunting grounds as these?"

Grek ground his teeth and looked around, conceding: "It is a good place, this valley. A good camp. If the winter does not last forever, it will serve us well."

And it did—for that winter, and for the next two winters.

But after the red dawn of their fourth autumn in the wonderful valley, many moons would rise and set before anything in Torka's world would seem so wonderful again.

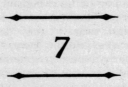

7

The great short-faced bear came by night, as do all true
horrors, for darkness is the accomplice of fear, making all
things that men dread seem larger and more dangerous.
But this animal was already so huge that the night could
do little to make him seem larger or more deadly. On all
fours, he stood well above five feet tall at the height of his
massively fat, thickly furred shoulders. Now, as he rose on
his hind limbs and sighted across the night, he was twelve
feet tall. By sheer girth and height and weight of mass, he
was one of the largest mammals ever to walk the earth. He
did not carry the fatty hump of his cousin the grizzly, but
he was larger by nearly a third, sleeker, and therefore
fleeter of foot. His oddly foreshortened face was not that of
an omnivore; the great short-faced bear of the Age of Ice
was exclusively a carnivore. His diet consisted of meat,
any meat—alive or dead, freshly killed or putrid.

And now his broad snout drew in the scent of the cache
pits, and the meat and hides that lay drying and stored
within the encampment of Torka's people. Salivating with
anticipation, the great bear began to move forward.

Slowly, long before the great bear was close enough to
be heard or scented, its presence began to rouse the
people and set them to sighing and thrashing restlessly in
their sleep. Soon, in each of the individual family pit huts,
the people of Torka lay wide awake and absolutely still.
Something was into the cache pits beyond the camp.

Snares and pit traps all around the encampment had

been carefully devised to keep predators away. For four autumns no predator had violated this safety system. But now a low, snapping sound that could have been the tripping of a snare line broke the silence of the dark.

In his hut, Torka listened, waiting, trying to put an image and a name to whatever was moving in the dark. He could hear it clearly now—soft paddings, softer exhalations, and low, slobbering gnawing barely audible above the constant sighing of the autumn wind. It sounded big, but in the dark, rodents could sound as large as wolves, and wolves could sound as large as lions, and—

Aar barked once from where he slept outside Karana's hut, but to Torka it sounded as if the dog was not certain of what he was barking at or if he was barking at anything at all. Because his man pack punished him when he woke them for no reason, Aar had long since learned not to alert them unnecessarily. Yet now, the dog was barking wildly, ferociously, fierce and mad with fear and aggression.

Torka pulled on his boots and was on his feet, his spear grasped in one hand and his bludgeon in the other before he reached out to sweep the weather baffle aside. Behind him, Umak was asking what was going on, and Lonit and Iana were both shushing the boy even as they told Torka to be wary. As though he needed their advice.

The hunter's heart was pounding as he warned his women and children to be still. His voice was so calm that for a moment he almost believed that he was not afraid. But he was afraid, for across the distance of time, he had lost a woman, a young son, and a suckling to a marauding mammoth.

Suddenly the intruder roared under the moonless sky. Torka heard a woman's scream of terror. *Wallah's.* And a man's curse. *Grek's.*

Trying to focus his night vision, Torka saw the bear, lit by dazzling starlight. Big it was, and fat from feeding throughout the endless days of light, but irritable—not only because it was near the time for its kind to den for the winter but because it had been driven away from its feeding by a circling, snapping wolf of a dog.

Across the encampment, from the lake of shadow that

lay before Grek and Wallah's pit hut, a woman was crying. *Mahnie*. Where was Karana?

Torka blinked; he could see clearly now. As the bear stood and wheeled, Torka saw Karana and Simu, two naked spearmen, screaming at the monster that loomed over them as the dog cut circles around its feet. There were two spears in the back of the bear; one was hanging loose, caught in fur and fat. Torka judged the other to be deep into muscle and bone by the way the bear was trying to paw it out.

He did not wait; he could smell it now, its big, meat-eating, animal stench, and sense its enormous weight moving in the dark. Karana and Simu were already hurling two additional spears. As the dog's hackles rose, Torka threw his own spear, but it went wide as the bear suddenly dropped to all fours and took off into the night with Aar at his heels.

Stunned, the three men stood in shocked silence. They came together instants later in an embrace of relief and satisfaction. The bear was gone! They had driven it away! Later they would wonder how much time had passed before they heard the crying of the women and children and the sobbing of the man, for Wallah lay bleeding from a gaping wound that began at the lower end of her hip where her right leg should have been.

Torka knew what must be done to stanch the flow of her blood. "As meat is seared in the flame, so it is with the flesh of man and woman," he said.

A look of disbelief and horror darkened the faces of the others.

"That which is burned will not bleed," he assured them. "This I was taught by Umak, spirit master, and this Karana was taught by the seeress and healer Sondahr. Our magic man had been taught in the ways of healing by both Umak and by the healers at the Great Gathering. For Wallah, mother of his woman, Karana will be a healer to his people. Now."

He stepped aside, and it was done. While compresses of hide were held against the wound, a stone was heated and laid against the flesh of the woman. Wallah fainted as the pain began. She awoke before it ended. But not once did the woman of Grek cry out.

Later that day the hunters found Wallah's leg but did not know what to do with it. After a brief but unsuccessful search for Brother Dog, they returned to camp. The band was happy the bear had not eaten of Wallah's leg; without it, she would become a crooked spirit, doomed to drag herself through the world of men as a ghost in search of her missing part. They brought it to her fire circle. After Mahnie had cleansed it, Grek stared at it and put it close to his woman, insisting that Karana make some sort of chant over it, as though the mutilated member might somehow fill with blood and life again and graft itself to her hip.

On the second day, the women lathered the severed limb in a purplish-red paint made of the reconstituted pulp of dried craneberries in hope that this would stimulate a responsive flow of blood. The leg, however, refused to return to life and rejoin itself to Wallah's body. There was talk of trying to sew it back on, but by then the leg had begun to putrefy. The people gathered stones and buried it in a shallow pit outside the encampment. They mounded stones over it, to keep it safe from predators, and all gathered around the little grave to honor the spirit of Wallah's leg.

On the third day, Brother Dog returned, battered and exhausted and missing most of his left ear.

For days the pain and fever took Wallah in and out of delirium. She slept, and moaned, and woke, and moaned. Grek stayed by her side. Mahnie tended him and her mother. Karana tried not to think of the severed limb lying in its grave as he made the chants of healing and waited to see if his magic would bring Wallah through her ordeal . . . and while he waited, he wondered what life would be like for a one-legged woman in an unforgiving world if it did.

Wallah slowly healed, but Torka's fear of the great bear did not. "If it lives, it may return. That is the way of its kind," he warned.

While Grek elected to stay with Wallah and the women and children, Torka, Simu, and Karana tracked the bear. It was not difficult; the animal had been bleeding profusely, and after a few miles, it was circling, stopping often, and dragging its hindquarters. They found it dead in lake country to the southeast, at the base of a range of broad, ice-free, cave-pocked hills. They skinned it, but not one of them wished to eat of its meat. In silence they removed their spearheads from the carcass and took the claws and hide.

There was no celebration of its death. The women were not even interested in the skin and claws.

"Who will sleep in a robe made of the skin of one who has eaten of our sister?" asked Lonit.

"*I* will sleep in it!" declared Wallah to everyone's surprise. Her face was unnaturally sallow, her features drawn and wan from hours of unrelenting pain, but her eyes were full of life for the first time since her dismemberment. "When all is said and done, Wallah thinks that it is better to be a one-legged woman than a dead bear without a skin!"

And so the bearskin was stretched and fleshed and cured for her.

As the skin was prepared, Torka, troubled, paced the camp. For the first time in longer than he could remember, he knew that he had erred, and badly. "We should have been more cautious," he admitted. "*I* should have been more cautious."

"Three winters is too long to stay in one camp." Grek's voice was hard, as were his eyes as he looked at Torka. "The spirits sour on men when they stay too long in one place. This man has said this before, and he says it again . . . but it is too late for Wallah."

"She lives!" Karana reminded him. "And from this time on, because we've found her limb, she will be especially favored by the forces of Creation. Not many women have lived to boast about running out of a pit hut in the black of night into the arms of a great bear—and ending up with the skin of the bear!"

Grek's head swung on his neck. The hardness in his eyes became sadness. "The spirits give with one hand and take away with the other! You, Magic Man, *you* tell my Wallah that she has been favored instead of cursed! Ask her which she would prefer to own—the skin of a bear or her own leg!" He sighed and closed his eyes, then opened them and fixed his gaze on Karana once again. "How long will she live with a wound like that? How long? You are a magic man. You tell me, yes! All the time she hurts so badly that she can barely sleep, and when she does, she wakes up looking for her leg, saying that she can feel it. She makes me look to see if her toes are wiggling, but there is nothing there. Nothing to hold up the weight of my Wallah if someday she might have to rise and run to save herself from another bear or lion or—"

"She will not have to run. Ever again," Torka told the old hunter. "In the hills above the bear's carcass, I saw caves—good, high, dry-looking, south-facing caves—and we could make a good camp in one of them. Wallah could be comfortable and safe for the rest of her days, and we could defend ourselves against any predator that would try to come against us."

"Men do not live in caves like animals!" protested Simu.

"Karana, Lonit, and this man have lived in caves. We are not animals," countered Torka.

Karana nodded. "And as magic man I tell you that both Grek and Torka have been right all along. It is not good for the people to stay too long in one camp. And in this new land, even Simu must learn new ways!"

A preliminary investigation proved that the caves were everything that Torka had hoped for and more. A good climb through scrubby spruce and birchwood along a spring-fed streambed was necessary to reach them. Water would be close at hand when it was needed, and large carnivores would pose no threat. Broad, dry, and deep, three of the caves had enough ceiling height for a man to stand with room to spare, and to Torka's increasing pleasure, the largest of the three had the best southern exposure, as well as the smoothest, flattest floor. He knelt and fingered the gritty dust beneath his feet. There was only a shallow layer; this was a good sign. In the depth of winter, as well as being insulated from the cold by the hills in which it lay, the interior was evidently protected from the vicious, subfreezing, snow-and-dust-laden bite of the wind.

Looking up and around, he saw no sign of seepage in the walls or ceiling. It was unlike the cave in which he had dwelled long ago; there had been a glacial ice pack atop the range of hills that leached through the ceiling of the caves, and in warming days, such masses of ice had presented the possibility of icefalls, which could mean disaster and death for any living thing that might be trapped within. Satisfied, Torka rose, wiping the dust from his fingertips.

Simu and Karana had already looked around and were standing at the broad, cornice-shaded entrance to the cave. The view was extraordinary: a vast, sweeping panorama of the lake country and surrounding valley, with vistas of soaring, glacier-ridden mountains to the southeast.

"It is good," Torka said, coming to stand between them.

"It is a cave," responded Simu, unconvinced of its merits.

"It is *our* cave," said Karana, and without another word he began the descent back into the valley to tell Grek and the women and children what they had found.

In the land to the far west, the world was red and gold and burnished umber, and all the way down from the cave of the wanawut, the beastling found himself pausing to draw in deep breaths of the autumn morning as he made small, staccato exhalations of delight in it. Something special was happening today. Something wonderful!

Mother stopped and turned back. Sister was following obediently; Sister always followed obediently. Mother stared past her female cub. Beneath her heavy brows, Mother's eyelids half closed as she looked directly at the beastling. She showed her teeth to signal her displeasure with him, then turned away and continued to pick her way down the mountain toward the vast and beautiful world.

The beastling frowned, his sense of wonder momentarily shadowed. He wished that he were more like Sister, who never disobeyed and was never distracted by the views. And Sister was bigger, stronger, and growing so much faster. Sister had claws and sharp, stabbing teeth, and Sister had fur—just like Mother's, long, thick strands of silky gray fur with a thick, mist-colored undercoat. The older Sister got, the more she resembled Mother.

He sighed. It made him sad to know that Mother was not pleased by his lack of fur. Whenever she groomed him, she frowned with worry and poked at his bare skin. The stringy, dark fur that grew from his head, at least, was growing very long. It hung to his shoulders now. It was odd fur, not at all like Mother's and Sister's. It made him think of the tails of the horses.

Below him on the mountain, Mother turned back once more. With a series of irritated hoots, she gestured him forward. He followed, tugging at his hair with one hand while he plucked at his tattered elkskin tunic with the other. It was a ragged, foul-smelling, ill-fitting garment. Mother had only recently given it to him, stripped from one of the legs of a lion-killed elk whose haunch she had stolen from the willow scrub where its killers had cached it. The tube of skin was still drying upon his body. Now it fit him like a casing, much too tightly across his shoulders and hips and much too loosely across his belly.

Given a choice, he would have preferred to be naked in the sweet yellow light of this golden autumn day. The wind was mild against his lean, lithe, nearly four-year-old body. But he knew that Mother would not tolerate his nakedness, and he did not want Mother to be angry with him. Not today, when, at last, she was guiding him down from the heights to the world below!

His sense of wonder in the day returned to him. For months, Mother had been leading her cubs out of the cave, teaching them to hunt on their mountain's boulder-littered summit. But never before had she taken them down the mountain. The way down from the cave was much steeper than he had imagined it would be.

Today he would learn to stalk with her and run at her side as he had so long dreamed of doing when he and Sister had been confined to the cave, where there had been little room to run—*really* run—as the herd animals of the world below ran from lions and leaping cats and wolves and dogs.

Mother was well ahead of him now, moving slowly, cautiously. Her leg was stiff—the one with the long shiny patch of exposed skin that ran from her hip to just below her knee. Now and again she rubbed the scar as she walked. The beastling gave this little thought. He could not remember a time when Mother had not favored her scarred leg.

He hurried on, and soon he was walking beside Sister. She was picking her way with infinite and indecisive care. New situations always frightened Sister as much as they intrigued him. She did not enjoy the forays from the mountaintop, and today Mother had had to cuff her to get her to leave the cave. The older they grew, the more there was about Sister that eluded him. She was as slow on her feet as he was swift, as quick to hang back as he was quick to run ahead. He huffed at her now, encouraging her with a loving touch. She mewed pathetically.

Mother looked back and grunted hard and loud. Sister fell silent. The beastling walked beside her, crouching down to use the knuckles of his hands for balance, although he found his own upright gait easier and more natural.

The angle of their descent lessened, and soon they were crossing the vast alluvial fan that opened onto the broad river-cut valley. With the sun on his back and the world looming all around him, the beastling could not contain the fire of joy that exploded within him. He began to run. For the first time in his life, he ran full out, upright like a boy, with his back erect and his strong young legs pumping and stretching beneath him. He ran with his head thrown back and his long black hair whipping in the wind. The feel of tundra beneath his feet was as natural and good as the feel of the grasses that whipped against his arms like stalks of warm, silken sunlight. He ran and kept on running, although he heard Mother screeching at him to come back.

Birds scattered and flew upward all around him. He laughed with delight and waved his arms as though he would join them. When a herd of antelope broke from the shelter of a scrub grove and ran ahead of him, he lengthened his stride to match theirs.

He was in deep grass now, but he did not slow his step. Somewhere ahead, wild dogs yipped and barked. The

sound filled him. With his arms flung high, he barked and
yipped in response as he ran wildly toward the river. He
broke through the high cover of the grass. The sun was
high, and the beastling was a part of the world's colors and
scents and wondrous sounds. Its hugeness failed to over-
whelm him. The spirits of ten thousand generations of
nomadic people of the tundra sang in his veins, and although he did not know the song, he sang it. As he ran
and ran it seemed to him that his very soul was bleeding
joyfully into the earth and sky.

And then, suddenly, he stopped dead. Wolves stood
between him and the river. He stared at them. Where
had they come from? How could he not have seen their
approach?

If he had possessed the gift of the language of his
ancestors, the word *careless* would have risen from his
memories. He remembered the dangers of the hunt on
the mountain summit, then realized that there were also
dangers in the world below.

He had never seen wolves close before. He had never
imagined that they were so tall and lean and long legged,
with coats like the grass of the steppe when it has been
frosted by new snow. The sun was in their eyes. Gold
eyes. Watching eyes. Hungry eyes. Predators' eyes.

His stomach lurched. He was hungry, too. Given time,
he would be a predator. But now he was only a small,
hairless cub with the uncured pelt of a dead elk around his
body.

The wolves smelled the dried blood and flesh of the
elkskin. The lead wolf was a big animal with the scars of
many a hunt and battle with his own kind on his ears and
muzzle. He took a step forward.

The beastling swallowed hard and did the same.

The wolf stopped.

The beastling stopped.

The wolf lowered its head.

The beastling did the same.

The wolf showed its teeth.

The beastling felt sick. The wolf's teeth were wonderful
things, but his own teeth were small and flat, no match for
the teeth of wolves. Intimidated, he took a step back.

The lead wolf's head went up as the wanawut suddenly came crashing through the grasses at a pounding, arm-swinging run. The wolves turned and ran.

The wanawut did not pursue them. She stopped just short of running over the beastling. With her errant cub cowering in her shadow, she waved her great hairy arms and showed her teeth as she screeched and roared with anger. When at last she looked down, he nearly lost control of his bladder. He had never seen Mother enraged before. It was a sight he would *never* forget.

Mother's wrath, however, lost its intensity when she looked at him. He knew she loved him. He was small and bald and of questionable value as a potential hunter, but he was her cub nonetheless. As her left arm swooped downward, the beastling messed himself and his elk skin, but Mother did not seem to mind as her massive fingers curled about his buttocks and brought him up into her embrace. She looked at him long and hard, but he could see that her eyes expressed reproach and relief. She turned toward where Sister was hiding, and, taking her man stone between her teeth, she picked the second cub up by the scruff of the neck without even slowing her stride.

They were back in the cave before the day was done. Mother cuffed him hard, sent him to the nest, and would not groom or cuddle him. He came close and did backward vaults to please her, but she remained unmoved by his antics, even when he peered at her upside down from between his legs, grinning in a broad attempt at apology. She eyed him coolly, grunted, and ignored him.

This will not happen again, he thought. *I will obey. I will learn. Mother* will *be proud of me.*

But in the days and nights that followed, the beastling had no chance to prove himself. Mother had lost confidence in him completely, and under her watchful eye, the cave became his prison.

It took Torka and his people many weeks to relocate their encampment completely. They managed it slowly, in several stages: first the women and children along with their sleeping and cooking supplies—and Wallah's dismembered leg, for she would not move from the encampment without it.

"It is a part of me," she said, "and a portion of my life spirit still lives within it! I will die without it. I know I will!"

It was Grek who dug up her leg, wrapped what was left of it in soft furs cross-laced with elkskin thongs, and carried her and it in his arms all the way to the cave. Wallah held her severed leg and was content even though she was in pain; with the leg in her possession, she did not think of herself as a one-legged woman.

The band's caches were left where they had originally put them, scattered across the land around the site of the now-abandoned encampment. Some stores were buried in deep pits, others were secreted in high, craggy places, and still others were within painstakingly erected cairns of heavy boulders. Despite their best efforts of concealment, the men acknowledged that some caches would be ransacked and destroyed. As a precaution, many had been made and filled with identical contents: dried food, bladder skins of water, spears, snares, sinew line, knapping blades, chisels, pounders, fishhooks, and nets, as well as extra boots, gloves, and warm furs. Emergency packs and bindings for injuries were stored, with packets of green willow stalk for pain relief, fire-making tools, and oil-soaked bones wrapped with dried grasses and roots, which would serve as quick, long-burning fuel to warm a hunter caught away from camp in a storm.

Now, at last, the old camp was no more. Lonit stood at the edge of the cave with Torka. It was night, and stars sparkled as though they were ice crystals strewn across the black skin of the sky. All along the horizon, the far ranges glistened like the fanged teeth of a predatory beast. Wolf song reverberated within distant canyons, and now and again mammoths called to one another as the wind wailed across the world, chilling the air with the promise of winter soon to come. The people of the band slept deeply within the warm, sheltering hollow of the mountain.

"Come, woman of my heart. It is late. You should sleep," said Torka.

"I cannot see to the west," she told him.

"The west is yesterday. It is behind us. It is good that we do not look back."

She knew that he was right; yet the sadness and longing for her lost twin was there. It was always there, deep within her heart . . . sleeping . . . waiting to be roused by a word or a thought or a dream. Would it never heal?

"Does Torka never look back and wonder? Does Torka never feel that one's presence or hear his voice calling on the wind? Does Torka not turn around and expect to see him following?"

With a broad, strong hand on her shoulder, he turned her toward him, bent, and kissed her mouth to silence her. It was a soft kiss, a deep kiss. It was a lover's kiss. And more than that, it was the kiss of one who knows the pain of another's soul and would ease it.

Lonit trembled. Her arms went around his neck. Her love for him was so intense that it hurt. From their first kiss to their last, it would always be the same for them. Like the mated pairs of great swans that graced the tundral ponds and lakes of summer, together they were one—one heart, one breath, one being, always and forever! How could she have asked him whether he felt the pain of the loss of their son? He was Torka! He had risked everything in the hope of saving the life of that poor, abandoned infant and bringing it back into the warmth and life of the band.

Breathless, she drew her mouth from his and looked directly into his face. Starlight illuminated the pain in his eyes—pain for a lost son and for the woman whose longing for that child could never be assuaged. His lips glistened with the moisture of her kiss. Once again she trembled. He was no longer the youth she had adored as a child and no longer the man whom she had loved from afar as a young girl. He was a mature hunter in the full power of his prime whose face and form were infinitely more wonderful than they had ever been. Strength and compassion were etched into his handsome features as though time had taken a blade and carved them there for all to see. No man in the world had a face as magnificent as Torka's. Not even the incomparably perfect Navahk—for his face, though handsome, had been as sharply drawn as the face of a raptorial bird, lean and cruel, and with odd, serrate-edged teeth.

She shivered. She had wanted Navahk once, long ago. Her wanting had had nothing to do with love, or even with liking, for she had detested the infamous magic man from the moment he had strutted brazenly into the Great Gathering at the head of his band. She had no desire to walk at the side of any man but Torka, but all women burned for Navahk. It was an enchantment that he put upon them.

In the end, the fire she had felt for him had been quenched by rape, yet in her heart she knew that at the moment he took her, although she had fought against him, she had wanted him and had nearly given herself—until she had looked into his eyes and had glimpsed his black soul. She had learned that to yield to him was to die. No, worse than that—to yield to him would have betrayed her love for Torka. And so she had fought him until the end, and when at last he had come to his savage release, she had ruined it for him by proclaiming:

"I am his woman, always and forever."

And although he had beaten her into unconsciousness, she had placed herself beyond his power. Yet the memory of the man still filled her with revulsion and shame at the knowledge that she had ever desired him in the first place.

Torka drew her close, held her gently. "You must put the sad things of the past behind you, Lonit. Come now, woman of my heart, in my arms you will forget."

And in the fold of one powerful arm he guided her into the cave and to the place where their sleeping skins lay piled upon a thick mattress of lichens and grasses. Iana had taken her bed furs to the fire of Grek and Wallah, so that she might aid the matron at her daily tasks and be there for her in the night; this allowed Grek to sleep and be strong for the days of hunting, and Mahnie to be at ease about her mother's care while she tended her own fire and the needs of Karana. Summer Moon, Demmi, and little Umak lay in a fur-covered heap nearby, close to the sod-and-stone curbing of the fire circle that Lonit had raised for her family.

"Come," whispered Torka, untying the soft thongs that held Lonit's dress in place. It fell around her hips, exposing her body to the chill of the night. He touched her, smiled at the sight of her, then lifted her in his arms and laid her down. When he had undressed, he lay over her, warming her. "The west is *yesterday*. This cave is *now*. Our children sleep safe in the night. Let us be one in the dark, and let there be no sadness between us."

A hard wind was driving snow before a rising gale. The last of late autumn's color was sheathed in white as animals sought shelter from the first cruel storm of winter. But within the cave in the hills above the lake country, the people of Torka were warm, dry, and relaxed in their fine encampment.

"Chant, Magic Man! Chant now in honor of the great spirits of the mammoth and the bear!"

As on the night of the great storm, Karana could not refuse the command of his headman. He took his place within the center of the cave, and as his people gathered around, he seated himself and began to chant. His song was long and thoughtful, honoring the power of the spirits of the mammoth, the bear, and the brave woman who had been dismembered but now sat propped up on her bed furs, leaning against Grek, her body swathed in the shaggy, well-combed skin of the beast that had maimed her, with one leg extended and the other lying across her lap in an elkskin bag. He chanted until he saw Wallah smile with wan pride, and when he thought that he could not say another word to praise her, the great bear spirit, or the great mammoth spirit, he closed his eyes and rested his hands upon his knees. He was surprised to hear Torka whispering in his ear.

The headman had come close and bent to provide the nearly inaudible directive: "The winter ahead will be long and dark. Rise now, Magic Man! You have made an aging, wounded woman happy, but you will need all the tricks of a shaman to keep my people from bickering in the long night of endless cold that lies ahead of us. Rise up, I say! Get up off your hunkers to make a show of your magic!"

Startled by Torka's sage but insulting advice, Karana looked at him, and had everyone else not been staring, he would have said: *I am not Navahk! Magic is not a show! Would you have me beguile our people in order to keep them content throughout the winter?*

Torka smiled. "Yes," he whispered.

Had he read Karana's mind? He suspected that Torka had. And now Karana read the headman's mind. He knew what Torka wanted, and scowling as he rose to his feet, the young man gave Torka what he asked for.

In the light of the fire circles of his people, Karana stood tall. In the dancing shadows of the flame-lit cave, Karana danced. And suddenly, as he moved to a powerful inner rhythm, he felt the magic rising in him . . . filling him . . . taking him out of himself as a transformation of spirit took place within his skin. He was no longer Karana at all. He was the great bear. He was twelve feet tall, and his blood was pounding with the power of his song.

He whirled. He roared. He postured with his arms up, neck arched, and hands curled into taloned paws.

His people cowered. Lonit was appalled. Never had Karana resembled Navahk more. Dak and Umak exclaimed with boyish delight as Mahnie gasped with pride and a woman's long-unsated hunger for her man. Beside her, Iana shivered as she also noted the magic man's resemblance to Navahk, as did Wallah, who shrank back within her fur as Grek put his arms around her, lest her shivering bring pain to the still-scabbed and oozing stump.

Demmi blinked and frowned, not wanting to acknowledge the power or handsomeness of a brother whom she had once adored but who had betrayed her trust with lies.

And Summer Moon, at nine almost a woman and already a beauty like her mother, gaped in wonder at the perfection and magnificence of a man whom she would never think of as her brother.

Outside, the wind dropped and snow fell as the evening passed. Beyond the storm a mammoth trumpeted, and its kindred answered. Within their cave Karana completed the headman's bidding, and the people bundled in their furs close to their fire circles slept.

Karana dreamed of another cave . . . of the wanawut standing in the darkness . . . its hideous face illuminated by the light of the rising sun.

"Karana?"

Did the monster speak his name? No. The dream was shifting now, deepening. The wanawut was gone; everything was gone; there was only blackness. A whisper, warm, languorous, and trembling, floated in the darkness . . . the warm seeking hands that stroked his body were trembling.

"Karana?"

Beneath his sleeping robe, a moist, sweet breeze fluttered at his neck and back, touching him, licking him, rousing him, enfolding him, melding with his flesh . . . moving . . . accepting as, in his dream, he was the bear again, dancing, thrusting, twelve feet tall and burning with power . . . until his body suddenly burst wide like river ice cracking open at spring flood. But the flood that rent him was not ice but molten fire—until he heard his name whispered again, and, gasping, he opened his eyes and . . . froze.

Mahnie was in his arms. She was joined to him, caressing him and kissing the hollow of his shoulder and looking at him with tears in her eyes and lashes. "Karana . . ." she whispered. "My magic man again."

"*Never* again!" he shouted, shoving her away as he rolled out from beneath the bed furs and, drawing one of them around himself, went to stand at the edge of the cave.

He knew that the eyes of everyone in the cave were on him. Let them look! He was beyond caring. Soon enough they would realize that there was nothing interesting about a man staring out into the night, and they would turn away and return to their dreams.

He drew back one of the hides and allowed the falling snow to touch him; he shivered but doubted he could ever be any colder than he was already. His face was flushed, his body throbbing. But his heart and spirit were of ice.

He did not know how long he stood there, glaring

sightlessly at the night, through the snow that fell straight out of the clouds, as silent as death, as white as his thoughts were black. He heard the mammoths call to one another again, the sound far away and muffled.

The wind was rising within him. It was the spirit wind, and it stroked his mood as tenderly as the hands of his woman had stroked his body.

A muscle twitched at the right side of his mouth, raising the corner of his lip into an expression that, in an animal, would have been taken as a snarl; but it was not a snarl, it was a smile—a dark and bitter and malevolent smile. *What a fool is Karana*, chided the spirit wind. *Always he broods. Always he turns his back upon his woman. Go back to your woman, Magic Man. A man must be a man. And if a child is put into the belly of Mahnie, why should you deny yourself the pleasure of its making? Because you fear that Navahk's spirit will find life again in its body? The life spirit of a man cannot be reborn into a female child. If it is a male child . . . true, it will be of the flesh of Navahk, but so are you. And as you sought to kill your father, so too may you seek to kill a boy-child of his flesh before it is ever accepted as a child. This is your right. As the son of Navahk, this will be your obligation. And what sweeter vengeance could you have upon him than to prevent his life spirit from ever being born into this world again?*

"None," he said aloud, smiling as he answered the spirit wind and, without hesitation, turned and walked back across the cave to Mahnie.

He did not notice the watching, sleepy eyes of little Umak, or note that as the child yawned and stretched, his face shone round and healthy in the soft glow of Torka's well-banked fire . . . a glow in which the boy's small, white serrate-edged teeth flashed bright for a moment before he rolled over and went back to sleep.

PART V

MAMMOTH MOON

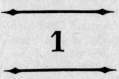

1

At the northeastern edge of the valley, less than half a day's walk from the encampment that Cheanah's people called the Place of Endless Meat, a reed-choked marsh surrounded several small tundral lakes. An old bull mammoth wandered into the wetlands by moonlight. Now, in the light of day, with vast wedges of white geese winging southward overhead, he was dying.

For hours he had lain on his side in a bog, fighting to rise from the swamp, but he made no sound during his travail except exhalations and whoofings of supreme effort and, eventually, huffings and sighings of despair. At no time did he expand his great lungs and lift his shaggy trunk to trumpet to others of his own kind who might have come to his aid. Perhaps he knew that it was his time to die.

Soon after the first of the carrion-eating birds had begun to circle his exhausted form, three hunters, sighting on the birds, had entered the marsh. Ank and Yanehva, sons of Cheanah, had refused to follow their brother as far as the russet, wind-combed shade of the reeds. They had hung back, reminding Mano that the northern edge of the valley was off-limits to them by their father's decree. When they warned of potential dangers, he had ignored them and plunged ahead.

"Mammoth!" Mano named his prey.

For a moment he thought that he had stumbled upon Life Giver, but a quick squint through the reeds convinced him otherwise. Its tusks were worn, discolored,

and broken at the tips. And it was small for its kind;
compared to the great mammoth spirit that had walked
ahead of Torka, this bull might well have been mistaken
for another species entirely.

But it *was* a mammoth, and Mano had never killed a
mammoth. Anticipation of a kill excited him. His left hand
encircled the slender shafts of the three stone-headed
spears that he carried balanced across his shoulder, and
slowly he shifted one into his right hand and readied
himself for a throw.

"Wait!" Ank implored sharply.

The boy's voice had been no more than a whisper;
nevertheless it broke Mano's concentration. His head swiveled to the right, and his small, sharp eyes fixed not only
Ank but Yanehva, as well. They had changed their minds
about following their brother and were standing ready to
protect him and themselves against unseen carnivores who
might turn from the dying mammoth and decide to dine
on man instead.

Mano's brow arched. He should have heard them coming. Yanehva was no longer the lean stretch of a youth
who had been able to slip through the grasses as though
he were a stalk himself; at nearly sixteen, he was a man
now. And Ank, almost eleven, was throwing a much longer
shadow than he had in the days before Man Who Walks
With Dogs had been banished from the Place of Endless
Meat. Several autumns had come and gone since then,
and now the time of endless light was gone, and another
autumn was on the brink of becoming winter.

"Come away," Yanehva said evenly. "Soon night will
darken the land, and Cheanah will be wondering about
us."

Mano's eyes narrowed. He did not like being told what
to do, and Yanehva, although two years his junior, had
fallen into a pattern of doing just that. "Has Yanehva lost
his vision or only his nerve? That is a *mammoth* out there!
A *mired* mammoth! We could kill it and bring much meat
back to our camp. Cheanah would be proud."

"Of what?" Yanehva inquired coolly. "If memory serves
me, mammoth is not the best meat. Cheanah has never
expressed a hunger for it. I do not think he will be pleased

to know that we have come so far north. And it takes no skill to kill a beast trapped in a bog."

Ank's eyes were wide. "It is forbidden to kill mammoths! Besides, mammoth meat is stinking, tough meat!"

Mano glowered at the boy. Now *Ank* was telling him what to do! He told him to shut his mouth. "What do you know of it? You were a suckling at our mother's teats when last we tasted mammoth!"

Ank wilted, and Yanehva put a consoling hand on the young boy's shoulder.

Beyond the screen of reeds, the mammoth tried to lift its head. Failing, it exhaled a mighty sigh as its massive skull settled more deeply into the bog. Water splashed and rippled outward. It sloshed around the hunters' heretofore relatively dry boots. Mano barely noticed. Yanehva looked down and shook his head, reminding his older brother that when men trekked into a marsh, they needed adequate footwear.

Mano squinted at Yanehva. There was a subtlety to his brother that eluded and annoyed him. The days had long since passed in which Mano had been able to bully him successfully. "Well?" he queried impatiently, looking up as the wings of a circling teratorn sent shadow across the marsh. "Are you going to hunt with me, or are you going to stand here while the creatures of the sky feed on what should be ours?"

Yanehva did not reply. He remained standing shoulder to shoulder with Mano, leaning forward, staring through the reeds.

Mano rolled his eyes. As always, Yanehva was taking more time than necessary to assess a situation. "Well?" he pressed again, irritably.

Yanehva straightened. "We must ask Cheanah."

Anger flared hotly within Mano; his temper had never needed much to kindle it. "*Why?* We are hunters. That is why we are out from camp—to *hunt!*"

"We are out from a meat-rich camp to teach our brother Ank to perfect his hunting skills," Yanehva corrected Mano coolly. "One of the most important things that we can teach him is the value of self-control: of when to hunt and when not to hunt, of—"

"It is *always* a good time to hunt! It is *always* a good time to kill! It is *always* a good time to take meat!" His face was flushed, his eyes bulging, and his right hand curled so tightly around the haft of his spear that his knuckles were white. "If we go back to camp and leave the mammoth here, it will be meat for the carrion eaters!"

"Then that is the will of the spirits who have brought it here to die!"

"Ngyah!" Mano spat a sound of pure disgust. "How does Yanehva know that *we* have not been led here by the will of those same spirits so that we would be the first to find this mammoth?"

"I do not," answered Yanehva. His hand was on Ank's shoulder again as he turned and began to walk away. "That is for Cheanah to say. He, not Mano, is headman of our band!"

It was the sight of the circling teratorn that drew the eyes of the beastling from the little circles that his finger was tracing in the thick dust that layered the floor of the wanawut's cave.

There were three circles in all: neatly drawn images of the full moon, half-moon, and quarter moon. And now, with his index finger poised over a partially completed rendering of a new moon, the beastling frowned, squinting against the glare from the hole in the sky and watching the teratorn circle above the distant marshes.

His brow furrowed. The teratorn was no longer alone. Others of its kind were winging out of the distance to join it in its circling. Something was down there in the marsh country—something dead. Maybe something good to eat. But he would never know what it was.

Nowadays when Mother left the mountain, she took Sister to hunt in the world below. Since he had nearly managed to feed himself to the wolves, he was not allowed this privilege. He sighed, miserable.

His belly gurgled with emptiness. Mother would want him to alert her to the gathering teratorns. Three days had passed since he had last eaten. Although his mind had begun to fill with images of meat, he did not want Mother to leave the cave today. The marsh country was far away, and Mother was tired. So tired, in fact, that he was frightened for her.

He turned to look into the shadowed recesses of the cave, where Mother was in the nest, asleep with Sister in the curl of her arm. For two days she had been off the mountain, hunting with Sister. When at last she had returned, it had been in the depth of the previous long night, and without meat. There was a deep gash on one of her upper arms, and her face had looked so drawn and full of hurt that he had wondered how she had managed to return at all.

But she *had* returned. She *always* returned. Only this was the first time that he had realized that a time might come when she would not. Now he exhaled a worried sigh as the enormity of this realization washed through him. What would happen to him then? And to Sister? If Mother were to become meat for some other animal . . . *No!* He would not think of this!

He turned and faced into the light of the hole in the sky. The teratorns were still circling. The air seemed colder than it had a moment before. He moved his hands over the moons that he had drawn in the dust, erasing them. Mother did not like it when he drew in the dust. It was the drawings of the beasts that upset her the most. He did not know why. They were merely little stick figures, as were his representations of animals, but when she saw them she always growled and stepped on them and rubbed them away before she sat on them as though the weight of her body would keep them from re-forming in the dust.

A sound of irritation formed in his throat, but he choked it back. He did not want to wake Mother, *especially* with vocalization, for his tongue-twisting attempts at articulation never failed to frustrate him as much as they irritated her. Why did he always manage to do things that annoyed Mother?

He swallowed hard, with great and ponderous resolve. If Mother did not want him to draw in the dust, he would not. If Mother wanted him to stay in the cave upon the mountain, he would stay. He would be as obedient as Sister until, at last, he regained Mother's trust.

Suddenly startled, he looked up to see that he was not

alone on the lip of the cave. Sister had awakened and
come out of the nest to stand beside him. How long she
had been there, he could not guess. But she had sighted
the circling teratorns, and with no thought of anything but
her own hunger, she screeched a series of high, happy
hoots as she jumped up and down and gesticulated wildly.

Mother awoke, arose, and limped heavily to the front of
the cave. Her low sounds of distress told the beastling that
the gash in her arm was still hurting.

Sister was so excited by the promise of a future meal
that she paid no heed to Mother's strained stance and
oddly pink, watery eyes.

The beastling was irked. What a self-serving creature
Sister was, attuned only to her own immediate urges,
fears, and needs. He cocked his head as he got to his feet.
Sister was hungry, but so was he, and hunger was not
such a bad thing. She could wait to eat until Mother was
rested and fit to hunt. Somehow, he knew that the bare
skin of Mother's broad, callused palm would be hot and
dry with fever even before he rose and took her hand in a
vain attempt to bring her back to the nest.

Mother pulled her hand free. Sister took it at once and,
yanking hard, urged Mother to come to the very edge of
the cave. Mother obeyed dully, responding to Sister's
excited hoots and jumps and waving.

The beastling glowered. He shoved Sister, slapped
at her long, gray-furred arm to keep her from pointing
toward the circling teratorns, but it was he who was slapped
away . . . by Mother. She did not hurt him—at least not
physically. Her slap had been gentle and controlled. His
inability to communicate his fear for her was excruciating
as Sister rubbed her belly and made Mother know that
she was hungry, that it was imperative that she be fed
now.

Mother sighed with acquiescence. With a low huff that
told the beastling that Sister had won the day, she went
into the depths of the cave to retrieve her man stone. She
gestured to him that he was to remain in the cave as she
turned and, with Sister at her side, began the descent.

He slunk back into the nest in despair. But suddenly his
own feelings seemed unimportant. He was out of the nest

and across the cave, standing at the lip of their aerie, watching Mother and Sister as they climbed downward. Mother was dragging her lame leg and favoring her injured arm. How slowly she walked! The droop of her shoulders betrayed the extent of her fatigue. She should not be out of the cave today! Instinctively, the beastling knew that she was in danger.

Leaning into the wind, with his hair blowing back over his shoulders and his bald little face puckered into an expression that fully revealed the depth of his fear for her, he screeched after Mother, pounding his fists against thin air until she turned and, with a wave of one of her own fists, warned him to stay where he was and be silent.

He felt sick as panic grew in him. Mother would not come back! In desperation, he screeched again as he jumped up and down. He thought that he would die of his anguish. If she would trust him, he would clamber up to the summit and find rodents to eat, while she rested. It would not be much, but it would keep Sister happy until Mother was herself again. Then they could all hunt together in the world below.

Deep within his throat, the sounds that Mother hated were forming. His tongue moved in his mouth. His throat constricted against the deep, pulling need to form a sound that would be more than a screech or a hoot or a howl, but an articulation that would make her understand exactly how he felt. And so, with his face thrust into the wind, he screamed not like a cub, not like a beastling, but like a child; and the scream was more than sound. It was a word . . . a word from out of his dreams . . . a word that he had heard long ago, on the wind.

"Mah . . . nah . . . rah . . . vahk—!"

But now, as then, the wind took the word and blew it away across the mountain. Mother kept on plodding downward across the stony scree of the mountainside. She did not turn back.

2

On the same burnished autumn day, miles from the bog in which the mammoth lay dying, Lonit stopped and stared westward. It was there again, deep in her heart: that terrible nagging sense of loss, that small tender voice calling to her out of time.

Mother! Where are you, Mother? I am here, waiting. Why have you left me all alone . . . far away . . . lost forever?

"Manaravak?" She spoke the name of her son and then realized that she had been a fool even to have thought of him. It was four-year-old Umak who had called to her. "Mother! Mother, *look!*"

She looked. She saw him, and the sadness left her. What a bright, bold, beautiful little boy he was, looking so much like her, and jumping up and down with Dak in the reeds, pointing with absolute delight as Mahnie's bola sang overhead.

Lonit's eyes followed its flight high across the wind-broken, frost-reddened grasses in pursuit of a goose that should not have lingered so long at the edge of the tundral pond to fatten itself further upon the last remaining seed heads and algae of summer. But the need to eat had outweighed the need to fly . . . until it heard the sloshing of Eneela and the children in the shallows and was easily flushed into a panicked flight.

The majority of the goose's kind had long since left the valley on their seasonal migration southeast. A few birds remained; unbeknownst to the goose that was now about to fly afoul of Mahnie's bola, more than a few of its kin were now strung through the beak on the carrying thong slung over Lonit's shoulder. The whirling, stone-weighted thong arms of Mahnie's bola wrapped themselves around the goose's neck, snapping its spinal column instantly. The bird plummeted to earth, dead before it landed, to the delighted exclamation of the children and the applause of Lonit and Eneela. Never before had Mahnie made such an exquisite kill with her bola.

Mahnie was not completely surprised by her achievement. She had been working long and hard under Lonit's supervision to perfect her skill and had killed many small animals and birds with the bola—but never a bird as fine as this, and never so quickly and with such absolute perfection. There had been something in the way the bola left her hand, a feeling of balance and coordination. . . .

She should have rejoiced with pride; yet, somehow, Mahnie felt an inexplicable lack of enthusiasm. There was so much to rejoice at in these days: the wonderful valley; the fine, dry, well-stocked encampment within the cave; the success with the bola—at last! And her happiness with Karana—at last! But now that had ended, and as she thought of him, she felt so miserable that she actually forgot for a moment that she had killed the goose at all. . . .

"We are *what*?" His question still rang in her head.

"I . . . we . . . are going to have a child."

"A child . . ." He had exhaled the words as though she had just told him that he was going to die.

"A child, yes. For Mahnie and Karana, at last."

"A male child or a female child?"

She had laughed out loud. "*You* are the magic man! You must tell *me*, if you can!"

He had not been amused. His face had gone as white as that of a corpse. Slowly, he had risen. Slowly, he had shaken his head. "A girl child. I will ask the spirits for a girl child."

Puzzled, she had shrugged and smiled, wanting only to please him. "Then I will do the same. But whatever comes of our love, male or female, it will bring joy to this woman's heart."

He had stared at her long and hard for a moment before turning away. And since that day he had not smiled, nor had he shared her bed skins with her. . . .

Beside her, Eneela now held her own bola in check as she looked with concern at Mahnie's suddenly pale face. "What is wrong?"

Mahnie shook her head. "Nothing . . ."

Eneela smiled knowingly. "We are all three of us carrying babies in our bellies. No doubt your mother has already told you that at this time it is perfectly natural for us to feel sick occasionally."

"I am not sick," Mahnie told her.

"You look sick," said Lonit, reaching to touch her brow.

Mahnie waved her hand away. Ahead of her, Summer Moon and Demmi were screeching with protest as Dak and Umak chased the older girls and made off with the goose and the bola, then circled back to Mahnie. She took her prize and her bola, thinking that yesterday she would have rejoiced at the sight of the children.

But now, as the boys wheeled away and ran off to harass the girls again, her heart beat slowly and her mouth turned down as her hand strayed to the taut span of her belly. She had not shed a woman's blood in over two moons now. Her breasts were tight and swelling. But how could she be happy when Karana was not?

"You must not fret as he frets," Lonit advised gently. "Karana has always been moody. Be patient with him. Perhaps he needs to commune with Life Giver and with the very forces of Creation to strengthen his magic for the good of us all."

"Do you think so?" Mahnie asked, hope welling within her. Sometimes, when everyone was asleep, she would know that Karana lay awake beside her, brooding and inwardly bleeding over deep thoughts that he would not share with her.

"Of course I do!" affirmed Lonit, and hugged the small young woman hard before releasing her and holding her close with a hand on each of her slim shoulders. "We all waited so long now for a child to take root in the belly of

Mahnie, we nearly gave up hope that it would ever happen. Perhaps it is so with Karana. And now that life is at last to come from the joining of the two of you, he worries about you. It is no easy thing, you know, this bearing of new life."

She felt better; Lonit could almost always make her feel better. "Karana has gone far from this camp and from his woman into the upland groves. But you think he is not angry with Mahnie?"

Eneela's wide, pretty face split with a grin. "Of course he is angry! Once Mahnie's belly starts to swell, for a very long while Karana will have no woman to join with in the night. In this small band, it will be the same for Simu and Torka." Her grin disappeared as she lowered her voice lest the frolicking children overhear. "In some bands—far away in the country out of which Torka has led us—Eneela has heard it said that some men who cannot couple with a woman howl like wolves and rut alone in their bed skins. Sometimes they take up their spears and travel to the camps of other bands to seek out women. And if the men in those camps refuse to share their women, there is killing, and the women are taken against their will, over the corpses of their men and children."

Mahnie's eyes went wide.

"It is true," Lonit affirmed, shivering against her memories. "Both Iana and this woman were taken captive by such men. Iana's newborn son was killed by them, and Summer Moon would have been had Torka and Karana not come to the rescue . . . in time for me, but not for Iana."

Eneela grimaced and shook herself. "Enough of such bad talk! Let us all be glad that we have left the country of such men. Simu has told this woman that among his people, going without a rut is a thing that a man must endure while his woman makes life."

"So it is with all men who care for their women," added Lonit. "Nevertheless, if a man sometimes grows a little bit restless at such times, a woman must understand—as Mahnie must understand. Besides, Karana will need many things if he is to keep us all well supplied with the special broths that shamans always brew for us in the dark time of winter! It is for the ingredients of this magic that he has no doubt gone from the camp. Mahnie should be glad for this."

Mahnie felt such relief that she reached out and hugged Lonit again. "You *are* the sister of my heart, Lonit, woman of Torka!"

To her surprise, Eneela embraced both of them. "In this good band we are *all* sisters," she said, kissing each of them on the cheek before stepping back and eyeing the fat, thickly feathered body of the goose that hung limply by the beak from Mahnie's hand. "Now let us gather up our children and get back to camp. Perhaps Mahnie will be willing to share this fat and beautiful goose?"

Torka was waiting to greet them as they returned from their birding. At least one hunter always accompanied the women and children when they left camp to set snares, dig for tubers, gather the last of the season's rapidly dwindling frost-and-wind-dried berries, or hunt with their bolas. Although they usually took Brother Dog on these expeditions to alert them to danger, a hunter nevertheless always checked the area for signs of predators before leaving them to their gossip, games, and female ways of hunting. But even when he left them, he remained close, watching from a nearby rise so they would be safe at all times.

"Father!"

Torka grinned when he caught sight of Umak and Dak racing toward him, well ahead of his daughters. The boys were both strong, lean little striplings, bright eyed and shiny faced with surplus energy. Soon they would be hunting big game with their fathers, but now they were still young enough to assist the females of the band. Umak did not quite manage to beat the older Dak up the hill from the marsh pond. They stopped before Torka to report that it had been a good day and that the women had done well.

"Despite the girls." Umak stated his opinion of his sisters' interference as Dak muttered that they were always in the way—just in time for the girls to come up behind them.

Demmi took a poke at Umak. He jumped forward but did not quite manage to avoid the blow. At seven, Demmi was still small, but she was taller than her brother and as fast on her feet as a well-thrown spear; if she had failed to outrun the boys, it was only because she had not tried. Summer Moon looked down her nose and turned up her chin as though such child's play was below her dignity.

Torka smiled down at his three children and Dak with love and pride as Lonit came walking up with Eneela and Mahnie. Although his woman boasted more of Mahnie's prowess than of her own, he saw at once that Lonit's shoulder thong held more birds. Karana's woman's face blushed a deep red, and her lips moved upward into a smile. Torka was glad to see that the day of birding had lifted her spirits.

"I heard Aar barking a little while ago. I think that Karana may be back from the groves," he told her.

She nearly cried out with delight as she hurried off.

"What about that goose?" called Eneela. "I thought that we were going to share it!" But Mahnie was oblivious to the protests. Simu's woman chuckled even though her own shoulder thong was devoid of birds. "Why do I suspect that this fine, fat goose is not going to be singed or roasted this night at all?"

Torka's brow shadowed his eyes as he slung an arm around Lonit's shoulder. "Karana should be singed and roasted if he doesn't start treating Mahnie with a little more concern."

"And when has he ever done that?" asked the woman of Simu, falling into step with Torka and Lonit as they began to herd the children back across the foothills toward the cave.

"It had been good between them for more than two moons," reminded Lonit. "Just in the last few days has life soured at their fire circle."

Eneela sighed. "I know that you call him Son and Brother, and I know that we owe our lives to his spirit powers, but I would not trade my Simu for him . . . not even if he *is* a most handsome magic man!"

Summer Moon took Torka's hand and proclaimed so all would hear: "Magic Man will be *my* man someday." She spoke confidently, as though her future were already decided.

"Surely, Daughter, it is far too early for you to think of this!" Lonit exclaimed, clearly startled.

Torka looked down at his older daughter and was dismayed to realize that it was *not* too early. Summer Moon was nine now. *Nine!* How could so many autumns have passed? Summer Moon *was* growing up and would need a man to take her to his fire circle. He frowned, annoyed with himself for not thinking of this before. Had he imagined that his daughters would remain little girls forever?

There was silence in the camp of Cheanah as Mano, Yanehva, and Ank stood before their father. The older two had respectfully stated their intent: Mano wanted to go back to retrieve the flesh, bones, and tusks of the mammoth; Yanehva did not.

Arms crossed over his chest, Cheanah stood tall before them in the posture of a man who was ready to listen and talk. He had listened, but instead of talking, he frowned and stared at them. Zhoonali, standing at his right, was certain that she would drown in her impatience with his silence.

Cheanah's frown became a scowl. "The meat of mammoth is an acquired taste," he said at last. "I, for one, have never acquired it. And my sons should not have been hunting so far to the north."

Zhoonali began to speak in defense of her grandsons, but Mano replied boldly: "It was the spirit of the circling teratorn that spoke to me, my father, and told me to lead my brothers into the marsh so that we might find the mammoth mired in the bog. We saw or heard no sign of the wanawut. But we saw the mammoth lying there, just waiting to be fleshed! Its long bones make the best spears, and from its great tusks we can make—"

"Mano had no idea what lay under the shadow of the condor before he ran off into the marsh country," Yanehva countered.

Zhoonali's mouth worked over what was left of her teeth. Her two older grandsons were quick and combative. No man would ever be able to fool either of them.

They were born to lead others. It was not so with their hesitant father. Cheanah did not know what to do, and his people could see that . . . his people were chafing against that.

Frustration and resentment toward Cheanah stirred deep within her withered breast. *Of all my sons, why is it that only the most dull witted survived?* Her old head shook on the tendoned stalk of her neck. It did no good to ask such questions; there were no answers for them.

Now, beside him, she stood as tall as she could within her ankle-length dress of white-feathered owl skins. It did not matter how many hours of stalking and snaring and meticulous workmanship had been involved in the accumulation, curing, and sewing of this garment. What mattered was that the dress set her apart from all other females. It made the mother of Cheanah special, and so it made *him* seem special, too. The dress affirmed her status; no longer was Zhoonali merely a midwife, wise woman, and mother of the headman—she was a magic woman, as well. This was an illusion that she fostered for the good of her son, the people of the band, and her own survival. Even in the worst of times, when the sick and old were the first to be sent away to walk the wind forever, a magic man or woman was needed to interpret the signs and omens, the one power that mere mortals possessed that might mean the difference between their lives and their deaths.

Zhoonali took out a badger-skin bag of dry, weather-whitened bone fragments and teeth gleaned from every type of animal that the band had killed and eaten ever since Karana had followed Torka out of the Place of Endless Meat and she had recognized her opportunity to become irreplaceable.

"If Cheanah wishes, this woman, who draws her power from his strength, will cast the bones for her people to determine what the spirits say."

And so the bones were cast, with Cheanah shadowing her and looking for all the world as though he, and not the scrawny woman in owl feathers, were in control of the moment.

As Zhoonali's old hands fingered the bones, she reminded herself: *This camp does not need the meat. But nowhere in this camp are there the long bones of mammoth. The hunters would be pleased if their headman led them to such bones, for it is true when Mano says that they make the best of spears. And its great tusks! What frame posts they would make for a new council hut for a headman.*

Her hands rested atop the bones. Kneeling, her body curled over them. She needed time to think, to analyze. *The words of this woman must cause the people to remember that they are Cheanah's band forever, with their own traditions and totems and taboos. It is time for them to set themselves forever apart from Torka by breaking with his totem, by committing themselves forever to the ways of Cheanah and their own ancestors!*

"Speak, Zhoonali! Tell us what the bones want us to do!" pressed old Teean.

Zhoonali's mouth puckered with annoyance. Teean's age gave him a false sense of worth and authority. *The bones see nothing, old man! It is what you believe that you see in the bones that matters.*

"Perhaps . . ." she began in a soft, well-practiced croak, which imitated what bones might sound like if they had spoken through a human body. "Perhaps . . . if the forces of Creation have caused the bull mammoth to become entrapped within a bog . . . perhaps if the great teratorn spirit led Mano to discover it . . . perhaps for the people of Cheanah *not* to take of its flesh and bones and tusks would be an affront to the great mammoth spirit and to those spirits who have given to the hunters of this band the gift of its life? . . ."

She drew back from the bones and remained hunkered on her haunches. Her face was set, but inside she was smiling. She had made no statement that might later be used against her; she had merely posed a question. How her people chose to answer it was up to them. But for brave men who knew the value of freshly taken mammoth bones and who believed implicitly in the power of spirits to speak through living beings, she had left them no response but one.

*   *   *

With no additional prodding from the old woman, the people of Cheanah responded with enthusiasm. They were people of the great bear and raven totems, and by now the mammoth was probably dead anyway, half-consumed by predators; but the spirits wanted them to have its bones and its tusks and what remained of its meat. The forces of Creation had decreed it through the talking bones of Zhoonali.

Yet, as Cheanah led his men and youths from camp, followed by the women with their butchering tools, Yanehva lagged behind.

"What is it?" asked Ank, who fell back to walk beside him.

"I don't like it. It was the great mammoth spirit of Man of the West who led our people to this valley. To eat of its flesh seems a sacrilege."

Ank frowned. "If our grandmother says it is all right and our father agrees, it must be so! The talking bones have spoken!" He paused. "Do you think Torka still lives?"

"That is unimportant. Whether Torka is dead or alive, it was still his totem that led us to this good land."

"He did have a pretty daughter," recalled little Ank dreamily. "Summer Moon, I mean." He ducked away, flame faced with embarrassment, as his brother cuffed him affectionately.

"Thinking of girls already, are you?"

"Girls grow up!" Ank snapped. "And so do boys. What girls worth thinking about do we have in this camp? Not one. You and Mano must share the women of others, and it will be years before the baby girls of Ekoh and Ram and the others are old enough to be taken from their fathers' fire circles. But if Summer Moon were still in this camp, she would be a woman soon, *my* woman maybe."

"She is not in this camp, nor will she ever be again. The daughter of Torka is unreachable! Thanks to our father, we will never see her or any of Torka's people again."

3

The beastling had stood alone at the edge of the cave, his little face thrust into the wind, and bawled like a mired camel as Mother and Sister completed their descent of the mountain.

Fear made him shiver against an inner cold. *Mother is tired. Mother is sick. Mother should not have left the cave today!*

By the time he took his first step down from the cave, he was able to justify his wanton disobedience. If he could keep Mother in sight, she would not disappear. If danger threatened her in the world below, he would be there to help her; even a *little* help would be better than no help at all. And if he was very, very careful, Mother would never know that he had ever left the cave.

He moved slowly. The wind was with him. Unless it reversed itself, they would catch no smell of him. To his relief, Mother was not looking back.

Unaware that he was following, Mother and Sister were well ahead, pushing their way deep into the high, frost-brittled auburn grasses of the steppe. Their movement formed a pathway that was easy for him to follow. He went on, deeper and deeper into the sea of grass, following confidently in their wake. His unprotected arms and legs itched and prickled against the grasses. And the wind was growing cold. He was shivering almost as fiercely as he was itching. If only he had fur!

He paused, momentarily distracted as shadows dulled the light of the hole in the sky. Long, translucent streamers of clouds struck a chord of warning; he knew their kind almost always appeared before storms . . . before *big* storms.

He continued to follow Mother and Sister's trail through the grassland. After a while, he could tell by the height of the breaks that Mother was carrying Sister. She must have grown tired. He understood why—never had he been so very far from the nest. His feet were raw and bleeding by the time Mother entered the marsh country. He was far behind her now, a small figure wincing and tight stepping against pain as he marveled at how Mother could forge ahead without stopping.

Unable to go on, the beastling paused to rest. The reeds were all around him, a wall separating him from Mother. They itched more than the grasses. Scratching himself irritably, he sat down. In a moment, his elkskin was soaked and his buttocks puckered against the icy sludge of muddy ooze underlying the reeds. The coolness of the marsh was welcome on his feet.

Then, suddenly, Mother screamed. The beastling was on his feet in an instant, his pain gone and his weariness a thing of the past. His heart was leaping in his chest. Carrion-eating birds were shrieking and winging from out of the reeds a good distance ahead of him. He cowered lest the larger hawks, eagles, or teratorns catch sight of him and decide to carry him away. The beastling realized that Mother was screaming to drive other carrion eaters from the carcass that she was about to claim for herself. Pride in Mother's power swelled in his chest.

His confidence disappeared when he heard the sloppy footfalls and pantings of a big animal moving just ahead of him. Instants later the reverberant growls of a lion had his heart beating so furiously that it seemed to lodge in his throat and he could barely catch his breath. The wind brought him the warm, wet, meat-eating stink of the lion.

The stench confused him, for it was a mixture of several highly individual body scents. He then heard the footfall of at least twelve paws. The beastling's eyes went round. There were several lions in the marsh, and they were moving toward Mother! She had driven them away, but now they were returning, walking slowly, deliberately, to close a circle from which they could attack.

The beastling felt sick with dread. Without hesitation, he shoved his way forward through the reeds, with all the speed that his small body would allow. He ran screaming at the top of his lungs, and the lions were so startled by his sudden appearance that they looked at him in amazement as he broke through their circle and raced ahead of them without looking back.

The wanawut looked up from her feast. Her man cub was racing toward her out of the reeds. She felt pride and gladness to see him, as well as righteous indignation at his disobedience. Beside her, her female cub looked up, eyed the man cub dully, and continued to eat from the shoulder of the dead mammoth.

Then the wanawut spotted the lions emerging from the surrounding wall of reeds. There were two large, shaggy females and three powerful albeit only half-grown adolescents. Standing now, the wanawut raised her arms and screamed at them, threatening them away with a show of teeth and claws and man stone.

The wanawut scooped up her female cub by the scruff of her neck as the lions moved forward toward the beastling. He was pounding toward her, his eyes bulging in terror, mouth agape, his step beginning to falter. The pursuing lions would be on him, and his life would be finished.

With a screech of rage, the wanawut leaped off the mammoth carcass, and as she came down hard into the shallow ooze of the marsh, pain burned in her leg and injured arm. She had no time for it. She snarled in frustration as she ran toward her cub, because she knew that her strength was not all that it should be.

The lions were closing on the beastling as a white, one-eyed, black-maned male joined them from the reeds. Memories flared within her. She knew this lion.

He stopped dead. She could see recognition in his ruined face. He shook his head and roared at her, displaying his killing teeth. But she kept on running, knowing that although he would not attack her, he would take her cub if he could. He roared again.

Ahead of him, the females and adolescents turned back

and stopped. Their tails twitched as they awaited a signal from him.

The wanawut did not wait for him to give it. The distance between her and her man cub was almost nonexistent now. With her man stone between her teeth and her female cub still dangling by the scruff of her neck, she reached out to him with her free hand. She had him now. He clung to her fur with the tenacity of a biting fly as she wheeled and ran. The gash on her arm had opened; she could feel it oozing from beneath the scab. The old injury on her thigh was threatening to cramp. She screamed against the betrayal of her body, but it was no use. Her leg gave out, and she fell, sprawled forward, her cubs sheltered beneath her.

The white lion was on her in an instant, like lightning striking from an unseen cloud. He was the weight of all the world crushing the life right out of her as he slapped at her with his huge paws, trying to turn her over so that he could get at her throat and belly. She felt him rip her shoulder as, gripping her man stone, she stabbed up and back with all her might. The lion roared in pain and arced straight up.

Still clutching her man stone, the wanawut scooped up her cubs in one arm. She fought to rise and run. Sounds that she had not heard in many moons came to her: Man sounds they were, hidden within the faraway grasses. She was running again, her cubs clinging to her. The female was burrowing between her breasts. The male was reaching over her shoulder as she ran, stuffing his little hands into the wounds that the lion's raking claws had inflicted upon her back. She knew that the beastling was trying to stanch the flow of hot blood, but lest he lose his balance she pulled him down into the protective press of her massive arm. She dared not let him fall! She dared not slow her pace! She had to keep on running, not only from the lions, but from the beasts whose voices she had heard.

They were coming with their flying sticks out of the southern grasslands. Soon they would be within the marsh. They would see her and hunt her, as their kind always hunted her kind . . . to the death. She could smell them now, coming ever closer.

The lions must have smelled them, too, for they were running at her side, no longer interested in hunting. To her relief they outdistanced her and kept on running until they disappeared into the grasses. She dared not slow her pace. Heading across the steppe toward the distant, stony hills, she followed them deep into the grassland.

The hole in the sky had vanished over the tangled, snow-covered horizon when, at last, straining against pain and exhaustion, she moved upward across the mist-shrouded highlands. If there was a moon, she could not see it through the clouds. She finally reached her cave, and with the cubs safe in the curl of her arm, she crawled into her nest to sleep in safety through the long autumn night.

In silence, the beastling stole from her embrace and stood above her in the cold dark. The smell of congealing blood was thick in the air. Mother was no longer bleeding. Her newest injury was not keeping her from sleep, nor was worry over Mother preventing Sister from smiling in her dreams.

The beastling turned away from them. Shivering against the cold, he went to sit at the edge of the cave. His stomach growled. Mother and Sister had eaten the flesh of the mired mammoth, but he had not. It did not matter; he had no appetite. He was deeply troubled. Once again she had returned to the cave with wounds upon her body . . . once again he was beset by the realization that someday she would leave the cave to hunt and would not return.

He sat very still, listening to the wind. Moonlight shone through apertures between the rivering clouds. He could see the world below almost as clearly as though it were day.

At the edge of the grassland, three beasts that walked on two legs stood together. The beastling held his breath. Never before had these strange-looking, upright beasts come so close to the mountain. The cub cocked his head as he observed them. Their torsos were as straight as the sticks that they carried . . . as straight as his own in those unguarded moments when Mother did not make him assume a correct bent-forward posture. And their arms were not long enough to allow them to lean comfortably on their knuckles. The beastling's frown deepened. His arms were not long enough for that, either! The arms of the beasts were down, and their fingertips reached to midthigh . . . like his own.

Their fur, he thought, was very strange. Not one of them possessed the same pelt. From this distance, it seemed that one of them had the body fur of a bear, the leg fur of a yak, and the shaggy arms of a bison. Another seemed to have the body fur of wolf, dog, and caribou, with long strips of horsehide running down its back. Two of them had big, puffy heads furred all around with what looked like fox or wolverine tails; if they had eyes, mouths, noses, or ears, the cub could not see them. But he could discern that the largest had a smaller head than the other two, and its face was bald . . . and the fur on its head was long and as black as the night, and as straight and smooth as a shaft of new grass.

He caught his breath. His hands flew to his head, and his fingers closed on two thick, tangled hanks of hair and pulled them forward. His own head fur was like the head fur of the beast that walked the world below. How could this be?

He stared down through the strands of his hair. The beasts were in a tight circle. The wind had changed, so he could hear them now, sounding to one another.

His hands left his hair and went to his throat. The beasts were sounding! They were not mewing or growling, screeching or huffing. Each sound had a shape, and within each shape was an inference of meaning that eluded him but was somehow calming to his spirit.

He closed his eyes, listening: One beast would sound, another would answer, and somehow a message was passed from one to the other. He could sense it; he could feel it. In an attempt at emulation, he inhaled deeply, pushed the air up and out of his chest, and held it captive within his mouth. He moved it over his tongue, shaped it, turned it, then slowly allowed it to escape as sounds.

"Ahh . . . kah . . . wah . . . mah . . ." Because the sounds made no sense to him, he did not know why it both pleased and saddened him to hear them.

"Mah . . . nah . . . rah . . . vak . . ." He intoned that utterance, then followed it with the one that Mother sometimes howled to a midnight moon: "Wah . . . nah . . . wah. Wah . . . nah . . . wut . . ." He opened his eyes. In the world below, the beasts turned and walked back into the grassland. The cub watched them.

At the back of the cave, Mother sighed in her sleep. The beastling needed no syllabic soundings to tell him that there was pain in the sound.

He rose and would have turned his back upon the night had a single flash of white not caught his eye. It was moving in the scrub growth near the river at the edge of the floodplain. He strained to focus his vision. He saw it clearly now. A white lion. The lion that had attacked Mother and hurt her.

He stood at the edge of the cave, glaring hatefully down at the world. As long as Mother remained weak and slow, that world would be the province of lions and wolves. It would not be safe for her or for Sister or for him.

A soft rain began to fall. The beastling turned and went into the cave. He stood over the nest, looking down at Mother and Sister. How deeply they slept within the safe, sheltering walls of the mountain.

Far away, beyond the clouds and rain, a lion roared. The beastling tensed, listening, knowing that Mother had recognized and feared that lion as much as it had feared her. Was the white lion responsible for the scar upon her leg as well as for the wounds in her back? Had Mother ruined its face and taken its eye? He hoped so.

Slowly, being careful not to wake Mother or Sister, he climbed into the nest and cuddled close to them. Sister briefly opened her eyes. She smiled and slung a long, gray-furred arm around him, then made smacking, contented little sounds as she settled back into her dreams.

The beastling lay very still. He was warm now.

Beyond the cave, rain turned to snow.

The white lion roared once more, then was still.

The beastling slept and dreamed. He saw himself fully grown, the man stone in his hand as he went down from the cave alone, to kill the white lion so that Mother would have no cause to fear it ever again.

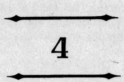

4

The sun disappeared over the western ranges, and winter settled over the land. Now was the time of the long dark, when day was only a memory and night went on forever.

Storms blew across the world. The sky was rarely clear, but when it was, the wonderful snow-covered valley and its surrounding hills and mountains sparkled beneath the light of the moon and stars, and the air was so cold that ice crystals hung suspended just above the earth in long rivers of subfreezing mist, which, if breathed too deeply, could fatally sear the lungs of man and beast alike.

Deep within the burrows and dens, the heartbeats of hibernating animals slowed as insulating layers of fat, feathers, and fur kept the cold away. Within lakes and rivers, fish sought deep water or died. And within wind-sheltered canyons, birds and predators hid from the storms as herd animals clustered, drawing warmth from one another's closeness.

Within Torka's capacious, richly stocked cave, weather baffles of hide kept the winter at bay, and as an additional guard against the loss of precious heat, the people raised a great hut in which life went on much as it would have done had they still been encamped upon the open steppe. In the light of a low-burning fire and tallow lamps, the laughter of children dispelled the shadows of the endless night.

Karana brooded in the winter dark. With the great dog Aar at his side, he walked the winter world whenever the weather permitted. Beneath the star-strewn skin of the night, he sought communion with the spirits on behalf of his people and implored the forces of Creation to make a female child within the belly of his woman—he knew in his heart that if it was a male, he must kill it for the good of the band lest through its flesh the bones and blood of Navahk take life again.

But how would Karana kill it? On what pretext? And when the time came, could he bring himself to do it? Would Torka allow him to murder the infant?

No matter. It would and must be done! And when it was accomplished, Karana knew with heart-sinking clarity that he would never be able to look into the eyes of his beloved Mahnie again. But the death of an infant and the death of his life with Mahnie were the prices he must pay, for he knew now that he had been unthinking and uncaring when he had chosen to be a man with her.

"You worry too much."

Torka's comment startled him. He had been sitting alone on a snow-blasted boulder, with a thick stand of willow scrub at his back. Aar had been gone for a while, leg lifting and sniffing out the land, tail up and whoofing low as though in conversation with himself. Karana swiveled and actually gasped in surprise when he saw Torka standing over him.

"And you should remember to watch your back!" Torka admonished evenly, bending into a crouch beside the magic man and resting his spears across his folded limbs.

Karana scowled. "I do not worry."

"You always worry . . . but not enough about yourself to cover your own back, it seems."

Karana felt cornered, ill at ease. "I am a magic man. The people expect me to worry. What are you doing here?"

"For much time have you been away from the cave. Mahnie worries, and Wallah's bones portend another storm. Summer Moon longs for you to share her joy in the good camp to which your visions of the wonderful valley have brought her people."

"You have come out alone across the land at the request of females?"

"I have come out alone across the land because I am

concerned about my son. You have been brooding too much, Karana—unless, of course, the Seeing wind has given you cause to be so preoccupied . . . and if this is so, then I think that you had better share the cause of your preoccupation with me."

"No!"

"Is that a refusal or a denial?"

Karana sucked in his breath; he had forgotten how easily Torka read his moods. "I make the songs *for* the People, and tell the stories *of* the People, and dance the dances *with* the People! What more must I do for them? I must take time to commune with the spirits. The responsibilities of a shaman are many! And since when is it wrong for a man to be concerned about his woman when she is with child?"

"It is not wrong. All the songs and dances and storytelling will not ease the burdens of Mahnie's pregnancy more than a simple smile and the open affection of her man."

"When the baby is born to us . . . when I see with my own eyes that all is well, then I will smile."

If it is a female child, he added in his own mind. *For if it is a male, after I have killed it, I do not think that I will ever smile again.*

Winter passed slowly.

With provisions stacked high all along the walls, the women and girls passed the hours sewing new garments from the many skins and yards of sinew thread that they had prepared during the time of light. The men had no real need to hunt, so when the moon bathed the world in blue light and dire wolves and wild dogs sang the songs of the pack and of the hunt, the men of the band listened and sighed against boredom.

"When do you think we will find bison in this good valley?" asked Grek. "Perhaps a good, fat hump steak would make my Wallah feel better, yes? Does Magic Man think that we will find bison soon?"

"Perhaps . . . yes . . ." replied Karana in the practiced tone of a seer.

But after the next series of storms, as Karana walked the valley's eastern edge with Brother Dog, he came upon bison sign and followed it to discover a half-grown calf that had become separated from a small herd that browsed the snow-covered tundral steppe only a few miles distant. The magic man returned to the cave at once, and in no more time than was necessary to gather up his spears and spear hurlers, Grek was off, with Karana leading the way and Torka and Simu following close. While the magic man stood aside, Grek made the kill before the others caught up with him.

"Not bad for an old man, yes?" he proclaimed, and after cutting out the tongue and two huge slabs of hump meat, he left them to take what they would of the animal as he ran practically all the way back to the cave in his eagerness to share his treasures with Wallah.

When Grek backhanded the weather baffle to stand before his woman, his happiness was quashed by Wallah's wan smile. She seemed to have lost her appetite along with her leg, and during the past moons, she was noticeably shrinking within the skin of the bear that had maimed her. Her wound was healing. The massive, crusted scab that had formed over it was gradually peeling away to reveal new and tender scar tissue. Nevertheless, Grek knew that she was still in constant pain.

"Hump steaks, woman! And bison tongue!" he announced. "To make my Wallah feel better in the winter dark!"

"This woman feels well enough!" she protested, and made a good effort to appear enthused as he knelt before her.

She was seated on her bed furs, stitching delicate feather trim onto the baby carrier that she was making for Mahnie. Her once-corpulent body looked small and wan.

Grek pretended not to notice. He took up his eating knife from in front of the large concave tallow lamp that he had carved for her years before out of an elongated green stone that had caught her eye. It had been a portion of her bride price.

Well paid, he thought, reminiscing how it had been between them in those long-gone days and marveling at how many years had passed between this moment and the time of the making of that lamp. An old, pain-ravaged woman sat across from him, and yet she was still Wallah, as he was still Grek. He looked down and ground his teeth. In his heart and bones and along the smooth, time-worn edges of his molars he knew that a lifetime *had* passed.

Behind her, the other women were raising life out of the well-banked main cooking fire. The children were running around it, singing the songs in praise of meat that Karana had taught them. It was a good sound, and it cheered him a little as he thought that soon his first grandchild would be joining them in their games and songs.

"This is a good camp for us," he said, slicing a ribbon of meat and handing it to Wallah.

"A good camp," she agreed, accepting the meat and eating it, making a show of her enjoyment.

Grek watched her and was not heartened. He could tell that she was forcing herself to eat because to do otherwise would make him unhappy. She did not ask him for a second portion, and when he handed one to her, she waved it away, and sighed apologetically. "Perhaps later I will be hungrier. Now Grek should eat. Please. It will make Wallah happy."

"Later," he said. "When the others return and Wallah joins them at their feast, Grek will eat then."

And so he did.

But much later, when the feasting was over and the people of his band slept, he lay naked beside Wallah beneath their bed skins. He enjoyed the warm privacy of their little fur-walled space inside the communal winter hut, but he worried as he stroked her back, as he often did, and felt how thin she was. What had happened to the big, broad, fleshy body that had once melded so perfectly to his?

"You must eat more. You are becoming a skinny woman," he told her.

"*Hmmph!* There is no pleasing some people! Out of your own mouth—and not so long ago—you were complaining that I was a fat woman . . . as fat as a rodent ready to go to ground for the winter!"

"It *is* winter," he reminded her gently. "In truth her fat

was indeed sweet to this man, and he would have it on her bones again!"

"Along with her leg, no doubt."

Her bitterness hurt him; it was a thing that he could neither soothe nor wish away, no matter how hard he tried, so he hugged her tightly, and careful not to rouse pain from her injury, he kissed the dry, narrow nape of a neck that had once been sweet and moist with the well-padded flesh of a woman who loved to eat. "Grek did not place five spears, a stone lamp, and twelve bison hides before the pit hut of your father in exchange for a leg! These things were given for a woman . . . a woman named Wallah."

"A *two*-legged woman named Wallah." Her whisper was thick with tears.

He sat up and moved so that he was facing her beneath their bed furs, holding her old tear-streaked, pain-worn face in his hands. "A bold-eyed, broad-bottomed, big-bosomed woman named Wallah." His hands stroked downward, caressed her breasts as his mouth found hers and tenderly kissed her. "What is a leg? When Grek still has his woman . . . his bold, bear-chasing woman! His Wallah!"

She sobbed softly and turned her face down, away from his kisses. "I am old and tired and so full of pain . . . and without a leg."

"We are old together, woman! Not many are lucky to say this, yes? Old and sharing a good camp, with a daughter swelling with life that will soon bring joy to us! And you still have your leg! There, in its elkskin bag. A part of you still, but not the best part. That is here . . . this." His hand rested between her breasts, over her heart. "My bold woman. My bear-hearted woman. My Wallah! You must eat and be strong again, if not for yourself, then for our Mahnie. She will need you when her time comes, and her baby will not be happy without a grandmother . . . and . . . " He paused and shook his head, then laid it down over her heart lest she see the tears that now filled his eyes. "No, my woman. Not for Mahnie, nor for her baby, but for this man. Because without his Wallah, Grek will have no heart to live at all!"

*   *   *

Change.

The people began to feel it happening long before the first wash of color began briefly to soften the darkness along the eastern horizon at that hour that should have been called dawn.

"Look, Father Mine! I think it is morning!" cried Demmi in delight.

And it was morning: a brief, lingering, dawn-gold promise of a sunrise that never came, of a day that was not quite born before the dark came down again.

"Between the storms there is now light in the sky, Father. When next you go to hunt with the others, will Dak and this boy Umak walk at your side?"

"Yes," agreed Torka when Simu had nodded in unspoken affirmation. "It is time."

"Yes, it *is* time," Lonit agreed after a moment.

"Make the songs for the coming day, Magic Man! For this girl longs for the return of lasting light!" Summer Moon implored.

Karana obliged her, and soon, after so many dawns that never quite yielded to sunrise, the sun showed itself above the peaks of the eastern range and the people gathered at the edge of the cave to rejoice in the days of light that were to follow.

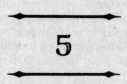

5

The wind was beginning to gust with the first stirrings of morning; but because it was the Month of the Starving Moon, it was still dark, and stars pricked a sky that showed no light except along the far eastern horizon. In this restless, fetal hour, Zhoonali glared up at her son and took hold of the fringes of Cheanah's sleeve. "Wait!" she whispered.

Cheanah paused just outside his new, larger pit hut. It was an impressive shelter, fit for the most commanding of headmen. The tusks and four of the ribs of the old, mired bull mammoth braced the vaulted ceiling, and the shaggy hide of the beast formed its outer covering.

With the scowling condescension of a man who had grown comfortable—and more than a little careless—with command, Cheanah turned and looked down at his mother. "You are up even earlier than usual, my mother. What is it?"

"The man need is on you *again*? Not even the great bear spirit is in rut *all* the time, Cheanah! The men of the band grow tired of rolling over in the winter dark so that you can ride their women."

The starlight shone like flecks of falling snow within the darkness of his narrowed eyes. "Go back to your bed furs, my mother. You have forgotten how it is with young men and women."

"Beware, Cheanah. Ekoh resents your preference for his woman. You must not abuse his generosity. And you *must* ease the fears that trouble your people."

He sighed. This was not the first time that she had come to him with this demand. "This is a good camp. My people want for nothing."

"No, they do not want. This *is* a good camp—so good, in fact, that your people wonder just how long the goodness can last! You have promised to kill the white lion but have failed to do so. Find the lion. Kill it. Skin it and hang its head from—"

"I would if I could." He sighed. "I have failed to find any sign of it since it disappeared into the foothills along with the wanawut and its cubs."

"You should not have boasted that you would kill it."

"Perhaps not. But one more skin in a camp full of prime pelts, what can it matter?"

"The skin means nothing. It is the word of Cheanah that counts."

"My word—? Byagh!" he sputtered, and waved her away. "The white lion will return to the northern edge of the marsh country with the sun. When it comes, I will hunt and kill it. And when I do, the people will know that not only Torka walks this world in the skin of lions . . . if, in fact, Torka still walks this world at all!"

Zhoonali watched him stride across the camp and disappear into the pit hut of Ekoh and his woman, Bili. She frowned, greatly disturbed. In this harsh, unstable season, when men were vulnerable to their fears, hardheaded headmen who would not heed them were the most vulnerable of all.

The sound of a hide weather baffle being slapped aside drew her eyes across the camp. Ekoh emerged stark naked from his hut and, dragging one of his bed furs, stood glaring up at the sky. The lean, usually mild-natured hunter clenched his fists, pulled his furs up around his shoulders, and, muttering furiously to himself, stalked off a few paces to the hut of Ram, his closest hunting companion, before turning and ejecting a stream of urine in the direction of his own pit hut.

Cheanah has won the enmity of that man, Zhoonali thought.

She wondered if Ekoh harbored second thoughts about not following Torka into the Forbidden Land. Ekoh had admired Man of the West. His woman, Bili, had mourned for many days over the absence of her sister, Eneela, woman of Simu; but Ekoh was a practical man. He treasured his young woman, mother of his son, Seteena, and would not risk them to the unknown.

Zhoonali sighed. Of all the women in this camp, why did Cheanah repeatedly single out Bili? He disliked the young woman. Furthermore, Bili had never made a secret of the fact that lying beneath Cheanah was something that she found unappealing.

"Dance!" Cheanah demanded.

"Choose another partner," Bili suggested as she strained against the press of his body.

He was naked over her, moving on her, mouthing her. "Dance!" he commanded again, ferociously, his command intensified by the strength of his hands as they worked her buttocks, forced her wide as the driving pressure of his man bone buried itself so deep that Bili gasped against the massive thrust of his invasion. "Come, you know you want it. Who else can ram so deep?"

She bit her lower lip as she fought against him.

"Move!" he shouted, biting her neck in frustration with her lack of response.

"Go away, Cheanah," she grunted, pushing at his shoulders, twisting her hips—not to please him but to be free of him.

He moved back, suddenly pulling out, and exhaled with satisfaction when he heard her gasp with surprise and pain. He took her breasts in his hands and began to manipulate them, working her nipples between his thumbs and index fingers. "If you can spread yourself for Ekoh, then you can spread yourself for me."

"Ekoh is my man! And you come too often!"

"I am your headman. Why do you not let yourself take pleasure in Cheanah? Who else has breasts like these? They are like your sister Eneela's, eh? But she is gone, into the Forbidden Land with her fine, big breasts made for babies and for men to suck. But it is good that she is gone, for Torka would not have shared his women. Here, now. Let me share the woman of Ekoh. Yes, like this, yes . . ."

He was mouthing her breasts. Again she gasped. When Ekoh did this, it set fire to her loins. It made her arch and open to him with sighs of delight. But Cheanah was not merely mouthing—he was not even kissing—he was suckling her, as an infant would suck, and at the same time fingering deep between her thighs, not to arouse her for her own sake as well as for his, but to test for readiness as he might have fingered roasting meat to see if it was hot enough for his tastes.

Bili was revolted by him. Cheanah demanded too much too often, and with absolutely no finesse at all.

"No!" she hissed, desperately trying to be free of him. But it was no use. He was too much for her. Briefly, she cursed Ekoh for yielding her body to Cheanah so easily. But she knew that it was not easy for her man. It was not easy at all.

Her open resistance was pure instigation to Cheanah. It was what he came for, what he never failed to arouse in her, and what excited him most about her. None of the other females in the band could be counted on to fight him. Tradition demanded that they yield. Tradition honored their men when their headman asked for them. He laughed, low and deep. How stupid women were. If only Bili knew why he came to ease his need in her, she would not resist; she would dance and sigh and open herself to him. Once she did, all of the pleasure of the hunt would be gone for him.

"Go . . ." she implored, anger spicing her voice.

"Soon . . ." He gripped her breasts, moved now to do that which always offended her and caused her to flail against him like a netted fish. He was a big man. Beneath the bed furs, he knew that he must look like a bear curling over a fawn as, gripping her arms and holding her limbs fast with his own, he bent to browse deep between her thighs, to send his tongue deep, probing, drawing the sweet taste of woman into his mouth until—

Something hurled itself against his lower back, growling and snarling. "Leave my mother alone!"

The blows of the boy Seteena were dulled by the thickness of the bed furs. One backward swipe of Cheanah's arm was enough to send the youngster flying. He turned, saw the boy sprawled across a collapsed pile of extra bed skins; close by, the three-year-old daughter of Bili and Ekoh was crying in distress.

Cheanah snarled in annoyance. "Get out," he ordered the boy. "Take your sister to one of the other pit huts. You dishonor your father by raising your hand against one whom he has welcomed into his hut and into his woman."

The boy's head went up. His nostrils flared. There was fire in his eyes as he looked to his mother.

"Go," she told him before he could speak, and when Cheanah looked down at her, he was gratified to see that she was terrified of what might happen to her only son as just punishment for his attack against the headman. "Take your sister to the hut of Ram. Your father will be there."

The boy, openly resentful, did as he was told.

Cheanah watched him pull on his boots and clothes and gather up his sister. He was small for his age. For a moment longer than was necessary, the boy stood with his back to the door flap, glaring at Bili.

When he was gone, Cheanah smiled and returned his attention to the woman beneath him. "Now," he slurred. "Where were we?"

"You will not hurt him? . . . He did not mean to—"

"It takes a brave boy to stand in defense of his mother. But it is a bad thing for a boy to offend an elder. He will have to be punished . . . perhaps put out of the band—"

"No! No, Cheanah, please. Now Bili will dance . . . for her son, yes? So Cheanah will not be angry with her son!"

And so she danced, moving in ways that she had never moved for him before, and he smiled and trembled in the ecstasy of his release in her, wondering why he had ever thought that an unwilling Bili was more pleasurable than the woman who lay beneath him now.

6

Violent, fitful storms continued to blow across the Forbidden Land, but they were no longer constant, and the savage bite of winter had left them: When snow fell, it was a softer substance; and when the sun rose, it stayed long enough in the sky to bring joy to Torka and his people.

In the night, the wind beat a gentler rhythm. Lonit, Mahnie, and Eneela listened, fingers laced across their swollen bellies as they smiled the small, secretive smiles of mothers-to-be, for the rhythm of the wind was no sweeter than the promise of life that stirred within them.

When the wolves and wild dogs howled in the darkness, Aar sat at the edge of the cave, his head cocked to one side, his one remaining ear up and twitching. The song of the dogs and wolves had changed. The dog sensed it long before Torka and his people did—but not before Karana and little Umak.

Umak was the dog's good friend now. "Aar listens to his brothers in the night," he remarked.

"Yes," agreed the magic man, sitting next to the dog at the edge of the cave. He always spent his nights and the bulk of his days here, away from Mahnie, away from everyone, along with his thoughts and his worries, with only the company of the dog to ease his increasingly troubled mind. He could talk to Aar, and Aar asked nothing except that they maintain their closeness and unwavering bond of mutual affection. Karana scowled as Umak seated himself on the other side of the dog and slung a fur-clad arm over Aar's broad shoulders.

"Brother Dog wants to be with his true brothers and sisters instead of with his man pack," said the boy. "He will soon go far away. A long time will pass before we see him again."

Karana's scowl deepened. The child rarely asked questions; he always made statements, and this last one was particularly annoying. "You cannot know that," he replied sternly. "And Aar is free to come and go as he chooses."

"He will go," repeated the boy quietly.

"Perhaps." Karana was ill at ease with the idea. He could barely remember a time when he and Aar had not been together, nor could he imagine a time in which the great grizzled dog would not be at his side.

"This boy will miss you while you are gone, Aar!" said little Umak, hugging the dog.

Aar turned his head and painted little Umak's face with a wet, sloppy lick. The boy licked him back and nestled close.

Karana's scowl deepened. Umak spoke to the dog as though the animal were a human brother fully capable of understanding his words—as Karana himself had always spoken, and old Umak before him. The scowl settled into a thoughtful frown, then disappeared entirely. He smiled. Old Umak would have liked to see his namesake and great-grandson sitting here with Aar. True, there was nothing of Torka or the old man in his face and form; the child looked like a miniature, masculine version of his mother. Nevertheless, he was Umak's great-grandson, and Karana sensed a strong feeling of continuation in the moment.

Continuation. His smile vanished. Behind him, deep within the cave, Mahnie slept warm and safe, his child within her. Never would there be a son for Karana. For Karana's life spirit, there would be no continuing.

"You are sad, Magic Man," Umak observed.

"Yes."

"My mother says that it is not a good thing for you to be sad so much." The boy sat very straight, peering at the magic man from over the shoulder of the dog. "Brother Dog will soon go away, but he *will* come back to us."

"You should not speak with such certainty of things you cannot know, Umak."

"Brother Dog *will* come back!"

Karana shook his head admonishingly. "He has not yet gone away."

"He will." The boy sighed and blinked sleepily. "Can this boy stay here with Magic Man and Brother Dog until the sun comes up?"

"Umak may stay."

The boy grinned happily as he settled himself back into the warmth of Aar's side. "This boy is glad to call Karana Brother," he admitted softly.

The confidence touched the magic man. If only he *were* the boy's true brother, Torka and Lonit's true son! All would be well, then. He would lie happily in Mahnie's arms and look forward to the birth of as many sons as she could bear.

He fell asleep before dawn and dreamed terrible nightmares of another cave and of another boy . . . of Torka's son Manaravak . . . and awoke with a start, sweated and sickened by memories.

Stars jeweled a moonless sky. Aar was gone. In the fold of Karana's arm, Umak, smiling, slept like a baby. The magic man drew him close. Umak had been right about the dog's intent to leave the cave. He had known that Aar was going to answer the call of wolves and wild dogs, when Karana, magic man of the band, had not. Indeed, the boy was the grandson of a spirit master!

Karana peered down at him. Even in the near darkness, Umak closely resembled his mother. He was a beautiful boy. Karana felt a brother's love for the boy. Now that he realized that they shared a similar gift, they would become closer. He could teach the child all that he had learned from old Umak and Sondahr and the shamans at the Great Gathering. When at last he was old and his spirit went to walk the wind forever, he might not die completely and forever, for Umak would remember his teachings and share them with future generations of magic men. Umak would be the closest thing to a son that Karana could ever hope to have. They *would* be brothers!

*   *   *

Once again, it was the time of the coming of the caribou. For many days before the first animals were sighted returning to the wonderful valley, the earth trembled beneath the weight of their hooves, and the air was thick with the scent of them.

"This is the first time of light in which Umak and Dak are old enough to stalk big game with their fathers," Torka announced proudly. "They will learn from their fathers and be blooded by the life spirits of the great herds of the animal that has always been the favorite meat of Torka's people."

"Caribou!"

In unison, Umak and Dak named their prey. The carcasses of two small caribou lay motionless at their feet. The boys' faces flushed with pride as their fellow hunters gathered around them and the fallen game.

Both animals were stringy—one sickly, the other old— but neither Dak nor Umak found them anything less than magnificent as the wind sang the Song of First Kill and the hooves of the departing herd thundered in the distance under the stampede's dust cloud, which now obscured the western horizon.

Observing the kill site from the cave, the women and girls cheered while the adult hunters formed a circle around the boys. In their stalking cloaks of caribou skins, the men seemed larger than life. Indeed, they did not look like men at all but like wondrous spirit forms that were half man, half caribou: The time-cured heads of the dead reindeerlike animals balanced atop their own, projecting forward over their faces, while the great, multipointed, curvilinear antlers branched up and out as though strange trees of twisted bone grew from the heads of each hunter.

Umak looked up at them with open adoration. Soon now Dak and he would wear such antlered cloaks. *Soon!*

He tried hard not to tremble visibly with anticipation as the hunters who had guided Dak and him to their first kill nodded with approval of their success. He drew in a deep breath. He was a hunter! It did not matter that he was small or that his spears were less than half the size of an adult's.

The boy frowned. The special moment was shadowed
by his realization that Dak had brought down his caribou
with one sure throw and had killed it with a second. It had
taken all four of Umak's slender, perfectly balanced spears
to accomplish the same thing, and his animal had been the
smaller. Had Torka noticed? Of course he had—everyone
had noticed!

No matter, thought the boy defensively. Now that the
deed was accomplished, he was confident he would do
better next time. Dak was older! It was only natural that
he was swifter and stronger. Umak was certain that he
would catch up with him in time. After all, he was the son
of the finest hunter of the band.

"Now . . ." said Torka, laying a hand on the shoulder of
each boy. "Not only have you stalked game alongside your
fathers in the winter dark, but you have both achieved
first kill . . . and the first to make first kill in this new
land!"

It was a wondrous and intoxicating moment. The shadows flew from Umak's mind and heart. Simu, Grek, and
Karana had odd, happy looks of nostalgia upon their faces.
The boy knew that they must be remembering their own
first kills.

"Praise now the life spirits of the game that, through the
skill of these new hunters, will nourish the People! Praise
now the life spirits of Umak and Dak and welcome them
into the brotherhood of the band, according to the ways of
our people."

And so it was done, with each adult male contributing
some small portion of ceremony in the way that he remembered from his own first kill. This melding of custom
brought them all closer than they had been before; from
this day forth, the ritual that they performed would be the
only ceremony.

Torka instructed the boys to withdraw their spears from
the slain caribou and to hand them up to their fathers.
They obeyed with alacrity. As Torka removed the spearhead from the shaft that had struck Umak's killing blow,
Simu followed suit with Dak's weapon. Simu watched
closely as the headman broke Umak's spears across his

thigh and, still holding the spearhead that had inflicted the actual kill, threw them down.

"These spears are cast away along with your childhood," Torka told the boys solemnly. "But the spearhead that makes a man's first kill of big game is to be kept always." He held Umak's spear reverently down to him on his upturned palm.

As the boy took the stone projectile point into his hand, Simu nodded, his expression revealing that this ritual was familiar to him. Simu proudly handed Dak's killing spearhead to him, then cracked the boy's spears in half across his raised thigh and threw them aside. "Now you will make new spears," he intoned. "The spears of men."

"And your next kills will be as those of hunters, responsible for the nourishment of the band." Torka tried not to smile as he looked down at the boys.

They hardly looked like men. Dak, whose age could be counted in the passing of six starving moons, was standing splay-legged with his narrow little boy's chest thrust out. His round, baby-cheeked face was set into the pugnacious expression of a self-satisfied owl.

Torka felt a stab of paternal tenderness. How much like his mother Umak looked, with his fine, straight, high-bridged nose, widely set, deeply lidded eyes, highly placed and rounded cheeks, and dimples. Umak grinned up at his father. He revealed a space where he had just lost a baby tooth, but all of his remaining small, white, sharply pointed little teeth were displayed like those of . . . *Navahk*.

Torka gaped at Umak, no longer seeing Lonit, but the man who had raped her. His heart was suddenly so cold that he clenched his fists and jaws. All feelings of tenderness toward the boy vanished. He stared at his son as though at a stranger.

Umak frowned at the sudden change in Torka. His little body tensed, waiting for his father's expression of approval and pride to return.

Karana spoke then, commanding the hunters' attention. "From this day on, the females will look to Umak and Dak for sustenance."

"And in starving times," added Grek somberly, "the old

and the sick will have no lives at all if Dak and Umak do not choose to share their youth and strength with them."

Torka saw the boys' eyes grow wide as they met the stern, steady gaze of the old hunter. Grek's words had made an impact on them. With Umak no longer smiling, the boy had the look of his mother again.

What a handsome, thoughtful child he is, Torka reminded himself. *What sort of a father am I to stand aloof from him, especially at such a time as this?*

The boys did not flinch against the responsibility that Grek had just handed to them. They were eager to take it on.

Torka felt a momentary pang of pity for them. *A man's life is hard, little hunters. Do not be so greedy for it.*

Umak's eyes sought Torka's approval again. He gave it with a nod and a smile. The boy beamed up at him.

"Now we must honor the spirit of the game," he said, and knelt to instruct the boys in the way that they must use their spearheads to slit their kills from throat to belly.

Blood spurted, entrails oozed and steamed. The hunters ate of the heart, liver, and kidneys of each animal, for these were the blood meats, and all knew that the spirit of the animal had drawn its life from these mysterious organs.

"Now that life is in you and in us," Karana told the boys. "The hunters of this band are united in the blood of the hunt."

The magic man dipped his fingers into the body cavities of the caribou and then reached to color each boy's forehead lavishly with blood.

A deep tide of sadness and emptiness swept through Torka. *Manaravak should be here now.*

His longing for his lost son was so intense that he winced when the magic man touched the blood of the caribou to his forehead.

"You are headman," said Karana. "It is for you to place the skins."

Torka nodded. The boys watched, enthralled, as he deftly fleshed and lifted the bloodied hides from the caribou, leaving the antlered heads and hooved limbs intact.

"From this day forth, in the skin of their kill shall Dak

and Umak stalk the caribou," said Torka as he placed the hides over the backs and heads of the new hunters.

Both boys staggered against the unexpected weight.

"Behold the new hunters of this band!" proclaimed Karana.

"*Aieeeh!*" exclaimed the others in unison, and circled the two drooping, massively antlered little figures in a hand-slapping, foot-stomping dance of celebration.

From the cave, the claps and song of the women and girls rode the wind to join the sounds of the men. Torka turned back, his eyes scanning the distance and lifting to the hills and the highlands beyond. He could see the cave and the little figures of the women and girls. Lonit stood taller than the others in her pale, fringed, and shell-beaded elkskin dress, with her long, plaited black hair blowing back over her shoulders. She was not singing or dancing. Her arms were raised. In thanksgiving to the forces of Creation for the successful hunt of her firstborn son? Of course. Torka knew she shared his pride in Umak's achievement. And yet she also shared his grief. As the wind brought the song of the women down from the hills, he spoke the name of his lost son aloud with terrible longing. "Manaravak . . ."

The other hunters did not hear him—they were too busy dancing, too busy singing. Dak, bent nearly double under the weight of his caribou skin, was strutting boldly in Simu's shadow; theirs was a rowdy, raucous song, full of laughter and love.

But beneath the heavy, antlered head of the caribou that he had killed, little Umak had heard him. The blood of the caribou, seeping from the animal's mutilated throat, trickled from the back of its severed jaw and ran into Umak's eyes and mouth, making him look as though he were crying tears of blood.

Torka saw and was instantly repentant, for surely he had not meant to cloud Umak's joy by speaking his dead brother's name aloud.

"Come," he said, extending a conciliatory hand to the boy. "We must celebrate your kill!"

Umak's expression remained tight as he backhanded the blood of the caribou from his face but inadvertently smeared it. "My brother, Manaravak, is dead, but he would have made a better kill than Umak! Manaravak would have made Torka proud!"

"No!" cried Torka, taking a step toward the boy, but it was no use.

With a sob of remorse, Umak turned and ran away.

The boy did not go far. The weight of the caribou skin slowed his steps. Besides, he really did not want to run away. He was glad when Torka caught up with him and insisted that he rejoin the others in celebration of first kill.

"Come, my son! The dance and song is in your honor."

"Dak has made a better kill than Umak."

"He is older, stronger. But Umak is my son. Torka's pride is in *him*."

The words were more welcome than the first rays of sunlight at the end of the time of long dark. Umak had no desire to challenge them.

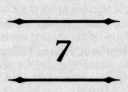

7

A daughter was born to Eneela under the Moon of River Ice Breaking. Simu accepted the tiny girl and named her Larani in honor of a long-dead sister. The people rejoiced, and the children were delighted with the newest member of their band.

But soon the Moon of River Ice Breaking set beyond the distant ranges. The nights grew short, and days grew noticeably longer. The Moon of the Green Grass Growing rose full and high. The great tusker Life Giver walked with his children in the wonderful valley and migratory birds returned to the Forbidden Land. Although the people rejoiced in the coming of summer, Karana did not share their happiness.

They saw him often, a solitary figure silhouetted against the fading light of day, arms raised skyward, head back, voice lifted. Sometimes he sang all night. Wolves and wild dogs answered him, but if Aar was with him, the people could not tell.

Then, on a day that was shadowed by swans winging softly across the sky, another girl-child was born to Lonit. They named the girl Swan, to honor the life spirit of the birds that had flown overhead at the time of her birth.

"Swan?" Umak tested the name on his tongue, not at all sure that he liked it. "Do you want a long-necked girl with wings and feathers?"

Torka laughed. "No, we want a girl as beautiful and loyal as that fine bird, for when it mates—like Torka and Lonit—the swan mates always and forever."

Then, on a cloudless dawn in which mammoths called to one another from the spruce groves at the far side of the wonderful valley, Mahnie went into labor. Her baby was born as quickly and easily as the morning. As the men, women, and children of the band rejoiced at the perfection of Karana's firstborn child, Torka left the cave in search of the young man.

It was time for the magic man to come home.

Karana stopped dead in his tracks. What had drawn him from his trance? He could not tell; his mind was too thick with black, substanceless dreams. He shook his head, willing the dreams away. They retreated sluggishly. He looked around, puzzled by his whereabouts and shocked that he was no longer fast asleep, curled up to the lee of a lichen-encrusted boulder within the lowlands.

It was quiet. The only sound was that of the wind and the restless lapping of semifrozen waves against a shore of stone and ice. The huge, ice-choked highland lake was behind him. As he turned to scan its miles-wide surface, a warning beat at the back of his brain. There was something black, ominous, and unsettling about this wide, cold body of water. The knot in his gut grew tighter as his eyes took in the soaring, weather-eroded sides of the glacier that walled its far shore. With a startled cry, he jumped back. The wonderful valley was *directly* below him. Had he taken one more step forward, he would have plummeted to certain death. He knew that he should be grateful to be alive, but a deep, all-pervasive emptiness told him that he was not.

Suddenly weary, he hunkered down, resting his forearms across his thighs. He had been searching for the elusive magic of his shamanistic powers so that he might use it to ease Mahnie's labor and ultimately to determine the gender of their baby. Instead he heard the high, frenzied yapping of dogs moving to a kill somewhere in the valley far below. He wondered if Aar was with them. Missing Brother Dog, he sighed, hoping that all was well with his boyhood friend.

His throat felt raw from endless chanting. Or was it

from the inner spirit voices biting at his throat and whispering in the winds of his mind?

You do not seek! *You do not* search! *You* run *from your people when they need you, Magic Man. You will never find the magic.* Never! *It is not for such as you . . . not for the son of Navahk . . . not for Karana, who has sworn to kill his own son and is afraid to do so!*

The foulness of that oath was suffocating. He rose, drew in deep, steadying breaths of the frigid morning, and faced directly into the rising sun. He shivered despite the warmth of the exquisite garments that Mahnie had stitched for him. *Mahnie! By now our child must be born! By now your pain must be over! By now you must wonder why I am not at your side!* The cold within his heart solidified into a vile, choking bitterness. *Be glad that I am not, for when I return to your side, if our child is a boy I will take it from your breast and kill it. I must! Even though I know that it will cost me your love and my place within the band if the killing is witnessed by others.*

He gasped, so miserable that he could barely breathe.

"I cannot allow his spirit to be reborn!" he cried aloud. "For in the end, he will see us all dead if he can!"

The sickness overcame him. He released it, violently. But there was nothing in his gut except the bile of his own commitment to his terrible purpose. Try as he might, he could not purge himself of it.

When Torka came upon him, Karana was on his way back to the encampment. His face was gray. He looked old and haggard and ill.

Until Torka spoke. Nine words—nine briefly stated words that caused the freshness of youth to flood back into the magic man's handsome face as tears of joy overflowed his eyes: "Mahnie is well. She has given you a daughter."

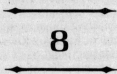

8

The daughter of Karana and Mahnie was called Naya, to honor the life spirit of her great-grandmother.

"A good and loving woman was Naya, who carried Grek in her belly and gave him life," the old hunter informed the band as they gathered to witness the acceptance of the newest daughter of the band by her father. "Grek thanks Karana for allowing his firstborn to honor the memory of Naya by carrying on her name."

Karana nodded circumspectly. *Better your ancestors than mine,* he thought as he raised the infant in his two strong hands and proclaimed before all: "I, Karana, accept this newborn girl child of my woman, Mahnie. May the ancestral spirit of Naya come to live again in the flesh of her great-granddaughter."

The baby stirred in Karana's upheld hands. The white caribou skin upon which she lay was smooth against his palms. His jaw tightened as the glow of first light washed the infant in a faint red-gold sheen. He thought of another child and of another caribou skin, red and sullied by the lies and blood of the magic man's self-inflicted wound.

He turned and looked at Torka as custom demanded, hoping that Torka would not see the haunted look in his eyes.

"Does the headman of this band accept the girl-child of this man and his woman?" he asked, continuing the ritual.

"With the permission of the band, the headman accepts this child of Karana and Mahnie," replied Torka.

"With our permission!" exclaimed the members of the band in full assent.

Karana watched dully as the infant was passed tenderly from one member of the band to the next. Each breathed into her nostrils, enacting the ancient custom that symbolized the sharing of life. Karana wished that he could share their joy and feel something other than relief and cold desolation—relief because the baby was not a boy, and so he would not have to kill it—desolation because, as he looked at Mahnie, he loved her and wanted her more than ever.

Their eyes met. His heart ached. Never again would she lie in his arms or feel the heat of his passion. Never.

He could not put himself through this torture again. This time the spirits had been kind. But they had also planted the seeds of warning in his heart: Next time Mahnie would bear him a son.

And so it was that later, when night filled the cave and the people slept content within it, Karana did not turn to look at Mahnie when she came from her bed furs to kneel beside him as he sat looking out across the night.

"Is my magic man sorry that his woman has not given him a son?"

"I am not sorry. I am glad for a daughter."

"The baby is a good baby. My breast milk flows for her. She sleeps and does not fuss."

He closed his eyes and thought of her breasts, of her soft, warm breasts.

"She is a strong, pretty girl."

Like her mother, he thought.

"Soon my time of birth blood will be over. Soon we will make another baby—a son . . . many sons would Mahnie give to her magic man."

Now he looked at her. "No!"

"I—I do not understand. I am your woman."

"No more!"

She shrank back from it. "I have offended you."

You could never offend me, my Mahnie.

"The child . . . you *are* displeased by the child."

He heard the quiver in her voice. He saw the look of despair in her eyes. He knew that he could not ease her heart, lest he lose his own. "I must be what I have been born to be, Mahnie. I was wrong to take you as my woman in the first place. A shaman needs no woman. Nothing must distract me from my magic. Not even--"—*my love for you*. He ached to speak the words. "There are too many distractions here for a magic man!" he said as he snapped to his feet and, wrapping his sleeping furs around himself, stalked out of the cave and into the night.

On the morning of the third day of his absence from the cave, Torka appeased a worried Grek and Mahnie and Summer Moon by taking up his spears and those of the magic man and following. He went alone, assuring Grek and Simu that he had no need of their assistance.

Karana had made no attempt to conceal his tracks. Torka caught up with him on the ridge where he sat alone overlooking the wonderful valley.

"Your woman worries about you," Torka told him.

"She need not."

"Perhaps."

Karana looked up, frowning at the drollness of Torka's tone.

"Here," said the headman and dropped Karana's spears across his lap. "With these in your hand, Mahnie will have less cause to fear for you."

"I have no need of them."

Torka shook his head. "A magic man is made of flesh and blood, as any other man. I doubt if the spirits will be offended if you seek to assist them in the protection of your hide. And even a shaman must hunt to eat once in a while."

Karana scowled, but he did not disdain his spears, nor did he refuse when Torka offered to share his traveling ration of cubed fat and dried meat.

They sat together in silence for a long time before Torka said thoughtfully: "You are alone too much. A new father should rejoice in the birth of his child."

Karana drew in a deep breath. "Go back to the cave.

Tell Mahnie that she has no cause to worry. I commune with the forces of Creation . . . on behalf of her and our child. I am a shaman, a magic man. This is what magic men are supposed to do."

Impatient with Karana's sullen mood, Torka left him to his meditations and headed back toward the cave. It was late, but days were longer than the nights at this time of year, and he was not concerned about traveling or sleeping alone. Trailing Karana at an easy jog, it had taken him nearly two days to reach the pass. It would take as many to get home. He stopped and turned back, taking in the awesome beauty of the heights before gesturing to Karana in hope that he would reconsider. If only he could teach the haunted, harried young man to put his sad, cruel, and tormented past behind him and learn to rejoice in each day as it came, for soon enough the final darkness must come to each man, and nothing—*nothing*—could stay its course.

The young man raised an arm and waved him away. With a sigh, Torka waved back, turned, and continued on. His mind was still filled with images of the ridge, with its wild vistas of the valley below, of open steppe and tumbled, encircling mountain ranges, of sprawling, distant ice fields, and of the strange, troubling beauty of the highland lake.

He frowned as he thought of the lake. He did not know why it should trouble him, except that if there were fish in its depths, no birds fed upon them. Nor had he seen sign of animals feeding along its stony shore. Now that he thought about it, he realized that it was like no lake he had ever seen before: a bleak, lonely place, devoid of the usual marshy embankments . . . a cold, barren stretch of iceberg-ridden water with ridges of stone and steep, discolored, weather-worn glacial walls surrounding its mountaintop basin.

He went on, glad to put the lake behind him. Somewhere within the trees ahead, a flock of small birds flew upward, startled by the sound of Torka's footfall. Glad for the distraction, he paused and looked back, hoping to see or hear Karana moving behind him. But there was no sign of him. For a moment, Torka regretted not insisting that Karana accompany him back to the cave. Then he rebuked himself. Karana was a man, and a man had a right to seek solitude when he had need of it . . . especially if he was a shaman. Torka went on, smiling again, amused that he was thinking like a father. When he was old and bent, with Karana growing old right behind him, would he still worry over him as though he were a boy whose life depended upon his father's protection? Yes, no doubt he would; it was the way of fathers. It did not matter that Karana was not the son of his own blood. He had raised him as his own. No father could love him more.

He deliberately forced the thought away before it brought him a ghost that he had no wish to see. Nevertheless, for an instant, the haunting was there: a whirling, dancing, obsidian-eyed ghost in the white belly skins of winter-killed caribou . . . Navahk . . . smiling his wolfish, carnivorous smile across the bleak, misted miles of time . . .

"You are *dead*, you treacherous, murderous, woman-stealing son of the past!" he shouted at the apparition as he found himself turning around and looking up through the trees into the gathering night. Was he there? Was *Navahk* there . . . in the mists . . . in the gathering clouds of the impending night? "No!"

He felt foolish for having shouted, and then more foolish because there was no mist. But something was moving in the undergrowth somewhere to his right. Whatever it was, it was large enough to make the tops of the shrubs sway and to send the little birds flying again. Torka wheeled. The ghostly vision of Navahk was so real that he hefted a spear and shouted in defiance, "I have seen you die! *Stay* dead! You are not welcome in this land!"

The undergrowth quivered, as if a wave of living shrubbery were moving toward him. He threw a spear. Hard.

Something yipped. The wave reversed itself, and now, through the gloom of twilight, Torka saw a tattered pyramid of grizzled fur moving atop the scrub growth, through it, away from him.

"*Aar!* Come back, Brother! Let me see what harm I have done to you!"

Although Torka called and called, the dog did not come back. Torka followed and retrieved his spear. To his relief he found no blood on the shaft, spearhead, ground, or shrubs. The dog's tracks were headed up the gorge, and two sets of smaller tracks were running alongside him.

Torka paused in the thickening dark and smiled. He sensed that the dog was watching him from the heights. With his spears in his hands, he raised his arms in salutation as he called: "Brother Dog! May you forgive a foolish man his moment of fearful impetuosity! Torka promises that there will always be a warm place at his fire for Aar and his females. *Always!*"

Night found Torka within the gorge. It was dark, very dark. He knew that it would be a while before moonrise allowed him to move on in safety. He seated himself with his back to the canyon wall. With his spears across his lap, he ate a wedge of fat and several slivers of dried meat before drifting off to sleep. Then he slept briefly, and not so deeply that he could not instantly wake up from the shallows of unconsciousness should danger threaten. When dogs began to howl high above him on the ridge he woke. The moon was up and full, so the gorge was bathed in cold blue light that was nearly as bright as day. Fully rested, Torka rose and walked on.

It was not quite dawn when he left the gorge and entered the broad, heavily forested alluvial hills that fanned downward toward the broad, rolling valley floor. The scent of mammoth was heavy in the air. Torka walked cautiously past a small herd of cows and calves. Then, cresting a heavily treed rise, he came to a clearing and found himself face to face with the Life Giver.

Squinting against the glare of dawn, Torka stopped dead. The mammoth stood so close that had Torka extended his arm, he could have touched the tips of its tusks. The animal towered above him. Eighteen feet tall at the shoulder, when it raised its twin-domed, shaggy head and lifted its hairy trunk, the earth shook beneath Torka's feet. Gasping in awe, he took an involuntary step back.

He had seen what death and destruction this animal

could deal. Since time beyond beginning, surely no mammoth had ever been larger, more cunning, or more deadly. But long ago a mystical covenant had been made between these two, so Torka respectfully stood his ground before the mammoth. Slowly, the great mammoth extended its trunk. Slowly, Torka extended his free hand. They touched. The moment was magic. Man and beast were one.

Without a sound, the mammoth turned and walked away. Without a word, Torka followed into the foothills where his people watched his approach from the cave.

When he entered the encampment, his heart was full and his blood was singing. As long as Life Giver walked ahead of him, his path would be the right path, for his woman, his children, his people, and himself.

"Where is Karana?" Summer Moon asked before Mahnie could speak.

"He will come soon. He seeks the magic . . . for us all," he told her, striding purposefully past her to his fire circle to embrace Lonit. As Torka held her, Umak smiled up at him in welcome, displaying teeth as white and even and serrated as Navahk's. The headman's mood went dark, and for the second time he was almost overcome by the knowledge that this boy might not be his son after all, but the spawn of Lonit's rape by Navahk.

Far away, Karana stood upon the heights and stared into the dawn. Aar was at his side. Two thin, leggy female dogs sat watching their big, grizzled, one-eared master of the pack in absolute puzzlement as he stood beside the man.

Karana barely noticed the dogs; he was transfixed by the sight of Torka walking into the sunrise with the mammoth. Their contact should have made him smile, for he could have asked for no better omen for his people.

Instead his spirit was dark, because last night, before the moon had risen, he had watched the stars and had known in his heart that the red star would return, the black moon would rise again . . . and in its shadow Manaravak would return to his people. Would he be as a man or a beast? And would Karana's half-human sister walk at his side?

What did it matter? Karana would keep watch. He would be ready for them lest Torka learn the truth of his betrayal. He would kill them both, as surely as he would have killed his own son. What else could he do?

PART VI

SUN OF ANGRY SKY

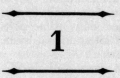

1

Many moons rose and set over the Place of Endless Meat. Two long, bitter winters and brief, cherished summers came and passed away, but still Cheanah had not fulfilled his promise to kill the white lion. He made excuses for himself: "It is a ghost lion. A man cannot kill a spirit."

Alone with him now outside the headman's pit hut, Mano eyed his father with thinly veiled contempt. "Long ago, Navahk killed the wanawut and danced in its skin. Surely if Cheanah wanted to, he could kill a lion, even if it *is* a ghost."

Cheanah glowered at his son. Mano's watchful avariciousness put him on edge. "Navahk was a magic man!" he defended himself hotly.

"He was also headman of his band."

As *I* am headman of *this* band!" Cheanah reminded him, furious at his son's obviously intended insolence. "Never forget that! *Never!*"

"I will not forget," replied Mano. "The question is: Do you always remember?"

In the autumn days that followed, Cheanah led his hunters and sons to stalk and kill with a wanton abandon that allowed Mano no doubt as to who was leading the band. Cheanah was a brave hunter and superlative tracker. Any animal that left so much as a hoof or paw print, a mound of scat, or an indentation in the grass or scrub growth was hunted and killed. Small or large, all were game to Cheanah and his hunters.

Soon the encampment was well stocked with meat and hides and the women were exhausted from overwork. Although their men still hunted, the women saw no cause to prepare the meat of their kills for storage. They took no sinew. They fleshed only prime pelts and ate only of tongue and eye, of intestine and haunch and hump. The rest was left for carrion.

By the first frost, game had already begun to become noticeably scarce in the once meat-rich hunting grounds. When winter came, the people were fat and ready to settle into camp. They feasted throughout the time of the long dark, confident that the great migratory herds of caribou, bison, and elk would return with the sun.

But this year the winter was colder and longer than any in memory. Food grew scarce. Babies wailed as their mothers' milk began to wane. The people grew thin and fearful as predators prowled close to the encampment. Wolves, wild dogs, and the wanawut howled against hunger in the endless, snow-driven dark.

"Do you think that the great mammoth spirit is punishing this band for having eaten of its flesh?" asked Honee. She was immediately sorry that she had asked the question, for Mano reached out and, across the meager fire of Cheanah's pit hut, smacked her across the side of the head so hard that her ears rang.

"That was long ago! *Long ago!*" he shouted. "And mammoth was totem to Torka and his band, not to us!"

Holding her head, Honee cowered in fear of another strike. She was grateful and surprised when Ank, instead of Zhoonali, spoke up in her behalf.

"It was your idea that we carve up the mammoth, Mano! Not the band's! Not even our father's! If the great mammoth spirits are angry, it is all your fault!"

Honee peered through her fingers in time to see Mano snarl and go for the boy, but Cheanah grabbed his eldest son by his long, greasy, unplaited hair and pulled him down hard. "Grown men do not beat boys or batter their sisters unnecessarily, Mano."

Honee looked across the flames to the men's side of the fire pit. Mano's features were twisted and engorged with anger and frustration. Mano frightened her. She wished that there were more women in the camp so that Mano could take one for himself and start his own family instead of sheltering with their father while sharing the women of the other men of the band.

"There is too much tension in the light of this fire . . . in this camp . . . in this people. It is not good, not good at all."

Honee looked up as her grandmother rose. Zhoonali was dwarfed by the high, shadowed tangle of antlers and mammoth bones that formed the arching roof of Cheanah's pit hut. In the flickering light of the central fire, the old woman looked so frail that Honee's heartbeat quickened in fear for her grandmother's life—until Zhoonali stood erect.

"Hear me! Spirits of the wind and storm, take pity on this people! Give to the land the gift of your warmth that is life!"

Zhoonali's prayer was answered. The gift of the sun was given, and the caribou came into the Land of Endless Meat from out of the eastern ranges. The blood of the men was up for hunting, so they did not notice that the herd was smaller than usual.

Cheanah led the way into an area of low hills, ahead of the caribou, where he positioned his fellow hunters on either side of the frozen river. Beneath the ice, the water was shallow; there would be little danger besides the cold if a man broke through. The broken ice would slow the caribou's movement, and the frozen embankments would cause a panicked animal to slip and fall. Those that did manage an escape would be vulnerable to the spears of those hunters positioned on the high ground of the surrounding hills.

The hunters patiently awaited the coming of the caribou to the river crossing. Then they ran. They howled. They yipped like frenzied wild dogs leaping to the kill.

"Enough!" cried Yanehva. "We have killed enough!"

Close at Yanehva's side, Mano laughed out loud. "*Never* can one kill enough!" He left Yanehva behind, spears in check. As Mano plunged forward through the shallows, young Ank raced after him, water and ice sludge spraying all around.

Mano's heart was pounding. His loins were hot; his penis was as hard and erect as his spears. The kill always affected him this way.

He was aware of Ank calling out to him, but he did not wait. Ank was young; he would soon learn that calling a man back from a kill was as futile as asking a man to hold back after an ejaculation had begun! The thought moved his mouth into a twisted smile as he waded deep into the fray.

The river was a boiling mass of men and caribou. Half of it fought for life; the other half fought to take life. Many caribou broke through the ice to become mired up to their chests in the shallows. Calves were drowning and cows were down, unable to rise, as Mano and his companions slogged their way through the bloodied, ice-thickened water, sloshing and stabbing and slashing.

Although buffeted by fear-maddened animals, Mano managed to hold his position. An antler raked his side; the pain was pleasure to him. He threw back his head and howled as he drove a spear deep into the side of a frantic, screaming cow. The animal ran a few steps, ran afoul of a downed calf, and fell forward, with Mano still stabbing. When her head came up out of the water, a section of some other caribou's intestine hung from her antlers.

He drove his spear deep again and again. "Die!" commanded Mano. "*Die!*"

The cow's tongue lolled, and the water was suddenly fouled with her final release.

Beside him, young Ank was stabbing at the same animal. Mano knocked the youth down. Ank fell sideways just as another cow leaped over him.

"Kill your own! This one is mine! And it is already dead!" Ank would sink or swim. Mano did not really care.

It was Yanehva who lunged through the morass of dead or dying caribou to save the boy. Mano cast a glance their way, then returned to the massacring until the strength was gone from his arms and he could find neither the energy nor the resolve to lift another spear.

By then the few surviving animals of the herd were

gone across the snow-covered hills. If the exhausted hunters were puzzled—in the past the herd was so large that it took many days to cross the land—they gave no thought to their puzzlement. They caught their breath and began to drag carcass after carcass onto the frozen embankment.

"You would have let the boy drown!" Yanehva accused Mano as the three brothers sat dripping beside Cheanah.

"You are too much the worrisome woman, Yanehva," Cheanah criticized.

"Ank was unconscious when I pulled him up!"

"Now, Brother, don't make so much of nothing!" Mano countered lightly.

The women and children arrived at the butchering site, but no butchering was done. They feasted instead. They ate until they could eat no more, and still more than half the number of slain animals had not been touched.

"We will never be able to eat them all," observed Ekoh with a thoughtful frown.

"We will eat the best parts!" Old Teean smacked his lips and sucked bits of raw tissue through his few remaining teeth.

"And store the rest." Ekoh nodded at the prospect.

"This woman will not skin all these caribou!" Kimm frowned darkly at Bili's man.

"We will take only the best skins and bring only the best meat back to camp!" proclaimed Cheanah, popping another eyeball into his mouth.

The people belched and dozed and cut wind, and then awoke to relieve themselves and to eat and rest again. When animals were heard howling and roaring in the distances of the night, they howled and roared back, and the hunters raised their spears and shook them at the sky.

"Listen," said Ank with trepidation. "Wolves and dogs have smelled our kill. Lions, too."

"Lions . . ." Cheanah tasted the word as if it were meat.

"And the wanawut," added Teean. "Did you hear it?"

Mano backhanded juices from his mouth. "Let them howl! I do not fear them. Mano's spears are sharper than their teeth!"

Cheanah looked at his son out of weary, sleep-bleary

eyes. "You boast too much. The life spirits of the animals you mock may take offense."

Mano forced up a belch and expelled it in Cheanah's direction.

The night was growing deep and cold. The women raised a fire. It was not a time for talk. The people slept on the bloodied earth, beneath the star-strewn, moonless sky. Only the hunter Ekoh lay awake with his woman, Bili, in the fold of his arm. She was pregnant again. By Cheanah—*again!* Ekoh's mouth turned down into a scowl of loathing and frustration.

The wanawut hunted with her young in the fading night. As always, her two cubs were well ahead of her—the female trailing the much smaller but bolder and fleeter beastling. She sighed and limped after them. When they found the game, she would help to kill it. A tremor of doubt passed through her. Her back continued to ache, and her shoulders felt hot and stiff. The thigh muscles of her lion-mauled limb had long since atrophied, shortening her leg and impairing her effectiveness as a predator. It was this that had forced her to remain in the hunting territory of man, where she and her young came to feed— and to depend upon the leftovers of the beasts.

She paused again, sniffing the wind as the fingers of her right hand curled around her man stone. Even with the aid of her dagger she knew she was no longer physically able to contest with other large carnivores for meat; she must be the first to reach a killing site or abandon all hope of a meal. Never could she risk a confrontation with the beasts and their throwing sticks. So it was that when she had led the cubs down from the cave, she turned away from the killing site and followed the surviving caribou. Some of the fleeing animals were injured; she had caught the scent of their fear and blood upon the wind. They would be easy to kill.

She went on again, certain that before the sun was up she and her cubs would eat well for the first time in longer than she could remember. With a sigh, the wanawut quickened her steps. She was growing old and slow, but her cubs had need of her still.

*   *   *

Mano awoke with the dawn and lay on his back in his bloodied stalking cloak. It was frozen as stiff with caked blood as the oiled exterior layering of his thigh-high boots. When he sat up, he could hear the cracking of the thin layer of ice that sheened his outer garments. He was warm within his thick, multilayered clothing, but his breath formed a cloud before his face and crystallized upon his stubby eyebrows and the sparse strands of brittle hair that he had neglected to pluck from his upper lip. It was not considered attractive for a man to have hair upon his face, but there were no women worth impressing since Cheanah had stopped allowing him to use Bili.

Mano was glad that Bili was pregnant again; now neither Ekoh nor Cheanah could use her. He had heard Cheanah mutter regretfully to himself about the loss of Torka's women. It was one of the few things that Mano had in common with his father. Mano could hear Ram and Kivan moving on their women. The sound stirred him. He looked around. Yes. The hunters had all moved to lie beside their women. Only Kimm, the children, and the old ones slept alone.

He rose, rubbing his gloved hands together. Stepping across the sleeping and mating forms of his people, he lamented his options. His father's second woman was the best he could hope for at the moment because Cheanah was joined with Xhan. He gave Kimm a sharp kick in her broad backside.

With a startled yelp, she rolled over and looked up, groaning when she saw who it was. Then she rolled onto her side again, pulling her sleeping skin over her head.

He kicked her again, hard, bent, and pulled away her carelessly groomed sleeping skin.

"Go away," she protested, but even as she spoke, she was arching her hips and reaching under her tunic to loosen her trousers.

"Roll over. On your belly," he commanded.

She complied.

Impatiently, he knelt and straddled her. Despite the long, hungry winter, Kimm was still plump. In the softly textured light of dawn, the two mounds of her buttocks shone up at him like twin moons cratered with fat. It was not a pretty sight, but it was the accepting end of a woman, and he came down on it eagerly, forcing penetration, ramming deep, pumping hard and fast, releasing quickly, and then moving slowly for a while until the last of his need was gone. Kimm was asleep before he was finished.

Disgusted, he withdrew and sat back, vexed to find that his sister Honee had been sleeping close to Kimm's back. The girl's small, closely set eyes were staring at him hatefully from beneath the soft, wind-rippled furs of her badger-skin hood.

"Except for hunting, is that all that you men know how to do?"

He snarled at her. "Be quiet, you ugly thing, or do you want me to give you some of what I have just given to your mother?"

"What makes you think I want you? Pound, pound. Quick, quick. That is what the women say of Mano."

The girl knew when to move in a hurry. She was up and away and settled safely in the dawn shadow of Zhoonali's sleeping form before Mano could make a grab for her.

He sat staring after her, despising her and wanting to hurt her, until he heard lions roar nearby.

Cheanah rose from where he lay with Xhan. Mano watched as the headman stood still, listening. The great cats sounded the deep, resonant growls of discontent as they prowled ever closer to the butchering site.

Mano went to Cheanah. "I would like to kill something this morning. Lions would do."

From somewhere in the darkness across the river, the wanawut howled in the hills above the frozen marsh country. The roar of a lion answered. They knew it was a big lion from the way its roar seemed to echo within its chest before it was released as a sound to rival thunder.

"Perhaps a white lion . . ." Speculation, not fear, colored Cheanah's voice, but there was hesitancy in it.

It did not pass Mano unheard. "Yes," he replied, eyeing his father. The speculation in his own voice had nothing to do with lions. "Perhaps it is time for Cheanah to take his white lion . . . if he can."

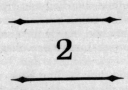

2

It was quiet in the twisting gully between the hills. The exhausted caribou milled restlessly, fetlock deep in a thick, rolling ground fog. They had heard the roaring of the lion, and it kept them alert, moving, heads up, ears and tails twitching.

The beastling crouched low. He listened for another roar to reverberate through the hills. None came. Nor was there a scent of lion. Sister was across the gully from him; he could just see the top of her head above the curve of the hill. Mother had moved to the canyon's head.

Now, for the first time, the caribou caught her scent. The heads of several cows went up. A *yuk-yuk-yuk* came from their throats. Clouds of vapor condensed above their muzzles as they began to circle.

The beastling looked on expectantly as Mother showed herself and raised her arms wide. She shook her fists and her man stone at the sky. She shrieked. The sound was a terrible thing to hear, but her visage was even more terrifying. The beastling's heart swelled with pride. Every movement hurt her, yet still she hunted for her cubs. How brave she was! How he loved her!

Today, with Sister to help him, he would try to make her see that she need not hunt at all. Her cubs were not fully grown, but thanks to her teaching they could provide for her as well as for themselves.

She shrieked again, and as he had been taught to do, the beastling shrieked back at her. Sister did the same, then followed the beastling's lead as he stood tall upon the hilltop, waving his arms and pounding at the sky with his fists. He gave his best imitation of the behavior and scream of a wanawut and then, howling and yipping at the top of his lungs, he raced downhill toward the startled caribou.

The herd scattered and ran. Mother stood directly ahead of them as the two screaming cubs advanced from the hills on either side. The panicked caribou turned back toward the neck of the little canyon. In the narrow gully, the turn was impossible for all but a few animals. Frenzied cows overran each other, and calves were hopelessly trampled, their bodies disappearing into the ground fog. Mother and Sister leaped upon them and began to feed.

The beastling, however, stood his ground, attracted to a fine, fleet-footed cow that raced ahead of the others. He stood poised on the hillside, ready to jump down as the cow ran under him. And then, with a shriek of delight, he was in the air. He was yipping and howling as he landed on her back. He grabbed her antlers and, straddling her, held on for his life.

As her panicked eyes bulged round and her nostrils flared and snorted in fright, she leaped and bucked and twisted, trying desperately to be free of him. With the wind in his hair and the saliva of the frenzied animal blowing back like warm snow against his face, he rode the fear-maddened caribou as she galloped out of the gully and back onto the open steppe. She ran on and on, full-out, with her heart pounding against her heaving ribs and her body as hot and wet as blood against his inner thighs. His head was filled with the thundering sound of the caribou's hooves.

Then, with no warning, she fell over, dead. The beastling, shocked, fell with her. The caribou was on her side, on top of him . . . and on top of the caribou was something big, growling and snarling ferociously as it grappled at the body of the dead cow with massive paws.

Blood ran into the beastling's eyes, but not before he glimpsed the color of those paws. Pale fur grew like soiled, blood-splotched grass around the enormous pads and claws of the white lion.

*   *   *

"Look! There in the mists ahead of us! There is the lion you seek!"

Mano and Cheanah had been brought to pause by the sight of a large caribou racing out of the hills ahead of them. The animal seemed to have something on its back, but distance made it impossible to say what it was. Nevertheless, when the caribou suddenly collapsed onto its side, neither Mano nor Cheanah failed to see the blur of white that suddenly leaped up out of the fog to fall upon it.

"The white lion . . ." Cheanah seemed to grow taller as he exhaled the words with the fire of pure intent. Then, without another word, he moved forward with a long, sure stride.

Mano, running beside him, was soon breathless. "The wind is in our favor, and the lion will not see us until we are within striking distance. No need to hurry."

Cheanah scowled as he ran. "I've waited too long to make this kill."

But as he and Mano closed on their prey, another form materialized out of the mists. Waist-deep in ground fog, it was big and gray. The way it ran upright on its hind legs was grotesquely human as it pounded, screaming, toward the lion and caribou.

"By the forces of Creation, what is *that*?" Mano's face revealed fear, revulsion, and horrified fascination as he stopped beside his father and stared ahead.

"Wind spirit . . . wanawut . . ." Cheanah trembled against frustration.

The white lion took one look over its shoulder and saw what was coming toward it, and instead of being driven away, it turned and faced its adversary. It lowered its great, pale, battle-scarred head and roared a warning, but the wanawut kept on coming. Cheanah and Mano saw the lion reach out and rake a broad, ripping swipe across the wanawut's face before leaping high and disappearing into the fog—but not before the wanawut's claws found its flank.

Cheanah cursed. The lion was gone. The wind spirit had driven it off, and perhaps mortally wounded it.

Mano raised a spear.

"Hold!" commanded Cheanah sharply, but it was too late.

Mano's spear struck the wanawut's shoulder, then fell, to disappear into the fog. The wanawut turned her gaze from the spear to the hunter who had thrown it. A broad set of bleeding tracks was laid by the lion across her hideous snout, and her left hand gripped her right shoulder. Blood oozed between her huge, furred fingers. She stared at the blood, her long, wide mouth working with anger and her lips lifting to bare teeth. She warned them back with a high, menacing screech, then she bent over the caribou carcass.

Mano spoke softly to his father, his eyes never wavering from the beast. "We could kill it. If we both ran forward now, if we both hurled our spears now before it could run away . . . Think of it! What would our people say to such a kill, eh? Better than a white lion, yes?"

"No! Men may not raise their spears against spirits."

Mano barked a harsh laugh. "Did you not see it bleed? It is no spirit."

Before Cheanah could stop him, Mano levered a spear, ran a few steps, and hurled the lance as hard as he could. He shouted in triumph as, to Cheanah's amazement, his spearhead buried itself in the upper back of the wanawut. The creature screamed and arched sharply backward. To their shock, she straightened again, reached behind her, and when she failed to pull the spear from her back, snapped the haft in two. With a hand's span of shaft still protruding from her shoulder, she turned and threw the remainder of the spear back at Mano.

With no projectile point to hold it on course, it went wide.

The two hunters were poised to run, but the wanawut did not move. She stood stiffly, obviously in agony. Then, slowly, she bent and reached down into the ground fog, where the antlers of the caribou showed above the mist. As Cheanah and Mano watched in disbelief, the wanawut lifted the carcass of the caribou, held it high above her head; then advanced on the men. Howling her rage, she hurled the limp, bleeding, lion-mauled body at them as though the thing weighed no more than an empty bladder bag.

It came at them so fast and so hard that Cheanah and Mano had no time to duck before it knocked them flat. One of the points of the antlers hooked under the left corner of Mano's mouth as he fell; when his head snapped to the right, he felt it tear his lip. He tasted blood through dizziness, anger, and fear. Beside him, Cheanah worked desperately to scramble free of the carcass. As he scuttled away on all fours, then began to run, he called back for Mano to follow before the wanawut fell upon him.

The young man's face twisted with resentment as he realized that his father had left him to fend for himself. He was on his feet and running now, touching his torn mouth with tentative fingers. His cheek lay open halfway to his ear; he would be scarred for life. And even though it would be a scar to boast about because he had won it in a contest with the wanawut, it would also be a reminder that when his life was in danger, his father had run off and left him.

But Cheanah had circled back through the rising fog, spears in hand, and stopped beside his son. "Look! We will be all right now. The wanawut runs into the hills. And it is not alone."

Holding his torn cheek, Mano glowered across the distance, where another, smaller, wind spirit ran at the side of the older one, arm in arm, leaning close, as though supporting the weight of the larger, wounded beast. Behind them ran a still smaller creature.

As the threesome disappeared into the distance, Cheanah frowned. "Did you see the black-haired one? I have never seen anything like it! When _ looked back, I saw the wanawut draw the black-haired one out of the mists, then check it for injuries. The littler cub must have been under the fallen caribou, and when the wanawut came out of the fog to attack the white lion, it was risking itself to save the life of its cub."

"Impossible." Mano measured his father with open contempt. "They are beasts. You are a man. And that is more than you were willing to do for me."

*   *   *

Mother was dying.

The beastling knelt at her side. Behind him, Sister whined pathetically as she circled within the cave. The beastling wished that she would stop; the scuffing sound of her feet annoyed him. Her whines, rapidly repeated high-pitched sounds, recalled the fear-choked peeps that cornered birds made just before he killed them. He did not want to think of death; just thinking of it seemed to bring it near.

Mother sighed. There was much pain in the sound. He signaled for Sister to be quiet and come to Mother's side, but although she clamped her mouth shut, Sister kept on circling and would not come. She deliberately kept her eyes on her feet. Anger rose in him; almost immediately it was cooled by pity. He had long since accepted the fact that Sister did not think as he thought. She was so easily confused and frightened.

Mother was lying on her side in a lake of blood. The long, gaping slashes in her face and arm were oozing. Blood bubbled from the corner of her mouth, as well as from the hole in her upper back where the broken bone protruded. He stroked her gently, so his touch roused no pain. Her skin rippled beneath his palm. Her eyes were on him—her beautiful mist-gray eyes, which were usually like the cool, clouded heights of the mountain that he loved so much. He cocked his head. There was nothing cool about them now. They were hot, glazed over, and pink with fever. As he watched, the gray suddenly became a narrowing ring around an expanding center. His own eyes went wide. The black center frightened him. It seemed to be opening inward into . . . what? He caught his breath. What had he seen within Mother's eyes? Emptiness. A terrible, black, and appalling emptiness, as though Mother was not within her body anymore—as though her skin and bones and fur were nothing more than a lifeless hide surrounding nothing . . . nothing at all.

She blinked. The black center of her eyes collapsed, and she stared directly at the beastling from out of the misted gray that he knew and loved. He sighed with relief. Mother was back inside her skin again. Her mouth opened. No sound came from it except the low, constant bubbling of blood that was welling from somewhere deep within her chest. Slowly, with great effort, she raised her hand. She still held her man stone. Her fingers opened, and the long, lanceolate dagger fell into the beastling's lap.

"Mah . . . nah . . . rah . . . vak . . ." Mother sighed, and there was so much pain in the sound of her voice that even though her hand dropped so heavily onto his shoulder that she came close to breaking it, he felt no pain except that which he shared with her.

"Mah . . . nah . . . rah . . . vak," he echoed, not really knowing why. He watched the grayness bleed out of Mother's eyes as her life ran out of her body along with her blood and breath.

He touched her, but she did not move. Her jaw hung lax, her tongue lolled, her eyes were open and empty and devoid of color. He shoved her. Yet even as he shoved, he knew that it was useless. Mother was dead, never to care for her cubs again.

Stunned, he sat staring, listening to Sister's whining and shuffling. The sounds were soothing to him now. Mother was gone, but Sister was still with him. He was not alone. As he looked at the man stone, he thought of the white lion and of the beasts and their throwing sticks. They had killed Mother. Now he would kill them.

His heart filled with hate—and with something even more bitter, self-recrimination and regret. It was his impetuosity that had led her to her death! If only he had not yielded to the impulse that had driven him to chase down his own kill, Mother would not have been forced to come to his rescue! She would still be alive. He looked down at her and touched her beloved face. The pain that welled within him was so pure and intense that he felt as though he would die of it.

Sister came to stand beside him. He knew from her blank expression that she did not understand that Mother was dead. He wondered if she would ever understand. He sighed as she seated herself beside him. She pressed close, seeking comfort in his warmth and nearness as she smiled at him. For the first time in his life, the twisted, upside-down smile of the wanawut came easily to his lips.

He wondered why his eyes were filling with a strange, burning liquid. It welled beneath his lids and ran down his cheeks, and suddenly he was sobbing as Sister frowned in worried puzzlement and drew her fingers across his face, then lifted them to her mouth to taste something that was unknown to the wanawut—or to any other beast. His tears . . . his fully human tears.

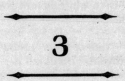

3

They tracked the white lion until the day was done.

"I tell you, it *is* a ghost lion," fumed Cheanah, for although the animal was wounded, it went on and on. Now, with night descending and the fog growing thicker, they lost it completely. They stopped in high hills at the base of a cloud-shrouded mountain. A fine, icy mist was beginning to rain.

Mano knelt, examined the stony ground, then rose and looked up, tense and eager. "Do you smell it?"

Cheanah scowled. "I smell no lion."

"No! It is the stink of the wanawut! It has gone there, up onto the mountain. We could follow."

"Follow a wind spirit into the clouds?"

"Why not? It has left us a trail of blood. Look, on the rocks at your feet. It is not from the surface wound of the lion. It is dark and thick. The thing has gone up onto the mountain to die. We could kill it and its young."

Cheanah scanned the heights with jaundiced eyes. Despite his swollen, sinew-sutured cheek, Mano's voice had been strong with the boundless enthusiasm of youth. It made Cheanah feel old and resentful. He had looked down upon the beast with his own eyes. He had no desire to confront such a monstrous thing again.

"It is time to go back. Soon the wind will rise and bring snow," he portended with the ease of one who speaks from a lifetime of experience.

Mano stared up at the misted heights. "Imagine what our people would say if you came back to them walking in

311

its skin, and I wore its teeth and claws around my neck and the pelts of its young across my back! That would be better than that elusive white lion of yours."

"It is not my lion."

"Apparently not."

Cheanah felt the sting of Mano's rebuke. His head went up as his eyes narrowed. "I *will* kill it."

"The wanawut may already have done that for you."

Cheanah frowned, wondering if other men disliked their sons as much as he disliked Mano. A sudden gust of wind swayed him on his feet, and the night was split by a heartrending wailing.

"It is one of the cubs that howls!" said Mano. "The adult must be dead! I *did* kill it!"

"Zhoonali would be proud to see her son Cheanah come back to camp in the skin of the wanawut. . . ."

Mano's eyes glittered. "It would even be better than a white lion. But if the wanawut is dead, *I* am the one who has killed it."

Cheanah did not appreciate the reminder. "And I am headman of our band! The skin is mine! You can take the pelts of the cubs!"

Mano agreed, then added quickly: "But only if I have your word that I can lie on any woman—including Bili— whenever I want, in return for my word to Zhoonali and the band that it was Cheanah's spear and not my own that killed the beast."

Cheanah's mouth turned down. His eldest son was as quick and as avaricious as a wolverine. "I should put my spear through your belly and leave you here for carrion," he growled. "Bili is nothing to me. When this night is over and the day that follows is done, if we return to the encampment with the skin of the wanawut, you may use her and any female of the band as you like."

Far away across the Forbidden Land, Umak awoke with a start. He sat upright and stared wide-eyed straight ahead into the darkness of the cave. His mouth was dry, his gut was tight, and his heart was pounding.

"What is it?" asked Dak, sitting up sleepily beside him on the bed skins that the two youths shared.

Umak shook his head. "A dream."

"Go back to sleep, then. Torka and Simu said that they would have us up before dawn so that—" He stopped. Umak was up and moving through the darkness toward the hide weather baffles that hung across the entrance to the cave.

As Dak squinted through the dark, he saw Umak sweep the weather baffle aside and stand naked against the starlight; he was panting, as if he had just run a race. Concerned, Dak rose, bundled his sleeping robe around himself, and went to stand beside his friend.

"What's wrong?" he pressed again, his voice very low.

"The dream . . . it was so real," Umak whispered.

He turned and looked at Dak. There were tears in his eyes as he confided softly: "If someone you loved died— your father . . . your *mother*—only then would you be as sad as I feel now."

"The dream's over. Now come back to sleep."

Umak took hold of Dak's sleeping robe. "Do you ever dream that you are someone else?"

Dak thought, then nodded. "Sometimes I dream that I am a hunter like my father, strong and bold and—"

"No. Someone *else*. And yourself at the same time. As though there were two Daks inside your body."

Dak felt a cold tide rush through him; the thought was unnerving. "No. Never."

"I do sometimes." Umak sighed. "And tonight I know that there is danger for him. I felt it, along with the sadness."

"*Him?*"

"My . . . my brother."

"Your brother is dead."

"Yes, but in my dreams I see him walking in mist, somewhere high. He is a boy like me, but he is dirty, wearing torn furs, with wild hair and—"

"If I had a brother who died the way yours did, I would dream of him now and again, too. Tell Karana. Magic men know about such things. Now let's get back to sleep before it's time to get up!"

*   *   *

Umak tried to do as his friend had advised. He did not sleep until the first glow of dawn began to shine blue and then pink around the edges of the hide weather baffles. He dozed heavily, to dream of terrible sadness and of imminent danger. In the dream he ran from it behind Dak, trying his best to close the gap between them but failing. Dak, seeming much wilder than in reality, turned back, shook his head, and laughed mockingly: "You will never catch me!"

But Dak was not Dak. He was another boy, a strange boy in tattered furs with unkempt hair and so much of Torka in his face that Umak raged at him: "*I* am the son of Torka!"

"No you are *not*!" cried the strange boy. "*I* am!"

"No!" Umak wept as the boy raced ahead of him into the mists of the dream.

Torka's touch roused him into instant wakefulness. He bolted upright, gasping, backhanding tears from his eyes.

"What is it?" asked Torka, kneeling close.

"Nothing . . ." Umak cried. "It was only a dream."

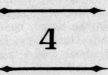

4

The beasts with their throwing sticks were coming, and there was nothing the beastling could do to prevent it. He watched them from the corniced lip of the cave. As he watched, his hatred of them grew in proportion to his fascination. They moved as he moved, erect on long limbs, with their backs nearly straight and their short arms swinging at their sides. Now and again they stopped and looked up. He doubted that they had seen him; he was too far above them, and the projecting lip of the cave entrance concealed him.

Sister came and knelt beside him. Leaning forward, she stared down the wall. When she saw the beasts she exhaled in worried confusion. Her brow furrowed so tightly that her little gray eyes almost disappeared. She looked at him as if expecting him to drive the beasts away. When he did not, she pounded her chest and screeched, then went back into the cave, bent and hooted over Mother's body, and poked her shoulder. Mother did not move.

He watched, wishing that he could make her understand that her circling, hooting, and poking were wasted on Mother. If the beasts were going to be turned back, Sister and he would have to be the ones to do it.

He went to gather fistfuls of pebbles and bits of refuse and began to throw these down at the ascending intruders. He thought that he had won the day. They paused and clung to the mountain, but in a moment they were climbing again. He hastily gathered bits of soiled nest grass, fecal matter, and discarded bones, but by the time he threw the refuse over the edge, the beasts were under the cornice, and the refuse fell harmlessly over them. Soon they would achieve their goal.

Panic grew within him. He looked back at Sister. She was so much bigger than he was, and her claws and fangs were weapons to envy. But Sister was no fighter. They would kill her and eat what they wanted of her, and he would be unable to stop them because they would kill him and eat him, too.

He growled deep in his throat. There was only one course of action open to him. He took it—but not without regret.

Cheanah and Mano reached the cave and stood with their spears ready, their bodies tensed. But the great gray corpse that lay on its side within the foul, stinking shadows of the interior of the cave presented no threat.

"Where are the cubs?" Cheanah's query was no louder than a whisper, as if he spoke within a sacred place.

"Gone into the mists above. But we need go no farther."

In silence, father and son set aside their spears, drew their skinning knives of stone, and knelt to make the first of many cuts.

All day the beastling and Sister hid within the shadows of the great, sheltering, lichen-clad boulders that lay in tumbled disarray upon the summit of the mountain. Far below something fell along the mountain wall. They heard it thud and roll several times. Stones broke loose wherever it hit, and soon they heard the cascading sound of a rockslide. A beast cried out, then there was silence. The cubs of the wanawut huddled together in the long, bitterly cold night, and although Sister held him close in her thickly furred arms, there was no warmth for the beastling. In his hand he held the man stone that Mother had given him, and in his heart he held the memories of uncounted days and nights of her love—a love that he would never know again.

Sister, restless and hungry, sniffed out a vole at dawn and ate it. He had no appetite, nor would he have until he returned to the cave and saw for himself what the beasts had done.

He knew the contours of the mountain as he had once known the contours of Mother's breasts. Even in the icy fog of daybreak, he led Sister easily, yet he hestitated before entering the cave. The smell of the beasts was strong, as was the smell of something else, which caused the beastling to grit his teeth and clench his fists so hard that the man stone cut his palm. Beside him, Sister made a sound of revulsion, but she did not hesitate to go on ahead. Silence followed her. Then she screeched. Only once.

The beastling drew in a breath to steady himself. He held it as he entered the cave, then exhaled as he stared ahead, so shocked that he could not move. Sister was mewing and whimpering and circling around and around in a frenzy. Never had he seen her so distraught, but then, never had he been as sickened and appalled as he was now. He stared past her at entrails and meat and piles of bloody, broken bones, all that was left of Mother.

They had opened and gutted her. They had skinned her and left her head and her hollowed-out arms and limbs intact. With these still attached to her hide, they had thrown the empty casing of her body down from the cave to save themselves the trouble of carrying it. That was the sound that he had heard! He forced himself to stare at the leavings of their desecration. He could not understand why the beasts would leave meat and take skin . . . the long, loving arms that had once held him . . . the breasts that had nurtured him. . . .

He could not bear it. He turned and went to the edge of the cave and howled in anguish. He howled and howled until, from out of the vastness of the world below, wolves howled back at him as though they recognized his pain and wished to ease it. He did not know when his keening became an ululation, or when his ululation became a song of perfect, albeit grief-torn lyric beauty. He only knew that he was in agony and that somehow the song allowed a release of pain.

Sister came to him. He saw a blank yet questioning look in her eyes and knew that she was afraid. She could not

understand the sounds that came from his mouth, compre-
hend why hot liquid was welling in his eyes and running
down his cheeks, or know why, as he drew her into a
brother's loving embrace, his body was wracked with con-
vulsive sobs.

He held her close. Comforted, her arms went around
him and hugged him tightly. When he hugged her back,
her eyes cleared and she began to purr softly. He knew
that his love was enough for her, but it was not enough for
him. Sister was a wanawut, and the beastling was beginning to understand that he was something less than that—
undefined, unfinished, and unable to take the world on its
own terms. Why was he so different? What was he? *Who*
was he?

And how would he and Sister survive in this world of
beasts without Mother?

Hatred congealed within him, thickening in his gut
and nostrils until he felt sick with it. His fingers
curled and uncurled around his man stone. They tightened
and squeezed until pain flared and blood seeped from his
palm. He wanted the pain. He wanted to leave a scar that
would be so deep that he could never forget. From this
moment on, whenever he looked at his palm he would
recall the agony.

With a start, he remembered the throwing sticks the
beasts had thrown at Mother. One had cut her arm and
then gone wide and disappeared into the fog. It must still
be there . . . as the white lion must still be there, weakened by its wounds. With his man stone and a throwing
stick he could kill the lion and skin it, as the beasts had
skinned Mother. And armed with his man stone and a
throwing stick, he could kill the beasts who had killed
Mother. Yes!

But first Sister and he would have to find another shelter, for the beasts had seen them flee with Mother and
had heard Sister screech at them as they had climbed the
mountain. Someday, when the mood was on them to hunt
wanawut once again, they would return to the cave.

At length Sister slept, and the fetid fog of his hatred
thinned into a clear, heady thing that filled him with
energy of pure purpose. While Sister slept peacefully on

the ledge, he rose and went down from the cave. He knew
that when she awoke, she would not go from the mountain
alone. Although he walked alone into the savage Arctic
night with his man stone in hand, he was not afraid. Soon
he would come back to Sister—with a throwing stick in his
hand and the skin of the white lion on his back.

5

The days of endless light poured out across the world. Life was good in the wonderful valley, full of the sounds of the newly born and of the laughter of the women and children of Torka's band.

Great flocks of birds nested in the wetlands around the lakes, streams, and rivers. Long-legged cranes and herons stepped high through the marshes. Phalaropes pirouetted in the shallows, beaks stirring the water into their favorite soup of crustaceans and larvae. A thousand ponds mirrored the reflections of loons and other waterfowl. To Lonit's delight, in the lake that was closest to Torka's cave a pair of black swans swam elegantly side by side, ahead of graceful wakes.

Once again the cave was stacked high with winter provisions. Once again the caches were full. Once again ribbons of meat, fish, and fowl hung like banners from the drying frames. Once again while the men and boys stood by and watched with infinite pleasure, the women and girls picked blossoms, festooning their braids and weaving browbands and necklaces and wristlets of riotous, sweet-smelling color.

With Aar at his side, Karana observed them from the ridge. He squinted across the distances.

Naya was walking and talking now. He could just make out her form in the valley far below—one of a trio of tiny flower-bedecked toddlers being supervised by the women and girls as they romped happily amid the flowers with the many pups that had been born to Aar and his two leggy mates.

Karana was lonely, and it was always cold on the mountain, but it was better that he stay on the heights and dwell in the small shelter of hides he had erected on the ridge.

It occurred to Karana that he was already living as an outcast and thus need not worry about Torka's banishing him from the band should his betrayal become known.

Karana frowned. Someone was coming up the canyon. He tensed, listening to the footfalls. They were slow and plodding, but they were also strong and true. It took no magic for Karana to know that Grek would soon stand before him.

Karana did not like the expression on the old man's face. "Speak."

"I come to talk two talks. The first is for Mahnie. Too long she is without a man. She does not eat or sleep as she should. She longs for you."

"I am a magic man."

"So? Where is the magic?" The old man's face was set. There was anger in it. "You must come down into the valley."

"I cannot."

Grek shook his head, then shrugged. "The spirit of a man may be dead in you here on your mountain, Karana. But life goes on. Down in the valley, Wallah and I grow old. Mahnie grieves. Simu and Eneela, Torka and Lonit, they make new babies. Children grow. Boys become men. And that brings me to my second reason for coming here to talk to you: Summer Moon will soon become a woman. Preparations must be made. There are things that must be attended to . . . things that only a magic man may do."

6

"I do not like the way Mano looks at me," Bili complained to Ekoh.

"He can look at you any way he likes, but as long as there is a baby in your belly, he will stay away, as will Cheanah."

"Like a pair of foxes—watching, waiting . . ."

Her head went up. Her nostrils flared. "You can tell them *no*!"

"I can tell them *nothing*!"

"Why?"

"Because one is headman, with the head of a wanawut over the entrance to his hut and the skin of the beast upon his back. The other is the headman's son! Tradition demands that I must say yes to whatever they ask."

"Tradition . . ." She sighed the word as if she could not bear its weight. "I only know that you must be careful, Ekoh, because once this baby is born, between Cheanah and Mano and the rest of the men of this band, you may soon have no woman left to share!"

His face became so congested with anger that for a moment Bili was certain that he was going to strike her. Instead, he pulled her close and held her tightly. "I wish we had gone into the Forbidden Land with Man of the West!"

"So do I," whispered Bili, and buried her face in his chest. "Oh, so do I!" For a moment, but only for a moment, she considered telling him her secret—that she had stuffed old skins beneath her tunic so that she would look pregnant and thus keep the "foxes" at bay. But she kept silent. This secret was hers alone. But how many moons could rise and set before someone noticed that this "baby" had been growing far too long?

Old Teean was busy following Honee as she carried fresh water to the headman's pit hut from the stream beyond the encampment.

"Go away," the girl told him.

He smiled an old man's ruined smile. "Why be in such a hurry to return to your hut? Wait . . ." He kept after her, displaying his old penis. "Look what I have just for you!"

She paused and stared at what he offered while those members of the band who were lounging out of the wind beside their pit huts looked on with open amusement.

"That is not a pretty sight!" Honee informed Teean. "Put it away, old man. No matter what you say or do, you will not be first with me!"

"In a band with no magic man to perform the rite of first piercing, some man must be first," he reminded her. "Cheanah has not said no to me!"

Her face flushed red. "He has not said yes, either! Zhoonali has said that I may wait as long as it pleases me."

"In a band with so few females, Zhoonali must know that you cannot put off your choice forever!"

"Perhaps just long enough for you to die!" She turned and walked off.

Laughter rose from the watchers. Teean did not care. Sooner or later, he would have his turn with her; all of the men of the band would. No man really wanted to take Honee to his fire circle; she was too homely, too fat, and much too nasty for anyone to want to cohabitate with on a permanent basis. Except old Teean. Her youth stirred him. He had only to think of her fat, tender little breasts, and of her taut, tender little nipples, and of the moist depths of her tight, unpenetrated secret place, and he was ready, his organ up and waving.

But the thought of first piercing made all men hard, and now several men called out to the girl.

"Come to my fire, daughter of Cheanah!" invited Buhl,

clucking his tongue lasciviously. "Come while you are still tight between your thighs. You will not regret it."

"No, come to mine, and afterward you will smile and ask for more!" invited Kivan as his woman came out of the hut of blood and, hands on hips, scowled across the camp at him.

As Teean glared, Ram lowered his head and, moving deftly, caught up with Honee. "Don't save it too long, girl. It may dry up."

Honee snarled and fixed him with black eyes as sharp and shining as obsidian splinters. "You are disgusting! All of you!" she said as, with a disdainful flourish, she walked on and disappeared inside her father's pit hut.

Aroused by the sight of her backside, Teean worked himself.

"Don't waste it, old man," cautioned Ram. "You may not have enough strength left to enjoy it when your turn comes!"

"My strength would surprise you . . . and her!" Teean worked himself to quick climax. When he was finished, he made a deliberate show of sighing, shivering, and shaking himself. Then he took his time sauntering to his own pit hut, where he seated himself next to old Frahn, out of the wind.

She was not moving. The sinew that she had been twisting and stretching into cord lay in her lap looped around her lax hands.

Teean picked a blackfly from his ear with his little finger, then leaned against his backrest and talked to Frahn about the advantages of having a young woman to help her with her workload. He droned on, justifying his hope of winning Honee.

After a while Frahn's lack of response caused him to realize that she was either asleep or dead. He looked closer. He winced—it had been a long time since Frahn had been a reasonable-looking woman. But now, as she leaned against her lichen-stuffed backrest, stiffening in her summer furs, she was not at all good to look upon. Her life spirit must have left her body hours ago.

Amazed, he stared at her. He had never really liked Frahn. If she had pleased him at all, it was because she had been a hard worker with a creative and insatiable appetite for coupling. Now that she had apparently breathed her last, Teean smiled.

"You have lived long enough," he told her, leaning forward and putting a resounding kiss on her brow. Frahn had just made Teean a man with no woman in a band where all mature females were spoken for. If Teean asked for Honee now, Cheanah would have to give her to him, whether the girl liked it or not. Zhoonali, the wise woman, would insist upon it. The traditions of their people since time beyond beginning would demand it!

"No!" yowled Honee.

Cheanah drew back in amazement at the loud, rude, and absolutely definitive sound. "I have asked Teean to reconsider, but he will not. You are the one he wants. You have no man. Custom decrees that you must go to him."

"I won't have him!" Honee lowered her voice; she looked like a cornered badger, all fat and glint eyed and showing her teeth. "It is my right to name the one who will be first with me! And I know who I want: Karana! Maybe he will come back someday soon and—"

"Karana! Karana is dead in the Forbidden Land along with Torka and all who followed him!" He was suddenly violently angry.

Zhoonali shook her head with obvious regret. "It is my fault. I have done wrong to spoil you. But in this matter, you must defer to the customs and traditions of your people. It must be so."

Honee's face was set. "Why? Why must it be so? I don't want Teean."

"What you want does not matter," the old woman informed Honee emphatically.

"It *does* matter." Honee's lower lip was quivering. "Teean is old. He has practically no teeth. I will have to chew his food for him! And his man thing is blue and crooked."

"Crooked?" Cheanah slapped his knees and laughed out loud.

Zhoonali shushed him. "It will straighten with the proper coaxing," she said sagely. "There is no room for laughter in this matter, Cheanah. The songs of first blood have been sung for Honee, and the dances of first blood have been danced. The song of first piercing has yet to be sung. Now the spirits have chosen a man for her."

Honee bit her lip. In childlike desperation she did the only thing that could possibly have won a victory for her. She sobbed like a hurt little girl and ran to the protection of her father's arms. "Cheanah does not have to let Zhoonali tell him what to do! You are Man Who Walks in the Skin of the Wanawut! Not even the spirits of the wind could make you say yes to one skinny old man with a crooked man bone!"

Zhoonali saw the girl's words work their magic on Cheanah's pride.

"There, there. I had no idea that you felt so strong an aversion to going to him. So you shall not go. What is the point of being headman if I cannot make my own decisions on such matters and—"

"No!" Zhoonali felt suddenly cold as a terrible wave of dread washed through her. "You are headman because the forces of Creation have chosen you to lead your people with the wisdom of your forefathers, to make decisions predicated on the traditions of the band and the customs of the ancients!"

Cheanah's head went up. He had made up his mind. When he spoke, his tone caused Zhoonali to shrink back. He was talking to her in a manner that allowed no rebuttal. He *was* headman! At last! For the first time in all of their years together, she knew that she had no power over him. "You are the wise woman of this band, but I am its headman. There is a difference between us. It is your role to advise. It is mine to listen to your advice and act upon it. You have advised. I have listened. And now that I have spoken, you will say no more. Is that understood?"

Slowly, the old woman rose to her feet. Her eyes were on Honee as she nodded and said with grim emphasis: "I understand more than you think." Then, with her head held high, she said coolly to Cheanah: "Beware. The forces of Creation are watching. The decisions that you make now are the decisions that your people will have to live with tomorrow and for all of the tomorrows to come."

7

Although Sister hung back, the beastling grew bold. He walked in the skin of the white lion now. It was a scarred, bedraggled-looking skin, for the lion had been dead when he found it, and he had no skill at all with Mother's man stone. He expected to feel anger toward the lion and gladness in its death; he felt neither. He took the pelt, leaving the head and paws, and after he had eaten, while Sister continued to gorge herself on the strong, stringy, unpalatable meat, he sat beside the head of the lion.

He touched the great, ruined head and let his fingers drift across its fly-eaten eye socket, its many scars, and its once-fine fur. *Give your wisdom and your strength to this cub, White Lion. I have found the throwing stick of the beasts. Make me bold and strong enough to use it against them, for they are the great wasters of life. When I kill them, I will kill for you as well as for Mother. I will be the white lion. The beasts will fear me and run from me as they once must have feared and run from you.*

It was no easy thing to find a new place in which to live after abandoning the cave. Sister tried to make him go back to the mountain, but the beastling refused. In the skin of the white lion, with Mother's man stone in one hand and the throwing stick of the beast in the other, he led her westward with no specific destination in mind. He knew only that if he was going to prey upon the beasts, he would have to remain in the vicinity of their hunting territory; besides, their wastefulness would make feeding easy for Sister and him as long as they were careful not to be seen.

His left hand clenched around the bone haft of the throwing stick. He had one stick; the beasts had *many*! He held it up and looked at it. The sharp tip was of stone. A wrapping of animal skin secured it to the stick. The stick itself was old bone, camel or bison. He brought it close to his face, smelled it, and tasted it with his tongue. It held the stink of fire. He frowned. How could this be? Where had the beasts found this stick? Where did they find *all* of their sticks?

His eyes narrowed. From far across the grasslands in the direction from which the beasts had come, there was the smell of smoke and burned meat and—charred bone! His eyes widened as he understood that the beasts had not found the thing; they had taken bone and stone and skin and somehow, with fire, had made a thing that had not been before . . . a throwing stick! And if they had made one, he could make one . . . and another . . . until he carried as many throwing sticks as he needed to kill the beasts!

It was an epiphany that staggered him with the pure, dazzling joy of revelation. He was breathless with euphoria as he lifted the throwing stick and shook it at the sky. And then he laughed. It was a light, bubbling, new sound that brought pure pleasure to his spirit. Sister huffed at him in worried puzzlement. He did not care. He was smiling as he turned and led her on. Now, at last, he knew exactly where he was going and what he was going to do when he got there.

He sought the hill country due north of the valley in which the beasts took shelter. Here, high on a south-facing slope that allowed him a broad overview of the hunting territory of the beasts, he found a perfect nesting site deep within an old rockfall, close to a shrub-choked stream.

Sister sulked. He knew that she was unhappy. Time and again, she tugged at his arm in a vain attempt to persuade him to return to the cave. Now that she knew that there was no hope of this, she would not help him to gather branches for their new nest. She chose a cool, relatively smooth boulder, sat on her broad, stub-tailed bottom, her long, hairy arms wrapped around her short, equally hairy legs. With her chin resting on her knees, she stared at him petulantly until the nest was done.

Then, suddenly curious, she ambled over, made low hoots of approval, and promptly climbed in and went to sleep. He laid a loving hand upon her heavy muscled shoulder; she twitched contentedly in her dreams. What a simple, uncomplicated creature she was.

The hole in the sky was warm, and its golden light filled him with a need for sleep. He lay down, closed his eyes, and dreamed . . . of Mother . . . of the white lion . . . and of a pair of black swans winging to the east, into that far, mountainous land where the sun was born.

Lonit stood at the edge of Torka's cave in her favorite, heavily fringed, elkskin dress, with necklaces of shells and feathers around her neck. In the valley far below, Umak and Dak were hunting with Aar for fresh meat, their contribution to the special feast that would be enjoyed later in the day. Their movements had caused the pair of black swans to rise from the lake.

Lonit stared westward, feeling sad. The old longing was back and her arms felt empty. "Manaravak . . ." she whispered.

"This is not a day for tears," said Torka, coming up behind her and putting his arms around her.

She turned and looked up at him, smiling, as he wiped the tears from her eyes, then bent to kiss her blossom-and-leaf-encircled brow. He had donned the full regalia of his rank: the head circlet of feathers drawn from the wings of eagles and hawks and the great black-and-white flight feathers of the condorlike teratorn, the massive collar of intricately woven sinew strands adorned with stone beads and fossilized shells, from which hung the paws and fangs of wolves, as well as the claws and stabbing teeth of the great short-faced bear he had killed so long ago. She caught her breath in wonder at the sight of him.

"How did you know that I was sad?" she asked, reaching up to touch his face lovingly.

"Because after all of our years together, I share your
spirit, Lonit. And I confide in you now that I, too, am sad.
But it is a sweet sadness that we share—reflections on our
youth, on all that we have endured together. Such great
distances, so many years, so many tears, so much laughter
and joy. On this day when our firstborn daughter is to be
welcomed into the band as a woman, it is good that we
should remember it all and long for the ones that we have
left behind." His hand moved to rest across the swollen
span of her belly. It pressed ever so gently, and yet, as if
in response to an unspoken command, a strong ripple of
movement stressed his palm. "Perhaps this one will be a
son. A brother for Umak, a son that I can—" He stopped,
obviously not wishing to speak the rest of his thoughts out
loud.

She looked up. His jaw was tense, and the sadness in
his eyes was so deep that she felt as though she would
drown in it. The white lion rose to roar within her from
out of the past, and the old fear was back again.

Does he suspect that Umak may not *be his son but the
son of . . . ?*

Torka looked down at her. "Do not look so concerned,
woman of my heart. Another daughter would please me."

Relief flooded her. The white lion disappeared. Torka
was not worried about Umak's paternity, after all. She
laughed out loud at her own foolishness. "It is all right for
Torka to say that he would prefer a son. If the forces of
Creation are listening, on this special day may they grant
your wish, for Torka honors the female spirits among them
by consecrating Summer Moon's maturity as a woman.
Not all bands celebrate the coming of age of their daughters. My father would never have celebrated my first time
of blood. He did not care whether I lived or died, except
when he could use me. As for Cheanah, I doubt if that
man would make much celebration except for his wolf-
eyed sons."

The corners of Torka's mouth worked with droll amusement. "Do you remember Cheanah's daughter? How
homely she was, and nasty."

"Still, I hope that Zhoonali has made a ceremony of
welcome for Honee. She would be a woman by now." She

sighed, painfully aware of the passing of time. "So long ago! I wonder what has become of her and of all those who chose to remain with Cheanah."

He held her close. "Forget them. Look. Karana comes toward us across the valley under the shadow of the circling swans. Today is not a day for the past. It is a day for the future."

8

At the back of the cave, Summer Moon lay naked within the little tent of woven dry branches that the women had raised for her, and in which she had ceremonially passed her first time of blood. The soiled scraps of fur that had absorbed the blood of her menses had been handed out one by one to the women who attended her every whim. The furs had been collected upon a special hide; later, she would come naked from the hut of first blood and would be given a burning brand, with which she would set fire to the furs and toss their ashes from the cave as a symbolic offering to the forces of Creation—the ashes of the "death" of her childhood.

Tears stung Summer Moon's eyes. She was afraid. Something important was about to happen, and she did not know how much it would hurt. She swallowed hard. She had seen babies born; could it be worse than that?

The girl sat up, listening. Outside the tiny tent, the women were talking low, secretively, conspiratorially, happily. Lonit had come to unlace the thongs that held the hide doorway closed. When it was parted, Lonit bent low and entered with her arms loaded with skin flasks. From outside, someone lashed the tent flap closed behind her.

"It is time to prepare you to be reborn as a woman," proclaimed Lonit, unburdening her arms and kneeling close.

Summer Moon swallowed hard and nodded. The fragrance of her mother's necklaces and armlets of leaves and blossoms filled the hut. Lonit looked beautiful and radiant.

"I am afraid," Summer Moon told her bluntly.

Lonit smiled tenderly. "On this day, dear one, you need not fear. You need only to bask in the love that we all feel for you. We are so proud! So glad for you!"

"When all is finished, must I go to Simu's fire?"

"Of course! A woman must *be* a woman! She cannot live with her father and mother. She must be with a man and make babies for the band."

"I would rather go to Karana's fire. He is younger and better to look upon, and—I . . . I have always loved him."

Lonit embraced her as though she were still a child. "Ever since he was a youth, all the girls and women have had an eye for Karana! But why would you wish to go to the fire of one who is as a brother to you? There is little enough for poor Mahnie to do. Karana would not make you happy. I doubt that he would give you any more babies than he has given to her."

"It is Mahnie who makes him sad. *I* would make him happy! And I am not sure that I want to make babies—unless they are Karana's."

"Nonsense! This band is small, and we need babies to make us strong. Besides, a woman without little ones is like a hunter without a spear—not of much use to the band at all! The blood that has been shed will not be unshed. Be glad! The forces of Creation smile upon you this day, for on the way from this tent to the fire circle of Simu, you must first stay awhile in the hut of rebirth, and there you will discover the magic that will surprise you."

Dak, Umak, and Aar intercepted Karana on his way to the cave.

"We hunt for gifts for Summer Moon and for Torka and Lonit!" declared Dak, proudly hefting the weight of a thong of fat geese.

"Special gifts for a special day," added Umak jubilantly, showing off two large, limp loons. "Have you seen omens for my sister?"

"Omens?" Karana growled. "I have seen no omens."

Dak frowned. Coming in contact with Karana was like bumping into a storm cloud and waiting for the lightning to strike. "Come on, Umak. I'm sure that the magic man has things to attend to at the cave before the ceremonies begin, and I want to take a few more geese before we return home."

"I'll meet you at the lake. I need to talk to Karana for a moment. About my dreams."

"Dreams!" Dak, openly annoyed, could not understand how Umak could be a normal friend one moment and a depressed, dreaming mystic the next. "Not about your brother again!"

"What sort of dreams?" Karana demanded.

Umak felt as though he were looking up at a wolf that would bite off his head if he said the wrong thing. "J-just dreams. I've told Dak about them, but . . . m-maybe this isn't the best time to bother you with—"

Dak took an inadvertent step back. He did not like the way the magic man's eyes had suddenly focused upon Umak as though in all the world there was nothing more important—or threatening—to him than that one middle-sized, antelope-eyed boy. "Come on, Umak. Karana has more important things to—"

The magic man's eyes spitted Dak. "There is nothing more important than dreams. *Nothing!* And believe me, boy, I am in no hurry to return to the cave this day!"

Dak gulped and nodded. He felt that he had ceased to exist for both Karana and Umak. He frowned, not liking the exclusion; on the other hand, he had no desire to be involved. "Well, then, if it's dreams you two want to talk about, I'll be off and leave you to it!"

Umak regretfully watched him go. Aar ran off with him.

"Dreams?" Karana's strong ungloved fingers gripped Umak's chin. "Tell me of your dreams, Umak."

Umak's eyes went wide. He saw the threat in Karana's eyes. "I . . . th-thought you could tell me what they m-mean. I've had them for a long time. Sometimes they aren't really dreams about my brother at all, but simply a *knowing.*"

Karana's face went as white as bleached bone. His eyes were as blank as the tundral steppe in the depth of the darkest winter night.

Umak decided that it was best simply to plunge ahead.

He would be glad to be away from the magic man. "I see my brother as a baby sometimes, all blue, with a thong around his neck. Always he looks like Torka but is very dirty. Sometimes I feel him inside me, lonely and sad, and very often, I have the feeling that he is in danger." He stopped. The look on Karana's face was terrifying. He *was* a wolf. He *would* eat him if he said another word about his dreams. He nearly dropped his thong of loons. "I'm sorry, Karana! Today is Summer Moon's day, not mine! Go on about whatever it is you have to do. I'll talk to Torka about the dreams another day when—"

"*No!*" Umak had already turned away, but Karana's hand gripped him by the arm and turned him back. "Your brother is dead, understand? And if you do not wish to make Torka angry or cause your mother pain, you will not speak of him again."

Umak wilted under the tirade. "But if he is in danger?"

"He cannot be in danger if he is dead, can he?"

"N-no."

"Then you will not speak of him again. Ever!"

"N-never," promised Umak, astounded and terrified by the twisted mix of wrath and anguish in Karana's face. "Never again."

Never had Umak seen a man's face as contorted with emotion as the magic man's was now. Wrath pulled the fine, even features into those of a snarling, moon-maddened wolf.

Madness. Yes. The boy had never seen it before, but surely it was madness that glittered in Karana's eyes and transformed his face into a visage of pure rapacious ugliness as he pulled Umak closer, twisting the boy's arm until Umak cried out, terrified.

"Could it be? Is it possible? Does he live in you?" Karana was muttering to himself, reasoning with himself. His eyes took in each and every one of Umak's features as though he had just seen him for the first time. "No. It could not be. It is not." The ugliness began to recede. He released Umak with a shove that sent the boy sprawling.

"Remember my warning, Umak. Speak no more of your dreams to me or anyone. For if you do, if I ever have cause to suspect that *his* spirit lives in you, I will seek you out even though Torka names you Son. In the night I will come, as an invisible owl with talons bared and poised to rip your throat. And when they find you dead, no one will know that it was my magic that stole your life. No one."

Torka stood at the base of the hills, and when Umak ran past him without so much as a word, he waited for Karana to stop before him.

"What did the boy want of you?"

"Words. Advice."

Torka sensed evasion. "He looked upset."

Karana met his gaze. "I tell you, it was nothing of importance."

Torka nodded. If the boy had gone to him for personal advice, the words they had shared were their own. "I am glad that you are here."

"I will not do what you and Grek have asked of me. I will make the songs and the smokes and lead the dances but no more than that."

"You must, Karana. Our people *must* have your magic. Grek and Simu agree. What we do now will be the honored rituals for the generations that come after us. Years from now, when Summer Moon is old and dry and barren, let her be able to draw her granddaughters around her and tell them that when she was a girl, before she went to the fire circle of her first man, there was a gift of magic given to the first new woman in this new land."

Karana scowled. "*Simu* has agreed to be her man. *He* can—"

"He is not a magic man, my son. There is no real love between him and Summer Moon. There is no 'first-love man' in this band for Summer Moon. There can be no magic for her, no fire, unless *you* create it for her."

Karana stared, silenced by the bitter truth. Yet could he give to Summer Moon what he denied to Mahnie? No! He could not, he would not, he *dared* not—not with her, not with any woman ever again. Yet he could not tell Torka why. "I . . . she . . . is my sister."

Torka waved the protest away. "A shaman is beyond such kinship. What I ask is common custom in many bands to the west. The ritual gift of opening may be of your devising. Gentling a girl into womanhood need not be a coupling. Only let it be magic, Karana! Magic in the darkness, in the firelight. A gift that will live in her heart forever."

He did not know how long he sat within the little hut of green branches. He entered it secretly sometime after Summer Moon came out of the hut of blood. Before that he had danced and drunk deeply of some half-bitter, half-sweet fermented brew that was passed too freely from hand to hand. During the dancing and drinking, Grek came close and growled a few words about lingering with Mahnie after the ceremony.

A special fire circle had been made and readied. With his "magic" kindling Karana made a "magic" fire, raised up "magic" smoke, and sang "magic" praise songs in honor of the new woman of the band.

And all the while he tried not to look at Mahnie or at little Naya. Mahnie looked tired, thinner and smaller than he remembered—frail almost—and yet so lovely and soft in a simple, membrane-thin summer tunic of doeskin, with flowers around her neck, wrists, and ankles and in her long, unplaited hair. Karana turned his back upon his woman and daughter lest he weaken, go to them, sweep them into his arms, smother them with kisses, and speak his love to them. And once he spoke he would never be able to go back into the cold, lonely mountains.

He was grateful when, with a great, clamorous shouting, the men and boys demanded that the new woman among them come forth. As Karana watched, Summer Moon came out of the hut of blood, naked and oiled and as glistening as a newborn baby.

But she was no infant and certainly no child. Amazed, Karana stared. Everyone stared as, guided by a proud Lonit, Summer Moon blushingly displayed a young woman's body for all to see. Torka handed her a burning brand. With this she strode to the entrance of the cave and ignited the pile of bloodied furs that the women had collected and covered with oil. When they had burned to ashes, Summer Moon proudly cast them to the wind.

Cries of delight went up, especially from Simu. Eneela

frowned and elbowed him in the side. He leaned close
and kissed her hard and long, then whispered something
to her that made her smile and kiss him back. Tears of
pride shone in Lonit's eyes. Torka took her hand as gar-
lands were placed around the new woman's neck and all
the members of the band gathered around.

Demmi, looking very regal and almost grown up in a
new fringed dress of elkskin similar to Lonit's, carried
little Swan up to Summer Moon and gave her big sister a
long and surprisingly tender embrace. Umak came forward with uncharacteristic shyness to murmur words of
congratulations.

Karana's heart went hard just looking at the boy. For
a moment he had actually believed that the boy was
Navahk's child. Ah, what a mockery that would be!
Unbeknownst to them all, Navahk, living among them,
insidiously working his evil will upon the band that had
destroyed him.

But no! If Umak's dreams were Vision, it was a gift
inherited through Torka's line and its generations of spirit
masters, not Navahk's. Nevertheless, if the power was
Umak's, would he know that Karana had lied to him?
Would he know the truth about Manaravak? Karana felt
sick. His head ached, and his belly felt queasy. He could
not stand to look at Umak or at Torka and Lonit, to whom
his lies had brought so much grief.

He escaped into the little hut of green branches. Away
from the fires, it was surprisingly cool and pleasantly
fragrant within the woven structure; but it was also dark,
and he could not stand upright inside it. He sat down
glumly, pleased to discover instant comfort upon the matting of soft new furs with which the women of the band
had carpeted the floor. The freshly gathered leaves, lichens, and blossoms that had been placed as extra cush-
ioning beneath the furs gave off a soothing summer scent.
Karana drew in their fragrance; the healing quality made
him feel better.

Clearheaded again, he looked around in the darkness.
There was nothing in the hut of rebirth except the furs on
the floor and, next to a small, fur-free area, a single white
feather, an antelope-skull container of oil, two bladder

flasks full of liquid—one of water, the other of fermented brew—and the neatly assembled makings of a fire.

The bow drill had the look of Lonit's workmanship, and the long, double upcurving lines that had been cut onto the main portion of the drilling stick looked like mammoth tusks and were clearly the same as the identification marks that Torka incised into his bludgeon, spears, daggers, and spear hurlers.

Karana smiled. He sensed their love and their unspoken hope for what must soon take place within this hut.

"Magic." He spoke the word and touched the objects that had been left for him . . . and for her.

Thoughtfully, he undressed and laid his clothes aside, then slowly, methodically anointed his body and his face with oil. He made a small fire and dipped the index finger of his right hand into the first of the ashes. With these he patterned himself across the brow and cheek, under his eyes and along both sides of his mouth, down along his arms and chest, belly, and limbs. Despite himself, he was aroused by the preparation for the ritual to come.

"No, it will not come to that for me—only for her," he decided.

It seemed to Karana that he sat alone for a long time. He grew warm and hungry and thirsty. He drank from the water flask. It cooled him but did nothing to alleviate either his hunger or his earlier intoxication. He grew warm again and dozed and dreamed of Mahnie . . . of their first time together, and of their last.

"Karana?"

He looked up.

Summer Moon caught her breath with wonder. Behind her, she could hear the women—all but Mahnie—tittering and whispering as they closed the door of woven limbs and leaves and walked away.

She was warm and sweated from dancing. Her head was swimming from too much drink, and the tips of her fingers and tongue and the surface of her skin felt hot and oddly tingling. The hut's ceiling was so low that she knelt, her arms folded shyly across her bare breasts as she looked across the fragrant, firelit, vaguely smoky shadows.

"Karana? Is it *you?*"

He sat straight and unmoving before the little fire; except for the dark tracings of ceremonial paint and a single white feather that lay upon his right thigh, he was as naked as she. His body shone with oil. He was so handsome and wantonly virile that he took her breath away.

"Karana is not here," he replied. "Only Summer Moon, the new woman, is here. The rest—what will now be between us—is magic." His left hand rose, gestured with incurling fingers. "Come. . . ."

Moving on her knees, she obeyed and paused before the fire. His eyes never left her body as he knelt across the flames before her. She gasped at the sight of him. If he was magic, he was also a man. She dropped her eyes and felt the heat of his presence in the dark.

"Come. . . ."

Again the invitation. She moved eagerly around the fire to face him. He reached out and drew her arms from her breasts. His eyes burned her. She felt a deep, subtle change within herself. She felt her face flame and was glad for the dark. He bent slightly, dipped his hands into an antelope-skull container, then anointed her shoulders, arms, and hands with oil.

"It feels good," she told him, wishing that the words would come more easily.

"Yes. It *is* good. For in this moment a woman is born, to be opened by man. You must not be afraid."

He spoke softly, with caring tenderness. Yet fear beat like a frightened bird at the back of her throat. She opened her mouth and released it with a sigh.

"I am not afraid," she told him, and knew that she was not as she closed her eyes and allowed her body to yield to the movement of his hands. "I have dreamed of this . . . with *you*, Karana—only with you. I have always loved you."

"No. Karana is not here . . . only the new woman . . . only the magic."

The anointing went on, slowly, purposefully. His arms circled her. She leaned close and felt the quick, hot, startled intake of his breath at her temple as her breasts touched his chest. Against her belly, that which she had always feared about men moved and hardened into a throbbing column of heat. Strangely, she had no fear of it now. She arched her hips, pressed its warmth hard against her belly, and once again gasped when she heard him suck in his breath.

For a moment he drew away from her and looked at her with stern measuring eyes.

"It *is* good," she whispered, lowering her eyes to look at him as she touched him tentatively . . . wonderingly.

Suddenly, with a sharp exhalation, he pulled her down upon the furs and allowed his hands to slide slowly downward over her breasts as he straddled her and knelt back.

She looked up at him. His eyes were as black and hot as the fire he had kindled in her loins—and within his own. She strained her limbs against his. He moved, allowed her the room that she instinctively sought as she opened herself to him . . . wide . . . wanting . . . moving to touch him again. She watched his face as, instead of lowering himself onto her, he reached back and took up the white feather from where he had set it aside. Slowly, as she handled him, he drew the feather around her breasts and downward between her ribs and over her belly and along her thighs and then back, slowly back, tracing lines of fire that caused her to cry out with pleasure. Suddenly his mouth closed over hers.

"No," he sighed. "Do not cry out. Mahnie must not hear."

"Mahnie!"

"Yes, Mahnie!"

His voice had changed. His hands gripped her wrists as he came down onto her, kissing her as no one had ever kissed her, as she had never even dreamed of being kissed. And when at last he entered her, pierced her deep and slow, bringing the pain that he had promised he would not bring, she yielded to it, and although his kiss smothered her cries of passion, cry out she did as she thrashed beneath him until the last thrum of pleasure was gone.

He shivered and held her tightly, continuing to move and thrust and tremble as he whispered, "It has been too

long . . . too long. . . . Ahh, Mahnie, how can I bear not
to have you ever again?"

She felt him tense just before, with a savage exhalation
of frustration, he threw himself off her and spilled his seed
beside her.

He lay still a moment, then sat up and shook his head.
"I'm sorry, Summer Moon. Simu will be better for you."

"This has not been magic!" she told him petulantly,
sitting beside him. In the center of the hut the fire was
still burning low, as it was within her loins. She touched
his brow. "I do not want Simu. I want you. . . . As it is
with Lonit and Torka, so it will be with us, always and
forever."

"No, Little One. It cannot be."

"Of course it can. You are a magic man. And I am not a
'little one' anymore. I am a woman! Here, in this place,
you have made it so!"

He pulled on his clothing and left the hut of rebirth. All
was subdued in the cave. Dak and Umak were playing
quietly. Umak looked up at him, paled, then looked away.
Everyone else seemed to have retired. Even the dogs
were asleep. It was Grek who called him back.

"Wait, you!"

Karana turned and glared at the old man, resenting his
openly abusive tone. "What is it?"

Grek strode toward him, head down, brows merged
into one mass of annoyance over the bridge of his nose.
"You're going now? Just like that? Without waiting for the
new woman to come out and accept her new man? And
with never a word to Mahnie?"

He looked around, wanting to see her, and then felt
relieved when he did not. "It looks to me as if everyone is
sleeping off the effects of the new-woman ceremonies. I
was not aware that Simu needed my presence in order to
accept his second woman. And is there something special
that you would have me say to Mahnie?" After the question was asked, he knew that it must have sounded as
callous to Grek as it did to him.

"No," growled the old hunter. "What should have been
said between you and Mahnie should have been spoken

long ago, before you misled her—and me—into thinking
that you were fit to take a woman!"

"He is fit!"

Karana wheeled around as Summer Moon came out of
the hut of rebirth, wrapped in furs and smiling lovingly at
him. He was stunned. She was not supposed to come out
of the hut until Simu called for her. And after what had
just happened between them, how could she look at him
as though he had just given her the greatest gift in all the
world?

"Bah!" Grek snarled in response to Summer Moon.
"Any male with meat between his legs is fit for that! But a
man needs more, here . . . and here!" He slapped his
chest, over his heart, and the side of his head. "You have a
daughter, Karana! And a woman who loves you! Although
why she does is a mystery to me! You have responsibilities!"

Karana shifted his weight restlessly. The old man's voice
had disturbed the sleepers. Couples were sitting up. From
where she had fallen asleep close to Wallah and Iana,
Mahnie looked toward him with a troubled frown. How
pale she looked, how drawn and sad.

He could not bear to look at her. In all the time they
had been together, she had never been less than fully
receptive and completely loving in his arms. But never
had she stirred the hard, driving, animal heat that Summer Moon had ignited. When the girl had touched him,
he had thought that he would explode with ecstasy. Never
had he experienced such absolute passion and release. He
was hard again just thinking of it and ashamed because
Mahnie's eyes were on him.

"I must go!" He turned abruptly and stalked toward the
lip of the cave.

"Karana?"

Mahnie had called. He stopped. He waited.

"May you walk in safety and come back to us soon, my
magic man."

Her gently spoken words of farewell struck him to his
heart, but he left without a word. He would not come
back soon! He dared not come back soon! He would need
time to recover from what he had nearly succumbed to.

"Never again!" he screamed at the wind and the sky and

the watching eye of the midnight sun when he was certain that he was out of earshot of the cave. "Never! Do you hear me, Navahk?"

The wind turned. Dust stung his eyes. He cursed the wind and the dust and the haunting memory of his father. And he cursed himself because as he walked he thought of his beloved Mahnie—but his soul was black and twisted inward with frustration, for although he thought of her, he hungered for the warm, eager, receptive body of the virgin girl whom he had called Sister all his life . . . and whom he would never think of as a sister again.

PART VII

WALKERS OF THE WIND

1

The wind blew across the Forbidden Land from the west and north, and all too soon it was winter again—a dry, dark, rock-hard winter of unremitting wind and storm.

Eneela went into labor for her third baby with the rising of the next moon. Even though they raised a large signal fire, Karana did not return across the valley to the cave in the hills. Umak was glad. Eneela's baby was born in the storm dark and was given the name of Nantu, to honor the memory of a boyhood friend of Simu's who had been killed many years before in the far land to the west.

"Karana should be here," said Simu, obviously irritated. "Why has my woman been deprived of his songs and his smokes?"

"And maybe some healing magic to stop Eneela's birth bleeding," added Wallah with visible annoyance.

"Karana would not leave us without his magic unless he could not come," Mahnie said. "Unless he was hurt . . . or unless he was . . ."

"We will see," said Torka, who began to put on his winter traveling clothes.

With Umak, Dak, Aar, and two of the now fully grown pups, he set out across the wonderful valley.

The beastling moved cautiously in the winter dark through the nesting place of the beasts. Clothed in the skin of the white lion, he was not only warm but nearly invisible.

For several moons now he had been watching the beasts, coming as close as he dared, to learn how they made their throwing sticks, how they commanded fire to leap from piles of grass, how they created clothes from animal skins. Closer and closer he came to their place of stinking shelters as the winter dark closed down upon the world. He came with his man stone and throwing stick, leaving Sister asleep within their nest. He did not want her at his side; she had not the disposition for the sort of hunt that he was on now.

He moved forward cautiously among the huts. The wind was strong, and snow was falling heavily. His observations had taught him that in stormy weather the beasts stayed inside their shelters, coming out only to relieve themselves or in packs to search for meat. Although the chance of any one of them coming out into the storm and darkness was minimal, that small chance thrilled him, heating his blood.

He went forward, searching. The largest shelter at the far side of the nesting site had stacked against its shaggy leeward wall the greatest number of that which he desired: throwing sticks.

Tall and white and beautiful, they stood upright, deep in the snow, with their wondrously worked stone tips secured with lacings of skin to the fire-hardened bone shafts. The beastling paused, salivating at the sight of them. His hand flexed around his own throwing stick. Silently he unlashed the thongs and drew six throwing sticks from the snow. Hefting them under his arm, he ventured around the front of the nest.

He stopped dead as he heard the long reach of footsteps across the hard-packed crust of the snow. A beast. A big beast!

He turned to run, but the wind struck him hard and the spears went clattering. *No!* He would *not* leave them. He bent, scooped them up, and, looking around to make certain that the beast was not coming at him, saw the head of Mother staring sightlessly into the night and storm.

Cheanah had gone to enjoy a little pleasure on Kivan's woman. On his return to his own hut, something flew past him. Instinct caused him to move sideways. A spear? Who would throw a spear at him in his own encampment? Then he saw it: a black-haired, white-maned thing crouching before the entrance to his pit hut, snarling with all of the menace of a cornered beast.

"Wanawut? Lion?" He stared, incredulous, then took a defensive stance, regretting that he had not bothered to take a spear.

And now a creature that had the look of man and beast and lion—a *white* lion!—was showing its teeth as it threw another spear at him, clearly trying to kill him. Again he sidestepped it. If it possessed neither strength nor skill, it did have speed and daring as, suddenly, with spears tucked under its arm, it raced past him for open land.

Fear rooted Cheanah's feet to the ground. His deep and aching terror began to gnaw at his self-confidence. The creature was a wind spirit! He had been right not to pursue it. Men could not kill phantoms! They would always come back in one form or another to exact vengeance.

His mouth was dry. The hide of the wanawut was suddenly inordinately heavy upon his back. He was painfully aware of the dried hands of the beast dangling over his chest. Despite the cold he broke into a hot sweat as it seemed to him that the hands were flexing at the wrists, reaching up, trying to choke him. He swirled the skin off his back.

"I should have stalked them more intently . . . the lion . . . the beast's cubs. I should have killed them. I—" He swallowed the rest of his words as he turned, suddenly aware that someone was staring at him.

It was Zhoonali. "I warned you to be wary of what you do, Cheanah. I warned you that the spirits would be watching."

Had she been standing in the entrance to the hut long enough to see her son standing weaponless before the spirits of the night as they threw his own spears at him? Could she smell the rankness of his fear, as he smelled it now? His face flamed with shame. "You have seen nothing!" he accused.

"I have seen enough," she replied, and without another word she turned and left him alone with the night and the wind and his own muddled fears.

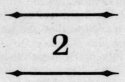

2

Despite his worry for Karana's safety, Torka was glad to be out of the cave, walking across the broad valley with Umak and Dak, and the dogs running out ahead.

They walked until Torka sensed a need in the boys to rest. Now he stopped and hunkered down. The dogs circled back and seated themselves close by, while the boys were silent, recouping their strength. Umak sat facing back toward the way they had come as if waiting for someone to follow or wishing himself home again; it had been his opinion that a magic man should not need to be summoned—his gift of Seeing should tell him when he was needed.

Torka eyed Umak thoughtfully. Something had happened between the boy and Karana prior to Summer Moon's becoming a new woman. It had shattered their former closeness, and this realization troubled Torka.

"I'm glad you brought us along," said Dak to Torka, chewing on his portion of fat and surveying the winter landscape. "It is too long a way for a man to go alone."

Dak's good-natured audacity caused Torka to grin. He heard a stomach growl. Umak's? His own? It did not matter. They had been gone from the cave a very long time. He passed out more wedges of fat and tossed a few to the dogs.

"Do you think my mother will be all right until Karana can bring his magic to her?"

Torka thought, nodded, and spoke his heart. "I do. Eneela is strong, and Wallah knows the way of healing in these matters almost as well as Karana. She cannot make magic, but she knows the way to stanch a flow of blood."

Looking back, Torka indicated the glimmering glow that was the signal fire that Simu and Grek were keeping on the lip of the cave. "Now that the storm has cleared, Karana will see the fire. Chances are he will meet us halfway across the valley." He hoped that his voice did not reveal his concern.

"He does not want to come," Umak declared.

It always annoyed Torka when Umak fell into the careless habit of making statements rather than suppositions. "You can't know that."

"Umak *always* knows things," informed Dak offhandedly. "Is that true, Umak?"

"Not always." The boy stood and stared across the way they had come. "For example, I was not sure that she would really have the nerve to follow."

"Who?" Torka was on his feet.

Dak shrugged, revealing his ignorance, but Aar was off and barking happily as a small figure plodding toward them raised an arm and called out.

"It's Demmi," answered Umak. "She's been trailing us for a long time now."

"And you said nothing?" Anger toward his son flared within Torka. "She is alone! She might have been attacked by—"

"Demmi's very good with a spear, and with a dagger and a bola, too," said Umak.

It was a while before the girl caught up with them. She was breathless, and her words were strained when she spoke. "You must come back to the cave, Father! Mother's labor has begun, but Wallah says that something is very wrong. Grek is coming along after me. He will go on with Dak to find Karana. You and Umak and I, we must go back to the cave now!"

For three long days Lonit labored to bring forth her baby.

"Too long . . . too long . . ." moaned Wallah, despairing of what to do. "Karana has special magic to relax a mother and bring a baby quick: oils, powdered bones,

drinks made of gland meats and green leaves and pounded
bark. From Sondahr and the shamans and healers at the
Great Gathering he has learned this magic. My knowledge
is small indeed when compared to his." She hesitated.
"Torka, I must speak truth to you. The infant is lodged
backward in the birth passage. I cannot feel a heartbeat."

From where she sat close at Lonit's side, Iana lifted her
sad eyes to Torka. "Perhaps it is time to think about using
the claw of taking."

Lonit roused herself. "No, Iana! Torka, tell her *no!*"

Bereft, he nodded, assenting to her will. Slowly, he
released his hope that he was soon to have another son,
one who, unlike Umak, would not have Navahk's smile.

"When Karana returns, the baby will come," Summer
Moon assured him, standing close at his side with little
Swan in her arms.

"Yes," agreed Mahnie. "When my magic man returns,
all will be well!"

Demmi glowered from where she sat soberly with Umak
at the other side of the cave. "If the baby's heart has
stopped, then it is already dead, and Karana's magic will
not bring it back to life. He should have been here days
ago. And if he truly has any power at all, he should have
known that there would be danger in this birth!"

Umak looked at her strangely.

Summer Moon glared at Demmi. "You know nothing of
men or of anything important!"

"*Shhh* now!" Eneela, propped against her backrest on
her bed furs with Simu, Nantu, and Larani, hushed the
siblings as if they were babies. "Enough! This is not a time
for arguing."

"It is time for *something!*" cried Demmi, rising and
curling her fists at her sides. "How long are we going to
wait for Karana while my mother grows weaker and her
baby refuses to be born? Whatever is to be done for her
must be done *now*, by those of us who are with her *now*."
Suddenly sobbing, she swept across the cave and fell in a
heap at Lonit's side. "This girl will help you! Is there not
something I can do?"

Beside her, Torka frowned, ashamed. Demmi was right!
Perhaps if the baby could be turned in Lonit's womb, not

torn to pieces with the claw of taking but turned by small, questing, and determined hands, Lonit could expel it, and both mother and child could be saved! Why had he not thought of it before? Because he had been waiting for Karana.

He lay one hand upon Demmi's back and the other upon Lonit's cheek. "I need Demmi's small, strong, and gentle arm, and I need the trust of the first woman of my heart. Do I have these things?"

"Always . . . and forever," whispered Lonit.

Demmi blinked and nodded.

"Good," said Torka and drew in a deep breath to give him courage. "I will hold my Lonit hard against the pain of what must come . . . as Demmi turns the child and draws it out."

It was done, but done too late. The baby, a boy, was dead. A son that might have been. Lonit wept, and Torka trembled against grief as Wallah took the infant from a sniffling, shaking, pale-faced Demmi and placed it in its father's hands.

"I'm sorry," Demmi whispered.

"It was a good try, girl!" Wallah told her. "But look at the cord. You see how it was wrapped around its neck? It was this that kept it from turning. There was danger to this one baby from the start."

"I knew," Umak said simply.

"Don't be silly, boy," the old woman rebuked him.

"I knew. In my dreams. My *brother*, lost and alone and in danger. I told Karana. I asked him what the dream meant. But he said that my brother was dead. He was so angry. He told me never to speak of it again, to anyone. He said he'd kill me if I did. But how can I keep silent now? My brother is dead, and Karana knew all along that it would happen. Unless he wanted this baby dead, Karana should have been here."

"I am here now," said Karana, picking up Umak's last few words as he came into the cave with Grek and Dak and the dogs. "What is it? Why do you all stare?"

Torka turned.

Karana had just loosed his hood. His face went white as he saw the corpse of the infant.

Slowly, as though in a trance, with his dead infant son held protectively in the fold of his left arm, Torka crossed the cave.

Karana never saw the blow that felled him. But suddenly his face was red with blood as one blow from Torka's fist knocked him flat.

"Why?"

The word struck Karana like a hard kick in his belly. Nauseated, he sat up, hand to his face, fighting against dizziness and pain. He knew that his nose was broken. Blood from his split upper lip was hot in his mouth. His upper teeth felt loose. His tongue moved to probe the extent of his injury, but it, too, was split and flapping wide in his mouth.

"Why?" Torka raged again. "In the name of all of the forces of Creation, why would you, whom I have named Son, threaten Umak and wish to keep such knowledge from me? Why would you deliberately stay away when you had the healing aids that might have quickened Lonit's labor and saved the life of my child?"

Something deep inside Karana's head seemed to snap. He heard it and felt it. The pain was excruciating. And then, out of a blackness that seemed to be boiling inside his brain, numbness came, and with it a low, deep rushing roar.

"I demand an answer! Why, Karana?"

Karana looked up at Torka and wondered if he had ever heard a more malevolent word. Torka's stillborn son, choked by its own cord. Yes, Umak had foretold his brother's death. *A boy . . . all blue . . . with a thong wrapped about its neck*. But he had not listened. Frightened, he had mistakenly thought that the boy was referring to the other vision, the one he and Umak shared: of the other twin, the wild boy dressed in fur, coming across the miles, walking with a beast on one side and the terrible specter of the truth on the other.

"Fool . . ." He whispered the recrimination. Pain flared within him. It was so intense that he nearly fainted. Blood was flowing fast now, welling in his nostrils and flowing back into his swollen sinuses; he could not breathe unless he sucked air through his mouth, but blood was pooling there, too, thick and hot.

Instead of sobbing in anguish at what he had done, he laughed. He did not know why, and he could not stop laughing any more than he could stop bleeding. Somewhere inside the black, roaring cloud boiling in his head, he could have sworn that he heard Navahk laughing—not with him, but *at* him. Squinting up, he saw the look of fury on Torka's face, and despite himself, he laughed again. "Fool . . . not to see, not to know. But couldn't speak . . . cannot speak . . . will not speak. This baby, it does not matter. . . . It—"

Karana glanced at those who stared at him, aghast and uncomprehending. Even Mahnie looked at him as though he were a stranger. Beside her, Umak, blank faced, stood staring back at him. Suddenly he fixed the boy with pure, unbridled rage. "Look!" How it hurt to speak; but speak he did and felt his tongue lying open in his mouth and the blood gushing from his face. "Look at what you have done to me! I will come for you in the night! I warned you not to—"

"No!" With his dead infant limp in the curl of one arm, Torka reached down with the other and jerked Karana by his hair to his feet. "Not another word! Not another threat! Get out! Go! This is the second time a son of mine has died because you have seen fit to wander the hills like a solitary wolf with your back turned to me and mine when we have needed you and depended upon you most. Had you been at my side on the night of the red sky and the black moon, your words of 'magic' could have changed the minds of ignorant, fearful people, and my son would not have become meat for the jaws of the wanawut, nor would I have been forced to leave the Place of Endless Meat to wander the Forbidden Land! Long ago, when you followed me out of the camp of Cheanah, you swore that it would not happen again. But it *has* happened! This stillborn son that I hold in my arms would be alive were it not for you! You have betrayed the trust and the love that have bonded us, Karana. No longer will I call you Son. Go, I say! Your 'magic' is not needed here. I am Torka!

The blood of many generations of spirit masters flows within me. It is time that I remembered this and drew strength from it. This band needs no magic man when Torka is headman, for at last I know that as long as Life Giver is my totem, my instincts will speak the wisdom of the spirits to me, and from this day until the ending of my days, when I have need of 'magic,' I will look into my own heart and know that the forces of Creation live there—as they live within any thinking, prudent man, under the guise of wisdom and common sense! So go from me now, Karana! Go! Be the wild, solitary thing you were when I first set eyes upon you. You are not my son. You are the son of Navahk, after all. I cast you out! Your people turn their backs upon you! No more shall we look upon your face!"

Karana stared. His laughter bubbled back into his throat along with his blood. The blackness in his head seemed to expand. For a moment, he saw through the pain and blood and anguish and knew that he did not want to go—not from Torka's side, not from the cave, not from the warm, loving embrace of his Mahnie, and not from the laughter of children and the fellowship of friends. He did not want to be a magic man. He only wanted to stay, to be a man among other men, no more, no less. To be forgiven. But how could Torka forgive him? How could he forgive himself? Torka was right: He was the son of Navahk, and from this there could be no reprieve.

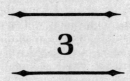

3

Winter deepened. If there had ever been a colder, stormier time of the long dark, the people of Cheanah could not remember it.

Zhoonali did not speak of the wind spirit's incursion into the encampment or of Cheanah's failure to pursue it into the storm. She kept his secret; as long as he was headman she would have a place within the band, no matter how long the winter lasted. As for the loss of some of his favorite spears, he soon crafted others.

Nevertheless, the winter went on and on, and if the sun rose briefly beyond the eastern ranges to mark the return of spring, they could not tell in the constant storms. And now, in the Place of Endless Meat, the people of Cheanah were down to the last of their moldering stores.

"Perhaps the spirits are angry with us," suggested Ank. "Perhaps Honee should have been given away to Teean according to the custom of the ancients. At least then we would not have to listen to her whining. And maybe it was not such a good thing to take the skin of a wanawut and—"

"Enough! I will hear no criticism from you, whelp!" Cheanah silenced the boy with a shout that allowed no argument.

"I am hungry," whined Honee.

Xhan observed the girl with open contempt. "You and everyone else!"

Old Teean had entered the headman's pit hut, hoping that at least one of the women might have snared some small vole or squirrel she would share. He overheard the

complaints of Honee and came closer. "You are still welcome to come to my bed furs, daughter of Cheanah, and
warm this hungry old man in the night. I will share my
meat with you."

The girl eyed him with revulsion. "Will you never give
up? I would rather starve than spread myself for you!"

The old man shook his head sadly as he shivered against
the cold, constant wind. "And well you may, before this
winter ends. Well may we all!"

An air of solemnity settled throughout the encampment.
Tempers grew short as men, women, and children began
to grow weak and sick.

"We should have stored more and eaten less," Ekoh
said tersely. "Cheanah should have insisted upon it!"

"We still have some stores left!" reminded the headman.

"Moldering fish and putrid fowl and fat so rotten that it
looks and smells like pus!" snapped Bili.

"Shut your mouth, woman of Ekoh, or you and yours
will eat nothing in the days to come, I promise you!"
warned Zhoonali.

Bili lowered her head and glared. "By my own initiative
I have seen fit to store more supplies than any woman in
this camp! And I have also seen fit to share them with you
and all the others! Do not threaten me, you old hag! If
there is meat on your bones, it is because of me!"

Zhoonali's head swung on her thin, tendinous neck as
she looked to Cheanah for support. "Speak for your mother,
my son! Will you allow this female to talk to me this way?"

Cheanah paused and stared at Zhoonali long and hard.
She had just unwittingly given him the opportunity to
shake the weight of some responsibility for the unending
winter off his back and onto hers. He smiled and shrugged.

"Bili should of course speak with respect to the wise
woman at all times, but in this she is right, my mother.
You *are* wise woman of this band. The talking bones speak
through you. But I do not remember your cautioning this
band about the severity of the winter to come . . . or
advising the women to set aside extra provisions for it."

The old woman drew herself up inside her bearskin.
Cheanah saw her features tighten, then expand.

"The talking bones speak *through* me. I do not speak. *They* speak. If anyone questions this woman's wisdom, then let *them* speak to the talking bones! Perhaps, in their mouths, they will speak great wisdom . . . or perhaps they will not speak at all!"

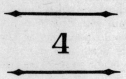

4

Alone, Karana made his way across the night. The wounds that Torka had left upon his face had healed; but his face was scarred, as was his heart. Like a solitary wolf he walked, outcast from the band, pacing his lonely territory—around the lake until the walls of the north-canyon glacier blocked his way, then back and around again. He found himself hoping that someday his pacing would end and he would be welcomed home once more.

The hope was troubling, causing him to remember that after Torka had banished him, he had almost blurted out the truth, as he spoke it aloud now: "Perhaps I am not responsible for the death of two sons, after all. The one who was abandoned long ago lives. He walks my dreams, even as he walks the dreams of Umak. The boy has foretold more than the death of this stillborn son! What he has also seen in his dreams is his living twin. Yes! It is so! I *lied*, so you would not follow the wanawut and discover what I truly am—not only the son of Navahk but the brother of beasts, unfit to walk in the company of men!"

From where he stood he could see tiny lights flickering in the flanks of the hills. The women were up in Torka's cave, rousing the cooking fire, igniting the tallow lamps. Soon it would be morning. Karana's mouth went dry with wanting.

He felt the madness growing in him, dark, disturbingly focused, and obsessive. He knew that Navahk had come to live within him upon the mountain, sharing his spirit and fighting for control.

Hardness toward beautiful Summer Moon congealed within his heart; it was to avoid her that he had deliberately ignored the signal fire that called him to Lonit's side. He saw it as a trick of Navahk's to get him to go back to the cave, to lie again with Summer Moon or Mahnie, so the evil Navahk would pour out of Karana and into the women to take life again and destroy Torka. Thus, although he had the magic to quicken Lonit's labor, he had withheld it from her.

Guilt struck him deep. He turned and began to run aimlessly, blindly, until he stumbled. He collapsed onto his knees in the darkness and was glad for the pain. It was no more than he deserved. He cursed and climbed to his feet. With a low growl of rage and anguish, Karana began to walk toward the place upon the high, black ridge where he had made his lonely, desolate home. He hoped that somewhere along the way he would die.

Far to the west, the great thaw finally came to the Place of Endless Meat. The steppe became a vast quagmire as meltwater poured out of the surrounding ranges. Avalanches and mudslides shook the mountains. Rivers roared and ran brown and thick with mud, suffocating the fish. Streams swelled and overran their banks.

The carcasses of animals that had frozen to death during the long, brutal winter were washed out of the canyons to litter the plains; birds and blackflies filled the gray, leaden skies as insects and starving carnivores came to compete with man for meat.

The starving people of Cheanah wailed as the wanawut howled with wolves in the night. Infants sucked at breasts that were nearly dry of milk. Although there was food to be had, the children sat hollow-eyed beside malnourished women who had stopped menstruating because their men were too weak to hunt effectively—even for carrion.

"I come to speak the truth," old Teean said with shaky deference as he stood before Cheanah within the headman's pit hut. "This man has done much thinking. It may be time for this band to go from this place. In this Place of Endless Meat, there is no meat. Never has this man seen so much rain. It is not a natural thing. The herd animals cannot come through the passes this year; the rivers are too deep and wide for the herds to cross them! Perhaps we should follow the way of Torka and walk into the face of the rising sun before it is too late."

With narrowed, resentful eyes Cheanah observed the wasted figure of the bow-backed old man. How had Teean managed to survive the winter? How had any of them survived it? "How far do you think that you—or any of us—could get, old man, if we took up our belongings and set out across this sodden country?"

The question hung in the air. Cheanah looked across the hut and eyed Zhoonali with grim speculation as she sat with her empty badger-skin bag in her lap, casting the bones of telling again and again. The bones clicked and rattled as they fell. Her hands resembled them—pale, dry, purely skeletal. She was wasted by malnutrition.

Guilt caused Cheanah to look away. Since the day he had shifted the responsibility for the weather onto her back, she had not nagged him or voiced an unsolicited opinion. She was his mother, but since being attacked in his own encampment by a spear-hurling wanawut, he had found himself thinking: *If Zhoonali dies, no one will ever know that it came into camp and that I failed to pursue it. No one will know that I lied about my stolen spears. What if Zhoonali is right? What if the forces of Creation have been angered by my wanton breaking with tradition?*

Beyond the pit hut, the rain intensified into a downpour. Honee put her head onto her knees and began to cry. Zhoonali's eyes narrowed as she looked long and hard at the girl, then at Teean, and lastly at her son. There was challenge in her eyes—and more than that, open castigation.

Resentment flared within Cheanah. He would *not* change his mind. "We will find food," he said, knowing that he would have to make good on his word. "When the rain slows, we will go out. And this time we *will* find meat."

The next day, Cheanah called for the starving hunters to assemble. The hunting party's destination was on the eastern horizon, where circling birds promised meat under their shadow.

The promise was not broken. The men found a small

pride of lions feeding on the carcass of a decaying elk. The wind blew the stink of the dead animal to the hunters. It had been dead a long time.

"Rotten meat is better than no meat," said Kivan, salivating. "My women told me to bring home something—*anything*—for the little ones."

"I count five females, all grown. They won't be easy to drive off." Ekoh's expression revealed his lack of enthusiasm.

"We have our spear hurlers," reminded Mano. "What's the matter, Ekoh? Lost your nerve? Been too long without a woman while waiting for Bili to free herself of that child she still carries?"

"You keep my woman's name out of your mouth!" Ekoh's face congested with anger. "Besides, we'll just get close enough to the lions to startle them off. And you, Kivan, could shut your women's mouths with a lion kill!"

Kivan nodded happily at the prospect.

"Maybe the lions will run," Yanehva volunteered. "But maybe they won't. They may be as hungry as we are."

Mano snorted a hot rebuke. "Always the cautious one, Yanehva! As tremulous as a first-time woman. I've been driven off by lions and bears from every carcass that the river's washed down from the hills since the thaw. I won't be driven off today."

Pride in Mano's assertiveness shone in Cheanah's eyes. "Mano is right. We can close from three sides. Teean, you stay here and yell. Your lungs are strong, but your legs and arms aren't what they used to be. You'll only be in the way."

It was a good plan. But the wind turned and the big cats scented the hunters before they could draw upon the element of surprise. The lions circled round, then charged them. The men scattered.

When the other females turned back to feed upon the elk, one of them kept on coming. Kivan screamed as a great, sweeping paw knocked him from his feet.

Ekoh and Ram positioned themselves to hurl their spears, but by then Kivan's screams had stopped; Cheanah called them back. The hunters turned their spear hurlers on the lions, driving them away, then dragged the mutilated remnants of the elk and of Kivan back to camp.

The women and children of Kivan mourned his death. Zhoonali made a little fire for Kivan and sang softly to his spirit while her people gorged themselves on the elk's meat. It was late in the night when the meat proved to be bad. Zhoonali alone was able to care for her winter-weakened people when they grew sick on it. Most she saved, others she could not.

Amazingly, old Teean survived, while Kivan's youngest widow died, as did Klee, Bili and Ekoh's little girl, and Shar, Cheanah's youngest daughter. One of the women of Ram succumbed, and after the bodies were abandoned to look upon the sky forever far out from camp, the people staggered back against illness and grief.

Zhoonali despaired. The breast milk of the meat-poisoned women made the surviving babies gravely ill. In a single night, one infant died, and three more girl babies were so sick that their fathers smothered them. As was customary during starving times, the bodies of the infants were taken well out from camp to serve as bait to lure small carrion eaters to the snares that were set around them.

That bleak, miserable night the people of Cheanah sat within the silent camp, listening to the wind, the rain, and the constant sound of water running over the land. Neither the wolves nor the wanawut howled or wailed, but the people sensed predators lurking . . . hungering . . . for the soft, sweet flesh of the naked infants.

"Whatever is found in the traps tomorrow, I will eat none of it," Bili whispered bitterly as she drew Seteena close within the pit hut of Ekoh; she ached inside when she felt the thinness of the boy, and she marveled at how he had survived when her outwardly stronger little girl had not.

"Do not speak so, my woman," soothed Ekoh. "Things will be better for us soon. We have endured bad years before."

She shivered. "Never like this."

Seteena patted his mother's face. "It will be all right, Mother. You will see."

"Your sister is dead," she reminded him gently.

The boy eyed her thoughtfully. "Maybe the child that grows within my mother has waited so long to be born because it has known that my sister would need a way to come back into the world. If it is a girl, we will name it after Klee! She will live again; you will see."

Bili sighed. The boy was so frail, yet so kind and brave. "I will always be sad, Seteena, for as long as we live within this band."

"What else can we do?" Ekoh asked.

"We could leave. We could walk to the east, as Torka walked. Perhaps we could find him. Oh, think of it, Ekoh! To see Eneela again, and Lonit and Iana, and to laugh at the wonderfully terrible jokes of Grek, and to be mothered by Wallah and—"

"Just the three of us? Half-starved and still weak with sickness, and you great with child? We would never reach them. Surely, Bili, we would die."

"We will die if we stay here. You will see. We will all die."

Within the pit hut of Cheanah, the sons of Cheanah lay awake within their warm, albeit moldering bed furs.

"Did you see the red star just before the weather closed in?" asked Yanehva, lying on his belly with his arms folded beneath his chin. "It looks like the same star that we saw long ago. You remember?"

Mano snorted. "Let's hope it isn't the same star. The sky caught fire, the earth shook, and the moon went black. We can do without that."

"The red star," Ank pondered. "If it shines when the sky is clear, maybe it will bring us luck. Maybe there'll be meat in the snares that we set around the dead babies. That would be something."

5

That was the first night that Sister led the way down from the hills. The beastling was not particularly hungry, but Sister, being fully grown, always had an appetite, and the smell of meat on the wind was sweet and enticing indeed.

His fingers curled now around the smooth hafts of his throwing sticks, which he could use very well. Whenever he left the nest, he always brought two along. He quickened his step. Sister was so far ahead of him that he could not see her now. The smell of the meat was stronger on the rain-misted wind. It was an odd smell, soft and sweet, but with the stink of beast to it.

And then he heard Sister scream.

"Did you hear it?"

"I heard," Cheanah replied to Zhoonali.

Mano was sitting up, shoving his feet into his boots. "Do you think it was one of the cubs, or another beast?"

"You said that the cubs of the wanawut were dead," Honee reminded him; fear put a wheedling tremor in her voice.

"Be quiet!" Cheanah's command stung the entire family to silence. Close at his side, little Klu, openly the headman's favorite since the day of his birth, stared up at his father questioningly.

"I'm afraid of the wanawut," Honee whimpered. "I wish its head did not hang outside this hut!"

Had the girl been within striking distance, she would have received the back of Cheanah's hand across her face.

"Stupid girl, you do not know a good thing when you see it! And do not put name to that which you have not seen lest you cause it to be!"

"Name it then, for I would gladly wet the head of my spear in wanawut blood!" said Mano.

Yanehva frowned at his older brother. "The skin of one wanawut has brought enough sorrow to this camp."

Other members of the band could be heard stumbling from their pit huts. In a moment they were standing close to Cheanah's, and he was up and opening the hide door.

"Did you hear it?" The question came from every mouth.

"Do you think we've snared it? Taken a wanawut alive?" Ram's voice held a tremulous edge.

The beastling found Sister on the ground, rolling on her back, curled up with her feet in the air and her hands desperately holding on to a long barb of bone that had somehow driven itself straight through her snout and palate. When he succeeded in gentling her by stroking her and sounding to her, she allowed him to pull it out. That was when the blood started to spurt and flow, and that was when she reflexively backhanded him ten feet through the air. He landed flat on his back, and the world went black.

When his head cleared and he was able to get to his feet again, he saw that Sister was down and half drowning in her own blood. He ran to her and pulled her to her feet; upright, she could breathe. While she was gasping and mewing in confusion and pain, he saw the meat and the snare. The beastling snarled at the cleverness of the device.

He frowned. It was starting to sleet. Instinct told him that the beasts must have heard Sister's screaming and that they would be coming soon. He must get her away.

"It has escaped," declared Cheanah, hopeful that the others had not heard the relief in his voice.

The sleet was stinging the ground with a fury.

"In this weather we have no chance of tracking it!" snarled Mano with obvious disappointment. "Look, the tracks have already washed away!"

Ank was on his knees. "Not all. Here are a couple. And blood. Yes. You can smell it if you bend close."

"Watch the snares, boy! They'll put a hole in a skull as small as yours!" cautioned Ekoh.

"Leave the snares set," Cheanah decided. "We can check them again in the morning."

Mano cast a hateful look up at the stormy night. "If we're lucky, we can pick up a few tracks then, in better light."

"If we do, it should prove interesting," said Yanehva as he knelt and touched the rapidly disappearing tracks. "There are *two* of them. And one wears boots!"

Late the next morning Mano roused Cheanah into reluctant leadership of a hunting party that went out under heavily clouded skies. The wanawut had not returned, but in one of the snares, the hunters found cause to smile: Eight foxes had come to feed upon the bodies of the dead babies. Six had been caught in the net. Mano broke their necks with his bare hands and laughed with the pleasure that the killing gave him. The other two were already dead in snares similar to the one that had injured the wanawut. No one spoke of that. The people were hungry, and the rain had washed away all signs of the beast; even to those who had clearly heard the scream, it seemed like a dream born of the storm of the previous night.

That day the people of Cheanah ate of the molting, malnourished foxes. If anyone thought about the dead infants that had served as bait, it was not mentioned. Food was food, and the babies had been dead anyway.

When the last of the muscle meat and marrow was gone, the women pounded the skulls and bones into fragments and dumped them into a large communal boiling bag with the ears, tails, snouts, sinews, and strips of hide. Rainwater was added to the bag, along with heated stones. The bag was then wrapped in several layers of water-saturated skins and buried in the ashes of the fire pit. The women periodically dug it up to add more heated stones and remoisten the outer layers of the skins to keep them from burning. After several hours, the bag was taken up and its contents strained into bowls of antelope skulls; the liquid that resulted was a thin but nourishing soup. They shared it, drinking it all. The men took the largest portion, as well as all the now moribundly tender ears, tails, snouts, sinews, and bits of hide.

When Ekoh reached out and handed a portion of one of the ears to Seteena, Zhoonali rose from the women's side of the fire and struck it from his hand.

"No! In starving times, that one has no right to eat! He is of no use to his people. Are there no traditions that will be maintained by this band?" Now her sharp, rheumy, hunger-haunted eyes challenged her son. "Tell him, Cheanah!"

He stared back at her as the fox ear he had just secreted under his tunic for little Klu dripped against his belly. He looked at Ekoh and the wasted form of Seteena. He did not like the boy and had not forgotten the way Seteena had attacked him in an imagined defense of Bili. But when Bili was at last free of her pregnancy, the headman knew he would need the boy's life as leverage; Bili would not be the same when he came to mount her once again.

"Do not be offended, old friend," he said equably to Ekoh. "Our wise woman speaks with valid concern. Your strength is needed to provide meat for the people."

"And for my son," replied Ekoh simply.

Cheanah observed the boy with unconcealed disapproval. "His mother may give to him what she will. You have lost a daughter. Let the boy eat of the child's share until the spirits smile once more upon this people."

"That may never be!" Bili retorted. She might have said more had Zhoonali not suddenly slapped her so hard that she fell sideways as blood spurted from her nose and mouth.

"Speak not so to the headman of this band, woman of Ekoh!"

Ekoh half rose but was kept in his place by the hard, steadying hand of Mano. "You are envied for your woman, Ekoh, but she talks too much."

Cheanah waved his hand in a conciliatory fashion. "As headman of this band I could command Ekoh to set his useless boy to walk the wind forever. But instead I say— generously, I might add—feed your useless one as you will, Ekoh, but not of a hunter's portion."

Zhoonali looked as though she would explode with anger, but a look from her son stung her to silence. "You have advised, wise woman. This headman has listened. Now he has spoken! You will speak no more!"

"My boy will die without more to eat!" protested Ekoh.

Cheanah shrugged. "Then he will die. As the spirits and the forces of Creation decree. Cheanah will hear no more!"

In silence, with eyes downcast, the people resumed their meal while Zhoonali began to cast her bones angrily, and the boy Seteena stared straight ahead in stoic silence. His gaunt face was set. His sunken eyes were hard with pride when Bili, bloody faced and beginning to swell around the mouth, offered him a portion of her broth. He ignored the cup, rose, and walked rigidly from the protection of the sodden tarpaulins to the pit hut of his parents.

"Let him go!" Cheanah shouted at Bili when she made to go after him. "The boy is nothing! Do as I say, or I will send him to walk the wind forever!"

It was late. The other members of the band slept undisturbed by the scuttlings of the youngest children as they went from their family pit huts to scavenge among the cooling embers of the big fire where the strainings of the soup had gone.

There was nothing left but fragments of bone and hairy hide, but the toddlers were hungry, so they chewed and sucked on these blissfully, spitting out the hair and splinters; until one of them discovered the only portions of the foxes that their elders had disdained—the potentially poisonous kidneys and spleens.

By morning the children were all sick. Weakened as they were by hunger and prolonged malnutrition, by nightfall all but one succumbed to the poisonous organs. Perhaps it was the ear of the fox that gave Klu, Cheanah's youngest and most beloved little son, the extra strength to live as long as he did. But Cheanah had taught all his sons to be bold, and Klu had managed to eat the largest portion of the stolen meat. He died at dawn.

And on that dawn, while the women wailed as they laid Klu to look upon the sky forever alongside the last of the toddlers of the band, Cheanah withered under the strain of his grief and cracked wide open under the crushing weight of his responsibilities.

The headman stood in absolute silence. Water poured off the skin of the wanawut as it lay across his back. In his hand, firmly spiked on a long stake of bone, was the head of the wanawut. Slowly, he raised the head of the beast. Slowly, he took off its skin, drove the stake that held the head deep into the sodden permafrost, then draped the robe over it.

With his head flung back and his arms flung wide, he cried out: "Take back that which is of the wind and storm and misted mountains! It belongs not on the backs of men! Take back the life of the wanawut, and restore our children to this man and to this people!"

Cheanah waited. His people watched. But the spirits did not take back the skin or the head of the wanawut. Trembling, he nodded as if to some inner voice, then pointed a finger at Seteena.

"That boy is not fit to live. That boy will not eat the food of this people! That boy will walk the wind forever!"

Ekoh stiffened and put a protective hand on his son's shoulder. "He will not walk alone!" he said boldly, but Cheanah was not listening.

The headman was advancing toward Honee. He dragged her by her hair and flung her toward Teean.

"Take her! She is yours! Pierce her *now*, before us all. Zhoonali is right. The spirits are watching! Let them see that the people of Cheanah honor their ancestors and the customs of those who have gone to walk the wind before us! Let them take back the bad luck that has come to this band!"

"No!" Honee screamed and turned to run, but Cheanah's fingers curled into her hair again and pulled her around.

As the band stood staring, Teean hesitated, for in these past few moons starvation had stripped away his arrogance. Now he stood sickly and shivering, loosening his clothes. His organ was flaccid. He worked it frantically to no avail.

Honee heard her father exhale a low hiss of frustration. He turned her and began to rip her garments away as she fought against him until, with a single slap, he sent her sprawling naked into the mud at his feet.

"Spread yourself! Now!"

Bitterly cold, sleet-driven rain stung her as she rolled to her hands and knees and tried to get up. But the ground beneath her was slippery, and she fell, gasping as Teean mounted her from behind.

"Mother! Zhoonali! Make him stop!"

Neither woman said a word as the band closed a tight circle around Honee and the old man. They stared down at her expressionlessly as old Teean grasped her breasts in a bony, pincer-hard grip and held her fast as he rammed his withered organ against her backside, seeking penetration . . . pumping but not penetrating.

Honee, sobbing and shivering against cold and shame, deliberately lurched forward and rolled sideways in the mud hoping to shake off the old man. It was no good; he lay locked to her, grimacing as he worked on her to no avail.

"The forces of Creation no longer give life to that old bone."

Honee looked up. Mano was standing over her, his own organ unsheathed and rigid in the rain.

"No . . ." Honee moaned. Yet it would be done. She knew it. She put back her head and screamed but knew it was no use.

The eyes of the men of her band had taken on the strange, fixed look that had transformed Mano's face. They were set and ready for rape. Starving they were, and weak and devoid of energy, but the sight of an unpierced woman lying naked and vulnerable in the rain had been enough to invigorate them. Even Cheanah was exposing himself.

She stared at him. "M-my father . . . no . . ."

His face was set. The circle was growing smaller; the women were no longer here. Even Ank was threatening and ready. Only Yanehva hung back until Cheanah raged at him.

"No! The forces of Creation are watching! It must be all of us! All!"

Yanehva slowly shook his head. "This is not right. She is a virgin."

"She is nothing!" Cheanah roared. "The potency of the band is everything!" He was like a great bear lowering himself, snarling impatiently as he forced a protesting Teean back and away.

"Time . . . a little more time!" begged the old man.

Honee hated them both as she sobbed and went lax beneath her father's cruelly questing hands. She wished that Mother Below would pull her down into her protecting embrace.

But it was not Mother Below whose command caused Cheanah to halt in the rape of his own daughter; it was Zhoonali. Honee looked up, hope flaring brightly. Then the girl saw the long claw of the giant ground sloth poised in her grandmother's hand.

"In the way of our ancestors, Teean will blood his woman—if not with his own bone, then with this!" declared Zhoonali.

"No!" screamed Honee, her eyes fixed on the claw. Twice the length of a man's hand, it was an oiled, blood-darkened menace. With a shriek, the girl flung herself ferociously free of her father's grasp and tried desperately to rise.

It was no use.

Cheanah caught her, brought her down again, and forced her onto her back as Mano grabbed her limbs and parted them wide—so wide that she thought she would go mad as young Ank and Ram took hold of one of her feet and Mano continued to grip the other.

"Hold," he whispered. "Imagine that I am entering you."

"Never!" she screamed, and then was amazed when her voice made no sound but a croak.

Zhoonali had given Teean the claw. He was coming toward her.

"Do not fight this, Honee," advised the old woman. "It will be done in the way of your ancestors since time beyond beginning, for the good of the band."

6

The star was rising out of the east and setting in the same place as the sun when it slipped over the edge of the world to the west. By night, Torka stared at it long and hard. By day, he thought about it long and hard.

"What troubles you, Torka? The star is a good omen, yes?"

He looked at Grek. "I don't know. The weather does seem to be improving. Come. Help me to train Aar's pups to carry a pack."

"Pups? These dogs are as big as wolves! And they do not smile at this man the way they smile at Torka, Karana, and Umak. You work with the dogs, my old friend. Why do you want the dogs to carry packs?"

"I have been thinking of moving next year to another camp, either across the valley or out of it entirely."

"My Wallah cannot walk."

"We will carry her, on a sledge, pulled by the dogs!"

Grek frowned thoughtfully. "It would be good to hunt in new lands again. But I am an old man, Torka, and this is good country. Why would you want to leave it?"

Torka sighed, suddenly irritable. "I have come to know that you are right: Men can stay too long in one place. I sense it. I grow restless with the need to walk into the face of the rising sun again."

Mano was livid. "Ekoh is gone, and Bili, too. They dropped their pit hut in the night and walked off with the boy!"

Cheanah sat cross-legged within his hut. They were alone. Cheanah had been dark and sullen since Klu's death; people tended to avoid him. "I sent the boy to walk the wind. It is his parents' right to walk it with him."

"You swore that I could have any woman that pleased me if I would keep your secret. I want Bili."

"Go after her, then. Bring her back . . . if Ekoh will allow it. But not the boy. Now that he is gone, the weather is improving. Now that Honee has gone to Teean and spreads herself for the men of this band, the game will return. Now that I have returned to the ways of our ancestors and put off the skin of the wanawut, the spirits will smile upon our people again. You will see."

"Hurry. I want to be in the eastern hills by nightfall," Ekoh urged.

Seteena, pale and panting, strained under the weight of his pack frame. "Mother is too big with baby to go so fast. Why would they follow? They *wanted* me gone from the band."

"It is not you they will come after. It is your mother."

Bili paused and looked back, then gave a startled cry. "Look! It's Mano and Ank!" Her face hardened as she remembered the hungry way Mano had been looking at her and the perversions he had worked on her before his father had forced all other men away, including her own Ekoh. She shivered with loathing. "We have a good start. If we hurry we can reach those stony slopes up ahead, where they will not be able to track us."

"But Mother, can you go fast enough?"

Bili smiled. Within a moment the bundle that she had secured under her tunic was exposed for what it was: a well-stuffed backrest. Ekoh and Seteena stared in amazement. "I'm sorry, Ekoh. I should have told you. But it has kept the wolves of Cheanah's band off me! I feared that you would have guessed. Mano was suspicious. So was Cheanah. No woman carries a child for over twelve moons!"

Ekoh pulled her close and winked at their son. "We will make our own band, my boy!"

They walked until the boy faltered and fell flat. Fighting against exhaustion, he tried to rise, but his malnourished body failed him. Bili took his pack, Ekoh hefted him in his arms, and they went on quickly. Only now and again did they stop, distracted by the sensation of being watched—by something above them in the gathering mists.

As the sound of the beasts' footfalls had come closer, the beastling had taken up his throwing sticks and his man stone, covered Sister with his lionskin to keep her warm, and walked naked out of hiding. He crouched behind boulders and observed the beasts.

They walked as if they were tired, yet they were hurrying, and he could smell their fear. The updrafts also brought him the scent of two other beasts walking far below. They were walking very fast, angrily, and there was no stink of fear on them.

Soon the shadows grew long, and the dark came down. He watched as the three beasts paused. They sat very close, ate something, and sounded softly to one another. Then they lay down and wrapped their arms around each other, much as Sister and he did when they sought warmth on a cold night.

It occurred to the beastling that this would be a good time to kill them, but their tenderness toward one another caused him to hesitate. With a sigh, he went back to the nest. Sister was feverish and howling for him. He hooted a greeting and put on the lionskin again. He was grateful for its warmth as he stayed by her side, stroking until she fell into troubled sleep. He was afraid she might die from the wound in her snout.

For a long while he lay awake, thinking of the three beasts sleeping on the hills below . . . and of the others that were climbing toward them. He took up his throwing sticks and his man stone and went from the nest to watch them again.

Snow fell heavily. He could find no sign of the three beasts; they had evidently continued on into the east. The two pursuers had turned back. He followed them. When the smaller slipped, the larger one kicked at it. The wind brought the mean, nasty edge of their vocalizing to him. It inspired him to hurl one of his throwing sticks at them.

He took careful aim at the larger beast, but the smaller went down screaming.

The beastling grunted in disgust. He showed his teeth and screeched loudly in frustration. One of his throwing sticks was gone forever.

The larger of the two pivoted, scanned the snow-driven heights, then bent, hefted its companion over its shoulders, and ran off into the driving snow. The throwing stick projected upward, out of the small one's back.

Once again there was mourning in the camp of Cheanah as a body was put out of camp to look upon the sky forever. In a driving snowstorm, Mano, standing above Ank's body, placed the spear that had killed his brother across his father's palms.

"*This* is what killed him! Your spear! Ekoh not only steals the best woman of the band, he dares to steal the weapons of our headman and then kill us with them when we follow!"

Cheanah stared at the spear. Mano had not guessed the truth, and mercifully, Zhoonali did not speak it. Cheanah broke the spear across his thigh and laid it over the body of his son.

Mano fixed his father with burning eyes. "When the weather clears, we must hunt Ekoh down. We must make him pay with his life!"

"There is not a man in this band who has the strength for such a trek," Yanehva pointed out soberly. "Let us mourn our dead in peace and leave Ekoh to his fate."

Cheanah frowned. It was difficult to think clearly. He was too hungry, too overwhelmed by the death of his children. He was headman of his people, and they were dying all around him. Why? Suddenly he knew the answer. It came to him with such cruel intensity that it staggered him. Yanehva had warned him long ago to hunt as Torka had hunted—to waste no meat, to decimate no herd. Within Cheanah's empty belly, hatred and resentment toward Torka rose like storm clouds boiling on the horizon of his thoughts. He would deal with them later. Now was the time to speak to his people of what must be.

His people closed a circle around him, sensing the change. He felt their eyes watching him.

"The bodies of our dead speak to Cheanah," he announced. "Have we eaten the last of the foxes that live in this land? Have we cracked the bones and spit the feathers of the last eagles and hawks and teratorns? Is there not one creature left alive to eat our dead? No! There is not! This is no longer the Place of Endless Meat. It is the Starving Land, and we must leave it! We must follow the animals to the east if we are to survive!"

Zhoonali's head went up within her snow-frosted bearskin hood. "We are too weak. We have no meat to give us strength to walk."

"We have meat," Cheanah said, and gestured downward toward the bodies of the little ones who had been placed to look upon the sky forever. "Our children will feed us. Our children will make us strong for the trek that lies ahead. We will feed on their flesh. It is for this that they have died—so that their people will live."

7

The beastling had been watching them in puzzlement as they knocked down their nests, packed them upon their backs, and walked away toward the east. They moved so slowly that by dark they still were not very far from where they had started. They stopped, put up some smaller nests, then crawled beneath them—to sleep, he supposed.

With the rising of the hole in the sky, the beasts were up again, taking down their nests, then walking around and around, gathering up things they had taken from their backs the night before. He was confused. Where were they going? *Why?*

As the days passed, only by moving greater and greater distances along the spine of the hills had he been able to keep a constant watch on them. Sister consistently refused to accompany him from the cave. Her wounded snout had healed, although it had left her with an ugly scar and a bad wheeze. She was well and strong and sound of appetite again, but it seemed to the beastling that somehow the experience had injured her spirit.

He was always able to find a good spot from which to view the beasts' progress, although sometimes he would have to walk for the equivalent of a full day and part of a night before he caught sight of them. Today he had traveled very far indeed. Sister would be upset with him when he returned.

She was always upset with him when he returned! And all of the long while that he was gone, when she was not sleeping, she howled and howled until he returned to assure her by his soundings and strokings that he would not leave her.

He fought against the fiercely protective thoughts that would not allow him to leave Sister. She needed him too much. But he had needs, too—to leave the nest, to walk the world in search of the beasts. He could not live in a world without beasts! He could not live in a world with no hope of killing them when he had learned all that he hungered to know.

He would kill them for what they had done to Mother. To Sister. To all the animals that lived beneath the hole in the sky. But until that day, he could not stay where he was while they walked away over the edge of the world. Sister would have to understand and follow . . . or she would have to stay behind.

Miserable but resolute, he turned and began the long walk back to the nest. He would gather up all his throwing sticks, his chips of stone, his drinking bowl—

He stopped. Sister was coming toward him. His spears were tucked under her arm, and his stone chips were chattering away in his drinking bowl, which she held out to him in one furred and massive hand.

For the first time in her life she sounded to him. It was the tremulous, quiver-lipped sound of one who fears that she is about to be abandoned. "Man-nah-rah-vak!" she cried, and as she stumbled into his welcoming embrace, he saw the completely unwanawutlike streams of moisture running from her eyes. He held her close, rocking her, but he did not try to wipe the wetness from her face. Tears were falling from his eyes, too.

In a world full of light, Karana felt much less like dying. The dark, twisted hauntings of his madness were diminished in the constant light of day. Now that the first signs of autumn were on the land, he spent most of his time gathering and gleaning, assembling a large medicine bag that was to be an offering to his people. True, they wanted no part of him or his magic, but healing ways and magic ways were two different things. His knowledge of healing was wasted upon the mountain, and he knew that it was not his to keep.

He owed his life and everything that he knew to Torka. If he had lost the gift of the spirit wind that had once opened his mind to the future, that was his fault, not Torka's. The spirits chose the vessels out of which they would be poured into the lives of men. They had chosen him, and he had proved unworthy. But before the time of the long dark came down again upon the world, Karana would give his healing gift back to Torka so that those whom he loved—most especially Mahnie and Naya—would know the ways to heal themselves.

The old restlessness stirred in him. He could see them as they went about their lives in the valley far below. As long as he could see them, he felt a part of their lives. They were safe from the evil machinations of Navahk as long as he stayed here. His purpose in life now was to protect his people from Navahk. And to protect himself from Torka's wrath, for the living lie, for which he could never be forgiven, was coming out of the west: Torka's son.

His head suddenly ached with confusion. He sensed danger walking with Manaravak. Should Torka not be warned of it? He lay back against the warm stone of the ridge and stared up at the sun. Light poured into him, warming him, and yet when he closed his eyes and fell asleep, his dreams were cold and dark and filled with falling stars. He was drowning in them.

Aar wakened him, rooted under his palm with a cold, wet nose. Karana smiled and sat up. Aar often saved him from dreams of drowning in darkness.

Come down the mountain into the world of men again, the dog seemed to say.

"I cannot, my brother, for if I come, Navahk will come with me."

The dog and man rose and walked together along the ridge, then back around the huge gray lake that gave life to nothing except icebergs, which broke off from the towering glacial cliffs that stood against its northern shore.

The dog whined softly. The lake lapped coldly, hungrily, against its stony banks and the icy wall that held it captive. Even with the sun shining, the glacier's weather-eroded, dust-encrusted surface failed to reflect the blue

sky. The lake's water was thick with silt . . . restless,
roiling, whitecapped by the invisible plucking fingers of
the wind that lived upon the mountain. It troubled Karana.
He stared, trying to place the source of his worry but
failing.

A desolate feeling caused by the age and decay overwhelmed the magic man. Because the entire highland
basin was a monstrous, ancient thing of ice that slowly,
inexorably moved and shifted and left behind the stony
bones of the mountain as rubble, Karana wondered why
he was drawn to walk here so often. He turned his steps
out onto the arm of the north-canyon glacier, which crawled
upward out of the gorge to dam the lake and keep it
locked within the broad sprawl of the highland basin.
Without the glacier, there would be no lake; the waters
would tumble from the heights down through the gorge
and inundate the wonderful valley.

The sound of boyish laughter rose up from far below.
Umak was swimming in the river after a day of hunting
alone. Karana frowned. Why was the youth alone so much?
Umak, the dreamer, who had so innocently turned Karana's
world upside down. He missed the friendship he had once
shared with Torka's son. But as Umak's laughter bubbled
up the gorge again, Navahk's ghost suddenly began to
laugh, and the smell of death was strong in Karana's
nostrils.

Whose death? Most assuredly his own.

"Come," he said to Aar as he began to walk back toward
his little shelter. "I have a gift—something that I would
have you bring to our band."

The dog stood patiently while he strapped to its back
the pack that he had so lovingly filled: healing herbs,
precious oils, and drawings on bark that would show his
people how to use the remedies.

And as the dog loped away, Karana watched his brother
go and wondered if he would ever see him again.

Cheanah's band found no sign of the great herds, but
they came upon remnants of the camps of Ekoh, Bili, and
Seteena . . . and of the old fire circles that Torka's band

had raised as they had trekked deeper into the Forbidden Land.

"I thought we'd find their bones drying in the wind," Ram remarked.

"Do you think they're all alive out there somewhere?" Weariness, hunger, and grief had etched deep lines into Yanehva's face. "If we find them, we could hunt with them again. There was always meat in Torka's camp."

Cheanah glowered, and his voice sounded strangely hollow. "Torka is our enemy. If we find him, we will take his meat, his fine women, and his shaman, as easily as I once stole his hunting grounds and his camp. But this time I will kill him. Now I know that Torka tricked us when he walked from our camp. He knew that his shaman would follow. And he knew that when Life Giver walked ahead of him, it would take our luck away. As long as that mammoth and Torka live, they will feed upon our luck— their shaman will see to it. We must find them and make them pay for our dead."

"You will not kill the women?" Mano pressed.

Cheanah looked up at his eldest son. "You and I will enjoy the women."

"And the girls, and Bili when we find her?"

"We will enjoy her, too. All of the men of this band will enjoy her! And Torka's girls."

At last they came to the confluence of two great rivers. Following the trails of Ekoh and Torka, they kept to the wider, easterly course. In the heart of a river-cut valley they sighted a small herd of bison.

Having eaten nothing but the remains of their toddlers, small game, birds, and fish since beginning their journey across the sodden land, they raised the first good camp in many moons. There they hunted and killed and feasted until their bellies could hold no more—all the while praising Cheanah for having had the courage and foresight to lead them out of the starving camp and into good hunting grounds again. Then Zhoonali threw her fortune-telling bones and predicted better days ahead, provided that the people of Cheanah abided by the wisdom of their ancestors.

They rested and ate until all the bison meat was gone. Only after the flies sang in the hollowed skeletons of the bison and the renewed energy of the hunters had been expended in hours of coupling with their women did they wake from glutted slumber, look around, and remember that the Place of Endless Meat had become a starving camp because of just such hunting practices as these. As a result, while the men hunted with circumspection in the days that followed, the women dried meat and stretched sinew.

The band broke camp and trekked eastward. Because their pack frames were heavily loaded, they had left a good deal of the bison meat behind. What they had packed was soon gone. Food remained scarce, and their hunts were few and far between.

Teean died a day before they sighted their first real game in weeks—a broken-legged camel and her calf. Honee rejoiced. Now there was one less man for whom she would have to spread herself, and never again would that bony old Teean pound her in the night while not once succeeding in filling her with the juice that the women said was the thing that put life into a woman.

The beastling and Sister were happy. They were thriving on the long trek across the new country. Sister was as cautious as the beastling was curious, but she followed readily now. Mother's disciplined training served them well. One good meal gave them energy enough for a two- or three-day walk. The beasts walked so slowly and noisily that, to the beastling's and Sister's delight, many small creatures scampered out of the band's way only to blunder into their path. They lingered on the site of the bison kill for many days. When at last they left it, the beastling carried bloody hump cuttings in a pouch that he contrived.

Now, after days of following the beasts through country where food was scarce, the smell of old meat drew them on. Soon they were driving off a small pack of wolves from something edible that the beasts had recently left behind.

Sister fell upon the meat at once. The beastling held back, realizing that the beasts had abandoned one of their own. He touched the hairless skin, then bent closer to smell it. Then he drew back, appalled. Could it be? Could he be one of *them*? Was this why he was so fascinated by them and drawn to learn from them? *No!* He was Mother's cub!

Sister looked up and held out a piece of mutilated hand. It was like his own hand, pale and hairless and clawless. He felt himself blanch and shiver as he refused her offering. He pulled his lionskin tighter and turned away, sitting with his back to Sister. Truth lay upon him like a freshly fleshed antelope skin: It felt as if his own skin had been turned inside out and left to bleed and cure in the wind. Moisture as salty as blood seeped from his eyes. He knew now that he was one of them—a *beast*, not Mother's cub, after all . . . but still and always he *would* be hers.

"Manaravak . . ." He exhaled it as a whisper. "Manaravak!" he shouted in the gathering darkness, beneath the light of the red star. He wept against the exquisite pain of the emotions that assaulted him. When that failed, he once again whispered . . . his own name.

And far across the world, Umak awoke with a start.

Dak eyed him and shook his head disparagingly as he sighed and snuggled back under his furs. "Dreams again?"

"No," replied Umak truthfully. Slowly, he rose and picked his way across the sleeping forms of his people. The dogs looked up and then down again; only Aar followed him to the edge of the cave.

Together they stood in the dark, looking across the world and the night at the red star.

"He is out there somewhere," Umak whispered to the dog. "I can feel him inside me and out there—alive somewhere."

Aar cocked his head.

Umak hunkered down and slung an arm around the dog's neck. "I will share a secret with you, old friend: I hope he dies, for I want no brother to shadow me. The sadness of the past has done too much of that already!"

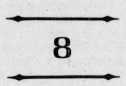

8

In the last days of autumn, with vast wedges of geese and other waterfowl winging overhead, Ekoh, Bili, and Seteena continued eastward, following the old campsites of Torka, until one day, with the smell of a coming snowfall bitter on the wind, Ekoh looked back and saw the tiny forms of travelers silhouetted against the far horizon.

"The whole cursed band!" he hissed. Then he looked at his little family and smiled. His woman and son looked well and strong. Seteena's eyes were bright, and he could walk for hours without complaint. "We will leave the trail and allow Cheanah to go on his way. We will find a place to spend the winter and ready a camp for the time of long dark."

Following the tracks of horses and elk into the hills, careful to leave no tracks of their own, they disappeared into a deep, wind-sheltered canyon.

Long before the sun disappeared into the west, the first storms of winter swept the Forbidden Land. In Torka's well-provisioned cave, the people knew neither cold nor hunger.

Torka looked up at Summer Moon when she came to stand close to his fire circle.

"Do you think he is all right, all alone on the far mountain, Father?"

He frowned. He had been thinking of the magic man a great deal these past dark days. "Karana can take care of himself. He has chosen his life."

Seated beside Torka with Swan in her lap, Lonit shook her head sadly. "No, the spirits have chosen it for him. They have not been kind. And yet Karana sent us a gift of his healing magic so we would not be without it in the winter dark."

"We were without it when our son died." Torka's voice was hard and unforgiving.

"Karana is our son," she reminded softly.

"No, he is not our son." The headman was relieved to be drawn from his brooding when Swan beamed at him, reached out with her pudgy little hands, and laughed.

Torka smiled as he lifted his daughter and held her high. "Leave it to a swan to lighten my heart. What do you think, little girl? If the weather continues as it has, shall your father set out across the valley and ask Karana to come home?"

"*Yes!*"

The word came not from the little girl but from everyone in the cave.

Torka nodded. "So be it, then."

Soon after, with Grek and Mahnie at his side, he set out with Aar.

Summer Moon, meanwhile, sat pouting at Simu's fire.

"You are my woman now. You will stay."

"I do not want to stay! Mahnie goes!"

"Mahnie is Karana's woman!" Simu retorted.

"But I make him happy. I would give him sons. If I were at his side, he would lie with me and be happy."

Eneela was angry. "You have been raised as Karana's sister and have no place at Karana's fire or in his heart."

"It was not as brother that he lay with me!"

Simu glowered at the girl, but it was Demmi who overheard and said: "You can make no one happy, Summer Moon. How can you, when all you do is think about yourself!"

Torka, Grek, and Mahnie walked until the need to rest became too strong, and then they stopped, raised a lean-to, and sat by the little fire that Mahnie kindled while the dog ran ahead.

Torka, chewing on the berry-impregnated wedges of

pounded fat that Mahnie handed out, watched the wolflike form disappear into the falling snow.

The next morning they entered the pass and made their way up the gorge. Travel was slow in the cold and dark; in places they lit the torches that they had brought and walked on under a cloud of their own smoke and oily light.

At last they reached the ridge. The torches were exhausted. Three more bundlings of oil-saturated sticks, lichens, and skins remained in their traveling packs; these they would save for the return trip. They went on, drawn by the scent of Karana's fire.

He and Aar watched them coming for hours, lights threading upward through the gorge, flickering in the misting snow and darkness.

So much darkness. Even for a magic man there could be too much darkness. It was inside him now, a living thing.

It spoke: *"Now . . . they come for you now."*

He cocked his head, listening.

"Hear the voices. You knew they would come!"

"Mahnie?"

"Yes, Mahnie. Soft and loving Mahnie." The darkness whispered on the wind all around him. He knew its voice as well as he knew his own. It was Navahk's. *"Now you will go back with them. Now I will be reborn!"*

"No!" he shouted. "Never!"

The dog growled. He lowered his head, put back his ear, and began to back away. Aar was brother to Karana, but he did not recognize the man who stood on the ridge before him now.

They stopped when they saw him.

"Go back," he warned. His voice was as flat and cold as the wind that moved down from the heights.

Torka's heart sank. "Too long have you been on the mountain, my son. It is time for you to come back to your people."

"I am *not* your son. I *have* no people. They are dead, beyond the Corridor of Storms, long ago."

"You are Karana. Grek and Wallah and Mahnie are survivors of your band. And you *are* my son and the magic man of Torka's band."

"I am Karana, son of *Navahk!* Grek and Wallah and Mahnie are of Torka's band now. They have no need of me. They have Torka for their magic."

"That is not enough." He wanted to say more, to speak his heart, to beg forgiveness from one to whom he had shown no forgiveness, but his grief was too great. What he saw in the face of Karana was almost more than he could bear: It was madness.

"This man has sent the gift of healing into the valley. Has Torka not received it? Have Torka's women failed to understand the meaning of the drawings—"

"They understand! I have received. But—"

"Then you have no need of Karana. Go."

"Karana? My magic man?" Mahnie's voice broke as she took a step forward, reaching out to him with all of the love in her heart.

"No! You will *not* come to me! Never! Never again!"

As Torka and Grek watched, appalled, the young woman put her arms around Karana only to be hurled to the ground as he turned and fled into the night.

For a long while Grek and Torka searched for him while Mahnie stayed on the ridge with Aar. Snow fell quietly at first, but when the wind changed, it took on the sting of the impending storm. She sat very still, watching it accumulate in her lap while the dog lay beside her. At length the two men returned.

"We've looked everywhere we could think to look!" Grek reported. "In his shelter . . . up around the lake . . . down toward the north-canyon glacier. There's no sign of him, the crazy fool. We'll never find him unless he wishes it; he knows the mountain too well."

"He has been alone too long," Torka said.

"Yes," Mahnie agreed. "But no longer. I am his woman. I will stay with him."

"No!" Grek was emphatic.

"I *will* stay, Father. It is my place to stay. A woman needs a man. And this man needs his woman! Did you see the way he looked? You will see: He will be better soon. When the coming storm is over, we will come from the mountain together. You must go before the weather closes in. Kiss Naya for me. Tell her I will try to be home with her father soon."

The two hunters stood in stunned silence. Mahnie's resolve made her seem taller and mature beyond her years. Torka understood her heart; Lonit would do the same for him.

"His shelter isn't much, but it seems to be adequately provisioned. There's a little bit of kindling and a stash of lichens and wood set by. You will be warm there until he returns. Come, I will show you."

Grek worried for his daughter, sputtered in fatherly confusion, but he knew that Torka was right. Mahnie had been wasting away with unhappiness without Karana. He thought about what he would be like without his Wallah. Empty. Yes. And that was what he had seen in the magic man's eyes: emptiness . . . loneliness . . . such terrible, black, aching despair. But to leave Mahnie here with Karana in the state he was in? "I don't like it," he muttered. "If the weather closes in, you may not be able to come off this mountain until the return of the time of light. And if ice should block the gorge, we may not be able to come up to you if you need us!"

"Nevertheless, I *will* stay." She moved to hold him in a loving embrace. She reached to push back the thickly furred projection of his ruff so she could kiss him and exhale the essence of her love onto each side of his broad face. "Go now, Father. Give this kiss to my mother and to Naya, and tell them both not to worry, even if I am here until spring! I will be with my magic man. Karana will keep me safe."

But Karana was not upon the mountain. Someone else walked in and out of his skin. He hid upon the heights and watched the torches disappear into the depths of the snow-driven gorge. Two figures, only two! Male by their dress. *She* had stayed behind!

Go to her . . . lie with her . . . love her. Yes, think of her warm body . . . of her mouth . . . of her breasts . . . of her soft thighs, and you between them. You will be one with her in the endless winter dark as I pour my life into her through you . . . and live again . . . yes. You would

*not have the courage to deny me life if she held me, all
newborn and tender, in her hands. She would hate you
and protect me against you if you did that. . . .*

"Yes . . ."

As the storm came down, Navahk whispered to him in
the wind. But he would not listen. He was back in his own
skin. He put his hands above his head and pressed upon
his ears, and when the voice of Navahk rose from within,
he howled defiantly into the night and the cold until he
could not hear it. He walked and walked until exhaustion
dropped him.

"Mahnie, I will not come to you. I cannot!"

He stayed where he was until he was stiff with cold and
his body ached and his mind felt drained of life. Hunger
drove him back toward his shelter . . . until he smelled
the fire that she had made and the meat that she was
roasting.

"No, I will *not* come to you."

He turned and stumbled away, back into the storm and
the night and the wind. He made a new shelter out of
snow in a new place and like a caribou lived on lichens.
He waited out the storm—and all the long, bitter storms
that followed. He had never known such cold.

He had no idea how much time had passed or how long
he had been away, but one morning he awoke, and it *was*
morning. The sun was rising to the east. He was certain
Mahnie must be gone from the mountain by now. Slowly,
he left his hut of snow and walked back to the place where
she had been waiting for him.

She *was* gone—at least her spirit was.

Her body was still waiting for him by the icy ashes of
the last fire that she had made, beside the few scattered
bone fragments that had been the last of his winter rations. She was frozen solid and must have been dead for
weeks.

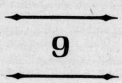

9

Winter refused to release its grip upon the land. It seemed that the sky had fallen onto the tundral steppe. A thin, constant snow blew across the world, causing Cheanah's people to wonder if the stars would ever shine for them again.

"We must go on," he told his hungry band. "Somewhere ahead of us there is bound to be meat. Somewhere ahead of us the shaman of Torka tells the spirits of the wind to put this bad weather upon us. We must find him and silence his song forever!"

They trekked on until meat was sighted—a sickly old stallion that had neither the strength nor the inclination to outrun the hunters; this was a good thing, for Cheanah and his hunters had little strength. The horse fell to their spears. At last they ate until the edge of their hunger was gone; what was left was for the women. Only Zhoonali was singled out to share in the larger portions of meat.

Kimm glowered jealously. "What about us?" she whined as annoyingly as her daughter. "Xhan and I have made your camps, carried your loads, and given you children! Do we not deserve as much meat as Zhoonali, or more?"

Cheanah eyed his women coldly across the pit hut. "As long as the talking bones and the wisdom of our ancestors speak through the mouth of Zhoonali to bolster the courage of our hunters as well as to affirm the wisdom of Cheanah, Zhoonali will not go hungry!"

Xhan's face twisted with resentment. "Zhoonali is indeed a wise woman."

"Yes," agreed Kimm with open sarcasm. "Wise enough to make herself important. Wise enough to say nothing definite when she speaks in the 'voices' of the bones! Wise enough so that no one can or will ever be brave enough to point a finger at her and say: 'Old woman, you are useless to this people! Go! Walk the wind forever and take your talking bones with you, for look where they have led us!'"

Cheanah hit Kimm so hard that he broke her jaw. "Never speak so against the mother of Cheanah! *You* are the useless one, you barren, sag-teated snorer. Why do I feed you at all? No sons have you ever made for me to replace those I have lost!"

Kimm was sobbing as through clenched and already swelling jaws she fought to speak in defense of herself. "Twin . . . shonnsh . . . onsh . . ." She could say no more.

"Twins! What are twins? Things forbidden by the forces of Creation!" Zhoonali, on her feet now, never took her eyes from Cheanah as she raged. "As Cheanah killed the twin sons of Kimm, so will he kill the twins of any woman. I tell you, Kimm, when those we seek die, you will cease to be barren. Then will our camp be full of meat. Then will Honee stop hating Mano for riding her in the night, for he will have Torka's women to use—and hurt as they deserve!"

Ekoh would watch for signs of Cheanah. Now and again, if the wind was right, they caught scent of his encampments or heard high, strident wisps of sound that they recognized as Zhoonali as she cried out in the 'voices' of her talking bones.

"It is amazing that she lives so long," Bili mused. She paused, suddenly troubled. "Why does Cheanah keep moving to the east? Is he also seeking Torka?"

"Why would he do that?" asked Seteena.

Ekoh paused to think. "Long ago, when we were still members of the band of poor old Zinkh, I heard it rumored that in bad times the people of Cheanah made their luck by stealing the luck of others—by raiding camps, by stealing meat and women! These are bad times. Perhaps Cheanah returns to his old ways?" He did not want to speak the thought aloud; the spirits might be listening. "It would be a good thing to find Torka before Cheanah does."

Several days after Cheanah broke Kimm's jaw, the headman's second woman became very ill as the result of complications from the injury. She moaned and muttered in fevered delirium, alternately snoring and snorting. In the darkness of Cheanah's pit hut, the headman lay naked with his daughter and tried not to listen. Impatient for release, he forcibly positioned Honee to his satisfaction while wishing someone would smother Kimm.

"Now . . ." he said, mounting the girl, forcing her wide, handling her, and easing entry as he began to probe the depths of his daughter's rigid and unyielding body with his equally rigid member.

"No!" She was crying, trying to push away from him.

He rammed deep, smiling with satisfaction; because she was tense, he was too big for Honee. When something tore inside her, he felt a long, hot shiver of ecstasy ripple through his loins. He thrust deeper and rode harder, pumping now.

Distracted by Kimm's endless moaning, his organ began to shrink, and the feeling of heat and pleasure began to ebb. With a curse he hurled himself off Honee and made certain that Kimm would not disturb him again. She resisted; it did no good. It only took a moment for a big man to smother a sick woman. When it was done, Cheanah looked around. Watching from the shadows, Mano smiled. Xhan nodded with approval. Zhoonali sat up and began to toss the bones of telling. Cheanah turned to intercept Honee as she tried to crawl out of the hut. He caught her by her heel and dragged her back to his sleeping skins. He was on her, mounted well and driving deep, before she could catch her breath. And when he was finished, drained but still probing, Mano came close.

"I have need," he whispered.

And for Honee, the pounding began all over again.

The beastling was glad to be back in the mountains, although the threesome of beasts seemed intimidated by the heights. The beastling watched them as they moved slowly through the canyons, searching for charred holes in the ground, which determined their path.

Meat was everywhere; although the beasts could not always find it, he hunted in the way of the wanawut and knew no hunger as he led Sister deeper into the range. He found himself thinking of the faraway mountain where Mother had taught him to hunt, and where he had learned how to survive in the wild land. How he wished that Mother could see the way he was caring for Sister, and how well he was living now.

The family of beasts continued to pick their way upward through the mighty range. They were ascending a narrow pass toward a high black ridge, beyond which was the smell of ice and open grassland far beyond.

Gradually, subtle changes were occurring in the land and sky. Each day the sun rose higher above the summits of the snow-clad peaks. Each night, the wind sang a different song and wolves howled in the far-flung canyons.

On clear nights, while Sister curled up close beside him, the beastling would lie on his back and stare up at the red star. Its tail seemed to be longer, and it was larger, brighter, redder, than when he first set eyes upon it.

And then one night, the sound of a lone wolf reached his ears, and he rose from his dreams as though the sound had the power to lift him to his feet. Although wolf song was a part of the night, this particular song touched him to his soul. The beastling stood very still, tensely listening. He turned toward the sound. He knew then that it was not a wolf but a beast sounding in the most terrible pain and anguish that he had ever heard:

"Mah . . . nee . . . my . . . mah . . . nee . . ." it cried. "Mah . . . nee . . . for . . . give . . . mee . . . mah . . . nee!"

He cocked his head. The sound went on and on, and it hurt him to hear it. Yet he strained to hear, to understand its meaning.

Sister awoke, sat up, listened briefly, then frowned, covered her ears, and gestured for him to come back to sleep.

He ignored her and stood transfixed, for the sounding of that faraway beast burned his senses and struck a chord of kinship within him . . . a need to soothe . . . a need to empathize.

Suddenly, although he did not intend to do it, he was sounding back, imitating the sound and forming his own articulation:

"Mah . . . nee . . . foh . . . giv . . . mee . . . mah . . . nee! My . . . mah . . . nee! Mah . . . na . . . rah . . . vak!"

The sounding stopped. He listened. It was gone. His hands went to his throat. It hurt him to breathe. He wanted the sound to continue. He *needed* it to continue.

"Mah . . . nee!" he cried to the wind. As tears welled beneath his lids, he threw back his head and howled, "Mah . . . nah . . . rah . . . vak!" He waited for the distant beast to hear him and howl back to soothe his pain as he had tried to soothe the pain of the beast.

But there was no answer to his cry.

"Did you hear it?" Torka was wide awake, cold, yet every nerve was aflame. "*Manaravak!* Someone called the name! Didn't you hear it?"

Lonit stirred beside him. "Only the wind . . . and wolves. Go back to sleep, man of my heart. You were only dreaming."

Torka was up, dressing, and pulling on his boots. Others had been disturbed by the sound, but not so much as he.

"What is it?" Simu asked, propping himself onto an elbow.

"Wolves in the mountains again, yes?" mumbled Grek.

"Not wolves or wind." Torka paused, squinting across the darkness of the cave. He saw that Umak was wide awake, staring straight at him.

"I heard the wind and wolves."

Torka frowned. Why did the boy look as though he was lying?

"I heard." It was Demmi, wide-eyed in the dark. "It was terribly sad. Two sounds: one crying for Mahnie. Then another crying my lost brother Manaravak's name!"

Umak turned to glare at his sister. "You don't know

what you heard! You hear with the ears of a girl, not of a hunter!"

Torka was across the cave, reaching for his spears. "By the forces of Creation, it has been too long since we have seen a fire on the western ridge. Something's wrong up there."

Simu and Grek were also on their feet now; the women were awake and staring as their men fumbled their way into their clothes.

"There is still ice in the gorge," cautioned Simu.

Grek bore an expression of grim determination. "My Mahnie is on the mountain! Ice or no ice, if the magic man has let her come to harm, I will break his neck with these two hands, yes!"

Torka laid a staying hand on the old man's arm. "You will not break any neck but your own, old friend. You stay here. Simu, Dak, Umak, take up your spears and ice-creepers and come with me!"

10

Although the time of year still made the way up the ridge cold and difficult, there was less ice than they anticipated, because the gorge faced directly into the rising sun. Once, briefly, they glimpsed a figure whirling and dancing on the ridge high above them . . . a man dressed entirely in the white skins of a winter-killed caribou . . . with black hair whipping in the wind, a braided forelock festooned with the white flight feathers of an Arctic owl . . . and a high-pitched chant vibrating with madness.

"Karana?" Torka's heart sank as he spoke the name. *Yes.* He knew the face, the form, and the set of the shoulders. And yet, impossibly, the figure that stood above him on the heights was not the boy he had raised to manhood; it was a haunting from the past. It was Navahk . . . Spirit Killer . . . alive within Karana's skin!

No! thought Torka. *It cannot be!* He wiped the back of his hand across his eyes; as he had hoped, when he looked again, the figure of the man was gone.

"Did you see him?" asked Dak. "Why would he dress like that? Why would he risk his safety by dancing to the edge of the ridge? Do you think he's all right?"

"No." Torka's voice was as bleak as the cold wind and as bitter as the scent of glacial ice and rotten rock that blew from the banks of the great highland lake and the north-canyon glacier. "Karana has not been all right for a long time now."

They went on in stunned silence. They found Mahnie laid out tenderly on a bed of lichens, with spruce boughs tented over her, and her body wrapped within furs that had once clothed the magic man. But of Karana, there was no sign. The little shelter in which Torka had last seen him had become a tomb for Mahnie. The feeling of death was strong around it. They drew the branches and the furs away just enough to see her face, to be certain that it was indeed the woman of Karana and the daughter of Grek and Wallah who lay alone upon the mountain. Time was usually quick to put its mark upon the dead; but it was still rarely above freezing this high on the mountain—neither time nor predators had disturbed her . . . or had Karana found a special magic to keep them both away?

They called to him. There was no answer. They waited. He did not come.

Simu drew in a steadying breath. "Mahnie had not been strong. Eneela was worried about her. I am sure that Karana did all that he could do to prevent—"

"Did you *see* him?" Within his black-maned winter tunic of golden lionskins, Torka was cold, and his face was granite hard. He told himself that he should feel pity for Karana, but he could find no room for pity in his heart. The image of the magic man dancing on the heights would not go away. "I am sure of nothing about Karana these days—except that he was right: He is not my son. He is Navahk's spawn. Where is he now? What is he now? If Mahnie took sick, why did he not bring her down to us, or come himself so that we could have helped her? Why does he not come now to tell us how she died? What sort of a man would leave his woman like this—alone, with no one to mourn her?"

"He mourns her, Torka," said Simu sadly. "He is a healer. If he could not help her, what could we have done?"

Simu's question was valid, but Torka was sick with grief and a terrible sense of failed responsibility. "*I* left her here. With Grek arguing against it, *I* allowed her to put her life into Karana's hands. *Again* I trusted him. And again, because of my misplaced trust, someone is dead!"

Simu rested a consoling hand upon Torka's shoulder. "This was Mahnie's choice. What has been done cannot be undone. We must take Mahnie back down the mountain.

Together her people will sing her life song. It is time for Grek and Wallah and Naya to grieve."

"But what about Karana?" Dak asked, genuinely concerned for the welfare of the magic man.

"What about him?" Umak shot back, sensing the darkness of Torka's mood, wanting to show that he was on his father's side. "If Karana wants to follow us, he will."

Torka looked down at the boy. "You were right, Umak: It *was* only the wind and a 'wolf' that I heard howling upon the mountain. I see it now. Let the wolf *be* a wolf. Long ago I found Karana living wild on a mountain. Now, on another mountain, I turn him loose and let him be what he was born to be—a wild animal that has shown me time and time again that he cannot be trusted. It has been wrong of me to expect him to be anything other than what he is: the son of Navahk, a deceiver who could not have sired anything but a wolf. Forget Karana. He cannot live among men . . . not even among those who have forgiven him repeatedly and have too long named him Son and Brother."

The Moon of the Green Grass Growing rose and set, and there was mourning in the wonderful valley as the spirit of Mahnie walked the wind forever. Grek sat brooding in the sun on the projecting lip of the cave and knapped his projectile points with a vengeance; he ruined most of them, gouged his fingers, and did not care. Wallah spent her days in the shadowed recesses of the cave, bundled in her bearskin with her leg across her lap as she sorted and resorted Mahnie's belongings. Iana tried to reinstill some small semblance of happiness into the old couple by reminding them of their responsibilities to their granddaughter. It did no good. If Naya cried for her mother in the night, it was Iana who came to her.

In lengthening days, an increasingly troubled Torka watched as Life Giver led his kindred farther and farther across the eastern edge of the valley to browse. Whenever Torka heard a lone wolf that was not a wolf howling in the western ranges, he shivered with grief.

Lonit listened and whispered sadly to her daughters that it was a bitter thing to have three sons to mourn.

"I wish that Father had let me be the one to go out to Karana in the winter dark," Summer Moon told Lonit.

"I think that if you had gone," Lonit replied quietly, "Karana would still be on the mountain, and I would be mourning you as well."

"It was your prodding of poor Mahnie that made her go off in the dead of winter in the first place," reminded Demmi coolly. "Your place is at Simu's fire."

"Simu is with Eneela now. He likes her better."

"So do I," said Demmi.

Lonit shook her head and wondered if the siblings truly disliked each other. Demmi's expression changed. She looked uncharacteristically and painfully sad. "You are such a selfish girl, Summer Moon. At least you have Simu. In this band, there is no man for me."

Lonit was taken aback. A man for *Demmi*? *Yes!* Soon it would be time. "You will have Dak," she said lightly. "If the forces of Creation grant their favor, Dak and Umak will both complete their final trial of endurance and survival skills before the land burns with the first color of autumn. They will be men of this band."

Demmi sighed. "But they are boys in my eyes and younger than I am!" There was no resentment or bitterness—only a sad acceptance. "There will never be a man for me, as Torka has been for you, Mother. Never."

Summer Moon smirked at her sister. "Or maybe Cheanah's band will come marching over the mountains, and you will have one of his—"

Lonit slapped her daughter hard across the face. *"Never!"* she cried. "Never speak so! Even in jest! The spirits may be listening."

Cheanah was sitting in front of his pit hut, setting a projectile point into the haft of a spear, when Mano sauntered by.

"Have you smelled the camp smoke on the wind?"

The headman did not bother to look up.

"I have."

"You don't seem excited."

"Since the caribou came through, this has been a good

camp. It has been good to eat again. Good to see the women smile. Soon there may be children again."

Mano nodded. "There will be better camps ahead."

Cheanah smiled. "Yes, through the black pass. But it is far, that pass. Yanehva and Ram have said that they are in no hurry to move on. They say we could spend the summer, store much more meat, then winter here. Perhaps stay on and see if the caribou come back through the pass as they return into the face of the rising sun before the coming of the time of the long dark."

Mano cast a sour look at his father. "And what does Cheanah say?"

The headman smiled. He enjoyed riling Mano. "Cheanah says there are too few women in this band. Cheanah says that he longs to have a virgin tight and hot around his man bone again. So Cheanah now says to Mano: Take Buhl and Kap and find the source of the smoke that brings to us the scent of the camps of men. If it is Ekoh, kill him and his whelp and bring Bili to me. In the meantime, Cheanah and the others will make new spears and flake new blades, for if you bring word that Torka's camp is ahead, we will be fresh and prepared to travel, to surround him while he sleeps, to kill him and Simu and the old man and the shaman. To take his women and girls . . . to eat of the flesh of his totem . . . and to take back the luck that Torka and his band have stolen from us!"

11

For days Karana watched smoke rising from the fires of the band encamped at the base of the western slope of the mountains. The pit huts were tiny from this height, the people no larger than insects, yet he knew them by the way they spaced their huts and by their wasteful manner of hunting. *Cheanah. Why?*

But the madness was on him, and the question seemed of little importance. No sooner had he turned away than he forgot Cheanah's encampment entirely. The thing that he most feared in the world was not in that camp. No! The thing that he feared was the abandoned son. Manaravak was following him, was on the mountain with him. He could feel the threat in the mist of his mind, rising and thickening with the coming of night, ebbing and thinning by day, driving him to stalk the heights, to prowl the canyons, to listen for the voice that had answered him one blue night . . . the voice that had echoed his own and spoken the name of the ghost that he was now set to destroy.

He walked on, a madman in white, hands pressed to his temples. He took himself to the west, and there he resumed the occupation that had driven him these past many moons: the setting of snare lines, the laboring over pit traps, the cutting of branches to conceal them—and the placement of deadly spikes and spring traps that he fashioned from the sinews and long bones of the animals that he killed.

Obsessed, he stopped making fires. If he ate at all he

ate his food raw. The white skin of the winter-killed caribou that he wore became bloodstained and foul, and when he slept, he slept like the dead—hard, black, and dreamless sleep—until the dreams came, and then he woke up screaming.

After a three-day fast, Torka and Simu had led Umak and Dak, as naked and weaponless as First Man, from the cave and to the base of the hills. The headman held out a forked breastbone of a teratorn and instructed Dak to take hold of one fork and Umak the other. Lonit and Eneela had snared the bird and dried and polished this bone for this day.

"Torka now holds before Umak and Dak the bone of choosing. The boy who breaks off the larger portion will walk to the east. The boy who breaks off the smaller portion of the bone will walk to the south. When you return from your final testing you will wear cloaks of its feathers and necklets of its talons. The teratorn has always been a sign of good fortune for this people. May you both return to us safely, clothed and with bellies full and with the weapon of a hunter of the band within your hand."

When Umak cracked off the larger portion, he suspected that things would go well for him. Hunger from the long fast sharpened his senses, and as he set off under the eye of the warm sun, dreams came to him. Dreams of food . . . wonderful piles of meat and eyeballs and intestines, steaming in a flood of red-hot blood that poured from the freshly opened bellies of some sort of prey animals. The dreams shifted subtly as the flood of blood became a flood of water pouring out of the mountains across the land—water so dark and deep that it filled the wonderful valley. Only the tips of the white mountains showed above it.

He trotted across the valley toward the distant ranges, alone and unafraid of anything but failure. But Torka had taught him well, as had Simu and Grek. A herd of dun-colored horses, each with a broad brown stripe running along its spine, nickered and wheeled away as he moved toward them. They were heading toward an area of broken country ahead. He could see their round eyes bright in the sun and their tails jabbing upward at the wind as they galloped away, trailing tides of blackflies.

The flies were his first challenge; a roll in the nearest bog bested them. He slathered mud over every inch of his body, including ears and genitals and the tips of his fingers. It dried on his skin and cracked in the wind. He did not mind; it disguised his body scent, and no flies could bite through it.

A great bear and her cubs digging for tubers in a broad meadow looked up at him as he went by. He gave them space, and they allowed him passage; he did not look like meat, nor did he smell like it.

Before the day was out, he had found his own little meadow and ate well of starchy, sweet roots that the great bear would have envied. He contrived crude snares, using the grasses of the steppe and tail hairs of horse, which he found tangled within the scrub growth. Soon he was eating birds and rodents.

He fashioned needles of bone and thread of sinew, then set himself to hunt larger game. He followed the horses farther east. From willow branches taken along a stream bank, he contrived a bow drill with which he could raise sparks and a fire when he collected sufficient kindling and burnable refuse. He saved the bones from every meal and gathered the leavings of grazing animals as he went. He took the time to break them up and dry them in the sun and wind before moving on.

After several days he reached the base of the far pass. He had gleaned enough dung and deadwood and collected enough bones from his many meals to make a fire for shaping and hardening the spear he would make. He had already found good-quality stone for the spearhead and a cast caribou antler that would serve as a perfect straightener for the shaft. He planned to create a spear of fire-hardened bone over which Torka would exclaim with pride.

With every ounce of skill that was his, he tracked the small herd of horses, set fire to a grassy area of broken hills, and panicked them into an uphill flight that sent them hurtling and screaming over the crest of a high knoll. From there they fell into a rocky defile, just as he had planned. He climbed cautiously down after them, burying himself under their twitching, broken bodies until the grass fire died.

He feasted on sweet horsemeat. He ate the eyes, and the intestines steamed in the air as he opened the bellies. This was what he had seen in his dream! He ate until he could eat no more; then after a brief rest, he examined his kill. If cured properly, horsehide could be soft. He skinned the animal that had the best and least-scorched pelt, fleshed it, and set it to dry while he fashioned the hafts of the spears not only for himself but for Torka, Simu, and Grek. These were gifts to honor those who had taught him so well. He was so filled with pride at his success, he raised his spears, shook them, and bellowed, "I am Umak! Son of Torka!"

His happiness lightened his step westward, back to the cave. Clad in horsehide and feathers, with his spears in hand, he returned to the encampment to learn that Dak had yet to come home. He smiled his widest smile while his people alternately sang and slapped at drums and blew upon bone whistles, and Torka came forward in his ceremonial finery proudly to proclaim him a man.

It was not long before Dak made his way to the encampment. The band drank the fermented juice of summer. The blood of the teratorn was mixed with it and streaked boldly across the brows and cheeks of the two young men, who sat unmoving and proud as Torka and Simu draped cloaks of black-and-white teratorn feathers across their backs.

Umak's euphoric bliss abruptly faded and grew cold as he stared westward. The sadness, the terrible, aching sadness of the boy inside him had broken his mood. *No,* he thought, gritting his teeth. *Not today! My brother will not come back to life today. I will not let you!*

"Is your gift for your parents ready?"

Umak nodded, grateful to Dak for the question; it made him feel better. "Yes," he said. "My gift is ready."

Distant music and beast sounding drew the beastling from his sleep. The wind carried the sound from the east, from somewhere beyond the blade-edged peaks that speared the clouds on either side of him. It was there one moment, gone the next.

The beastling sat up. He went to look at the little beast family. They still slept undisturbed under their shaggy dead animal skins. The more he had watched the beast family, the less inclined he was to kill them. Their erect form and their gait were so much like his own. But how unlike the quarrelsome beasts traveling in their wake! The family, which he recognized as being a male and female and their cub, cared for each other and shared their food willingly.

The music and singing drifted to him again. He was captivated, enthralled.

Only half aware that Sister was trailing him, mewing for him to come back, he moved eastward. Sister tugged at his arm. Briefly he considered whether he should heed her and go back. But a neatly arranged circle of stones caught his eyes and invited further investigation. Fire had not lived in the charred hollow within the stones for a long time; but beast scent lay there, so tenuous that he could barely perceive it. Perceive it he did, and he reacted to it as though some inner portion of himself were being tweaked by memories. But memories of what? Instinctively he knew that the answer lay ahead.

He went on and up until at last he found himself within a broad highland basin. He came upon an enormous gray lake in which islands of ice shifted and groaned. The look of the lake disturbed him. It seemed a captive thing, restless and brooding.

He veered south, turned east, and paused for a moment. Was danger here? The east wind distracted him with the scent of music and distant beast-made smokes. There was the smell of roasting meat and dripping fat and of the beasts themselves—not rank and foul like the other beasts in the far western camp, but a good scent. It was similar to the essence he had just picked up from the charred hollows—disturbingly, painfully familiar.

He hurried on, knowing that he was on his way to something important. Sister grasped his shoulder and tried forcibly to draw him back. He knew that she was frightened by these strange surroundings and longed to run away. But the beastling held his ground, annoyed by her persistent attempts to pull him away.

He crouched on the ridge; dark, lichen-encrusted boulders allowed him cover as, with Sister peering over his shoulder, he looked across a valley of such magnificent proportions that it took his breath away. He saw at last what he had come to see: the distant encampment of the singing beasts. Of his own kind? *Yes!*

Now, for the first time, he accepted the truth. He was a beast, like the old corpse on the plain, like the ones who had injured and killed Mother. But also like the three who were plodding up the canyon, caring for and nurturing one another. He was touched to the quick by a sense of oneness with them.

He strained to see but could not see enough; it was too far away. And yet he was just close enough to the encampment to make out tiny figures. All made wonderful sounds while two young males stood apart from the rest, being celebrated. They were wearing collars of the feathers of great black-and-white birds. The beastling's hand went to his throat, for an excruciating longing to be with them became a terrible sadness, then a devastating loneliness.

He started to sound back to them, but Sister shoved him hard. For the first time in his life, he saw her as being alien to him. She was a furred, fanged, clawed wanawut, and her fear of everything she did not understand bound him to her as surely as lichen was bound to a rock. He snarled and struck out at her so hard that he nearly knocked her down.

Frightened and bewildered, she stared wide-eyed at him. He knew at once that he had hurt her, but his feeling of resentment had not yet passed. He snarled again and gestured threateningly. With a wail of anguish, she turned and fled, hooting and screeching.

He wept with a violent suddenness. He stood on the ridge with the sound of song and laughter and music beating in his brain, and he wept. If he went to them now across that broad and beautiful valley, would they recognize him as one of their own and accept him? He would never know. Bereft, his deep love and concern for Sister's safety caused him to tear himself away and follow her.

*   *   *

Yanehva crested the ridge just as something big and gray went screeching past him in the mists. Something else followed it—white and maned like a lion. His heart pounding, Yanehva turned to look. But whatever had gone racing past him had disappeared into the mists before he had got a good look.

He stood dead still, listening. *Wind spirits?* Yes, he thought, and gripped his spears more tightly; this was a good place to see wind spirits. Fortunately they had not seen him.

He went on slowly, measuring each step. Only a few more paces brought him to look out across the most magnificent valley he had ever seen. The music and singing had attracted his gaze right to Torka's encampment. He was actually sorry to have found it.

He did not want to be here. He had no heart for what Cheanah planned for Torka or what Mano intended to work upon the little camp of Ekoh; with his brother and Buhl in the spear-sharp mood for murder and rape, he had known that it would have done him no good to try to stop them.

So, tired from the climb and shaken by the sighting of the apparitions, Yanehva rested. Hungry, he reached into the larder pouch at his belt and pulled out a few strips of dried bison tongue. It was a little moldy, but during a wet season, that was to be expected. He ate slowly, watching the distant camp, listening to the celebratory songs and observing the dancing. Pleasant memories of life as it had been long ago, when Torka had been headman of his band, cut the acrid taste of the mold; for a moment it actually tasted good to him—until he heard Bili scream. He jumped to his feet, knowing that no matter what the risk to himself, he could not allow his brother to work murder and rape upon those who deserved better.

Honee cowered behind the rockfall. She had been having second thoughts about her decision to follow her brothers and Buhl secretly in the hope that she would be able to discover Torka's camp, run ahead of the others, and beg the man for refuge. But each time she experienced doubt, she remembered why she had run away in the first place. Now Bili's scream had brought her to pause, her heart pounding. She could not move, for what was happening in the little camp of Ekoh was too frightening to look at . . . and too fascinating not to observe.

Mano and Buhl had taken Ekoh unaware. Mano thrust a spear into Ekoh's belly, pinning him to the ground. Bili boldly rose and, with a spear in her hands, threatened the attackers. They laughed at her. She had told them that her boy had been hurt in a snare and begged them to take pity on Seteena. Mano went to the child and cut his throat.

Honee clasped her hand over her mouth to keep from being sick. The boy was still fighting against death as Ekoh, making terrible gurgling sounds and gripping the spear embedded within his gut, tried to rise. He might have succeeded had Buhl not come to work the weapon even deeper. Bili flew to the defense of her man, screaming her rage and hatred, but Mano tripped her. The spear flew from her hand, then Mano was on her, straddling her, then pulling her back.

Honee felt a terrible nausea sweep over her. Seteena was dead in a lake of blood now, but neither Buhl nor Mano even looked at him. Buhl was holding Ekoh's head up by the hair, telling him to watch and enjoy his last moments of life. Mano was ripping at Bili's clothes, hurting her, choking her into semiconsciousness before mounting her, all the while taunting Ekoh.

Suddenly a howling scream of pure animal rage echoed up and down the canyon. A spear came flying as though from out of nowhere. It struck Buhl through the neck with such force that he went down backward with the spearhead clean through his throat and protruding out the other side.

"Yanehva?" Honee squinted up.

The beastling hurled one throwing stick as hard as he could, although not at the beast who was hurting the female for fear that he might accidentally strike her. He screeched with pleasure when he saw the other male go over backward, grasping at his throat; he would die slowly, and in agony. That made the beastling smile.

He came down on the shoulders of the beast on the female, but the beast did not react in blind panic as a caribou or antelope might have done. Instead, he skillfully reached up and sent the beastling flying heels over head to the ground.

The beast with a scarred face was standing over him with a spear at his throat while, far off upon the mountain, the sounds of Sister squealing in agony and terror rent the beastling to his heart.

Scarface looked startled and turned toward the terrible sounds that Sister was making . . . and then not making at all.

With one ferocious roll and lunge, the beastling was on his feet, making for the rockfall. He was dizzy. His thoughts were running wild. Sister was dead; the beastling knew it. He ran full out and began to climb over the rocks. Sister needed him now. When he heard one high, pitiful, lost cry, he sounded out to her. "Man-ara-vak!" he screamed, just as something from behind hit him hard across the back of the head, and he went sprawling.

Torka could not remember when he had felt better. The boy had performed superbly! Now Umak stood before him, wearing the cloak of teratorn feathers. "For my parents, from whom my life has sprung and whose names I speak with pride and honor, I give these special gifts, symbolic of their love for each other and for their band. For they are as the great black swans that have always flown out of the face of the rising sun to give heart to the people—always and forever, to Torka and Lonit, Umak gives these cloaks!" Umak brought them forth and held them high, one in each hand. "For many moons I have been making them in secret just for you."

Torka stared. Everyone in the cave stared at two full-length cloaks sewn entirely of the skins of white swans—except for the shoulder portions; these were black. The two rare black swans would never again fly out of the face of the rising sun at the return of the time of light. Umak had killed them both. He had slit them open, then stretched them wide. He had gutted them and dried them and softened them with infinite care so no feathers would be lost. Out of the great outstretched wings he had fashioned hoods, stitching the wings to the long extended necks so that when worn, the heads of the swans would extend over the heads of the wearers with beaks still attached and eyes replaced with polished stones.

Torka could not look away from the cloaks or from Umak's beaming face. Umak's wide, white smile displayed his fine, strong, serrate-edged teeth. Suddenly, as Lonit looked away from the cloaks and, weeping, buried her face in Torka's shoulder, the headman gasped as though someone had dealt him a deathblow.

With shaking hands he forcefully struck the cloaks from Umak's hands. The boy's face collapsed into hurt and shock. Although he was no longer smiling, all that Torka could see of him was his smile! His cursed, wolfish smile! It might as well have been Karana staring up at him in pale-faced disbelief. Karana . . . son of Navahk . . . *brother* of Umak?

The likelihood struck him like a spear in the belly. He almost vomited. It *must* be! The child of rape, the child of Navahk, sent to torment him for the rest of his days. Torka's heart was aching and empty. Would he never have a son who would bring joy to his life?

"Father! I worked so hard to m-make something th-that would p-please you."

"Please me! These cloaks are a gift of pain!" he raged, and as he drew Lonit, sobbing, into a protective embrace, he vented his anger and frustration. "What kind of son makes a gift by killing his parents' symbols for life and love? What kind of son makes his mother weep? No son of mine!"

In that moment, sounds reached them from afar—disembodied sounds, screams of pain. And one word, faint, yet so clear and full of agony that no one in the cave failed to hear it or be touched by it: "Man-ara-vak!"

And as Torka and Lonit looked west, they knew it was a lost and abandoned boy answering Torka's anguished cry of so long ago, when he had stood in the wind upon a distant mountain and had cried out to the forces of Creation to save the life spirit of his son. And now, at last, it was time to bring Manaravak home.

12

Torka, Simu, and Dak donned their traveling clothes, took up their spears, and were about to leave the cave when Lonit joined them.

"I will go!" she declared. "If my *son* is there, Torka, I want to be with you when you find him! Do not forbid me to come."

He did not.

From the cave, a devastated Umak stood with his two older sisters and watched them go. "I was not asked."

"No one was *asked*," Summer Moon retorted. "Who knows what dangers they will find? The only reason Grek volunteered to stay behind with us is that he is slow and might turn out to be a hindrance instead of—"

"Grek stays behind to protect us in case we should have need of him! The only hindrance in this band is your mouth, Summer Moon!" Demmi snapped at her sister. She turned to her brother. "Torka didn't mean the things he said."

"Of course he meant them!" countered Summer Moon. "What a stupid thing to do . . . to kill the black swans! Why didn't you go after Life Giver while you were at it? Torka will never forgive you!"

"He will," Demmi consoled.

"Why should he?" Umak glared straight ahead. "No matter what I do, it always ends up wrong in his eyes."

At that moment Iana came to place a loving hand upon Umak's shoulder. "You must go with your father, Umak."

The boy looked at her, mouth set, eyes hard and accusing. "*Is* he my father, Iana?"

The woman's expression changed. "In truth, Umak, sometimes I wonder. I was at your birth. You came first and hard—tearing your way into this world. Manaravak came much later—and gently, for he was so small that the midwife who took him said that he looked unready to be born, as though he had taken life within Lonit later than you. I do not know if it is possible for a woman to carry the sons of two different fathers within her belly at the same time. Sometimes, when I see you smile, I see the ghost of Navahk in your face. But who can say? That man is long dead. I do know that you *are* your mother's firstborn son and that Torka has risked everything so that you might live and walk beside him as his own. If he questions the circumstances of your birth, he keeps those questions hidden. What more can you ask of him, you foolish boy? He is the only father you will ever know! You erred in judgment when you killed the swans—but you did it out of love, and when Torka's anger cools, he will know this. So now I say to you, if you *are* Torka's son, be his son! Do not allow the ghost of Navahk to have his way in this world as Karana has done. Put the shadows of the past behind you. They cannot hurt you, Umak, unless you let them! Go now, be a son to Torka. Help to bring your brother home."

Circling birds led them to the place where Ekoh and Seteena had died. Nearby they found Honee in shock, huddled beside a rock. Lonit set down her spear and drew the frightened girl into a motherly embrace while Torka, Dak, and Simu formed a caring circle around her. In gasps and sputters, she told them what had happened.

"They took Bili and the beast boy to the camp of Cheanah. I thought Mano was going to kill him, but Yanehva threatened to bash in Mano's head with his own spear if he tried. So in the end, they trussed the wild boy like a dead antelope, and Yanehva slung him across his shoulders. He was growling and snarling like an animal and he was very dirty, but he *was* a boy—a wild boy in the skin of a white lion. He had your face, Man of the West. And he was very brave."

"The skin of a white lion?" Tears were streaming down Lonit's cheeks. Torka's heart broke to see the pain in her expression. "When the twins were born, I thought I would die of the unending pain. In my mind I became a wolf. A white lion rose within me, threatening, standing between me and my sons!"

"The people of Cheanah are wolves, but they will not kill the white lion."

The words startled her. They startled everyone.

Torka turned and saw that Umak had come over the rockfall to stand behind them. Aar was at his side. Torka's eyes narrowed. Umak looked as though he had been physically pummeled; words had done that to him. Torka fiercely regretted that he had spoken so rashly.

Whatever doubts he might have about Umak's birth, it was wrong to hold the boy responsible. Umak had not chosen the circumstances of his birth—no child could do that. And what about the lost twin? Might he not also be Navahk's spawn?

The question ripped through him. He cursed it. All he could ever be sure of was that the force of Navahk's power had twisted the spirit of Karana, driven him to lie, then driven him mad. Was he going to allow Navahk's ghost to destroy Umak, too? *No!* He had taken Umak from his mother's arms and defended his life against the people of Cheanah and the forces of Creation! He had raised the boy and loved him as a son. The boy was his—from this moment on, without question! "I am glad that you have come," he told him, then added strongly: "Umak. My son."

Umak's head went up defensively. "Truly?"

Honee looked around in the manner of a hunted animal. "We must go! Cheanah and his men will soon come over the mountain, marching the beast boy ahead of them. Mano said that because Torka will not want to see the boy die twice, he will let them come across the valley and into his cave."

Torka scanned the heights and nodded. "Come, let us take Ekoh and Seteena to the overview of the valley, where they may lie upon the ridge together and look upon the sky forever. It is a good place. Their spirits will watch us as we go back to the cave and await the coming of the son of Zhoonali."

"But Cheanah and his hunters will kill you!" cried Honee, terror sparkling in her black, beadlike little eyes. "They have sworn it! They will kill you all, and then they will hunt and eat your totem. And as they feast upon its flesh and build feast fires with your bones, they will lie upon your women and girls and say that the forces of Creation have smiled upon them, for they will have taken back their luck from those who have stolen it!"

"We will see," said Torka. "We will see."

Cheanah stood tall, wearing the ragged skin of the white lion draped over his shoulders. The wild boy thrashed around at his feet, snarling and growling up at him.

"The pelt of the white lion is mine now, as I always swore it would be," the headman said to the boy. "Whether you have killed it or found it dead somewhere does not matter. What matters is that it is mine now. And when I have put you to my purpose, Manaravak, son of Torka, you too will die."

Zhoonali came to stand beside him. "It is a spirit. Be wary of what you do with it. With my own hands I put that child to look upon the sky forever. It must be dead!"

Cheanah planted his booted foot on his captive's throat and raised his spear. Slowly, he moved the projectile point downward from the boy's chest to his belly, opening a long, shallow line of red. "That which bleeds can die."

Her brow furrowed. "You are too bold these days, Cheanah."

Cheanah nodded, eyeing Zhoonali thoughtfully. The years were beginning to tell upon her at last. "Have you not always taught me that risk is essential? That a headman must be bold if he is to keep his people's respect and affection? Think of it, my mother: Torka's cave, high and dry on a good, south-facing slope. Think how comfortable you would be there!"

Her lips twitched into a smile. "Yes. It will be a good thing. But it will also be dangerous."

"She is right." Yanehva eyed his father with disgust; it was clear from his expression that he considered the wild boy who thrashed and howled and strained against his tethers to be less bestial than the headman, who had enjoyed several ruts upon Bili since Mano had brought her dazed and battered back to camp. "Again I ask you to reconsider. Why must there be bloodshed among our two peoples? The valley that lies ahead is enormous, with game enough for all. Loose the boy. Clean him up a bit. Let us go peacefully into that fine valley and offer to hunt as brothers with Torka, with the past behind us. And as a gift of our good faith, this son of Torka's, who is little more than an animal because of us."

Mano came by, dragging Bili by her matted hair. He shoved her to the ground as he spoke to his brother with unconcealed contempt. "You have forgotten that this wild thing killed Buhl. And Honee has disappeared; no doubt the dark magic of Torka's shaman has called her forth. His men are using her by now . . . like this." He went down on Bili; she lay like a limp doll beneath him, staring ahead, motionless as he came to a quick release and stood up. There was blood on Mano's organ as he dropped his tunic over it.

Yanehva frowned. "Every man in the camp has been on Bili again and again. You will kill her if you keep this up. Look at her eyes. They have no life in them. How will she bear children in the future if she is too badly torn?"

"That won't matter," Mano said. "There are better women in Torka's camp. They will bear our children."

Cheanah slung an arm around Mano's shoulders with obvious affection. "And soon we will pierce them all!"

"Look! The mammoths are leaving the valley!" Demmi called out, distraught.

"Yes, Daughter. And we must leave it, too."

Torka's words settled heavily.

Demmi did not understand. "But you have returned from the western range without our brother!"

"And without Karana!" added Summer Moon.

"We must leave," he replied sternly. "Now. Enemies are coming toward us. They outnumber us two to one, and

I will not risk losing control of this band to such as they, or risk any of our number to their spears. We must go. As Life Giver walks, so must the people who name him totem walk, into the face of the rising sun."

Demmi glowered at her mother, unable to understand how Lonit could leave now, when she knew at last that Manaravak was alive.

As Grek stood looking at his beloved old Wallah, his big face sagged with worry. "This has been a good camp for us. It could be defended. . . ."

"Bah!" To everyone's surprise, Wallah was on her foot, leaning on fine new crutches, which Umak had made for her. "Sadness lives in this camp now. Our Mahnie's life spirit will walk with us wherever we go, for she lives in our hearts and in our memories. And Naya has yet to walk free across the open steppe and beneath the open sky. Too much do you worry about this old woman, old man! If Torka says we must go, then we must go! Never has he led us wrongly. This woman does not question. Nor should you."

Grek was dumbfounded. "But the way ahead may be long, too much up and down for a one-legged woman!"

She gestured broadly toward her bed furs. "I have both my legs! What is the difference if I walk on one and carry the other?"

For the first time since Torka's denouncement of his gifts, Umak was happy. They were actually going! They were going and leaving Manaravak behind.

For days now, Karana had lingered around the pit into which the beast had fallen. Before that, he had watched it all: the murder of Ekoh and Seteena, the rape of Bili, the bold and magnificently selfless attack by Manaravak. He had watched but had done nothing. When they had knocked Manaravak down, he had thought, *Good, they have killed him!* And when they had carried him off, he had thought, *Now he will never come back!*

Then he had been drawn by the wanawut's screams and moans. When he had seen it—gray and furred and hideous—he had taken up a stone and had poised himself, ready for the kill. He had set the snares and dug these pits

so he could kill the beast, the child of Navahk and the
wanawut . . . his sister! The haunting that had driven him
slowly and undeniably insane.

But as he had looked down into the pit, with the heavy
stone in his fist, poised to be hurled against the creature's
head, she looked up at him out of fevered, pain-racked,
mist-gray eyes. She raised a hand and feebly gestured to
him as she mewed softly, like a dying friend sighing in
relief as it sighted a long-lost, beloved companion. "Man
. . . a . . . ra . . . vak?"

The beast spoke! The beast was *not* a beast! The rock
fell from his limp hand as he stood, slack jawed, staring
into the pit. If Navahk had been her sire, none of his spirit
lived within her. Her eyes were open and guileless and
full of love for him, and as he looked into them, his mind
was swept clean of madness as though a cool and loving
hand had soothed his furrowed brow.

Karana wept as he climbed down into the pit. He sobbed
and stood still as her long, softly furred arm lifted, and a
huge, clawed, grotesquely human hand touched his mouth
and drifted adoringly across his face. The long mouth of
the beast turned downward, and then, with great effort, it
turned upward and twitched at the corners into a smile of
such unquestioning love and radiance that Karana drew
the creature close. She gasped as her body was drawn
upward over the bone stakes. She shivered, then relaxed
as he cradled her, whispering in her ear and soothing the
beast with his embrace. He rocked his sister in his arms
until she died, and as she died, his madness died with
her. And in the arms of the wanawut, Karana was reborn.

The people of Torka left the cave. They walked in
silence, dogs loaded with packs, children running ahead
and calling out as though it were all a wonderful game.

Summer Moon kicked at stones and clumps of grass. "It
was wrong to leave Karana. He is our brother, our magic
man."

"Torka is magic man enough for us," Lonit reprimanded
her daughter, but there was sadness and unmistakable
tension in her voice.

They walked for many miles, stopping at their various

cache pits and withdrawing from them the best of their stores.

"We will leave nothing for the people of Cheanah," Torka vowed, and although this meant that their loads became heavier, their hearts became lighter as the men of the band urinated upon what was left in the pits.

After two days, they reached the far side of the valley and the neck of the pass. As they looked back a rain of meteors streaked across the sky.

Torka looked up. He has seen so many shooting stars since the red star had appeared, it troubled him. He put his hand on Umak's shoulder. "The way ahead will be long and new. Many unknown dangers lie ahead."

"Life Giver walks ahead of us. I am not afraid!" the boy replied.

"A wise man lives with fear as though it were his second skin, my son. Only through fear does a man learn caution, and only a cautious man may hope to survive. You are a man now, Umak—both you and Dak—and I will count on you in the days ahead to stand with Grek and Simu as you follow Life Giver into the face of the rising sun, seeking new hunting grounds for our women and children."

Demmi's eyes went wide. What was her father saying?

It was Grek who asked. "Proud will this man be to walk at the head of Torka's people with Simu and Dak and Umak. But where will Torka be?"

"I must seek the one who was abandoned and who lives."

"Why should you risk yourself for him when you would not do as much for Karana?" Summer Moon asked petulantly.

"Karana has chosen the way of a solitary. He will live or die according to his own will. Manaravak is but a boy, and he *is* my son. I will not abandon him to those who will surely kill him when they discover that we have gone. And so in the days that follow, this band must be strong. If I do not return, you—Grek, Simu, Dak, and Umak—must lead our people. The spirits have been warning me for many moons that it was time to leave the valley. I should have put my faith in my own instincts long ago, not in the word of Navahk's shaman son. If it is the will of the spirits,

I will find Manaravak and follow you with him. If it is not their will, then you will be safe—and my son who has lived alone will, at least, not die alone."

"No!" cried Lonit. "We will go together. Iana, Summer Moon, and Demmi can look after Swan. Umak is grown. They will be safe with the band. But I must be at your side, my love, always and—"

"No!" He stopped her. "Not this time. If you were at my side, my concern for you would put us both at risk. Knowing that you wait for me will strengthen me—as your presence will strengthen our people. You are the first woman of this band, the mother of Torka's children and generations to come. If the spirits do not allow me to return to you with our son . . ." He stopped and looked at Umak, then smiled. "With our *lost* son," he corrected himself. "And now to Umak, firstborn son of Torka and Lonit, the twin brother of Manaravak, I put this in trust."

The boy stared with wide-eyed, openmouthed incredulity as slowly, with great ceremony, Torka drew his bludgeon of fossilized whalebone from the spruce-bark sheath that hung at his side. He held the weapon outward to Umak across his palms, then paused, aware of Lonit, standing tall, so full of pride in him. His eyes sought hers.

She smiled. *Yes*, said her eyes. *What you do is right! What you do is what* must *be done! You will come back. You will!*

He nodded, his heart full of love. *But if I do not come back, no man could have wished for more in a lifetime than to have walked at your side, Lonit! Always and forever.*

He moved his gaze back to Umak. He saw Lonit's face in the boy's and her love in his eyes. "Look to the bludgeon, my son. Across the long miles I have incised in the stone the story of our people's wanderings. If I do not return, it will be for you to continue that responsibility. You must tell our tales to our children, and to our children's children, until you, in turn, will pass the bludgeon to your eldest son, and the tales will live on through him. *I* will live on through him, and those who come after us will know how it was when Torka led his people in the shadow of the great mammoth Life Giver."

There were tears in the eyes of the boy as Torka pressed the bludgeon into his hands.

"Be strong, Umak, first son of Torka, grandson of Manaravak, and great-grandson of Umak. Our lives are in your care. You must live and be a man of the wild steppe, the open tundra, and the misted heights of the great ranges. When I die, it is through you that my life spirit will be reborn. And so now I say to you, before all who are assembled here, what I should have said long ago: As Lonit and I are one, so too are we—you and I—my son, my flesh and spirit, *one* . . . always and forever!"

13

Cheanah had brought his people to pause along the western shore of a strange, ice-islanded lake. Above the soaring, ice-capped ranges, a meteor shower flamed across a golden sky to reflect tracings of fire into the surface of the great highland reservoir. Sitting alone upon a snowy embankment, Zhoonali looked up. The old woman did not like the falling stars, the lake, or the high, cold mountains that held the huge, restless body of water captive. The mountains made her feel small, insignificant.

Once again, a bright finger of light streaked across the sky to mirror its image briefly in the surface of the lake. The increasing frequency of falling stars defied Zhoonali's understanding. She had always found them beautiful—but these stars fell by day and in groups. That was unusual, and so to be feared.

There was also something ominous about the lake, as though some monstrous spirit lived deep beneath its surface, causing the waters to churn and the islands of ice to shift and groan.

Bili cried out. Scowling, Zhoonali looked toward the sound and shook her head. Mano and two others were on that woman again. The men lay together under a single blanket of several joined bison hides to keep the cold wind off their backs as they worked the woman. Close by, the captive beast boy sat naked, wrists bound behind him, glaring at them, refusing to eat, allowing himself no sleep, waiting for his chance to leap at those who had captured him. Twice now he had attempted to defend Bili; twice now he had been badly beaten. He seemed oblivious to pain or was defiant of it in the face of his captors. Truly he *was* Torka's son.

She looked away, wishing they had never found him, wishing that he had died long ago. But even as she thought this, she knew that her wish was a foolish one. The beast boy was a gift of the spirits. His presence would allow them to insinuate themselves into Torka's band under the guise of friendship.

Briefly, she thought of Honee and wondered if her granddaughter had found death or the man of her dreams beyond the mountains.

Karana. The old woman's eyes scanned the sky. Perhaps it was his magic that was calling down the fires of the sky. It could well be. He had been only a youth when he had walked out of Cheanah's band, but the powers of Seeing and Calling had been his. Now that he was a man, his magic would be great indeed. She had made a silent invocation against the magic man and his people as she hunkered within her bearskin robe and longed for warmth.

Soon you will have a warm camp. Yanehva has seen it. Cheanah has promised it! She sighed, drew up her badger-skin bag, and shook the bones of telling into her lap. The bones would confirm her thoughts and warm her in this cold mountain wind. She scooped them into her palms and cast them onto a small circle of hide. The bones clacked hollowly as they fell.

Zhoonali gasped. Her hands flew to her face. For the first time in her life, she saw in the fall of bones not what she wanted to see, not what she had contrived, but a true reading that nearly overwhelmed her. She leaped to her feet.

"What is it, my mother?" Cheanah had come to stand beside her.

"The bones speak to me of death."

He smiled. "Yes," he confirmed, drawing her close in a loving embrace. "The death of all who would dare to stand against the son of Zhoonali as he goes forth to claim what is rightfully his!"

*   *   *

In the days that followed, Cheanah led his people out across the wonderful valley, with Zhoonali carried like a queen on furs laid over the interlocked arms of Mano and Yanehva, while the beast boy walked at Cheanah's side, tethered by a thong noosed around his neck.

For days Karana had observed their approach, and for days he had watched Torka's band's departure. Karana would follow his people, but first there was something that he must do: He had stolen Manaravak from Torka. Now he must return him.

Cheanah's people made their final camp and raised smokes to alert Torka of their presence. The cave lay ahead, but there was no sign of life in it.

"They should have seen us by now," said Yanehva. "Why is no one coming out to us?"

Mano grinned. "They're probably waiting in the cave, to see why we come and what we bring to them, eh?"

Bili sat by herself in quiet misery as the others ate and prepared for what they hoped would be a day of wondrous pleasures partaken in death and rape. Cheanah was donning his headman necklet of feathers and readying his favorite spears.

Not far from Bili, the beastling sat hunched up. Bruised, swollen, and shaking, he was tethered to a stake by a single thong, his hands behind his back.

Bili watched him. She could see that he was dying, his spirit bleeding out of him. But then, so was hers. They would kill her when they reached the cave and found others to sate themselves upon. Mano had promised it. She sighed. Without Ekoh and little Seteena, with Torka's people murdered and his women enslaved, she had no wish to live. None.

And so, while the others ate and boasted of what was to happen this day, she moved slowly . . . so slowly that no one noticed that the distance was closing between her and the wild boy. They never witnessed the moment in which she freed him; it happened too quietly.

He stared at her.

"Go!" she whispered, gesturing across the valley. He

took her hand to pull her along with him, but she shook her head. "Run now, before it is too late."

Mano's spear struck her through the back and pierced her heart. And even as she died, she knew that it did not matter. Her heart was broken anyway. And the boy, Torka's son, was free.

Mano loosed another spear.

"Stop!" Yanehva screamed, but it was too late.

Mano did not intend a killing blow; he had merely wished to intimidate the wild thing by striking close and thus prevent him from fleeing. To his shock, the son of Torka not only kept on running, he managed to snatch his spear in midflight. Turning as deftly as a steppe antelope, the boy wheeled, hurled the spear back, and kept running.

The weapon struck true. Mano went down, his eyes bulging with shock and disbelief, knowing that the boy had killed him. Now, as he fell facedown and watched the world grow dark within his own head, he knew that with Bili's death, he had killed once too often. With that final murder he had succeeded in killing himself.

Manaravak ran. The others were after him, so he lengthened his stride. He was fast—as fast as a white lion running for his life. He ran and ran, as Mother had taught him to run from predators. He ran until he could run no more, and then he collapsed, gasping, knowing that they were coming, coming across the distances. Although he had put a huge gap between himself and them, it was only a matter of time before they caught him and killed him.

Panting, he splayed his hands upon the ground and willed himself to rise against the burning protest in his chest. But, impossibly, he was jerked to his feet from behind. For an instant, before the beast hefted him over his shoulders and broke into a pounding race for the far hills, he looked into its face. Its eyes were shining and full of moisture; its mouth was split wide in the most beautiful smile he had ever seen.

"Manaravak!"

The sound of the beast was *his* sound. "Man-ara-vak!" he responded in kind.

And the father threw back his head and howled with triumph as he turned and, with his son in his arms, raced toward the eastern edge of the valley without looking back.

Had he done so, he would have seen the solitary figure in the white belly skins of winter-killed caribou, dancing and whirling on high ground between him and his pursuers.

"Go!" cried Karana to Torka. "Now, in this moment, I give you back your son! Now, in this moment, I loose my spirit to walk the wind! And now, in this moment, I kill Navahk forever!"

With his spears in his hand and his black hair whipping in the wind, Karana was a figure of pure power as he ran toward the west, to intercept the men of Cheanah and cause them to stop dead in their tracks.

As a meteor shower burned across the sky above him, five spears brought him down. Even then he lived to see the great star fall, its tail burning across the sky as it plunged to earth, striking the western mountain and burying itself in the great, gray highland lake.

The waters rose. They boiled and steamed. And the upper arm of the north-canyon glacier tore away to loose the watery nightmare vision.

With the north-canyon glacier demolished, there was nothing to hold back the tumultuous waters of the high-land lake. Cheanah stood in shock, Zhoonali clinging to his side, as a roaring explosion of water and boulders erupted from the gorge in a boiling, misting rage. It shook the world and leveled the forests of the foothills as it raced out of the mountains and across the wonderful valley toward them.

"The bones! The death they foretold was ours!" cried Zhoonali, her voice barely audible above the thunderous deluge. "Help me, Cheanah! Carry me to Torka's cave and safety!"

He turned on her, his teeth bared. "You lied! The magic man is dead, but my luck is still gone." He turned and bolted, leaving the old woman to face her death alone.

Suddenly Yanehva appeared at her side as Cheanah raced off to the east, squealing like a madman.

"He will never make it," Yanehva told the old woman as he lifted her in his strong arms and ran for high ground.

"You?" Amazement half choked her. "*You* came back for me? I have held nothing but contempt for you. You might have reached the cave, Yanehva."

"Yes, you always said there was too much softness in me, but until this day, I never knew how right you were!"

She was light in his arms, so light that he did not feel her die as he raced full out and even faster, scrambling after the others for the high ground of the cave and reaching it.

Only his own band were here. Torka was not here . . . luck was not here. It had flown with Torka and his son to the east.

As the need for breath clutched at his throat, Yanehva looked down at Zhoonali. Her jaw hung slack in death. He looked around. Here there was death. *His* death. The death of his people. Yanehva held his grandmother firmly in his arms as he turned to face it.

"Come, then!" he cried defiantly at the wall of roiling water. It moved across the land at a speed that intensified the power of its mass. And in that last moment of his life, he wished that the old woman could have seen that he alone among all his people was unafraid of death. It came with an ear-splitting roar that smashed into the cave and shattered the people within.

Their bodies washed up as debris, limp and broken, as the great wave poured on to override the hills and to fill the wonderful valley until it was no more.

"Karana!" Torka cried out the name even as the edge of the great wave caught him and took him down, carrying him away into black, suffocating darkness. "No!" he cried out to the forces of Creation. "For the sake of this boy, if not for me, let death not find us now!"

But death was a merciless, implacable force with no eyes or ears or compassion. Water filled his mouth and seared his lungs and the hollows of his head as, in desperation, he clutched the boy to him. The power of the water fought to wrench Manaravak from his arms.

Torka's eyes were open, bulging and burning, as he was

assaulted by a cold, debris-laden wave. Something big and white went shooting past him—a lion or a man? Somehow both. The churning, rushing waters brought the thing back toward him. He saw it now; it was Cheanah, eyes popping, mouth gaping wide in death, arms and legs flailing lifelessly in the maelstrom. As the corpse struck him, he tried in desperation to hold on to his long-lost son. But the force of the impact of the dead man yanked the boy from his arms. Drowning, Torka screamed in anguished rage as he saw his son swept away in a wave of blackness.

"Manaravak! Man-ara-va . . ."

He awoke but knew not how much time had passed. Aar, faithful friend, was licking life and circulation back into his face.

Grek was bending over him, and Lonit and Umak and Demmi. All of the band were looking down at him. Only Honee hung back. Of Manaravak there was no sign. The falling star and the angry sky had taken back their son. Torka could not speak; he had no heart to form the words.

Lonit gave him fresh water, and when he was able to walk, they went on. He stopped often to look back. He knew he would always look back, for a portion of his heart would always remain with Karana and Manaravak in the drowned valley, beneath the new lake that had been born of the red star that had plunged from the angry sky.

A warm, welcoming wind was blowing out of the land to the east, beckoning the tiny group of survivors. Torka and his people trudged on and on, weighed down by their pack frames and grief. There were no words to lessen the pain from a son twice lost. At last they left the pass and the mountains towering behind them.

Well ahead, Life Giver trumpeted as he plodded on with his kindred.

"Where does the great mammoth walk to, Father Mine?" asked Summer Moon. "Do you think he knows, or does he simply walk onward, deeper into the Forbidden Land?"

Torka looked at the girl sadly. But she was not a girl anymore. She was a woman—a sad woman. And yet, as he put a gentle and loving arm around her shoulders, it seemed as if she were the same little girl who had stood beside him so long ago, voicing the same question, trying not to give in to the same fears. "No man may say. No man may know. But we are the people of the dawn, and we will follow as we have always followed."

"Look!" Demmi's exclamation was so full of joy and wonder that it took the sadness from the moment.

Torka turned, and as he did, Summer Moon turned with him. When she saw what had alighted upon Demmi's outheld hand, tears of happiness filled her eyes.

"Longspur!" Demmi exclaimed. She was crying, too. "Look, everybody! As Karana promised, it is Longspur! He said I would find him in the wonderful land! Oh, he has not broken his promise, after all!"

While Aar cocked his head and whined softly, Umak stared wide-eyed at the little bird. It ruffled its feathers, then rose into flight, eastward. "He is with us. Karana is with us. His spirit leads us into—"

"—the face of the rising sun!" Lonit's voice was a song.

And so they went on, one people, one band, with the wind singing of the past behind them, and the little bird winging ahead to alight on the towering shoulders of Life Giver, who led them deeper into the Forbidden Land. At last they crested the great pass. When they looked back, it seemed that they saw themselves, the spirits of the past, waving them onward, wishing them a good journey across the Forbidden Land.

As Simu led the others on, Umak stood staring back across the distances. Torka turned back and joined him with his little family, and together they gazed across the magnificent, ice-ridden ranges and the flooded valley they had once called home. So much joy. So much sadness.

"Come," Torka urged. "It is time to go. We must put the past behind us. It will walk with us as it will, my son."

"Yes," replied Umak in a somber tone. "It will." Then, impulsively, in a voice that sang out across the miles, he called out his brother's name. "Manaravak! Walk at my side as my brother! It will be better than living in my dreams!"

Torka and Lonit exchanged concerned glances as the wind took Umak's words into the mountain vastnesses, across the drowned valley, and through the black and desolate range that lay beyond.

"Come," urged Torka again, and then, just as he was about to turn away, a figure emerged to stand silhouetted against the western sky.

"Look!" cried Demmi and Summer Moon.

In Lonit's arms, Swan squirmed and pointed off. "Boy!" exclaimed the little girl. "Look! Boy!"

Torka and Lonit did look, then embraced and laughed and wept aloud with joy as the girls jumped up and down and danced and called their long-lost brother's name across the miles.

"Manaravak!" they shouted as the figure in the west began to move toward them.

"Man-ara-vak!" he answered from afar.

Demmi and Summer Moon, waving their arms over their heads and calling out their brother's name, began to run toward him. Torka scooped Swan into his arms and, with Lonit, followed after them.

"He is coming," said Umak to Aar, and smiled because for the first time in his life the words made him glad. "My *brother* is coming! I've known it all along."

AUTHOR'S NOTE

Since setting to the task of creating The First Americans Series, I have often been asked how I am able to project myself into the past to re-create life as it must have been for those first bands of men and women who walked out of Asia to people the Americas so many millennia ago. The answer is a simple one—and it does not lie completely in the often staggering amount of reading, research, and legwork that goes into each book. The bones, burins, and "graveyards" of the past permit inferences of how they lived, what they looked like, how they hunted, where they walked. But *who* were they, these first Americans? What did they think, feel, fear, love? Ah . . . now there's the rub.

I have walked the high tundra of Torka's world, but often when working on my manuscripts I seek inspiration in timbered mountains that surround my home in California's Big Bear Valley. Glaciers once lay on the summits of the highest peaks; above the marshy, mysterious *ciénagas* that lie in the high canyons of the eleven-thousand-foot San Gorgonio massif, a hiker can climb beyond tree line to explore cirques and hanging valleys formed by vanished alpine glaciers. In the high playas below the summits, giant sloths once grazed while saber-toothed tigers hunted them. I know. I have seen and touched their bones and walked along the spine of an eight-thousand-foot ridge that allows views due east, "into the face of the rising sun."

With the mountains falling away to the vast crucible of the Mojave Desert, time rides the wind, and the desert extends beyond the curve of the horizon. Great rubble heaps of ancient cinder cones stand against the sky. Long black scars of lava flows stretch like veins that once ran hot with the molten blood of the earth.

The world below is as it has always been: savage, hostile, magnificent. A road intrudes here and there; ruler straight, hair thin—a tenuous intrusion across the land that has remained virtually untouched by Man since time beyond beginning . . . since Torka's descendants first walked out of the great passes some forty thousand years ago to observe what was in the Age of Ice not a desert but a great and wondrous grassland.

As one stands on the ridge with wind-driven banks of cloud moving eastward like the ghosts of ancient bands of Paleo-Indian people, inspiration comes like a gift from the spirits of the past. It is easy to imagine that it is indeed the Age of Ice—or could be again, if the forces of Creation decreed it.

Four times during the last two million years, global weather patterns have changed, and the world has grown cold. Now, despite our best scientific efforts, no man knows why, if, or when the next Ice Age will come. We only know that if it does, we will have to find ways to survive and to accommodate ourselves to a new way of life.

And so, in this way as in all ways, we are no different from our most ancient ancestors. Despite our technocracies and great cities and urban sprawl, beneath the veneer of the complex and multifaceted civilization in which we clothe—and all too often hide—ourselves, we are still the same furless, fangless, clawless hunting "beast" that speared mired mammoths in the Arctic tundra and competed with saber-toothed tigers for the meat of the giant ground sloth in the high playas of the San Bernardino Mountains. We smile not only to show pleasure but, as the great apes smile, to show our teeth in snarling rage or leering threat. Strip away the veneer of all we consider civilized, and life becomes primeval again; we are cavemen again, joined together around the soft glowing fires of our mutuality. We love. We hate. We dream. And unlike any other creature that we know of in this world, we laugh out loud to express our pure, driving joy in being alive. We dare to ask "Why?" of the Infinite as we defy the forces of Creation by inventing new and better ways to accomplish the daily tasks of life and to assure our own survival.

Primitive man still lives, and not only in the ever-dwindling wild places of this world, in jungles or deserts or far-flung mountain ranges. He lives in *us*, in each and every one of us. The more civilized we become, the more deeply we bury that truth, but it is there in the legends of all the world's diverse peoples, a mythos created by a creature who, in its physical weakness, fears the world and so, in order to survive, has fought to hold dominion over it.

Perhaps this is why so many find comfort in cities . . . in the lights, the noise, the tension, the comforting environs of everything man-made, man controlled. It is soothing fiction. But simply turn off the lights in any big city and people cluster and cower like prey animals beneath the vast black skin of the night, while others howl like wolves and become purely predaceous. The instincts are there, buried in our psyches. They will save us or destroy us in the end, for we are now what we have always been: predator and prey . . . Navahk and Karana . . . darkness and light . . . animal and human . . . modern and ancient Man living in the same skin.

One people, still looking at the stars and asking "Why?" . . . still staring into the face of the rising sun and, like Torka and his band, still daring to follow.

Once again, my thanks to all the staff at Book Creations who have eased the way of Torka's people ever deeper into the New World, and most especially to Laurie Rosin, editorial director, who knows well why the thanks are so fully given!

William Sarabande
Fawnskin, California

Experience all the passion and adventure life has to offer in these bestselling novels by and about women.

Bantam offers you these exciting titles:

Titles by Jean Auel:

☐ 28091 CLAN OF THE CAVE BEAR $5.50
☐ 28092 THE VALLEY OF HORSES $5.50
☐ 28094 THE MAMMOTH HUNTERS $5.50

Titles by Cynthia Freeman:

☐ 26161 DAYS OF WINTER $4.95
☐ 26090 COME POUR THE WINE $4.50
☐ 25433 FAIRYTALES $4.50
☐ 26092 NO TIME FOR TEARS $4.50
☐ 24790 PORTRAITS $4.50
☐ 27743 WORLD FULL OF STRANGERS $4.95

Titles by Barbara Taylor Bradford:

☐ 27790 A WOMAN OF SUBSTANCE $4.95
☐ 25621 HOLD THE DREAM $4.95
☐ 26253 VOICE OF THE HEART $4.95
☐ 26541 ACT OF WILL $4.95

Titles by Judith Krantz:

☐ 25917 MISTRAL'S DAUGHTER $4.95
☐ 25609 PRINCESS DAISY $4.95
☐ 26407 I'LL TAKE MANHATTAN $4.95

Bantam Books, Dept. FBS2, 414 East Golf Road,
Des Plaines, IL 60016

Please send me the books I have checked above. I am enclosing
$_____ (please add $2.00 to cover postage and handling).
Send check or money order—no cash or C.O.D.s please.

Mr/Ms _____

Address _____

City/State _____ Zip _____

FBS2—4/89

Please allow four to six weeks for delivery. This offer expires
10/89. Prices and availability subject to change without notice.

Special Offer
Buy a Bantam Book
for only 50¢.

---

*Now you can have Bantam's catalog filled with hundreds
of titles plus take advantage of our unique and exciting
bonus book offer. A special offer which gives you the
opportunity to purchase a Bantam book for only 50¢.
Here's how!*

*By ordering any five books at the regular price per
order, you can also choose any other single book
listed (up to a $5.95 value) for just 50¢. Some
restrictions do apply, but for further details why not
send for Bantam's catalog of titles today!*

*Just send us your name and address and we will send
you a catalog!*
